The World's Best Short Stories

Anthology & Criticism

Volume V

Mystery and Detection

THE WORLD'S BEST SERIES

The World's Best Short Stories

I. *Short Story Masters: Early 19th Century*
II. *Short Story Masters: Late 19th & Early 20th Centuries*
III. *Famous Stories*
IV. *Fables and Tales*
V. *Mystery and Detection*

Forthcoming:
VI. *Horror and Science Fiction*
VII. *Characters*
VIII. *Places*
IX. *Cultures*
X. *Research and Reference: Criticism and Indexes*

The World's Best Poetry

Foundation Volumes I-X

Supplements:
I. *Twentieth Century English and American Verse, 1900-1929*
II. *Twentieth Century English and American Verse, 1930-1950*
III. *Critical Companion*
IV. *Minority Poetry of America*
V. *Twentieth Century Women Poets*
VI. *Twentieth Century African and Latin American Verse*
VII. *Twentieth Century Asian Verse*

CoreFiche: *World's Best Drama*
Microfiche with companion reference

The World's Best Short Stories

Anthology & Criticism

Volume V

Mystery and Detection

Stories by Alarcón, Brown, Chesterton, Christie, Collins, Dahl, Conan Doyle, Futrelle, Hammett, Hardy, McBain, Macdonald, Baroness Orczy, Paretsky, Poe, Prather, Ellery Queen, Rendell, Sayers, Thompson

Prepared by
The Editorial Board

 Roth Publishing, Inc.
Great Neck, New York

ISBN   0-89609-307-7
ISBN for 10 Volume Set   0-89609-400-6
Library of Congress Catalog Card Number 89-60440

Manufactured in the U.S.A.

Contents

Mystery

Detection

Case Studies

Preface

The World's Best Short Stories is designed to give both the serious student and the general reader a large selection and broad range of stories from around the world. Its ten volumes organize the stories into seven reader-friendly groupings:

> *Short Story Masters* (Volumes I and II)
> *Famous Stories* (Volume III)
> *Fables and Tales* (Volume IV)
> *Mystery and Detection* (Volume V)
> *Horror and Science Fiction* (Volume VI)
> *Characters* (Volume VII)
> *Places* (Volume VIII)
> *Cultures* (Volume IX)

Volume X is a research and reference guide and includes a cumulative index to all the volumes.

The arrangement of the stories suggests the multiple approaches for using these volumes. *Short Story Masters* focuses on the author; it contains stories that demonstrate the development of the short story as a conscious art form. *Famous Stories* is the volume to go to for well-known stories by authors who may or may not themselves be well-known. *Fables and Tales* includes fairy tales and other short non-realistic literature, as well as tales that are ancestors of the short story form. Volumes V and VI contain genre fiction; they act as a kind of counterpart to *Short Story Masters*. Whereas *Masters* places the short story in the tradition of an evolving art, these genre-centered volumes put it at the disposal of the general reader and the popular imagination. *Mystery and Detection* makes the case for a genre that has been continuously popular and critically treated since Poe, while *Horror and Science Fiction* looks at two different styles of fantastic literature—one finding its elements in the supernatural, the other in the superscientific.

The later volumes contain stories that are remarkable for a salient feature. The stories in *Characters* are portrait studies: their primary function is to examine the character of the hero or heroine. *Places* compiles stories that evoke a setting in a way that is memorable and important to the being of the story. Finally, *Cultures* uses ethnicity as its backdrop. It carries stories that are informed by their cultural setting.

The organization, variety, and breadth of **The World's Best Short Stories** makes it a unique anthology collection that can be used for study or read for pleasure.

Introduction

This and the following volume of **The World's Best Short Stories** focus on genre fiction. This volume contains stories of Mystery and Detection, stories that are firmly grounded in the realistic tradition of literature but of a type: there is a problem that needs to be solved; sometimes a detective is required. Its companion, Volume VI, contains Horror and Science Fiction, genres that introduce *super*-natural or *supra*-natural elements, respectively, to stories that in other ways seem realistic enough.

These four types—mystery, detection, horror, and science fiction—are not intended to stand in for all of genre literature. There are many genres not covered in these volumes, including adventure, the western, romance, historical romance, and fantasy, as well as emerging ones, like steampunk, splatterpunk, and cyberpunk. Another two books could have been devoted to these types. We have chosen not to represent them as genres (though individual stories appear elsewhere in this short story series) for several reasons, not the least of which is space. Additionally, the paucity of short stories in some genres, like historical romance and fantasy, ruled them out. Other genres simply do not have the variety, tradition, and acceptance that mystery, detective, horror, and science fiction have.

The four genres represented in Volumes V and VI, then, are strong genres with an equally strong contribution from the short story form. They have been written about by scholars and argued over by fans. Even then, the issue so often comes back to first principles. What is a genre?

An Historical Definition of Genre

The American Heritage Dictionary defines a genre as "a category of literature marked by a distinctive style, form, or content." This definition falls short, for genre literature is also, always, popular literature, read by a general readership that may not even be consciously aware of the genre as a concept.

Like the short story itself, the genre was an invention of the early nineteenth century, and was produced to meet some of the same needs. An increasingly literate populace had made the mass production and distribution of periodicals a viable venture for entrepreneurs. Throughout the better part of the 1800's, these periodicals provided entertainment for the growing middle classes. Toward the end of the century, when magazines such as *The Strand* (which published the Sherlock Holmes stories) and *Graham's* lowered their prices to make themselves accessible to an even wider readership, there was fierce competition to acquire the stories of proven and popular authors, like H.G. Wells or W.W. Jacobs, to help sell the magazines. In the days before copyright, editors would ask for stories based on previously published material or require stories similar in tone and subject matter to that of the popular authors of the day. Publishing historian Sam Moscowitz tells of brief manias for cannibal plant stories or helpful-insect tales that proliferated in the magazines at the turn of the century. Some of these stories edged on the plagiaristic (like the "sequel" one author wrote to *The War of the Worlds*), but mostly it was the tone, not the subject matter, that was copied.

Certain authors were celebrated for their talents, and magazines capitalized on their fame. Stories were trumpeted as being a "scientific romance in the style of Mr. Verne," or "a mystery in the manner of Mr. Arthur Conan Doyle." This was only one step away from assigning a genre label.

By the 1930's, it was feasible for a publisher to devote an entire magazine to one genre. These magazines, printed on a cheap woodpulp paper (thus the name "pulps"), gave rise to some of the greatest writers the genres have known. H.P. Lovecraft and Robert

Bloch saw their early stories published in *Weird Tales,* while the legendary John W. Campbell guided the early careers of such giants as Isaac Asimov and Theodore Sturgeon in *Astounding*, and *Black Mask* started its own school of detective fiction by publishing the work of Dashiell Hammett.

The pulps died out in the 1950's, to be replaced by digest-sized magazines like *Ellery Queen's Mystery Magazine* and *The Magazine of Fantasy and Science Fiction* (occasionally joined by larger-sized efforts like the horror-themed *Twilight Zone* magazine). But by that time, the genres had become firmly entrenched in the mass culture. Presses specializing in specific genres (most importantly Arkham House, the training ground for Ramsey Campbell, and the Mysterious Press) produced works geared toward a growing group of fans.

While the four genres represented here have been treated by critics and academicians as "serious" literature, they are foremost popular literature. That's the basic ingredient: a genre tale must entertain. Whether it does so by frightening us or infusing us with a sense of wonder is irrelevant—the impulse to amuse the reader is paramount (although there are some writers, like Philip K. Dick and Ross Macdonald, who have additional things on their agendas), and that is how a genre tale must be judged. While the style, form, and content of the stories in these two volumes vary greatly, all of them can be said to do one thing, and do it well. Every one of them entertains.

Mystery and Detection

There is a great deal of argument as to what constitutes a "mystery story." Indeed, some claim that the first mystery is the story of Oedipus, whose detective-like hero discovers that he himself is the murderer of his predecessor king. The mystery story as we know it came about in the wake of the creation of, and debate over, the science of criminology.

The development of criminology and the formation of the first official police department by Eugene Vidocq became one of the most discussed subjects among the intellectuals of Europe and America. Each had his own theories as to the validity of the fledgling science, and writers tended to present their theories in the form of stories. People like Hardy and Alarcón would use their fictitious crimes to give their views of the changing methods of justice and law enforcement. Poe's own theory would prompt him to create the first series detective.

The stories presented here have been chosen with an eye toward creating a cross-section of the traditions evident in these two genres. Early mysteries were very formulaic in terms of storytelling. It was only later, as the mystery genre became more accepted, that different approaches became acceptable. Although Pedro Alarcón was the first to look at crime in terms of the people committing them, it would have been unthinkable for him to write of the events in "The Nail" from the point of view of its murderous widow; thus, the story is told by a virtual bystander in the proceedings. By 1947, Roald Dahl was able to write from the murderess' point of view in "Lamb to the Slaughter," and even makes light of the situations surrounding her. By the 1960's, Jim Thompson's stories specialized in psychotic and criminal "heroes," like the aspiring thief of "Exactly What Happened." The most recent story in this collection, Ruth Rendell's "A Needle for the Devil," finds nothing wrong in showing sympathy for its murderess, and finds humor and affection for her besides.

Just as the detective story split into the formal ("whodunit") and hard-boiled (Hammett/Chandler) schools, the mystery story generated its own sub-genres. The earliest sub-genre was the "thriller," of which Wilkie Collins's "A Terribly Strange Bed" is a prime example: the mystery is totally secondary to the chill elicited by the titular smothering device. A later sub-genre was the "suspenser," where the question is not "Whodunit?" but "Will it be done sucessfully?" The style of a suspenser is darker, and often experimental: Fredric Brown's suspenser, "Don't Look Behind You," casts the reader in the role of victim. Another sub-genre, the police procedural, focuses on the methods a police department uses in solving a crime, like the line-up depicted in Ed McBain's classic "First Offense."

In the case of the detective genre, the stories presented here try to inidicate the evolution of the detective-hero by giving the reader examples of the deductive genius (C. August Dupin), the scientific detective (The Thinking Machine), the amateur sleuth (Jane Marple), as well as private detectives both soft (Ellery Queen) and hard-boiled (The Continental Op). By reading the stories in sequence, one can see the archetypal detective go from the unfeeling, almost callous seeker of truth typified by Sherlock Holmes to the too-caring V.I. Warshawski, who sometimes wonders if she's more of a social worker than a detective.

The type of crimes taken on by detectives in these stories reflect their genre leanings. The "formal" detective typified in this collection by characters like Dupin, Father Brown, and Lord Peter Whimsey, tends to solve "problem crimes": locked-room mysteries like "Murders in the Rue Morgue," mysteries springing out of supernatural incidents like "The Eye of Apollo," mysteries of identity like "The Four Suspects," or the simply bizarre case of "The Superfluous Finger." In this tale, the Thinking Machine endeavors to find out why a woman would willingly subject herself to mutilation. Despite the fantastic nature of the crimes, the mysteries are always soluble by means of superior ratiocination, and the criminals all turn out to be outsiders. They are foreigners like the Nazi spy of "The Four Suspects," charlatans like the religious leader of "The Eye of Apollo," or even nonhuman like the culprit in "Murders in the Rue Morgue."

Because the formal detective's crimes have a touch of the fantastic, their solutions tend to revolve around strange devices. Whimsey is able to determine the identity of a thief from his misuse of his native language in "The Entertaining Episode of The Article in Question." Ellery Queen determines the identity of the last Januraian—and the killer—by engaging in a simple word game. Miss Marple uses her knowledge of "the language of flowers" to find the murderer among "The Four Suspects." While the methods they use to reach their conclusions seem unorthodox, the culprit never goes unpunished. Those that seem to get away with their crimes, like the unmasked murderer in "The Eye of Apollo," are brought misfortune by other means.

By comparison, the "hard-boiled" detective's crimes are much more mundane. No dastardly fiends with ingenious murder methods here; the deed is done quickly and without frills. What little ornamentation there is, comes from covering up, rather than committing, the crime, as in "Death and Company." While a hard-boiled detective may cross paths with career criminals, like Shell Scott in "Squeeze Play," he will more often deal with normal people caught up in their own passions. In some cases, the apparent crime hides something worse. In "Death and Company," a kidnapping is a ruse to cover up a murder and the identity of the murderer. While the crime in the formal detective story is usually the result of long-held animosity or greed, the crime in a hard-boiled story usually results from passion of the moment—and the subsequent cover-up. This is not to say that motivations in the formal detective story are unique and distinct from the motivations in the hard-boiled story—the murder in Ross Macdonald's "Sleeping Dog" is the result of a decades-long thirst for revenge.

The thing that most differentiates the formal and hard-boiled school is one of tone. The formal detective is sophisticated, crisp, and smooth; the hard-boiled detective tends to be unrefined, world-weary, and rough. The crime in the formal detective story emphasizes the impossible and will be long-planned; the crime in the hard-boiled story leans toward the mundane and will be performed spontaneously. The formal detective bases his solutions on wordplay, esoteric knowledge, and strange dying messages; the hard-boiled detective uses psychology, street knowledge, and footwork to catch his culprit. The formal detective solves the problem and is hailed by his fellows; the hard-boiled detective is in opposition to the police and shunned, unless he is absolutely needed. The formal detective's world is one that seems brighter and gayer; the hard-boiled detective's world seems dingy and gray. There are exceptions (the determinedly cheerful tone of Richard Prather's "Squeeze Play" is as out of place as the dour sense of tragedy in Ellery Queen's "The Inner Circle," yet there is no way you can imagine them being written any other way), but the contrast in story-telling technique is what separates an Agatha Christie from a Ross Macdonald.

The fascination the public has for mysteries is as much a mystery as some of the stories. The Case Studies section presents a chronology and three critiques that suggest the variety and number of detectives and attempts to answer why they are so popular. In tracing the contributions of Edgar Allen Poe to the detective genre, Robert Lowndes gives some credence to the theory of the mystery as an intellectual puzzle. William Aydelotte, on the other hand, presents us with the idea of mystery as therapy. Raymond Chandler, himself a practitioner of the hard-boiled school, claims for that school an art, while relegating formal detective fiction to mere escapism.

Yet any theory is irrelevant in light of what mysteries and detective stories were originally meant to do. Self-conscious artists like Sayers aside, these stories were written primarily to amuse the reader. There are different styles and different approaches. But no matter the differences, each story entertains. So be prepared to amuse yourself with twenty stories from some of the very best mystery writers.

Mystery

The Nail

Pedro Antonio de Alarcón

Pedro Antonio de Alarcón (1833-1891) was born and raised in Gaudix, Spain. During his teens, Alarcón gained some experience as an editor. When he was 22, he moved to Madrid to be closer to the center of Spanish literary life. In 1855, he wrote his first novel, *The Final Aria of Norma*. Alarcón served as an editor for *El laligo*, writing a large number of stories, essays, and poems that were collected in *Tales, Articles, and Novels* in 1859. That year, he traveled to Morocco to report on the Spanish campaign there. Upon his return a year later, Alarcón became interested in politics and was elected to the state legislature. He published little until 1874, when he published his collection *The Three-Cornered Hat*. Alarcón was again involved in politics when he was elected to the Council of State the following year. During his tenure, he published two more novels (*Scandal*, 1875; *Captain Poison*, 1881), as well as the first volume of his short story collection, subtitled *Stories of the Nation* (1881). After he retired from politics in 1881, he published another novel, *The Prodigal Woman* (1882), as well as the final two volumes of his collection, *Tales of Love* and *Improbable Narratives* (both 1882). Alarcón suffered a series of strokes throughout the 1880's, and his output declined. He produced little before his final stroke in 1891.

"The Nail" is considered Alarcón's greatest short story. Its triple-layered story is masterfully told. It also shows the sort of criminological theories many of the literary community were exploring in the first half of the nineteenth century.

WHAT IS MOST ardently desired by a man who steps into a stagecoach, anticipating a long journey, is that his companions be pleasant, that they have the same tastes (and possibly the same vices), that they be well educated and know enough not to become too familiar.

When I opened the door of the coach I felt afraid that I might encounter an old woman suffering with asthma—an ugly one who could not bear the smell of tobacco smoke, one who gets seasick every

3

time she rides in a carriage—and little angels who would be continually yelling and screaming for God knows what.

You yourself might have hoped some time to have had a beautiful woman for a traveling companion—for instance, a widow of twenty or thirty years of age (even, let us say, thirty-six) whose delightful conversation would help you pass away the time. But if you ever had this idea, as a reasonable man you would have quickly dismissed it, for you would have known that such good fortune does not fall to the lot of the ordinary mortal. Nevertheless, these hopes were in my mind when I opened the door of the stagecoach at exactly eleven o'clock on a stormy night in the autumn of 1844. I had ticket No. 2 and I was wondering who No. 1 might be. The ticket agent had assured me that No. 3 had not been sold.

It was pitch dark within. As I entered I said, "Good evening," but no answer came. "The devil!" I said to myself. "Is my traveling companion deaf, dumb, or asleep?" Then I said in a louder tone: "Good evening," but once more there was no reply.

During all this time the stagecoach was whirling along, drawn by ten horses.

I was puzzled. Who was my companion? Was it a man? Was it a woman? Who was the silent No. 1—and, whoever it might be, why did he or she not reply to my courteous salutation? Lighting a match would have been helpful, but I had given up smoking at that time and carried no matches with me. What should I do? I came to the conclusion that I could rely upon my sense of touch, and wondering whether I would feel a silk dress or an overcoat, I stretched out my hand to where No. 1 should have been—but there was nothing there. At that moment, a flash of lightning, herald of a quickly approaching storm, lit up the night and I perceived that (except for myself) there was no one in the coach at all. I burst into a roar of laughter. Yet, a moment later, I could not help wondering what had become of No. 1.

A half hour later we arrived at the first stop. I was just about to ask the guard (who flashed his lantern into the compartment) why there was no No. 1, when she entered. In the yellow rays I thought it was a vision: a pale, graceful, beautiful woman dressed in deep mourning.

Here was the fulfillment of my dream, the widow I had hoped for.

I extended my hand to the stranger to assist her into the coach, and she sat down beside me, murmuring: "Thank you, señor. Good evening"—but in a tone so sad that it reached my very heart.

"What a pity," I thought. "There are only fifty miles between here and Malaga. Too bad this coach isn't going all the way to Kamschatka." The guard slammed the door, and we were in darkness. I wished that the storm would continue and that we might have a few more flashes of lightning. Instead, the storm relented and finally fled away, leaving only a few pallid stars whose light amounted practically to nothing. I made a brave effort to start a conversation.

"How are you feeling?"

"Are you going to Malaga?"

"Did you like the Alhambra?"

"Do you come from Granada?"

"Isn't it damp out tonight?"

To which questions she respectively replied:

"Very well, thank you."

"Yes."

"No, señor."

"Yes!"

"Awful!"

It was quite clear that my traveling companion was not inclined to conversation. I tried to formulate something original to say to her, but since nothing occurred to me I began to lose myself in thought. Why had this woman boarded the stage at the first stop instead of at Granada? Why was she alone? Was she married? Was she really a widow? Why was she so sad? I certainly had no right to ask her any of these questions, but they interested me because *she* interested me. I wished the sun would rise. In the daytime one may talk freely, but in the darkness of night one feels a certain oppression, as if one were seizing an unfair advantage.

My unknown companion did not sleep a moment during the night. I could tell this by her breathing and by her sighing. It is probably unnecessary to add that I did not sleep either. Once I asked her: "Aren't you feeling well?" and she replied: "I'm all right, thank you. I'm sorry if I've disturbed your sleep."

"Sleep!" I exclaimed disdainfully. "I don't want to sleep. I was just afraid that you might not be feeling well."

"Oh, no," she said in a voice that contradicted her words. "I'm feeling quite well."

At last the sun rose—and how beautiful she was! (I mean the woman, not the sun.) But what deep suffering had lined her face and still lurked in the depths of her beautiful eyes!

She was elegantly dressed and evidently belonged to a good family. Every gesture bore the imprint of distinction. She was the kind of woman you might expect to see in the principal box at the opera, resplendent with jewels, surrounded by admirers.

We breakfasted at Colmenar. After that my companion became less reserved and I said to myself when we again entered the coach: "Philip, you have met your fate. It's now or never."

II

I regretted the very first words I mentioned to her regarding my feelings. She became a block of ice and I lost at once all that I might have gained in her good graces. Yet she spoke to me very kindly: "It's not because it is you, señor, who speaks to me of love—but love itself is something which I hold in horror."

"But why," I asked.

"Because my heart is dead. Because I loved someone to the point of delirium and I was deceived."

I felt that perhaps I should talk to her in a philosophic way and there were enough platitudes on the tip of my tongue, but I refrained from uttering them. I knew that she meant what she said. When we arrived at Malaga, she said to me in a tone I shall never forget: "I can't thank you enough for your kindness during the trip, but I hope you'll forgive me if I don't tell you my name and address."

"You mean then that we won't meet again ?"

"Never. But you—especially, you—should not regret it." And then with a smile that was utterly without joy she extended her exquisite hand to me and said: "Pray to God for me."

I pressed her hand and made a low bow. She entered a handsome victoria that was awaiting her and as it moved away she bowed to me again.

Two months later I met her once more.

At about two o'clock in the afternoon I was jogging along in an old cart on the road that leads to Cordoba. The object of my journey was to examine some land which I owned in that neighborhood and to pass three or four weeks with one of the judges of the Supreme Court, an intimate friend of mine who had been my schoolmate at the University of Granada.

He received me with open arms. As I entered his handsome house I could not help but note the perfect taste and elegance of the furniture and decorations.

"Ah, Zarco," I said. "You've gotten married and you never told me about it. Is this the way to treat a man who was such a close friend?"

"I am not married and what is more, I never will marry," the judge answered sadly.

"I will believe that you're not married, old fellow, since you say so. But I can't understand the declaration that you never will. You must be joking."

"I'm telling you the truth," he replied. "I can swear to it."

"But what a metamorphosis!" I exclaimed. "You were always a partisan of marriage. In fact, for the past two years you have been writing me and advising me to take a wife. Whence this wonderful change, my friend? I hope nothing has happened to you—nothing unfortunate?"

"To me?" the judge answered, somewhat embarrassed.

"Yes, to you. Something has happened and you are going to tell me all about it. You live here alone, have practically buried yourself in this huge house. Come on, tell me everything."

The judge pressed my hand. "All right, I'll tell you everything. You'll get to know why I feel like the most unfortunate man in the world. But listen—this is the day when everyone in Cordoba goes to the cemetery and I must be there, if only for the sake of form. Come along with me. It's a pleasant afternoon and the walk will do you good after riding so long in that old cart. The cemetery is in a beautiful location and I'm sure you will enjoy the walk. On the way I'll tell you about the incident that ruined my life and you can judge for yourself whether I'm justified in my hatred of women."

As we walked together along the flower-bordered road, my friend told me the following story:

Two years ago when I was Assistant District Attorney in ...., I obtained permission from my chief to spend a month in Sevilla. In the hotel where I stayed, there was a beautiful young woman who passed for a widow. But her background, as well as her reasons for living in that town, were a mystery to everyone. Her manner of living, her wealth, her total lack of friends and acquaintances, the sadness of her expression, together with her incomparable beauty, gave rise to a thousand conjectures.

Since her rooms were directly opposite mine, I frequently met her in the hall or on the stairway, only too glad to have the chance of bowing to her. But she was unapproachable and it was impossible for me to secure an introduction. Two weeks later, fate was to afford me the opportunity of entering her apartment. I had been to the theater that night, and when I returned I thoughtlessly opened the door of her apartment instead of that of my own. The beautiful woman was reading by the light of the lamp and she started when she saw me. I was so embarrassed by my mistake that for a moment I could only stammer a few unintelligible words. And my confusion was so evident that she could not doubt for a moment that I had made a mistake. I turned to the door, intent upon relieving her of my presence as quickly as possible, when she said with most exquisite courtesy: "In order to show you that I do not doubt your good faith and that I'm not at all offended, I ask that you call upon me again, *intentionally.*"

Three days passed before I got up sufficient courage to accept her invitation. Yes, I was madly in love with her. Accustomed as I am to analyze my own feelings, I knew that my passion could end only in the greatest happiness or the deepest suffering. At the end of the third day I went to her apartment and spent the evening there. She told me that her name was Blanca, that she was born in Madrid, and that she was a widow. She sang and played music for me and asked me a thousand questions about myself, my profession, my family, and every word she spoke increased my love for her. From that night my soul was the slave of her soul. Yes, and that's how it will be forever.

I called on her again the following night, and thereafter every afternoon and evening I was with her. We loved each other, but not a word of love was ever spoken between us.

One evening she said to me: "I married a man without loving him. And shortly after marriage I hated him. Now he is dead. Only God knows what I suffered. Now I understand what love means—it is either heaven or hell. For me, until now, it has been hell."

I could not sleep that night. I lay awake thinking over these last words of Blanca's. Somehow this woman frightened me. Would I be her heaven and she my hell?

My leave of absence expired. I could ask for an extension, pretending illness, but the question was: *should* I do it? I consulted Blanca.

"Why ask me?" she said, taking my hand.

"Because I love you. Am I doing wrong in loving you?"

"No," she said, becoming very pale, and then she put both arms about my neck and her beautiful lips touched mine.

Well, I asked for another month and, thanks to you, my friend, it was granted. They would never have given it to me without your influence.

My relations with Blanca were more than love—they were delirium, madness, fanaticism, call it what you will. Every day my passion for her increased, and each tomorrow seemed to open up new vistas of happiness. And yet I could not avoid feeling at times a mysterious, indefinable fear. And I knew she felt this as well as I did. We both feared to lose each other. One day I said to Blanca:

"We must marry—as quickly as possible."

She gave me a strange look and said, "You wish to marry me ?"

"Yes, Blanca. I'm so proud of you that I want to show you to the entire world. I love you and I want you—pure, good and saintly as you are."

"I cannot marry you," answered this incomprehensible woman. She would never give a reason.

My leave of absence finally expired and I told her that on the following day we must separate.

"Separate ? It's impossible!" she exclaimed. "I love you too much for that."

"Blanca, you know that I worship you."

"Then give up your profession. I am rich. We will live our lives out together," she said, putting her soft hand over my mouth to prevent my answer.

I kissed the hand and then, gently removing it, I answered: "I would accept this offer from my wife, although it would be a sacrifice for me to give up my career. But I will not accept it from a woman who refuses to marry me."

Blanca remained thoughtful for several minutes. Then, raising her head, she looked at me and said softly, but with a determination that could not be misunderstood:

"I will be your wife, and I won't ask you to give up your profession. Go back to your office. How long will it take you to arrange your business affairs and secure from the government another leave of absence to return to Sevilla ?"

"A month."

"A month ? All right, I'll wait for you here. Return within a month and I will be your wife. Today is the fifteenth of April. Will you be here on the fifteenth of May ?"

"You can be sure of that."

"You swear it?"

"Of course I swear it."

"You love me?"

"More than my life."

"Then go—and return. Farewell."

I left on the same day. The moment I arrived home I began to arrange my house to receive my bride. As you know I solicited another leave of absence, and so quickly did I arrange my business affairs that at the end of two weeks I was ready to return to Sevilla.

I must tell you that during this fortnight I did not receive a single letter from Blanca, although I wrote her six. I set out at once for Sevilla, arriving in that city on the thirtieth of April, and went at once to the hotel where we had first met.

I learned that Blanca had left there two days after my departure without telling anyone her destination.

Imagine my indignation, my disappointment, my suffering. She had gone away without even leaving a line for me, without telling me where she was going. It never occurred to me to remain in Sevilla until the fifteenth of May to ascertain whether she would return on that date. Three days later I took up my court work and tried to forget her.

A few moments after my friend Zarco finished the story, we arrived at the cemetery.

It was only a small plot of ground covered with a veritable forest of crosses and surrounded by a low stone wall. As often happens in Spain, when the cemeteries are very small, it is necessary to dig up one coffin in order to lower another. Those that are disinterred are thrown in a heap in a corner of the cemetery, where skulls and bones are piled up like a haystack. As we were passing, Zarco and I looked at the skulls, wondering to whom they could have belonged, to rich or poor, noble or plebeian.

Suddenly the judge bent down and picking up a skull, exclaimed in astonishment:

"Look here, my friend. What is this? It must be a nail."

Yes, a long nail had been driven into the top of the skull which he held in his hand. The nail had apparently been hammered into the head and the point had penetrated what had been the roof of the mouth.

What could this mean ? He began to speculate and soon both of us felt filled with horror.

"I recognize the hand of Providence!" the judge cried out. "A terrible crime has obviously been committed and would never have come to light had it not been for this accidental discovery. My duty is clear and I won't rest until I've brought the murderer to the scaffold."

III

My friend Zarco was one of the keenest criminal judges in Spain. Within a very few days he determined that the corpse to which this skull belonged had been buried in a rough wooden coffin that the grave digger had taken home with him, intending to use it for firewood. Fortunately, the man had not yet burned it up, and on the lid the judge managed to decipher the initials: "A. G. R." together with the date of interment. He immediately searched the parochial books of every church in the neighborhood, and a week later found the following entry:

"In the parochial church of San Sebastian of the village of..., on the 4th of May, 1843, the funeral rites as prescribed by our holy religion were performed over the body of Don Alfonso Gutierrez Romeral, and he was buried in the cemetery. He was a native of this village and did not receive the holy sacrament, nor did he confess, for he died suddenly of apoplexy at the age of 31. He was married to Doña Gabriela Zahura del Valle, a native of Madrid, and left no issue of him surviving.

The judge handed me the above certificate, duly certified by the parish priest, and said excitedly: "Now everything is as clear as day. I'm positive that within a week the murderer will be arrested. The apoplexy in this case happens to be an iron nail driven into the man's head, bringing quick and sudden death to A. G. R. I have the nail and I'll soon find the hammer."

According to the testimony of the neighbors, Señor Romeral was a young and rich landowner who originally came from Madrid, where he had married a beautiful wife. Four months before the husband's death, his wife had gone to Madrid to spend a few months with her family. The young woman returned home about the last day of April—that is, about three months and a half after she had left her husband's residence for Madrid. The death of Señor Romeral occurred about a week after her return. So great was the shock caused to the widow by the sudden death of her husband that she became ill and informed her friends that she could not continue to live in the same place where everything would remind her of the man she had lost. And just before the middle of May she left for Madrid, ten or twelve days after the death of her husband.

Further details were obtained from the testimony of the servants of the deceased: The couple did not live amicably together and they frequently quarreled. The separation of three and a half months (which preceded the last eight days the couple lived together) was practically an understanding that they were eventually to be parted from each other on account of mysterious disagreements that had existed between them from the date of their marriage. On the day of the death of the deceased, the couple were together in the husband's bedroom. At midnight the bell was rung violently and the servants heard the cries of the wife. They rushed to the room and were met at the door by the wife, who was very pale and extremely upset. She cried out: "It's apoplexy! Run for a doctor! My poor husband is dying!" When they entered the room, they found their master Lying upon a couch and he was dead. The doctor who was called certified that Señor Romeral had died of cerebral congestion.

Three medical experts testified that death brought about as this one had been could not be distinguished from apoplexy. The physician who had been called in had not thought to look for the head of the nail, which was concealed by the hair of the victim, nor was he in any sense to blame for this oversight.

Without delay the judge issued a warrant for the arrest of Doña Gabriela Zahara del Valle, widow of Señor Romeral.

"Tell me," I asked the judge. "Do you think you will ever capture this woman?"

"I'm positive of it."

"Why ?"

"Because in the midst of all these routine criminal affairs there occurs without fail what may be termed a dramatic fatality. To put it another way: when the bones come out of the tomb to testify, there is very little left for the judge to do."

In spite of my friend's confidence, Gabriela was not found and three months later she was, according to the laws of Spain, tried *in absentia,* found guilty and condemned to death.

I returned home after promising Zarco to join him again the following year.

IV

I spent that winter in Granada. One evening I had been invited to a great ball given by a prominent Spanish lady. As I was mounting the stairs of the magnificent residence, I was startled by the sight of a face that was easily distinguishable even in this crowd of southern beauties. It was she, my unknown companion, the mysterious woman of the stagecoach. I made my way toward her, extending my hand in greeting. She recognized me at once.

"Señora," I said, "I've kept my promise not to search for you. I did not know I'd meet you here. Had I suspected it I would have held myself back from coming, for fear of annoying you. Now that I am here, tell me whether I may recognize you and talk to you."

"I see that you're vindictive," she answered graciously, putting her small hand in mine. "But I forgive you. How are you?"

"To tell the truth, I don't know. My health—I mean the health of my soul, because you wouldn't ask me about anything else in a ballroom—depends upon the health of yours. What I wish to say is that I can only be happy if you are happy. May I ask if that wound of the heart, which you told me about when I met you in the stagecoach, has healed?"

"You know as well as I do that there are wounds that never heal."

With a graceful bow she turned away to speak to an acquaintance. A friend of mine was passing and I asked him: "Can you tell me who that woman is?"

"A South American whose name is Mercedes de Meridanueva."

On the following day I paid a visit to the lady, who was residing at that time at the Hotel of the Seven Planets. Receiving me as if I were an intimate friend, the charming Mercedes invited me to walk with her through the wonderful Alhambra and then to dine with her. During the six hours we were together she spoke of a variety of things, and since we always returned to the subject of disappointed love, I felt impelled to tell her the unhappy love experience of my friend, Judge Zarco.

After listening to me attentively, she laughed and said: "Let this be a lesson to you not to fall in love with women you don't know."

"Now please don't think that I've invented this story."

"Oh, I don't doubt the truth of it," she said. "Perhaps there is a mysterious woman in the Hotel of the Seven Planets of Granada, but perhaps she doesn't resemble in the least the one your friend fell in love with in Sevilla. So far as I'm concerned, though, there's no risk of my falling in love with anyone—because I never speak three times to the same man."

"Señora! That's the equivalent of telling me that you refuse to see me again."

"No. I only wish to inform you that I leave Granada tomorrow and it is probable that we will never meet again."

"Never? You told me that during our memorable ride in the stage-coach. And you see that you're not a good prophet."

She suddenly turned quite pale and rose abruptly from the table, saying: "Well, let's leave that to fate. For my part I repeat that I am bidding you an eternal farewell."

Having solemnly articulated these last words, with a graceful bow she turned and ascended the stairway that led to the upper story of the hotel.

I must confess that I was somewhat annoyed at the disdainful manner with which she chose to terminate our acquaintance. Yet this feeling was lost in the pity I felt for her when I perceived her expression of suffering.

And so that was to be our last meeting. Would to God that it was our last! Man proposes, but God disposes.

V

A few days later some business matters brought me to the town where my friend Judge Zarco resided. I found him as lonely and as sad as at the time of my previous visit. Although unable to discover anything about Blanca, he could not for a moment forget her. This woman was unquestionably his fate—his heaven or his hell, as my unfortunate friend would put it.

Meanwhile we were soon to learn that his judicial superstition was to be fully justified.

The evening of the day of my arrival we were seated in his office, reading the latest reports of the police, who had been vainly attempting to trace Gabriela, when an officer entered and handed the judge a note:

"In the Hotel of the Lion there is a lady who wishes to speak to Judge Zarco."

"Who brought this," the judge asked.

"A servant."

"Who sent him?"

"He gave no name."

After gazing thoughtfully at the smoke of his cigar for a few moments, the judge said: "A woman! To see me? I don't know why, but this thing frightens me. What do you think about this, Philip?"

"That it is your duty as a judge to answer the call, of course. Maybe she can give you some information about Gabriela."

"You're quite right," answered Zarco, rising. He thrust a revolver into his pocket, threw a cloak over his shoulders and left.

He returned two hours later.

I saw at once by his face that some great happiness must have come to him. He clasped his arms around me and embraced me convulsively. He said with uncontrolled emotion: "Oh, Philip, if you only knew, if you only knew!"

"But I don't know a thing," I answered. "What on earth has happened to you?"

"I'm simply the happiest man in the world."

"But what is it?"

"The note that called me to the hotel was from *her.*"

"But from whom? From Gabriela Zahara?"

"Oh, stop such nonsense! Who's thinking of those things now? It was she, I tell you—the other one!"

"In the name of heaven, be calm and tell me whom you are talking about."

"Who could it be but Blanca, my love, my life?"

"Blanca," I answered with astonishment. "But the woman deceived you."

"Oh, no. That was all a foolish mistake on my part."

"Explain yourself."

"Listen—Blanca adores me!"

"Oh, so you think she does? Well, go on."

"When Blanca and I separated on the fifteenth of April, it was understood that we were to meet again on the fifteenth of May. Shortly after I left she received a letter calling her to Madrid on urgent family business, since she didn't expect me back until the fifteenth of May, she remained in Madrid until the first. But, as you know, in my impatience I couldn't wait. I returned fifteen days before the agreed day. Not finding her at the hotel I jumped to the conclusion that she had deceived me and that was why I didn't wait for her. I've gone through two years of torment and suffering—all due to my own stupidity.

"But she could have written you a letter."

"She explained that. She said that she had forgotten the address."

"Ah, my poor friend," I said. "I see that you are trying to convince yourself. So much the better. Well, when does the marriage take place? I suppose that after so long and dark a night the sun of matrimony will rise radiant."

"Better be serious," said Zarco. "You are going to be my best man."

"With much pleasure."

Man proposes, but God disposes. We were still seated in the library, chatting together, when there came a knock at the door. It was about two o'clock in the morning. The judge and I were both startled, but neither of us could have said why. After the servant opened the door, a man dashed into the library so breathless from hard running that he could scarcely speak.

"Good news, Judge—great news!" he said when he recovered his breath. "We've won!"

The man was the prosecuting attorney.

"Explain yourself, my dear friend," the judge said, motioning him to a chair. "What could have happened to bring you here in such a rush and at this time of night?"

"We've arrested Gabriela Zahara."

"Arrested her?" the judge exclaimed joyfully.

"Yes, señor, we have her. One of our detectives has been on her trail for a month. He finally caught her and now she's locked up at the prison."

"Then let's go there right now," the judge said eagerly. "We'll interrogate her tonight. Do me a favor—please notify my secretary. And owing to the gravity of the case, you yourself must be present. Also notify the guard who's in charge of the skull of Señor Romeral. It's been my opinion from the beginning that this woman would not dare deny the murder when she was confronted with the evidence of her crime. As far as you're concerned," said the judge, turning to me, "I will appoint you assistant secretary so that you can be present without violating the law."

I could not answer. A horrible suspicion had been growing within me—a suspicion that, like some infernal animal, was tearing at my heart with claws of steel. Could Gabriela and Blanca be one and the same? I turned to the assistant district attorney.

"By the way," I asked casually, "where was Gabriela when she was arrested?"

"In the Hotel of the Lion."

Although my suffering was frightful, I could say nothing without fear of compromising the judge is some way. Besides, I was not yet sure. Even if I were positive that Gabriela and Blanca were the same person, what could my unfortunate friend do? Feign a sudden illness? Flee the country? The better alternative was to remain silent and let God work it out in His own way. The judge's orders were communicated to the chief of police and the warden of the prison. Even at this hour the news spread through the city and idlers began gathering in hope of catching a glimpse of the rich and beautiful woman who would eventually ascend the scaffold. I still clung to the slender chance that Gabriela and Blanca would not prove to be the same person. But on the way to the prison I staggered like a drunken man and was compelled to lean upon the shoulder of one of the officials, who anxiously asked me if I were ill.

VI

We arrived at the prison at four o'clock in the morning. Inside the large and brilliantly lit reception room, the guard was awaiting us, holding in his hand a black box containing the skull of Señor Romeral.

The judge took his chair at the head of the long table, with the prosecuting attorney sitting at his right and the chief of police standing by with his arms folded. The secretary and I sat at the judge's left. About six or seven police officers and detectives stood near the door.

Touching his bell the judge said to the warden:

"Bring in Doña Gabriela Zahara."

I felt as if I were dying. Instead of looking at the door, as did the others, I watched the judge to see if I could read in his face the solution of this fantastic problem.

I saw him become livid and clutch his throat with both hands, as if to seize and suppress a cry of agony, and then he turned to me with a look of infinite supplication.

"Keep quiet!" I whispered, putting my finger to my lips. And then I added: "I knew it."

Stunned, he arose from his chair.

"Judge!" I exclaimed, and in that one word I conveyed to him the full sense of his duty and of the dangers that surrounded him. Slowly controlling himself, he resumed his seat. But were it not for the light in his eyes, he might have been taken for a dead man. Yes, the man was dead—only the judge still lived.

After I had convinced myself of this, I turned and glanced at the accused. Good God! Gabriela Zahara was not only Blanca, the woman so deeply loved by my friend, but she was also the woman I had met in the stagecoach and subsequently at Granada, the beautiful South American, Mercedes!

All these fabulous women had now merged into one—the real one who stood before us, who had been condemned to die for the murder of her husband.

There was, of course, still a chance that she might be able to prove herself innocent. Could she do it ? This was my supreme hope, as it was that of my poor friend.

Gabriela (we will call her now by her real name) was deathly pale, but apparently calm. Was she trusting to her innocence or to the weakness of the judge? This doubt was soon settled. Up to this moment the accused had looked at no one but the judge. I did not know whether she desired to encourage or menace him, or to tell him that his Blanca could not be a murderer. But noting the impassiveness of the magistrate and that his face was as expressionless as that of a corpse, she turned to the others, as if seeking help from them. Then her eyes fell upon me, and she blushed slightly.

Awakening from his stupor the judge asked harshly:

"What is your name?"

"Gabriela Zahara, widow of Romeral," answered the accused in a soft voice.

Zarco trembled. He had just learned that his Blanca had never existed; and it was she who told him so—she who only three hours before had consented to become his wife!

Fortunately, no one was looking at the judge. All eyes fixed upon Gabriela, whose marvelous beauty and quiet manner conveyed to everyone an almost irresistible conviction of her innocence.

The judge recovered himself. Like a man staking more than life upon the cast of a die, he ordered the guard to open the black box.

"Señora," said the judge sternly, his eyes flashing. "Come forward and tell me whether you recognize this head."

At the judge's signal the guard opened the black box and lifted out the skull.

A cry of mortal agony rang through the room—one could not tell whether it was of fear or of madness. Shrinking back, her eyes dilating with terror, the woman screamed: "Alfonzo, Alfonzo!"

Then she seemed to fall into a stupor. Everyone turned to the judge and nodded as one man murmured: "She's guilty all right."

"Do you recognizc this nail which took the life of your husband?" said the judge, arising from his chair as a corpse might ascend from its grave.

"Yes, señor," Gabriela replied mechanically.

"That is to say, you admit that you murdered your husband?" the judge asked in a voice that trembled with emotion.

"Señor," she said, "I really don't care any more about living. But before I die I would like to make a statement."

After falling back in his chair the judge asked me with a look: "What can she possibly say?"

For myself, I was almost stupefied by fear.

Standing with her hands clasped and a far-off look in her huge dark eyes, Gabriela said: "I am going to confess and my confession will be my only defense—although it will not be sufficient to save me from the scaffold. Listen to me, all of you! Why deny what is self-evident? I was alone with my husband when he died. The servants and the doctor have testified to this. So, only I could have killed him. Yes, I committed the crime—but another man forced me to do it."

I could see a shiver of emotion pass through the judge. But courageously dominating his feelings, he said:

"The name of that man, señora? Tell us at once the scoundrel's name."

Regarding the judge with an expression of infinite love, as a mother would look at the child she worshiped, Gabriela answered: "By a single word I could drag this man into the depths with me. But I will not. No one will ever know his name, because he loved me and I still love him. Yes, I love him, although I know he will do nothing to save me."

Half rising from his chair the judge extended his hands beseechingly, but she looked at him as if to say: "Be careful! You will betray yourself without doing a bit of good."

After he slowly sank back into his chair, Gabriela continued her remarks in a quiet, but firm voice:

"I was forced to marry a man I hated. I hated him more after I married him than I did before. I lived three years in this state of torture. One day there came into my life a man whom I loved. He demanded that I marry him, that I fly with him to a heaven of happiness and love. He was a man of exceptional, noble character, whose only fault was that he loved me too much. Had I told him: 'I have deceived you, I am not a widow, my husband is living'—he would have left me at once. Although I invented a thousand excuses, he always answered: 'Be my wife!' What could I do? I was bound to a man of the vilest character and habits, a man I loathed. Well, I killed this man, letting myself believe that I was committing an act of justice—and God punished me, for my lover abandoned me. And now I am very, very tired of life, and all I ask of you is that death may come as quickly as possible."

Gabriela fell silent. The judge had buried his face in his hands, as if he were thinking, but I could see that he was shaking like an epileptic.

Gabriela then spoke again: "Your honor, please grant my request that I may die soon."

The judge made a sign to the guards to remove the prisoner. Before following them, she gazed firmly into my eyes and in her look there was more pride than repentance.

I do not wish to enter into details of the judge's condition during the following day. Let it suffice to say that in the great emotional struggle that took place, the officer of the law conquered the man, and he confirmed the death sentence.

Within the next twenty-four hours the papers were transmitted to the Court of Appeals. Zarco then came to me and said: "Wait here until I return. Take care of this poor woman, but do not visit her, because your presence would humiliate rather than console her. Do not ask me where I am going, and do not think that I am going to commit the very foolish act of taking my own life. Goodbye for a while—and forgive me all the worry that I have caused you."

Twenty days later the Court of Appeals confirmed the sentence, and Gabriela Zahara was escorted into the death cell.

When morning came on the day fixed for the execution, the judge still had not returned. The scaffold had been erected in the center of the square and an enormous crowd had gathered. I stood by the door of the prison. Although having obeyed my friend's wish that I not call on

Gabriela in prison, I believed it my duty to represent him in this tragic moment by accompanying the woman he loved to the foot of the scaffold.

When she appeared, surrounded by guards, I hardly recognized her. She had grown very thin and seemed hardly strong enough to lift to her lips the small crucifix she carried in her hand.

"I am here, señora. Can I be of service to you?" I asked her as she passed by me.

She raised her deep, sunken eyes to mine and when she recognized me, she exclaimed:

"Oh, thanks, thanks! This is a great consolation for me in my last moment of life. Father," she said to the old priest who stood beside her, "may I speak a few words to this generous friend?"

"Yes, my daughter," the priest said.

Then Gabriela asked me: "Where is he ?"

"He is not here—"

"May God bless him and make him happy. When you see him, ask him to forgive me even as I believe God has already forgiven me. Tell him I still love him, even though this love is the cause of my death."

We had arrived at the foot of the scaffold, where I had to leave her. A tear, perhaps the last one left in her heart, rolled down her cheek. Once more she said: "Tell him I died blessing him."

Suddenly there came a thunderous roar from the crowd. In the huge throng, people began to shout, dance and laugh like maniacs—and above all this tumult one word rang out clearly:

"Pardoned! Pardoned!"

A man on horseback entered the square and galloped madly toward the scaffold. Waving a white handkerchief he continued to shout above the clamor of the crowd:

"Pardoned! Pardoned!"

It was the judge. Reining up his foaming horse at the foot of the scaffold, he handed a paper to the chief of police.

Gabriela, who had already mounted a few steps, turned and gave the judge a look of infinite love and gratitude.

"God bless you," she said weakly and then fell senseless.

As soon as the signatures and seals upon the document were verified by the authorities, the priest and the judge rushed to the prisoner to undo the cords from her hands and arms and to revive her.

All their efforts proved useless. Gabriela Zahara was dead.

The Three Strangers

Thomas Hardy

Thomas Hardy (1840-1928) was born in Higher Bockhampton, England. The son of a stone mason, Hardy stayed in Dorset county until he was 22. He studied architecture at Dorcherster, concentrating on church restoration. A voracious reader, Hardy taught himself French, Latin, and Greek. In 1862, he travelled to London to open his architectural practice. Hardy started writing poetry at this time, but his efforts to get published met with no success. He gave up his architectural practice in 1867 to write full-time. Hardy had no success until editors expressed an interest in seeing him write fiction. Hardy submitted a story to George Meredith and John Morley in 1868. Meredith refused to print it, but helped Hardy write his first published novel, *Desperate Memories* (1871). Hardy began to write other novels in serial form to support himself; *The Greenwood Tree* (1871), *A Pair of Blue Eyes* (1873), *Far From The Maddening Crowd* (1874), *The Return of the Native* (1878), *The Trumpet Major* (1880), and *A Story of To-Day* (1881) are among the best known. In the mid-1880s, Hardy began to write more political works like *The Mayor of Casterbridge* (1886), *Tess of the D'Urbervilles* (1891), and *Jude the Obscure* (1895). Hardy returned to writing poetry, exclusively, in his later years, and his first collection, *The Wessex Poems,* appeared in 1898. This and later collections like *Poems of the Past and Present* (1901) and *Satires of Circumstances* (1914) contained new poems and old ones. His last great work, an epic poem called *The Dynasts,* was produced in three parts over a period of time from 1904-1908.

"The Three Strangers" is a story of identity and justice set in the area Hardy knew best.

AMONG THE FEW features of agricultural England which retain an appearance but little modified by the lapse of centuries, may be reckoned the high, grassy, and furzy downs, coombs, or ewe-leases, as they are indifferently called, that fill a large area of certain counties in the south and southwest. If any mark of human occupation is met with hereon, it usually takes the form of the solitary cottage of some shepherd.

Fifty years ago such a lonely cottage stood on such a down, and may possibly be standing there now. In spite of its loneliness, however, the spot, by actual measurement, was not more than five miles from a county-town. Yet that affected it little. Five miles of irregular upland, during the long inimical seasons, with their sleets, snows, rains, and mists, afford withdrawing space enough to isolate a Timon or a Nebuchadnezzar; much less, in fair weather, to please that less repellent tribe, the poets, philosophers, artists, and others who "conceive and meditate of pleasant things."

Some old earthen camp or barrow, some clump of trees, at least some starved fragment of ancient hedge is usually taken advantage of in the erection of these forlorn dwellings. But, in the present case, such a kind of shelter had been disregarded. Higher Crowstairs, as the house was called, stood quite detached and undefended. The only reason for its precise situation seemed to be the crossing of two footpaths at right angles hard by, which may have crossed there and thus for a good five hundred years. Hence the house was exposed to the elements on all sides. But, though the wind up here blew unmistakably when it did blow, and the rain hit hard whenever it fell, the various weathers of the winter season were not quite so formidable on the coomb as they were imagined to be by dwellers on low ground. The raw rimes were not so pernicious as in the hollows, and the frosts were scarcely so severe. When the shepherd and his family who tenanted the house were pitied for their sufferings from the exposure, they said that upon the whole they were less inconvenienced by "wuzzes and flames" (hoarses and phlegms) than when they had lived by the stream of a snug neighboring valley.

The night of March 28, 182—, was precisely one of the nights that were wont to call forth these expressions of commiseration. The level rainstorm smote walls, slopes, and hedges like the clothyard shafts of Senlac and Crecy. Such sheep and outdoor animals as had no shelter stood with their buttocks to the winds; while the tails of little birds trying to roost on some scraggy thorn were blown inside-out like umbrellas. The gable-end of the cottage was stained with wet, and the eavesdroppings flapped against the wall. Yet never was commiseration for the shepherd more misplaced. For that cheerful rustic was entertaining a large party in glorification of the christening of his second girl.

The guests had arrived before the rain began to fall, and they were all now assembled in the chief or living room of the dwelling. A glance into the apartment at eight o'clock on this eventful evening would have resulted in the opinion that it was as cosy and comfortable a nook as could be wished for in boisterous weather. The calling of its inhabitant was proclaimed by a number of highly-polished sheep-crooks without stems that were hung ornamentally over the fireplace, the curl of each shining crook varying from the antiquated type engraved in the patriarchal pictures of old family Bibles to the most approved fashion of the last local sheep-fair. The room was lighted by half-a-dozen candles, having wicks only a trifle smaller than the grease which enveloped them, in candlesticks that were never used but at high-days, holy-days, and family feasts. The lights were scattered about the room, two of them standing on the chimney-piece This position of candles was in itself significant. Candles on the chimney-piece always meant a party.

On the hearth, in front of a back-brand to give substance, blazed a fire of thorns, that crackled "like the laughter of the fool."

Nineteen persons were gathered here. Of these, five women, wearing gowns of various bright hues, sat in chairs along the wall; girls shy and not shy filled the window-bench; four men, including Charley Jake the hedge-carpenter, Elijah New the parish-clerk, and John Pitcher, a neighboring dairyman, the shepherd's father-in-law, lolled in the settle; a young man and maid, who were blushing over tentative *pourparlers* on a life-companionship, sat beneath the corner-cupboard; and an elderly engaged man of fifty or upward moved restlessly about from spots where his betrothed was not to the spot where she was. Enjoyment was pretty general, and so much the more prevailed in being unhampered by conventional restrictions. Absolute confidence in each other's good opinion begat perfect ease, while the finishing stroke of manner, amounting to a truly princely serenity, was lent to the majority by the absence of any expression or trait denoting that they wished to get on in the world, enlarge their minds, or do any eclipsing thing whatever—which nowadays so generally nips the bloom and *bonhomie* of all except the two extremes of the social scale.

Shepherd Fennel had married well, his wife being a dairyman's daughter from a vale at a distance, who brought fifty guineas in her pocket—and kept them there, till they should be required for ministering to the needs of a coming family. This frugal woman had been somewhat exercised as to the character that should be given to the gathering. A sit-still party had its advantages; but an undisturbed position of ease in chairs and settles was apt to lead on the men to such an unconscionable deal of toping that they would sometimes fairly drink the house dry. A dancing-party was the alternative; but this, while avoiding the foregoing objection on the score of good drink, had a counterbalancing disadvantage in the matter of good victuals, the ravenous appetites engendered by the exercise causing immense havoc in the buttery. Shepherdess Fennel fell back upon the intermediate plan of mingling short dances with short periods of talk and singing, so as to hinder any ungovernable rage in either. But this scheme was entirely confined to her own gentle mind: the shepherd himself was in the mood to exhibit the most reckless phases of hospitality.

The fiddler was a boy of those parts, about twelve years of age, who had a wonderful dexterity in jigs and reels, though his fingers were so small and short as to necessitate a constant shifting for the high notes, from which he scrambled back to the first position with sounds not of unmixed purity of tone. At seven the shrill tweedle-dee of this young-ster had begun, accompanied by a booming ground-bass from Elijah New, the parish-clerk, who had thoughtfully brought with him his favorite musical instrument, the serpent. Dancing was instantaneous, Mrs. Fennel privately enjoining the players on no account to let the dance exceed the length of a quarter of an hour.

But Elijah and the boy, in the excitement of their position, quite forgot the injunction. Moreover, Oliver Giles, a man of seventeen, one of the dancers, who was enamored of his partner, a fair girl of thirty-three rolling years, had recklessly handed a new crown-piece to the musicians, as a bribe to keep going as long as they had muscle and wind. Mrs. Fennel, seeing the steam begin to generate on the counte-nances of her guests, crossed over and touched the fiddler's elbow and put her hand on the serpent's mouth. But they took no notice, and fearing she might lose her character of genial hostess if she were to interfere too markedly, she retired and sat down helpless. And so the dance whizzed on with cumulative fury, the performers moving in their planet-like courses, direct and retrograde, from apogee to perigee, till the hand of the well-kicked clock at the bottom of the room had traveled over the circumference of an hour.

While these cheerful events were in course of enactment within Fennel's pastoral dwelling, an incident having considerable bearing on the party had occurred in the gloomy night without. Mrs. Fennel's concern about the growing fierceness of the dance corresponded in point of time with the ascent of a human figure to the solitary hill of Higher Crowstairs from the direction of the distant town. This person-age strode on, through the rain without a pause, following the little-worn path which, further on in its course, skirted the shepherd's cottage.

It was nearly the time of full moon, and on this account, though the sky was lined with a uniform sheet of dripping cloud, ordinary objects out of doors were readily visible. The sad wan light revealed the lonely pedestrian to be a man of supple frame; his gait suggested that he had somewhat passed the period of perfect and instinctive agility, though not so far as to be otherwise than rapid of motion when occasion required. At a rough guess, he might have been about forty years of age. He appeared tall, but a recruiting sergeant, or other person accustomed to the judging of men's heights by the eye, would have discerned that this was chiefly owing to his gauntness, and that he was not more than five-feet-eight or nine.

Notwithstanding the regularity of his tread, there was caution in it, as in that of one who mentally feels his way; and despite the fact that it was not a black coat nor a dark garment of any sort that he wore, there was something about him which suggested that he naturally belonged to the black-coated tribes of men. His clothes were of fustian, and his boots hobnailed, yet in his progress he showed not the mud-accustomed bearing of hobnailed and fustianed peasantry.

By the time that he had arrived abreast of the shepherd's premises the rain came down, or rather came along, with yet more determined violence. The outskirts of the little settlement partially broke the force of wind and rain, and this induced him to stand still. The most salient of the shepherd's domestic erections was an empty sty at the forward corner of his hedgeless garden, for in these latitudes the principle of masking the homelier features of your establishment by a conventional frontage was unknown. The traveler's eye was attracted to this small building by the pallid shine of the wet slates that covered it. He turned aside, and, finding it empty, stood under the pent-roof for shelter.

While he stood, the boom of the serpent within the adjacent house and the lesser strains of the fiddler, reached the spot as an accompaniment to the surging hiss of the flying rain on the sod, its louder beating on the cabbage-leaves of the garden, on the eight or ten beehives just discernible by the path, and its dripping from the eaves into a row of buckets and pans that had been placed under the walls of the cottage. For at Higher Crowstairs, as at all such elevated domiciles, the grand difficulty of housekeeping was an insufficiency of water; and a casual rainfall was utilized by turning out, as catchers, every utensil that the house contained. Some queer stories might be told of the contrivances for economy in suds and dish-waters that are absolutely necessitated in upland habitations during the droughts of summer. But at this season there were no such exigencies; a mere acceptance of what the skies bestowed was sufficient for an abundant store.

At last the notes of the serpent ceased and the house was silent. This cessation of activity aroused the solitary pedestrian from the reverie into which he had lapsed, and, emerging from the shed, with an apparently new intention, he walked up the path to the house-door. Arrived here, his first act was to kneel down on a large stone beside the row of vessels, and to drink a copious draught from one of them. Having quenched his thirst he rose and lifted his hand to knock, but paused with his eye upon the panel. Since the dark surface of the wood revealed absolutely nothing, it was evident that he must be mentally looking through the door, as if he wished to measure thereby all the possibilities that a house of this sort might include, and how they might bear upon the question of his entry.

In his indecision he turned and surveyed the scene around. Not a soul was anywhere visible. The garden-path stretched downward from his feet, gleaming like the track of a snail; the roof of the little well (mostly dry), the well-cover, the top rail of the garden-gate, were varnished with the same dull liquid glaze; while, far away in the vale, a faint whiteness of more than usual extent showed that the rivers were high in the meads. Beyond all this winked a few bleared lamplights through the beating drops—lights that denoted the situation of the county-town from which he had appeared to come. The absence of all notes of life in that direction seemed to clinch his intentions, and he knocked at the door.

Within, a desultory chat had taken the place of movement and musical sound. The hedge-carpenter was suggesting a song to the company, which nobody just then was inclined to undertake, so that the knock afforded a not unwelcome diversion.

"Walk in!" said the shepherd promptly.

The latch clicked upward, and out of the night our pedestrian appeared upon the door-mat. The shepherd arose, snuffed two of the nearest candles, and turned to look at him.

Their light disclosed that the stranger was dark in complexion and not unprepossessing as to feature. His hat, which for a moment he did not remove, hung low over his eyes, without concealing that they were large, open, and determined, moving with a flash rather than a glance round the room. He seemed pleased with his survey, and, baring his shaggy head, said, in a rich deep voice, "The rain is so heavy, friends, that I ask leave to come in and rest awhile."

"To be sure, stranger," said the shepherd. "And faith, you've been lucky in choosing your time, for we are having a bit of a fling for a glad cause—though, to be sure, a man could hardly wish that glad cause to happen more than once a year."

"Nor less," spoke up a woman. "For 'tis best to get your family over and done with, as soon as you can, so as to be all the earlier out of the fag o't."

"And what may be this glad cause?" asked the stranger.

"A birth and christening," said the shepherd.

The stranger hoped his host might not be made unhappy either by too many or too few of such episodes, and being invited by a gesture to a pull at the mug, he readily acquiesced. His manner, which, before entering, had been so dubious, was now altogether that of a careless and candid man.

"Late to be traipsing athwart this coomb—hey?" said the engaged man of fifty.

"Late it is, master, as you say.—I'll take a seat in the chimney-corner, if you have nothing to urge against it, ma'am; for I am a little moist on the side that was next the rain."

Mrs. Shepherd Fennel assented, and made room for the self-invited comer, who, having got completely inside the chimney-corner, stretched out his legs and his arms with the expansiveness of a person quite at home.

"Yes, I am rather cracked in the vamp," he said freely, seeing that the eyes of the shepherd's wife fell upon his boots, "and I am not well fitted either. I have had some rough times lately, and have been forced to pick up what I can get in the way of wearing, but I must find a suit better fit for working-days when I reach home."

"One of hereabouts?" she inquired.

"Not quite that—further up the country."

"I thought so. And so be I; and by your tongue you come from my neighborhood."

"But you would hardly have heard of me," he said quickly. "My time would be long before yours, ma'am, you see."

This testimony to the youthfulness of his hostess had the effect of stopping her cross-examination.

"There is only one thing more wanted to make me happy," continued the newcomer "And that is a little baccy, which I am sorry to say I am out of."

"I'll fill your pipe," said the shepherd.

"I must ask you to lend me a pipe likewise."

"A smoker, and no pipe about 'ee?"

"I have dropped it somewhere on the road."

The shepherd filled and handed him a new clay pipe, saying, as he did so, "Hand me your baccy box—I'll fill that too, now I am about it."

The man went through the movement of searching his pockets.

"Lost that too?" said his entertainer, with some surprise.

"I am afraid so," said the man with some confusion. "Give it to me in a screw of paper." Lighting his pipe at the candle with a suction that drew the whole flame into the bowl, he resettled himself in the corner and bent his looks upon the faint steam from his damp legs, as if he wished to say no more.

Meanwhile the general body of guests had been taking little notice of this visitor by reason of an absorbing discussion in which they were engaged with the band about a tune for the next dance. The matter being settled, they were about to stand up when an interruption came in the shape of another knock at the door.

At sound of the same the man in the chimney-corner took up the poker and began stirring the brands as if doing it thoroughly were the one aim of his existence; and a second time the shepherd said, "Walk in!" In a moment another man stood upon the straw-woven door-mat. He too was a stranger.

This individual was one of a type radically different from the first. There was more of the commonplace in his manner, and a certain jovial cosmopolitanism sat upon his features. He was several years older than the first arrival, his hair being slightly frosted, his eyebrows bristly, and his whiskers cut back from his cheeks. His face was rather full and flabby, and yet it was not altogether a face without power. A few grog-blossoms marked the neighborhood of his nose. He flung back his long drab greatcoat, revealing that beneath it he wore a suit of cinder-gray shade throughout, large heavy seals, of some metal or other that would take a polish, dangling from his fob as his only personal ornament. Shaking the water-drops from his low-crowned glazed hat, he said, "I mut ask for a few minutes' shelter, comrades, or I shall be wetted to my skin before I get to Casterbridge."

"Make yourself at home, master," said the shepherd, perhaps a trifle less heartily than on the first occasion. Not that Fennel had the least tinge of niggardliness in his composition; but the room was far from large, spare chairs were not numerous, and damp companions were not altogether desirable at close quarters for the women and girls in their bright-colored gowns.

However, the second comer, after taking off his greatcoat, and hanging his hat on a nail in one of the ceiling-beams as if he had been specially invited to put it there, advanced and sat down at the table. This had been pushed so closely into the chimney-corner to give all available room to the dancers, that its inner edge grazed the elbow of the man who had ensconced himself by the fire; and thus the two strangers were brought into close companionship. They nodded to each other by way of breaking the ice of unacquaintance, and the first stranger handed his neighbor the family mug—a huge vessel of brown ware, having its upper edge worn away like a threshold by the rub of whole generations of thirsty lips that had gone the way of all flesh, and bearing the following inscription burnt upon its rotund side in yellow letters:—

THERE IS NO FUN

UNTIL I CUM

The other man, nothing loth, raised the mug to his lips, and drank on, and on, and on—till a curious blueness overspread the countenance of the shepherd's wife, who had regarded with no little surprise the first stranger's free offer to the second of what did not belong to him to dispense.

"I knew it!" said the toper to the shepherd with much satisfaction. "When I walked up your garden before coming in, and saw the hives all of a row, I said to myself, 'Where there's bees there's honey, and where there's honey there's mead.' But mead of such a truly comfortable sort as this I really didn't expect to meet in my older days." He took yet another pull at the mug, till it assumed an ominous elevation.

"Glad you enjoy it!" said the shepherd warmly.

"It is goodish mead," assented Mrs. Fennel, with an absence of enthusiasm which seemed to say that it was possible to buy praise for one's cellar at too heavy a price. "It is trouble enough to make—and really I hardly think we shall make any more. For honey sells well, and we ourselves can make shift with a drop o' small mead and metheglin for common use from the comb-washings."

"O, but you'll never have the heart!" reproachfully cried the stranger in cinder-gray, after taking up the mug a third time and setting it down empty. "I love mead, when 'tis old like this, as I love to go to church o' Sundays, or to relieve the needy any day of the week."

"Ha, ha, ha!" said the man in the chimney-corner, who, in spite of the taciturnity induced by the pipe of tobacco, could not or would not refrain from this slight testimony to his comrade's humor.

Now the old mead of those days, brewed of the purest first-year or maiden honey, four pounds to the gallon—with its due complement of white of eggs, cinnamon, ginger, cloves, mace, rosemary, yeast, and processes of working, bottling, and cellaring—tasted remarkably strong; but it did not taste so strong as it actually was. Hence, presently the stranger in cinder-gray at the table, moved by its creeping influence, unbuttoned his waistcoat, threw himself back in his chair, spread his legs, and made his presence felt in various ways.

"Well, well, as I say," he resumed, "I am going to Casterbridge, and to Casterbridge I must go. I should have been almost there by this time; but the rain drove me into your dwelling, and I'm not sorry for it."

"You don't live in Casterbridge?" said the shepherd.

"Not as yet; though I shortly mean to move there."

"Going to set up in trade, perhaps?"

"No, no," said the shepherd's wife. "It is easy to see that the gentleman is rich, and don't want to work at anything."

The cinder-gray stranger paused, as if to consider whether he would accept that definition of himself. He presently rejected it by answering, "Rich is not quite the word for me, dame. I do work, and I must work. And even if I only get to Casterbridge by midnight I must begin work there at eight tomorrow morning. Yes, het or wet, blow or snow, famine or sword, my day's work tomorrow must be done."

"Poor man! Then, in spite o' seeming, you be worse off than we," replied the shepherd's wife.

"'Tis the nature of my trade, men and maidens. 'Tis the nature of my trade more than my poverty.... But really and truly I must up and off, or I shan't get a lodging in the town." However, the speaker did not move, and directly added, "There's time for one more draught of friendship before I go; and I'd perform it at once if the mug were not dry."

"Here's a mug o' small," said Mrs. Fennel. "Small, we call it, though to be sure 'tis only the first wash o' the combs."

"No," said the stranger disdainfully, "I won't spoil your first kindness by partaking o' your second."

"Certainly not," broke in Fennel. "We don't increase and multiply every day, and I'll fill the mug again." He went away to the dark place under the stairs where the barrel stood. The shepherdess followed him.

"Why should you do this?" she said reproachfully, as soon as they were alone. "He's emptied it once, though it held enough for ten people; and now he's not contented wi' the small, but must needs call for more o' the strong! And a stranger unbeknown to any of us. For my part, I don't like the look o' the man at all."

"But he's in the house, my honey; and 'tis a wet night, and a christening. Daze it, what's a cup of mead more or less? There'll be plenty more next bee-burning."

"Very well—this time, then," she answered, looking wistfully at the barrel. "But what is the man's calling, and where is he one of, that he should come in and join us like this?"

"I don't know. I'll ask him again."

The catastrophe of having the mug drained dry at one pull by the stranger in cinder-gray was effectually guarded against this time by Mrs. Fennel. She poured out his allowance in a small cup, keeping the large one at a discreet distance from him. When he had tossed off his portion the shepherd renewed his inquiry about the stranger's occupation.

The latter did not immediately reply, and the man in the chimney-corner, with sudden demonstrativeness, said, "Anybody may know my trade—I'm a wheelwright."

"A very good trade for these parts," said the shepherd.

"And anybody may know mine—if they've the sense to find it out," said the stranger in cinder-gray.

"You may generally tell what a man is by his claws," observed the hedge-carpenter, looking at his own hands. "My fingers be as full of thorns as an old pincushion is of pins."

The hands of the man in the chimney-corner instinctively sought the shade, and he gazed into the fire as he resumed his pipe. The man at the table took up the hedge-carpenter's remark, and added smartly, "True; but the oddity of my trade is that, instead of setting a mark upon me, it sets a mark upon my customers."

No observation being offered by anybody in elucidation of this enigma, the shepherd's wife once more called for a song. The same obstacles presented themselves as at the former time—one had no voice, another had forgotten the first verse. The stranger at the table, whose soul had now risen to a good working temperature, relieved the difficulty by exclaiming that, to start the company, he would sing himself. Thrusting one thumb into the arm-hole of his waistcoat, he waved the other hand in the air, and, with an extemporizing gaze at the shining sheep-crooks above the mantelpiece, began:—

> "O my trade it is the rarest one,
>   Simple shepherds all—

My trade is a sight to see;
For my customers I tie, and take them up on high,
And waft 'em to a far countree!"

The room was silent when he had finished the verse—with one
exception, that of the man in the chimney-corner, who, at the singer's
word, "Chorus!" joined him in a deep bass voice of musical relish—

"And waft 'em to a far countree!"

Oliver Giles, John Pitcher the dairyman, the parish-clerk, the engaged man of fifty, the row of young women against the wall, seemed
lost in thought not of the gayest kind. The shepherd looked meditatively on the ground, the shepherdess gazed keenly at the singer, and
with some suspicion; she was doubting whether this stranger were
merely singing an old song from recollection, or was composing one
there and then for the occasion. All were as perplexed at the obscure
revelation as the guests at Belshazzar's Feast, except the man in the
chimney-corner, who quietly said, "Second verse, stranger," and
smoked on.

The singer thoroughly moistened himself from his lips inwards, and
went on with the next stanza as requested:—

"My tools are but common ones,
            Simple shepherds all—
    My tools are no sight to see:
A little hempen string, and a post whereon to swing,
    Are implements enough for me!"

Shepherd Fennel glanced round. There was no longer any doubt that
the stranger was answering his question rhythmically. The guests one
and all started back with suppressed exclamations. The young woman
engaged to the man of fifty fainted half-way, and would have proceeded but finding him wanting in alacrity for catching her she sat
down trembling.

"O, he's the—!" whispered the people in the background, mentioning the name of an ominous public officer. "He's come to do it! 'tis to
be at Casterbridge jail tomorrow—the man for sheep-stealing—the
poor clock-maker we heard of, who used to live away at Shottsford and
had no work to do—Timothy Summers, whose family were a-starving,

and so he went out of Shottstord by the high-road, and took a sheep in open daylight, defying the farmer and the farmer's wife and the farmer's lad, and every man jack among 'em. He" (and they nodded towards the stranger of the deadly trade) "is come from up the country to do it because there's not enough to do in his own county-town, and he's got the place here now our own county man's dead; he's going to live in the same cottage under the prison wall."

The stranger in cinder-gray took no notice of this whispered string of observations, but again wetted his lips. Seeing that his friend in the chimney-corner was the only one who reciprocated his joviality in any way, he held out his cup towards that appreciative comrade, who also held out his own. They clinked together, the eyes of the rest of the room hanging upon the singer's actions. He parted his lips for the third verse; but at that moment another knock was audible upon the door. This time the knock was faint and hesitating.

The company seemed scared; the shepherd looked with consternation towards the entrance, and it was with some effort that he resisted his alarmed wife's deprecatory glance, and uttered for the third time the welcoming words, "Walk in!"

The door was gently opened, and another man stood upon the mat. He, like those who had preceded him, was a stranger. This time it was a short, small personage, of fair complexion, and dressed in a decent suit of dark clothes.

"Can you tell me the way to—?" he began: when, gazing round the room to observe the nature of the company amongst whom he had fallen, his eyes lighted on the stranger in cinder-gray. It was just at the instant when the latter, who had thrown his mind into his song with such a will that he scarcely heeded the interruption, silenced all whispers and inquiries by bursting into his third verse:

"Tomorrow is my working day,
            Simple shepherds all—
    Tomorrow is a working day for me:
For the farmer's sheep is slain, and the lad who did it ta'en,
        And on his soul may God ha' mercy!"

The stranger in the chimney-corner, waving cups with the singer so heartily that his mead splashed over on the hearth, repeated in his bass voice as before:

"And on his soul may God ha' merc-y!"

All this time the third stranger had been standing in the doorway. Finding now that he did not come forward or go on speaking, the guests particularly regarded him. They noticed to their surprise that he stood before them the picture of abject terror—his knees trembling, his hand shaking so violently that the door-latch by which he supported himself rattled audibly: his white lips were parted, and his eyes fixed on the merry officer of justice in the middle of the room. A moment more and he had turned, closed the door, and fled.

"What a man can it be?" said the shepherd.

The rest, between the awfulness of their late discovery and the odd conduct of this third visitor, looked as if they knew not what to think, and said nothing. Instinctively they withdrew further and further from the grim gentleman in their midst, whom some of them seemed to take for the Prince of Darkness himself, till they formed a remote circle, an empty space of floor being left between them and him—

"...circulus, cujus centrum diabolus."

The room was so silent—though there were more than twenty people in it—that nothing could be heard but the patter of the rain against the window-shutters, accompanied by the occasional hiss of a stray drop that fell down the chimney into the fire, and the steady puffing of the man in the corner, who had now resumed his pipe of long clay.

The stillness was unexpectedly broken. The distant sound of a gun reverberated through the air—apparently from the direction of the county-town.

"Be jiggered !" cried the stranger who had sung the song, jumping up. "What does that mean?" asked several.

"A prisoner escaped from the jail—that's what it means."

All listened. The sound was repeated, and none of them spoke, but the man in the chimney-corner, who said quietly, "I've often been told that in this county they fire a gun at such times; but I never heard it till now."

"I wonder if it is *my* man?" murmured the personage in cinder-gray.

"Surely it is!" said the shepherd involuntarily. "And surely we've zeed him! That little man who looked in at the door by now, and quivered like a leaf when he zeed ye and heard your song!"

"His teeth chattered, and the breath went out of his body," said the dairyman.

"And his heart seemed to sink within him like a stone," said Oliver Giles.

"And he bolted as if he'd been shot at," said the hedge-carpenter.

"True—his teeth chattered, and his heart seemed to sink; and he bolted as if he'd been shot at," slowly summed up the man in the chimney-corner.

"I didn't notice it," remarked the hangman.

"We were all a-wondering what made him run off in such a fright," faltered one of the women against the wall, "and now 'tis explained!"

The firing of the alarm-gun went on at intervals, low and sullenly, and their suspicions became a certainty. The sinister gentleman in cinder-gray roused himself. "Is there a constable here?" he asked, in thick tones. "If so, let him step forward."

The engaged man of fifty stepped quavering out from the wall, his betrothed beginning to sob on the back of the chair.

"You are a sworn constable?"

"I be, sir."

"Then pursue the criminal at once, with assistance, and bring him back here. He can't have gone far."

"I will, sir, I will—when I've got my staff. I'll go home and get it, and come sharp here, and start in a body."

"Staff!—never mind your staff; the man'll be gone!"

"But I can't do nothing without my staff—can I, William, and John, and Charles Jake? No; for there's the king's royal crown a-painted on en in yaller and gold, and the lion and the unicorn, so as when I raise en up and hit my prisoner, 'tis made a lawful blow thereby. I wouldn't 'tempt to take up a man without my staff—no, not I. If I hadn't the law to gie me courage, why, instead o' my taking up him he might take up me!"

"Now, I'm a king's man myself, and can give you authority enough for this," said the formidable officer in gray. "Now then, all of ye, be ready. Have ye any lanterns?"

"Yes—have ye any lanterns?—I demand it!" said the constable.

"And the rest of you able-bodied—"

"Able-bodied men—yes—the rest of ye!" said the constable.

"Have you some good stout staves and pitchforks—"

"Staves and pitchforks—in the name o' the law! And take 'em in yer hands and go in quest, and do as we in authority tell ye!"

Thus aroused, the men prepared to give chase. The evidence was, indeed, though circumstantial, so convincing, that but little argument was needed to show the shepherd's guests that after what they had seen, it would look very much like connivance if they did not instantly pursue the unhappy third stranger, who could not as yet have gone more than a few hundred yards over such uneven country.

A shepherd is always well provided with lanterns; and lighting these hastily, and with hurdle-staves in their hands, they poured out of the door, taking a direction along the crest of the hill, away from the town, the rain having fortunately a little abated.

Disturbed by the noise, or possibly by unpleasant dreams of her baptism, the child who had been christened began to cry heart-brokenly in the room overhead. These notes of grief came down through the chinks of the floor to the ears of the women below, who jumped up one by one, and seemed glad of the excuse to ascend and comfort the baby, for the incidents of the last half-hour greatly oppressed them. Thus in the space of two or three minutes the room on the ground-floor was deserted quite.

But it was not for long. Hardly had the sound of footsteps died away when a man returned round the corner of the house from the direction the pursuers had taken. Peeping in at the door, and seeing nobody there, he entered leisurely. It was the stranger of the chimney-corner, who had gone out with the rest. The motive of his return was shown by his helping himself to a cut piece of skimmer-cake that lay on a ledge beside where he had sat, and which he had apparently forgotten to take with him. He also poured out half a cup more mead from the quantity that remained, ravenously eating and drinking these as he stood. He had not finished when another figure came in just as quietly—his friend in cinder-gray.

"O—you here?" said the latter, smiling. "I thought you had gone to help in the capture." And this speaker also revealed the object of his return by looking solicitously round for the fascinating mug of old mead.

"And I thought you had gone," said the other, continuing his skimmer-cake with some effort.

"Well, on second thoughts, I felt there were enough without me," said the first confidentially, "and such a night as it is, too. Besides, 'tis the business o' the Government to take care of its criminals—not mine."

"True; so it is. And I felt as you did, that there were enough without me."

"I don't want to break my limbs running over the humps and hollows of this wild country."

"Nor I neither, between you and me."

"These shepherd-people are used to it—simple-minded souls, you know, stirred up to anything in a moment. They'll have him ready for me before the morning, and no trouble to me at all."

"They'll have him, and we shall have saved ourselves all labor in the matter."

"True, true. Well, my way is to Casterbridge; and 'tis as much as my legs will do to take me that far. Going the same way?"

"No, I am sorry to say! I have to get home over there" (he nodded indefinitely to the right), "and I feel as you do, that it is quite enough for my legs to do before bedtime."

The other had by this time finished the mead in the mug, after which, shaking hands heartily at the door, and wishing each other well, they went their several ways.

In the meantime the company of pursuers had reached the end of the hog's-back elevation which dominated this part of the down. They had decided on no particular plan of action; and, finding that the man of the baleful trade was no longer in their company, they seemed quite unable to form any such plan now. They descended in all directions down the hill, and straightway several of the party fell into the snare set by Nature for all misguided midnight ramblers over this part of the cretaceous formation. The "lanchets," or flint slopes, which belted the escarpment at intervals of a dozen yards, took the less cautious ones unawares, and losing their footing on the rubbly steep they slid sharply downwards, the lanterns rolling from their hands to the bottom, and there lying on their sides till the horn was scorched through.

When they had again gathered themselves together, the shepherd, as the man who knew the country best, took the lead, and guided them round these treacherous inclines. The lanterns, which seemed rather to dazzle their eyes and warn the fugitive than to assist them in the exploration, were extinguished, due silence was observed; and in this more rational order they plunged into the vale. It was a grassy, briery, moist defile, affording some shelter to any person who had sought it; but the party perambulated it in vain, and ascended on the other side. Here they wandered apart, and after an interval closed together again to report progress. At the second time of closing in they found themselves near a lonely ash, the single tree on this part of the coomb, probably sown there by a passing bird some fifty years before. And here, standing a little to one side of the trunk, as motionless as the trunk itself, appeared the man they were in quest of, his outline being well defined against the sky beyond. The band noiselessly drew up and faced him.

"Your money or your life!" said the constable sternly to the still figure.

"No, no," whispered John Pitcher. "'Tisn't our side ought to say that. That's the doctrine of vagabonds like him, and we be on the side of the law."

"Well, well," replied the constable impatiently; "I must say something, mustn't I? and if you had all the weight o' this undertaking upon your mind, perhaps you'd say the wrong thing too!—Prisoner at the bar, surrender, in the name of the Father—the Crown, I mane!"

The man under the tree seemed now to notice them for the first time, and, giving them no opportunity whatever for exhibiting their courage he strolled slowly towards them. He was, indeed, the little man, the third stranger; but his trepidation had in a great measure gone.

"Well, travelers," he said, "did I hear ye speak to me?"

"You did: you've got to come and be our prisoner at once!" said the constable. "We arrest 'ee on the charge of not biding in Casterbridge jail in a decent proper manner to be hung tomorrow morning. Neighbors, do your duty, and seize the culpet!"

On hearing the charge, the man seemed enlightened, and, saying not another word, resigned himself with preternatural civility to the search-party, who, with their staves in their hands, surrounded him on all sides, and marched him back towards the shepherd's cottage.

It was eleven o'clock by the time they arrived. The light shining from the open door, a sound of men's voices within, proclaimed to them as they approached the house that some new events had arisen in their absence. On entering they discovered the shepherd's living to be invaded by two officers from Casterbridge jail, and a well-known magistrate who lived at the nearest country-seat, intelligence of the escape having become generally circulated.

"Gentlemen," said the constable, "I have brought back your man— not without risk and danger; but every one must do his duty! He is inside this circle of able-bodied persons, who have lent me useful aid, considering their ignorance of Crown work. Men, bring forward your prisoner!" And the third stranger was led to the light.

"Who is this?" said one of the officials.

"The man," said the constable.

"Certainly not," said the turnkey; and the first corroborated his statement.

"But how can it be otherwise?" asked the constable. "Or why was he so terrified at sight o' the singing instrument of the law who sat there?" Here he related the strange behavior of the third stranger on entering the house during the hangman's song.

"Can't understand it," said the officer coolly. "All I know is that it is not the condemned man. He's quite a different character from this one; a gauntish fellow, with dark hair and eyes, rather good-looking and with a musical bass voice that if you heard it once you'd never mistake as long as you lived."

"Why, souls—'twas the man in the chimney-corner!"

"Hey—what?" said the magistrate, coming forward after inquiring particulars from the shepherd in the background. "Haven't you got the man after all?"

"Well, sir," said the constable, "he's the man we were in search of, that's true; and yet he's not the man we were in search of. For the man we were in search of was not the man we wanted, sir, if you understand my everyday way; for 'twas the man in the chimney-corner!"

"A pretty kettle of fish altogether!" said the magistrate. "You had better start for the other man at once."

The prisoner now spoke for the first time. The mention of the man in the chimney-corner seemed to have moved him as nothing else could do. "Sir," he said, stepping forward to the magistrate, "take no more trouble about me. The time is come when I may as well speak. I have done nothing; my crime is that the condemned man is my brother. Early this afternoon I left home at Shottsford to tramp it all the way to Casterbridge jail to bid him farewell, I was benighted, and called here to rest and ask the way. When I opened the door I saw before me the very man, my brother, that I thought to see in the condemned cell at Casterbridge. He was in this chimney-corner; and jammed close to him, so that he could not have got out if he had tried, was the executioner who'd come to take his life, singing a song about it and not knowing that it was his victim who was close by, joining in to save appearances. My brother looked a glance of agony at me, and I knew he meant, 'Don't reveal what you see; my life depends on it.' I was so terror-struck that I could hardly stand, and, not knowing what I did, I turned and hurried away."

The narrator's manner and tone had the stamp of truth, and his story made a great impression on all around. "And do you know where your brother is at the present time?" asked the magistrate.

"I do not. I have never seen him since I closed this door."

"I can testify to that, for we've been between ye ever since," said the constable.

"Where does he think to fly to?—what is his occupation?"

"He's a watch-and-clock-maker, sir."

"'A said 'a was a wheelwright—a wicked rogue," said the constable.

"The wheels of clocks and watches he meant, no doubt," said Shepherd Fennel. "I thought his hands were palish for's trade."

"Well, it appears to me that nothing can be gained by retaining this poor man in custody," said the magistrate; "your business lies with the other, unquestionably."

And so the little man was released off-hand; but he looked nothing the less sad on that account, it being beyond the power of the magistrate or constable to raze out the written troubles in his brain, for they concerned another whom he regarded with more solicitude than himself. When this was done, and the man had gone his way, the night was found to be so far advanced that it was deemed useless to renew the search before the next morning.

Next day, accordingly, the quest for the clever sheep-stealer became general and keen, to all appearance at least. But the intended punishment was cruelly disproportioned to the transgression, and the sympathy of a great many country-folk in that district was strongly on the side of the fugitive. Moreover, his marvelous coolness and daring in hob-and-nobbing with the hangman, under the unprecedented circumstances of the shepherd's party, won their admiration. So that it may be questioned if all those who ostensibly made themselves so busy in exploring woods and fields and lanes were quite so thorough when it came to the private examination of their own lofts and outhouses. Stories were afloat of a mysterious figure being occasionally seen in some old overgrown trackway or other remote from turnpike roads; but when a search was instituted in any of these suspected quarters nobody was found. Thus the days and weeks passed without tidings.

In brief, the bass-voiced man of the chimney-corner was never re-captured. Some said that he went across the sea, others that he did not, but buried himself in the depths of a populous city. At any rate, the gentleman in cinder-gray never did his morning's work at Casterbridge, nor met anywhere at all, for business purposes, the genial comrade with whom he had passed an hour of relaxation in the lonely house on the coomb.

The grass has long been green on the graves of Shepherd Fennel and his frugal wife; the guests who made up the christening party have mainly followed their entertainers to the tomb; the baby in whose honor they all had met is a matron in the sere and yellow leaf. But the arrival of the three strangers at the shepherd's that night, and the details connected therewith, is a story as well known as ever in the country about Higher Crowstairs.

A Terribly Strange Bed

Wilkie Collins

Wilkie Collins (1824-1889), the most important mystery writer after Poe and before Doyle, was the son of noted painter William Collins. In 1836 and '37, Collins travelled Europe with his family. In 1839, he was sent to private school. While there, Collins was made to tell stories to the class by the prefect. He left in 1841 to take an apprenticeship with a tea importer. Never very interested in the importing business, Collins left it in 1846 to study law at Lincoln's Inn. He became a barrister shortly afterwards, but never practiced. In 1848, Collins published a biography of his father, and followed it with the historical romance *Antonia* (1850). In 1851, he first met Charles Dickens, who would become his best friend. Dickens encouraged his literary ambitions, and published some of his work in *Household Words. Basil: A Story of Modern Life,* was published in 1852. In 1859, Collins met Caroline Graves, who inspired him to write *The Woman in White* (1860) for Dickens' *All the Year Round.* The two lived together openly until Caroline left to marry another man. He then began an affair with Martha Rudd, with whom he fathered three children. During this period, Collins wrote his best work, including *No Name* (1862), *Armadale* (1866), *The Moonstone* (1868), *Poor Miss Finch* (1872), and *My Lady's Money* (1878). In 1879, Collins began to suffer from ill health, and Caroline Graves returned to help nurse him. He became addicted to opium, and later novels like *Heart and Science* (1883) and *The Evil Genius* (1886) show signs of his deterioration. A sickly Collins finally succumbed to his illness in 1889.

"A Terribly Strange Bed," Collins' most famous piece of short fiction, originally appeared in his collection *After Dark* (1856).

SHORTLY AFTER my education at college was finished, I happened to be staying at Paris with an English friend. We were both young men then, and lived, I am afraid, rather a wild life, in the delightful city of our sojourn. One night we were idling about the neighborhood of the Palais Royal, doubtful to what amusement we should next betake ourselves. My friend proposed a visit to Frascati's; but his suggestion was not to my taste. I knew Frascati's, as the French saying is, by heart; had lost and won plenty of five-franc pieces there, merely for amusement's sake, until it was amusement no longer, and was thoroughly tired, in fact, of all the ghastly respectabilities of such a social anomaly as a respectable gambling-house. "For Heaven's sake," said I to my friend, "let us go somewhere where we can see a little genuine, blackguard, poverty-stricken gaming with no false gingerbread glitter thrown over it all. Let us get away from fashionable Frascati's, to a house where they don't mind letting in a man with a ragged coat, or a man with no coat, ragged or otherwise." "Very well," said my friend, "we needn't go out of the Palais Royal to find the sort of company you want. Here's the place just before us; as blackguard a place, by all report, as you could possibly wish to see." In another minute we arrived at the door and entered the house.

When we got upstairs, and had left our hats and sticks with the doorkeeper, we were admitted into the chief gambling-room. We did not find many people assembled there. But, few as the men were who looked up at us on our entrance, they were all types—lamentably true types—of their respective classes.

We had come to see blackguards; but these men were something worse. There is a comic side, more or less appreciable, in all blackguardism—here there was nothing but tragedy—mute, weird tragedy. The quiet in the room was horrible. The thin, haggard, long-haired young man, whose sunken eyes fiercely watched the turning up of the cards, never spoke; the flabby, fat-faced, pimply player, who pricked his piece of pasteboard perseveringly, to register how often black won, and how often red—never spoke; the dirty, wrinkled old man, with the vulture eyes and the darned great-coat, who had lost his last *sou,* and still looked on desperately, after he could play no longer—never spoke. Even the voice of the croupier sounded as if it were strangely dulled and thickened in the atmosphere of the room. I had entered the place to laugh, but the spectacle before me was something to weep over. I soon found it necessary to take refuge in excitement from the depression of spirits which was fast stealing on me. Unfortunately I sought the nearest excitement, by going to the table and beginning to play. Still more unfortunately, as the event will show, I won—won prodigiously; won incredibly; won at such a rate that the regular players at the table crowded round me; and staring at my stakes with hungry, superstitious eyes, whispered to one another that the English stranger was going to break the bank.

The game was *Rouge et Noir.* I had played at it in every city in Europe, without, however, the care or the wish to study the Theory of

Chances—that philosopher's stone of all gamblers! And a gambler, in the strict sense of the word, I had never been. I was heart-whole from the corroding passion for play. My gaming was a mere idle amusement. I never resorted to it by necessity, because I never knew what it was to want money. I never practiced it so incessantly as to lose more than I could afford, or to gain more than I could coolly pocket without being thrown off my balance by my good luck. In short, I had hitherto frequented gambling-tables—just as I frequented ballrooms and opera-houses—because they amused me, and because I had nothing better to do with my leisure hours.

But on this occasion it was very different—now, for the first time in my life, I felt what the passion for play really was. My success first bewildered, and then, in the most literal meaning of the word, intoxicated me. Incredible as it may appear, it is nevertheless true, that I only lost when I attempted to estimate chances, and played according to previous calculation. If I left everything to luck, and staked without any care or consideration, I was sure to win—to win in the face of every recognized probability in favor of the bank. At first some of the men present ventured their money safely enough on my color; but I speedily increased my stakes to sums which they dared not risk. One after another they left off playing, and breathlessly looked on at my game.

Still, time after time, I staked higher and higher, and still won. The excitement in the room rose to fever pitch. The silence was interrupted by a deep-muttered chorus of oaths and exclamations in different languages, every time the gold was shovelled across to my side of the table—even the imperturbable croupier dashed his rake on the floor in a (French) fury of astonishment at my success. But one man present preserved his self-possession, and that man was my friend. He came to my side, and whispering in English, begged me to leave the place, satisfied with what I had already gained. I must do him the justice to say that he repeated his warnings and entreaties several times, and only left me and went away after I had rejected his advice (I was to all intents and purposes gambling drunk) in terms which rendered it impossible for him to address me again that night.

Shortly after he had gone, a hoarse voice behind me cried: "Permit me, my dear sir—permit me to restore to their proper place two napoleons which you have dropped. Wonderful luck, sir! I pledge you my word of honor, as an old soldier, in the course of my long experience in this sort of thing, I never saw such luck as yours—never! Go on, sir—*Sacré mille bombes!* Go on boldly, and break the bank!"

I turned round and saw, nodding and smiling at me with inveterate civility, a tall man, dressed in a frogged and braided surtout.

If I had been in my senses, I should have considered him, personally, as being rather a suspicious specimen of an old soldier. He had goggling, blood-shot eyes, mangy moustaches, and a broken nose. His voice betrayed a barrack-room intonation of the worst order, and he had the dirtiest pair of hands I ever saw—even in France. These little personal peculiarities exercised, however, no repelling influence on me. In the mad excitement, the reckless triumph of that moment, I was ready to "fraternize" with anybody who encouraged me in my game. I accepted the old soldier's offered pinch of snuff; clapped him on the back, and swore he was the honestest fellow in the world—the most glorious relic of the Grand Army that I had ever met with. "Go on!" cried my military friend, snapping his fingers in ecstasy—"Go on, and win! Break the bank—*Mille tonnerres!* my gallant English comrade, break the bank!"

And I *did* go on—went on at such a rate, that in another quarter of an hour the croupier called out, "Gentlemen, the bank has discontinued for tonight." All the notes, and all the gold in that "bank," now lay in a heap under my hands; the whole floating capital of the gambling-house was waiting to pour into my pockets!

"Tie up the money in your pocket-handkerchief, my worthy sir," said the old soldier, as I wildly plunged my hands into my heap of gold. "Tie it up, as we used to tie up a bit of dinner in the Grand Army; your winnings are too heavy for any breeches-pockets that ever were sewed. There! that's it—shovel them in, notes and all! *Credié!* what luck! Stop! another napoleon on the floor! *Ah! sacré petit polison de Napoleon!* have I found thee at last? Now then, sir—two tight double knots each way with your honorable permission, and the money's safe. Feel it! feel it, fortunate sir! hard and round as a cannon-ball—*Ah, bah!* if they had only fired such cannon-balls at us at Austerlitz—*nom d'une pipe!* if they only had! And now, as an ancient grenadier, as an ex-brave of the French army, what remains for me to do? I ask what? Simply this, to entreat my valued English friend to drink a bottle of champagne with me, and toast the goddess Fortune in foaming goblets before we part!"

Excellent ex-brave! Convivial ancient grenadier! Champagne by all means! An English cheer for an old soldier! Hurrah! hurrah! Another English cheer for the goddess Fortune! Hurrah! hurrah! hurrah!

"Bravo! the Englishman; the amiable, gracious Englishman, in whose veins circulates the vivacious blood of France! Another glass?

Ah, bah!—the bottle is empty! Never mind! *Vive le vin!* I, the old soldier, order another bottle, and half a pound of *bonbons* with it!"

"No, no, ex-brave; never—ancient grenadier! *Your* bottle last time; *my* bottle this. Behold it! Toast away! The French Army! the great Napoleon! the present company! the croupier! the honest croupier's wife and daughters—if he has any! the Ladies generally! everybody in the world!"

By the time the second bottle of champagne was emptied, I felt as if I had been drinking liquid fire—my brain seemed all aflame. No excess in wine had ever had this effect on me before in my life. Was it the result of a stimulant acting upon my system when I was in a highly excited state? Was my stomach in a particularly disordered condition? Or was the champagne amazingly strong?

"Ex-brave of the French Army!" cried I, in a mad state of exhilaration, "*I* am on fire! how are *you?* You have set me on fire. Do you hear, my hero of Austerlitz? Let us have a third bottle of champagne to put the flame out!"

The old soldier wagged his head, rolled his goggle-eyes, until I expected to see them slip out of their sockets? placed his dirty forefinger by the side of his broken nose; solemnly ejaculated "Coffee!" and immediately ran off into an inner room.

The word pronounced by the eccentric veteran seemed to have a magical effect on the rest of the company present. With one accord they all rose to depart. Probably they had expected to profit by my intoxication; but finding that my new friend was benevolently bent on preventing me from getting dead drunk, had now abandoned all hope of thriving pleasantly on my winnings. Whatever their motive might be, at any rate they went away in a body. When the old soldier returned, and sat down again opposite to me at the table, we had the room to ourselves. I could see the croupier, in a sort of vestibule which opened out of it, eating his supper in solitude. The silence was now deeper than ever.

A sudden change, too, had come over the "ex-brave." He assumed a portentously solemn look; and when he spoke to me again, his speech was ornamented by no oaths, enforced by no finger-snapping, enlivened by no apostrophes or exclamations.

"Listen, my dear sir," said he, in mysteriously confidential tones— "listen to an old soldier's advice. I have been to the mistress of the house (a very charming woman, with a genius for cookery!) to impress on her the necessity of making us some particularly strong and good coffee. You must drink this coffee in order to get rid of your little amiable exaltation of spirits before you think of going home—you *must,* my good and gracious friend! With all that money to take home tonight, it is a sacred duty to yourself to have your wits about you. You are known to be a winner to an enormous extent by several gentlemen present tonight, who, in a certain point of view, are very worthy and excellent fellows; but they are mortal men, my dear sir, and they have their amiable weaknesses: Need I say more? Ah, no, no! you understand me! Now, this is what you must do—send for a cabriolet when you feel quite well again—draw up all the windows when you get into it—and tell the driver to take you home only through the large and well-lighted thoroughfares. Do this; and you and your money will be safe. Do this; and tomorrow you will thank an old soldier for giving you a word of honest advice."

Just as the ex-brave ended his oration in very lachrymose tones, the coffee came in, ready poured out in two cups. My attentive friend handed me one of the cups with a bow. I was parched with thirst, and drank it off at a draught. Almost instantly afterward, I was seized with a fit of giddiness, and felt more completely intoxicated than ever. The room whirled round and round furiously; the old soldier seemed to be regularly bobbing up and down before me like the piston of a steam-engine. I was half deafened by a violent singing in my ears; a feeling of utter bewilderment, helplessness, idiocy, overcame me. I rose from my chair, holding on by the table to keep my balance; and stammered out that I felt dreadfully unwell—so unwell that I did not know how I was to get home.

"My dear friend," answered the old soldier—and even his voice seemed to be bobbing up and down as he spoke—"my dear friend, it would be madness to go home in *your* state; you would be sure to lose your money; you might be robbed and murdered with the greatest ease. *I* am going to sleep here; do *you* sleep here, too—they make up capital beds in this house—take one; sleep off the effects of the wine, and go home safely with your winnings tomorrow—tomorrow, in broad daylight."

I had but two ideas left: one, that I must never let go hold of my handkerchief full of money; the other, that I must lie down somewhere immediately, and fall off into a comfortable sleep. So I agreed to the proposal about the bed, and took the offered arm of the old soldier, carrying my money with my disengaged hand. Preceded by the croupier, we passed along some passages and up a flight of stairs into the bedroom which I was to occupy. The ex-brave shook me warmly by the hand, proposed that we should breakfast together, and then, followed by the croupier, left me for the night.

I ran to the wash-hand stand; drank some of the water in my jug; poured the rest out, and plunged my face into it; then sat down in a chair and tried to compose myself. I soon felt better. The change for my lungs, from the fetid atmosphere of the gambling-room to the cool air of the apartment I now occupied, the almost equally refreshing change for my eyes, from the glaring. gaslights of the "salon" to the dim, quiet flicker of one bedroom-candle, aided wonderfully the restorative effects of cold water. The giddiness left me, and I began to feel a little like a reasonable being again. My first thought was of the risk of sleeping all night in a gambling-house; my second, of the still greater risk of trying to get out after the house was closed, and of going home alone at night through the streets of Paris with a large sum of money about me. I had slept in worse places than this on my travels; so I determined to lock, bolt, and barricade my door, and take my chance till the next morning.

Accordingly, I secured myself against all intrusion; looked under the bed, and into the cupboard; tried the fastening of the window; and then, satisfied that I had taken every proper precaution, pulled off my upper clothing, put my light, which was a dim one, on the hearth among a feathery litter of wood-ashes, and got into bed, with the handkerchief full of money under my pillow.

I soon felt not only that I could not go to sleep, but that I could not even close my eyes. I was wide awake, and in a high fever. Every nerve in my body trembled—every one of my senses seemed to be preternaturally sharpened. I tossed and rolled, and tried every kind of position, and perseveringly sought out the cold corners of the bed, and all to no purpose. Now I thrust my arms over the clothes: now I poked them under the clothes; now I violently shot my legs straight out down to the bottom of the bed; now I convulsively coiled them up as near my chin as they would go; now I shook out my crumpled pillow, changed it to the cool side, patted it flat, and lay down quietly on my back; now I fiercely doubled it in two, set it up on end, thrust it against the board of the bed, and tried a sitting posture. Every effort was in vain; I groaned with vexation as I felt that I was in for a sleepless night.

What could I do? I had no book to read. And yet, unless I found out some method of diverting my mind, I felt certain that I was in the condition to imagine all sorts of horrors; to rack my brain with forebodings of every possible and impossible danger; in short, to pass the night in suffering all conceivable varieties of nervous terror.

I raised myself on my elbow, and looked about the room—which was brightened by a lovely moonlight pouring straight through the window—to see if it contained any pictures or ornaments that I could at all clearly distinguish. While my eyes wandered from wall to wall, a remembrance of Le Maistre's delightful little book, *Voyage autour de ma Chambre,* occurred to me. I resolved to imitate the French author, and find occupation and amusement enough to relieve the tedium of my wakefulness, by making a mental inventory of every article of furniture I could see, and by following up to their sources the multitude of associations which even a chair, a table, or a wash-hand stand may be made to call forth.

In the nervous unsettled state of my mind at that moment, I found it much easier to make my inventory than to make my reflections, and thereupon soon gave up all hope of thinking in Le Maistre's fanciful track—or, indeed, of thinking at all. I looked about the room at the different articles of furniture, and did nothing more.

There was, first, the bed I was lying in; a four-post bed, of all things in the world to meet with in Paris—yes, a thorough clumsy British four-poster, with a regular top lined with chintz—the regular fringed valance all round—the regular stifling, unwholesome curtains, which I remembered having mechanically drawn back against the posts without particularly noticing the bed when I first got into the room. Then there was the marble-topped, wash-hand stand, from which the water I had spilled, in my hurry to pour it out, was still dripping, slowly and more slowly, on to the brick floor. Then two small chairs, with my coat, waistcoat, and trousers flung on them. Then a large elbow-chair covered with dirty-white dimity, with my cravat and shirt collar thrown over the back. Then a chest of drawers with two of the brass handles off, and a tawdry, broken china inkstand placed on it by way of ornament for the top. Then the dressing-table, adorned by a very small looking-glass, and a very large pincushion. Then the window—an unusually large window. Then a dark old picture, which the feeble candle dimly showed me. It was a picture of a fellow in a high Spanish hat, crowned with a plume of towering feathers. A swarthy, sinister ruffian, looking upward, shading his eyes with his hand, and looking intently upward—it might be at some tall gallows at which he was going to be hanged. At any rate, he had the appearance of thoroughly deserving it.

This picture put a kind of constraint upon me to look upward too—at the top of the bed. It was a gloomy and not an interesting object, and I looked back at the picture. I counted the feathers in the man's hat—

they stood out in relief—three white, two green. I observed the crown of his hat, which was of conical shape, according to the fashion supposed to have been favored by Guido Fawkes. I wondered what he was looking up at. It couldn't be at the stars, such a desperado was neither astrologer nor astronomer. It must be at the high gallows, and he was going to be hanged presently. Would the executioner come into possession of his conical crowned hat and plume of feathers? I counted the feathers again—three white, two green.

While I still lingered over this very improving and intellectual employment, my thoughts insensibly began to wander. The moonlight shining into the room reminded me of a certain moonlight night in England—the night after a picnic party in a Welsh valley. Every incident of the drive homeward, through lovely scenery, which the moonlight made lovelier than ever, came back to my remembrance, though I had never given the picnic a thought for years; though, if I had *tried* to recollect it, I could certainly have recalled little or nothing of that scene long past. Of all the wonderful faculties that help to tell us we are immortal, which speaks the sublime truth more eloquently than memory? Here was I, in a strange house of the most suspicious character, in a situation of uncertainty, and even of peril, which might seem to make the cool exercise of my recollection almost out of the question; nevertheless, remembering, quite involuntarily, places, people, conversations, minute circumstances of every kind, which I had thought forgotten for ever; which I could not possibly have recalled at will, even under the most favorable auspices. And what cause had produced in a moment the whole of this strange, complicated, mysterious effect? Nothing but some rays of moonlight shining in at my bedroom window.

I was still thinking of the picnic—of our merriment on the drive home—of the sentimental young lady who *would* quote "Childe Harold" because it was moonlight. I was absorbed by these past scenes and past amusements, when, in an instant, the thread on which my memories hung snapped asunder; my attention immediately came back to present things more vividly than ever, and I found myself, I neither knew why nor wherefore, looking hard at the picture again.

Looking for what?

Good God! the man had pulled his hat down on his brows! No! the hat itself was gone! Where was the conical crown? Where the feathers—three white, two green? Not there! In place of the hat and feathers, what dusky object was it that now hid his forehead, his eyes, his shading hand?

Was the bed moving?

I turned on my back and looked up. Was I mad? drunk? dreaming? giddy again? or was the top of the bed really moving down—sinking slowly, regularly, silently, horribly, right down throughout the whole of its length and breadth—right down upon me, as I lay underneath?

My blood seemed to stand still. A deadly paralyzing coldness stole all over me as I turned my head round on the pillow and determined to test whether the bed-top was really moving or not, by keeping my eye on the man in the picture.

The next look in that direction was enough. The dull black, frowzy outline of the valance above me was within an inch of being parallel with his waist. I still looked breathlessly. And steadily and slowly— very slowly—I saw the figure, and the line of frame below the figure, vanish, as the valance moved down before it.

I am, constitutionally, anything but timid. I have been on more than one occasion in peril of my life, and have not lost my self-possession for an instant; but when the conviction first settled on my mind that the bed-top was really moving, was steadily and continuously sinking down upon me, I looked up shuddering, helpless, panic-stricken, beneath the hideous machinery for murder, which was advancing closer and closer to suffocate me where I lay.

I looked up, motionless, speechless, breathless. The candle, fully spent, went out; but the moonlight still brightened the room. Down and down, without pausing and without sounding, came the bed-top, and still my panic terror seemed to bind me faster and faster to the mattress on which I lay—down and down it sank, till the dusty odor from the lining of the canopy came stealing into my nostrils.

At that final moment the instinct of self-preservation startled me out of my trance, and I moved at last. There was just room for me to roll myself sidewise off the bed. As I dropped noiselessly to the floor, the edge of the murderous canopy touched me on the shoulder.

Without stopping to draw my breath, without wiping the cold sweat from my face, I rose instantly on my knees to watch the bed-top. I was literally spellbound by it. If I had heard foot steps behind me, I could not have turned round; if a means of escape had been miraculously provided for me, I could not have moved to take advantage of it. The whole life in me was, at that moment, concentrated in my eyes.

It descended—the whole canopy, with the fringe round it came down—down—close down; so close that there was no room now to squeeze my finger between the bed-top and the bed. I felt at the sides, and discovered that what had appeared to me from beneath to be the ordinary light canopy of a four-post bed was in reality a thick, broad mattress, the substance of which was concealed by the valance and its fringe. I looked up and saw the four-posts rising hideously bare. In the middle of the bed-top was a huge wooden screw that had evidently worked it down through a hole in the ceiling, just as ordinary presses are worked down on the substance selected for compression. The frightful apparatus moved without making the faintest noise. There had been no creaking as it came down; there was now not the faintest sound from the room above. Amid a dead and awful silence I beheld before me—in the nineteenth century, and in the civilized capital of France—such a machine for secret murder by suffocation as might have existed in the worst days of the Inquisition, in the lonely inns among the Hartz Mountains, in the mysterious tribunals of Westphalia! Still, as I looked on it, I could not move, I could hardly breathe, but I began to recover the power of thinking, and in a moment I discovered the murderous conspiracy framed against me in all its horror.

My cup of coffee had been drugged, and drugged too strongly. I had been saved from being smothered by having taken an overdose of some narcotic. How I had chafed and fretted at the fever fit which had preserved my life by keeping me awake! How recklessly I had confided myself to the two wretches who had led me into this room, determined, for the sake of my winnings, to kill me in my sleep by the surest and most horrible contrivance for secretly accomplishing my destruction! How many men, winners like me, had slept, as I had proposed to sleep, in that bed, and had never been seen or heard of more! I shuddered at the bare idea of it.

But ere long all thought was again suspended by the sight of the murderous canopy moving once more. After it had remained on the bed—as nearly as I could guess—about ten minutes, it began to move up again. The villains who worked it from above evidently believed that their purpose was now accomplished. Slowly and silently, as it had descended, that horrible bed-top rose towards its former place. When it reached the upper extremities of the four posts, it reached the ceiling, too. Neither hole nor screw could be seen; the bed became in appearance an ordinary bed again—the canopy an ordinary canopy—even to the most suspicious eyes.

Now, for the first time, I was able to move—to rise from my knees—to dress myself in my upper clothing—and to consider of how I should escape. If I betrayed by the smallest noise that the attempt to suffocate me had failed, I was certain to be murdered. Had I made any noise already? I listened intently, looking towards the door.

No! no footsteps in thc passage outside—no sound of a tread, light or heavy, in the room above—absolute silence everywhere. Besides locking and bolting my door, I had moved an only wooden chest against it, which I had found under the bed. To remove this chest (my blood ran cold as I thought of what its contents *might* be!) without making some disturbance was impossible; and, moreover, to think of escaping through the house, now barred up for the night, was sheer insanity. Only one chance was left me—the window. I stole to it on tiptoe.

My bedroom was on the first floor, above an *entresol,* and looked into a back street. I raised my hand to open the window, knowing that on that action hung, by the merest hair-breadth, my chance of safety. They keep vigilant watch in a House of Murder. If any part of the frame cracked, if the hinge creaked, I was a lost man! It must have occupied me at least five minutes, reckoning by time—five *hours,* reckoning by suspense—to open that window. I succeeded in doing it silently—in doing it with all the dexterity of a house-breaker—and then looked down into the street. To leap the distance beneath me would be almost certain destruction! Next, I looked round at the sides of the house. Down the left side ran a thick water pipe—it passed close by the outer edge of the window. The moment I saw the pipe I knew I was saved. My breath came and went freely for the first time since I had seen the canopy of the bed moving down upon me!

To some men the means of escape which I had discovered might have seemed difficult and dangerous enough—to *me* the prospect of slipping down the pipe into the street did not suggest even a thought of peril. I had always been accustomed, by the practice of gymnastics, to keep up my schoolboy powers as a daring and expert climber; and knew that my head, hands, and feet would serve me faithfully in any hazards of ascent or descent. I had already got one leg over the window-sill, when I remembered the handkerchief filled with money under my pillow. I could well have afforded to leave it behind me, but I was revengefully determined that the miscreants of the gambling house should miss their plunder as well as their victim. So I went back to the bed and tied the heavy handkerchief at my back by my cravat.

Just as I had made it tight and fixed it in a comfortablc place, I thought I heard a sound of breathing outside the door. The chill feeling of horror ran through me again as I listened. No! dead silence still in the passage—I had only heard the night air blowing softly into the room. The next moment I was on the window-sill—and the next I had a firm grip on the water-pipe with my hands and knees.

I slid down into the street easily and quietly, as I thought I should, and immediately set off at the top of my speed to a branch Prefecture of Police, which I knew was situated in the immediate neighborhood. A Sub-prefect, and several picked men among his subordinates, happened to be up, maturing, I believe, some scheme for discovering the perpetrator of a mysterious murder which all Paris was talking of just then. When I began my story, in a breathless hurry and in very bad French, I could see that the Sub-prefect suspected me of being a drunken Englishman who had robbed somebody; but he soon altered his opinion as I went on, and before I had anything like concluded, he shoved all the papers before him into a drawer, put on his hat, supplied me with another (for I was bare-headed), ordered a file of soldiers, desired his expert followers to get ready all sorts of tools for breaking open doors and ripping up brick flooring, and took my arm, in the most friendly and familiar manner possible, to lead me with him out of the house. I will venture to say that when the Sub-prefect was a little boy, and was taken for the first time to the play, he was not half as much pleased as he was now at the job in prospect for him at the gambling-house!

Away we went through the streets, the Sub-prefect cross-examining and congratulating me in the same breath as we marched at the head of our formidable *posse comitatus*. Sentinels were placed at the back and front of the house the moment we got to it; a tremendous battery of knocks was directed against the door; a light appeared at a window; I was told to conceal myself behind the police—then came more knocks and a cry of "Open in the name of the law!" At that terrible summons bolts and locks gave way before an invisible hand, and the moment after the Sub-prefect was in the passage, confronting a waiter half-dressed and ghastly pale. This was the short dialogue which immediately took place:

"We want to see the Englishman who is sleeping in this house?"

"He went away hours ago."

"He did no such thing. His friend went away; *he* remained. Show us to his bedroom!"

"I swear to you, Monsieur le Sous-prefect, he is not here! he—"

"I swear to you, Monsieur le Garçon, he is. He slept here—he didn't find your bed comfortable—he came to us to complain of it—here he is among my men—and here am I ready to look for a flea or two in his bedstead. Renaudin!"—calling to one of the subordinates, and pointing to the waiter—"collar that man and tie his hands behind him. Now, then, gentlemen, let us walk upstairs!"

Every man and woman in the house was secured—the "Old Soldier" the first. Then I identified the bed in which I had slept, and then we went into the room above.

No object that was at all extraordinary appeared in any part of it. The Sub-prefect looked round the place, commanded everybody to be silent, stamped twice on the floor, called for a candle, looked attentively at the spot he had stamped on, and ordered the flooring there to be carefully taken up. This was done in no time. Lights were produced, and we saw a deep raftered cavity between the floor of this room and the ceiling of the room beneath. Through this cavity there ran perpendicularly a sort of case of iron thickly greased; and inside the case appeared the screw, which communicated with the bed-top below. Extra lengths of screw, freshly oiled; levers covered with felt; all the complete upper works of a heavy press—constructed with infernal ingenuity so as to join the fixtures below, and when taken to pieces again, to go into the smallest possible compass—were next discovered and pulled out on the floor. After some little difficulty the Sub-prefect succeeded in putting the machinery together, and, leaving his men to work it, descended with me to the bedroom. The smothering canopy was then lowered, but not so noiselessly as I had seen it lowered. When I mentioned this to the Sub-prefect, his answer, simple as it was had a terrible significance. "My men," said he, "are working down the bed-top for the first time—the men whose money you won were in better practice."

We left the house in the sole possession of two police agents—every one of the inmates being removed to prison on the spot. The Sub-prefect, after taking down my *procès verbal* in his office, returned with me to my hotel to get my passport. "Do you think," I asked, as I gave it to him, "that any men have really been smothered in that bed, as they tried to smother *me?*"

"I have seen dozens of drowned men laid out at the Morgue," answered the Sub-prefect, "in whose pocketbooks were found letters stating that they had committed suicide in the Seine, because they had lost everything at the gaming table. Do I know how many of those men entered the same gambling-house that *you* entered? won as *you* won? took that bed as *you* took it? slept in it? were smothered in it? and were privately thrown into the river, with a letter of explanation written by the murderers and placed in their pocketbooks? No man can say how many or how few have suffered the fate from which you have escaped.

The people of the gambling-house kept their bedstead machinery a secret from *us*—even from the police! The dead kept the rest of the secret for them. Good night, or rather good morning, Monsieur Faulkner! Be at my office again at nine o'clock—in the meantime, *au revoir!*"

The rest of my story is soon told. I was examined and re-examined; the gambling-house was strictly searched all through from top to bottom; the prisoners were separately interrogated; and two of the less guilty among them made a confession. I discovered that the Old Soldier was the master of the gambling-house—*justice* discovered that he had been drummed out of the army as a vagabond years ago; that he had been guilty of all sorts of villainies since; that he was in possession of stolen property, which the owners identified; and that he, the croupier, another accomplice, and the woman who had made my cup of coffee, were all in the secret of the bedstead. There appeared some reason to doubt whether the inferior persons attached to the house knew anything of the suffocating machinery; and they received the benefit of that doubt, by being treated simply as thieves and vagabonds. As for the Old Soldier and his two head myrmidons, they went to the galleys; the woman who had drugged my coffee was imprisoned for I forget how many years; the regular attendants at the gambling-house were considered "suspicious" and placed under "surveillance" and I became, for one whole week (which is a long time) the head "lion" in Parisian Society. My adventure was dramatized by three illustrious playmakers, but never saw theatrical daylight; for the censorship forbade the introduction on the stage of a correct copy of the gambling-house bedstead.

One good result was produced by my adventure, which any censorship must have approved: it cured me of ever again trying *Rouge et Noir* as an amusement. The sight of a green cloth, with packs of cards and heaps of money on it, will henceforth be for ever associated in my mind with the sight of a bed canopy descending to suffocate me in the silence and darkness of the night.

Lamb to the Slaughter

Roald Dahl

Roald Dahl (1916-1990), one of the masters of short mystery and
suspense fiction, graduated from Repton School in 1932. He joined the
East African division of Shell Oil after graduation, but left after a short
time to pursue a career as a free-lance writer. In 1938 he enlisted with the
Royal Air Force. Trained as a fighter pilot, Dahl served with the RAF for
seven years, and used his experiences as the basis of his first short story
collection, *Over to You* (1946). Dahl began writing the stories he was
famous for in the late 1940's, spending upwards of six months on each
tale. In 1953, Dahl's second collection, *Someone Like You* was published.
That same year, he won his first Edgar and married actress Patricia Neal.
After one more collection (*Kiss, Kiss;* 1960), Dahl began writing children's books, beginning with *James and the Giant Peach* (1961), and
including *Charlie and the Chocolate Factory* (1964). During the 1960's,
Dahl became involved in screenwriting, penning the script for such films
as *You Only Live Twice* (1967) and *Chitty Chitty Bang Bang* (1968).
During this time, Dahl also hosted a short-lived television series known
for its gruesome effects, *Far Out* (1968). Dahl produced two more
collections, *Switch Bitch* (1974) and *Tales of the Unexpected* (1977). Dahl
began hosting the British anthology program *Tales of the Unexpected* in
1979. In 1990, he produced his last book, a collection of poetry entitled
Rhyme Stew. A long time resident of Buckinghamshire, he died late that
year of heart failure.

"Lamb to the Slaughter" is one of the most famous mystery stories
of all time. It has been adapted for television twice since its publication in
1953.

THE ROOM WAS WARM and clean, the curtains drawn, the two
table lamps alight—hers and the one by the empty chair opposite. On
the sideboard behind her, two tall glasses, soda water, whiskey. Fresh
ice cubes in the Thermos bucket.

Mary Maloney was waiting for her husband to come home from
work.

Now and again she would glance up at the clock, but without anxiety, merely to please herself with the thought that each minute gone by made it nearer the time when he would come. There was a slow smiling air about her, and about everything she did. The drop of the head as she bent over her sewing was curiously tranquil. Her skin—for this was her sixth month with child—had acquired a wonderful translucent quality, the mouth was soft, and the eyes, with their new placid look, seemed larger, darker than before.

When the clock said ten minutes to five, she began to listen, and a few moments later, punctually as always, she heard the tires on the gravel outside, and the car door slamming, the footsteps passing the window, the key turning in the lock. She laid aside her sewing, stood up, and went forward to kiss him as he came in.

"Hullo darling," she said.

"Hullo," he answered.

She took his coat and hung it in the closet. Then she walked over and made the drinks, a strongish one for him, a weak one for herself; and soon she was back again in her chair with the sewing, and he in the other, opposite, holding the tall glass with both his hands, rocking it so the ice cubes tinkled against the side.

For her, this was always a blissful time of day. She knew he didn't want to speak much until the first drink was finished, and she, on her side, was content to sit quietly, enjoying his company after the long hours alone in the house. She loved to luxuriate in the presence of this man, and to feel—almost as a sunbather feels the sun—that warm male glow that came out of him to her when they were alone together. She loved him for the way he sat loosely in a chair, for the way he came in a door, or moved slowly across the room with long strides. She loved the intent, far look in his eyes when they rested on her, the funny shape of the mouth, and especially the way he remained silent about his tiredness, sitting still with himself until the whiskey had taken some of it away.

"Tired, darling?"

"Yes," he said. "I'm tired." And as he spoke, he did an unusual thing. He lifted his glass and drained it in one swallow although there was still half of it, at least half of it left. She wasn't really watching him, but she knew what he had done because she heard the ice cubes falling back against the bottom of the empty glass when he lowered his arm. He paused a moment, leaning forward in the chair, then he got up and went slowly over to fetch himself another.

"I'll get it!" she cried, jumping up.

"Sit down," he said.

When he came back, she noticed that the new drink was dark amber with the quantity of whiskey in it.

"Darling, shall I get your slippers?"

"No."

She watched him as he began to sip the dark yellow drink, and she could see little oily swirls in the liquid because it was so strong.

"I think it's a shame," she said, "that when a policeman gets to be as senior as you, they keep him walking about on his feet all day long."

He didn't answer, so she bent her head again and went on with her sewing; but each time he lifted the drink to his lips, she heard the ice cubes clinking against the side of the glass.

"Darling," she said. "Would you like me to get you some cheese? I haven't made any supper because it's Thursday."

"No," he said.

"If you're too tired to eat out," she went on, "it's still not too late. There's plenty of meat and stuff in the freezer, and you can have it right here and not even move out of the chair."

Her eyes waited on him for an answer, a smile, a little nod, but he made no sign.

"Anyway," she went on, "I'll get you some cheese and crackers first."

"I don't want it," he said.

She moved uneasily in her chair, the large eyes still watching his face. "But you *must* have supper. I can easily do it here. I'd like to do it. We can have lamb chops. Or pork. Anything you want. Everything's in the freezer."

"Forget it," he said.

"But darling, you *must* eat! I'll fix it anyway, and then you can have it or not, as you like."

She stood up and placed her sewing on the table by the lamp.

"Sit down," he said. "Just for a minute, sit down."

It wasn't till then that she began to get frightened.

"Go on," he said. "Sit down."

She lowered herself back slowly into the chair, watching him all the time with those large, bewildered eyes. He had finished the second drink and was staring down into the glass, frowning.

"Listen," he said. "I've got something to tell you."

"What is it, darling? What's the matter?"

He had now become absolutely motionless, and he kept his head down so that the light from the lamp beside him fell across the upper part of his face, leaving the chin and mouth in shadow. She noticed there was a little muscle moving near the corner of his left eye.

"This is going to be a bit of a shock to you, I'm afraid," he said. "But I've thought about it a good deal and I've decided the only thing to do is tell you right away. I hope you won't blame me too much."

And he told her. It didn't take long, four or five minutes at most, and she sat very still through it all, watching him with a kind of dazed horror as he went further and further away from her with each word.

"So there it is," he added. "And I know it's kind of a bad time to be telling you, but there simply wasn't any other way. Of course I'll give you money and see you're looked after. But there needn't really be any fuss. I hope not anyway. It wouldn't be very good for my job."

Her first instinct was not to believe any of it, to reject it all. It occurred to her that perhaps he hadn't even spoken, that she herself had imagined the whole thing. Maybe, if she went about her business and acted as though she hadn't been listening, then later, when she sort of woke up again, she might find none of it had ever happened.

"I'll get the supper," she managed to whisper, and this time he didn't stop her.

When she walked across the room she couldn't feel her feet touching the floor. She couldn't feel anything at all—except a slight nausea and a desire to vomit. Everything was automatic now—down the steps to the cellar, the light switch, the deep freeze, the hand inside the cabinet taking hold of the first object it met. She lifted it out, and looked at it. It was wrapped in paper, so she took off the paper and looked at it again.

A leg of lamb.

All right then, they would have lamb for supper. She carried it upstairs, holding the thin bone-end of it with both her hands, and as she went through the living-room, she saw him standing over by the window with his back to her, and she stopped.

"For God's sake," he said, hearing her, but not turning round. "Don't make supper for me. I'm going out."

At that point, Mary Maloney simply walked up behind him and without any pause she swung the big frozen leg of lamb high in the.air and brought it down as hard as she could on the back of his head.

She might just as well have hit him with a steel club.

She stepped back a pace, waiting, and the funny thing was that he remained standing there for at least four or five seconds, gently swaying. Then he crashed to the carpet.

The violence of the crash, the noise, the small table overturning, helped bring her out of the shock. She came out slowly, feeling cold and surprised, and she stood for a while blinking at the body, still holding the ridiculous piece of meat tight with both hands.

All right, she told herself. So I've killed him.

It was extraordinary, now, how clear her mind became all of a sudden. She began thinking very fast. As the wife of a detective, she knew quite well what the penalty would be. That was fine. It made no difference to her. In fact, it would be a relief. On the other hand, what about the child? What were the laws about murderers with unborn children? Did they kill them both—mother and child? Or did they wait until the tenth month? What did they do?

Mary Maloney didn't know. And she certainly wasn't prepared to take a chance.

She carried the meat into the kitchen, placed it in a pan, turned the oven on high, and shoved it inside. Then she washed her hands and ran upstairs to the bedroom. She sat down before the mirror, tidied her hair, touched up her lips and face. She tried a smile. It came out rather peculiar. She tried again.

"Hullo Sam," she said brightly, aloud.

The voice sounded peculiar too.

"I want some potatoes please, Sam. Yes, and I think a can of peas."

That was better. Both the smile and the voice were coming out better now. She rehearsed it several times more. Then she ran downstairs, took her coat, went out the back door, down the garden, into the street.

It wasn't six o'clock yet and the lights were still on in the grocery shop.

"Hullo Sam," she said brightly, smiling at the man behind the counter.

"Why, good evening, Mrs. Maloney. How're *you?*"

"I want some potatoes please, Sam. Yes, and I think a can of peas."

The man turned and reached up behind him on the shelf for the peas.

"Patrick's decided he's tired and doesn't want to eat out tonight," she told him. "We usually go out Thursdays, you know, and now he's caught me without any vegetables in the house."

"Then how about meat, Mrs. Maloney?"

"No, I've got meat, thanks. I got a nice leg of lamb from the freezer."

"Oh."

"I don't much like cooking it frozen, Sam, but I'm taking a chance on it this time. You think it'll be all right?"

"Personally," the grocer said, "I don't believe it makes any difference. You want these Idaho potatoes?"

"Oh yes, that'll be fine. Two of those."

"Anything else?" The grocer cocked his head on one side, looking
at her pleasantly. "How about afterwards? What you going to give him
for afterwards?"

"Well—what would you suggest, Sam?"

The man glanced around his shop. "How about a nice big slice of
cheesecake? I know he likes that."

"Perfect," she said. "He loves it."

And when it was all wrapped and she had paid, she put on her
brightest smile and said, "Thank you, Sam. Goodnight."

"Goodnight, Mrs. Maloney. And thank *you*."

And now, she told herself as she hurried back, all she was doing
now, she was returning home to her husband and he was waiting for
his supper; and she must cook it good, and make it as tasty as possible
because the poor man was tired; and if, when she entered the house,
she happened to find anything unusual, or tragic, or terrible, then
naturally it would be a shock and she'd become frantic with grief and
horror. Mind you, she wasn't *expecting* to find anything. She was just
going home with the vegetables. Mrs. Patrick Maloney going home
with the vegetables on Thursday evening to cook supper for her
husband.

That's the way, she told herself. Do everything right and natural.
Keep things absolutely natural and there'll be no need for any acting
at all.

Therefore, when she entered the kitchen by the back door, she was
humming a little tune to herself and smiling.

"Patrick!" she called. "How are you, darling?"

She put the parcel down on the table and went through into the living
room; and when she saw him lying there on the floor with his legs
doubled up and one arm twisted back underneath his body, it really
was rather a shock. All the old love and longing for him welled up
inside her, and she ran over to him, knelt down beside him, and began
to cry her heart out. It was easy. No acting was necessary.

A few minutes later she got up and went to the phone. She knew the
number of the police station, and when the man at the other end
answered, she cried to him, "Quick! Come quick! Patrick's dead!"

"Who's speaking?"

"Mrs. Maloney. Mrs. Patrick Maloney."

"You mean Patrick Maloney's dead?"

"I think so," she sobbed. "He's lying on the floor and I think he's dead."

"Be right over," the man said.

The car came very quickly, and when she opened the front door, two policemen walked in. She knew them both—she knew nearly all the men at that precinct—and she fell right into Jack Noonan's arms, weeping hysterically. He put her gently into a chair, then went over to join the other one, who was called O'Malley, kneeling by the body.

"Is he dead?" she cried.

"I'm afraid he is. What happened?"

Briefly, she told her story about going out to the grocer and coming back to find him on the floor. While she was talking, crying and talking, Noonan discovered a small patch of congealed blood on the dead man's head. He showed it to O'Malley, who got up at once and hurried to the phone.

Soon, other men began to come into the house. First a doctor, then two detectives, one of whom she knew by name. Later, a police photographer arrived and took pictures, and a man who knew about fingerprints. There was a great deal of whispering and muttering beside the corpse, and the detectives kept asking her a lot of questions. But they always treated her kindly. She told her story again, this time right from the beginning, when Patrick had come in, and she was sewing, and he was tired, so tired he hadn't wanted to go out for supper. She told how she'd put the meat in the oven—"it's there now, cooking"—and how she'd slipped out to the grocer for vegetables, and come back to find him lying on the floor.

"Which grocer?" one of the detectives asked.

She told him, and he turned and whispered something to the other detective, who immediately went outside into the street.

In fifteen minutes he was back with a page of notes, and there was more whispering, and through her sobbing she heard a few of the whispered phrases—"...acted quite normal...very cheerful...wanted to give him a good supper...peas...cheesecake...impossible that she..."

After a while, the photographer and the doctor departed and, two other men came in and took the corpse away on a stretcher. Then the fingerprint man went away. The two detectives remained, and so did the two policemen. They were exceptionally nice to her, and Jack Noonan asked if she wouldn't rather go somewhere else, to her sister's house perhaps, or to his own wife, who would take care of her and put her up for the night.

No, she said. She didn't feel she could move even a yard at the moment. Would they mind awfully if she stayed just where she was until she felt better? She didn't feel too good at the moment, she really didn't.

Then hadn't she better lie down on the bed? Jack Noonan asked.

No, she said. She'd like to stay right where she was, in this chair. A little later perhaps, when she felt better, she would move.

So they left her there while they went about their business, searching the house. Occasionally one of the detectives asked her another question. Sometimes Jack Noonan spoke at her gently as he passed by. Her husband, he told her, had been killed by a blow on the back of the head administered with a heavy blunt instrument, almost certainly a large piece of metal. They were looking for the weapon. The murderer may have taken it with him, but on the other hand he may've thrown it away or hidden it somewhere on the premises.

"It's the old story," he said. "Get the weapon, and you've got the man."

Later, one of the detectives came up and sat beside her. Did she know, he asked, of anything in the house that could've been used as the weapon? Would she mind having a look around to see if anything was missing—a very big spanner, for example, or a heavy metal vase.

They didn't have any heavy metal vases, she said.

"Or a big spanner?"

She didn't think they had a big spanner. But there might be some things like that in the garage.

The search went on. She knew that there were other policemen in the garden all around the house. She could hear their footsteps on the gravel outside, and sometimes she saw the flash of a torch through a chink in the curtains. It began to get late, nearly nine she noticed by the clock on the mantle. The four men searching the rooms seemed to be growing weary, a trifle exasperated.

"Jack," she said, the next time Sergeant Noonan went by. "Would you mind giving me a drink?"

"Sure I'll give you a drink. You mean this whiskey?"

"Yes please. But just a small one. It might make me feel better."

He handed her the glass.

"Why don't you have one yourself," she said. "You must be awfully tired. Please do. You've been very good to me."

"Well," he answered. "It's not strictly allowed, but I might take just a drop to keep me going."

One by one the others came in and were persuaded to take a little nip of whiskey. They stood around rather awkwardly with the drinks in their hands, uncomfortable in her presence, trying to say consoling things to her. Sergeant Noonan wandered into the kitchen, came out quickly and said, "Look, Mrs. Maloney. You know that oven of yours is still on, and the meat still inside."

"Oh *dear* me!" she cried. "So it is!"

"I better turn it off for you, hadn't I?"

"Will you do that, Jack? Thank you so much."

When the sergeant returned the second time, she looked at him with her large, dark, tearful eyes. "Jack Noonan," she said.

"Yes?"

"Would you do me a small favor—you and these others?"

"We can try, Mrs. Maloney."

"Well," she said. "Here you all are, and good friends of dear Patrick's too, and helping to catch the man who killed him. You must be terribly hungry by now because it's long past your suppertime, and I know Patrick would never forgive me, God bless his soul, if I allowed you to remain in his house without offering you decent hospitality. Why don't you eat up that lamb that's in the oven? It'll be cooked just right by now."

"Wouldn't dream of it," Sergeant Noonan said.

"Please," she begged. "Please eat it. Personally I couldn't touch a thing, certainly not what's been in the house when he was here. But it's all right for you. It'd be a favor to me if you'd eat it up. Then you can go on with your work again afterwards."

There was a good deal of hesitating among the four policemen, but they were clearly hungry, and in the end they were persuaded to go into the kitchen and help themselves. The woman stayed where she was, listening to them through the open door, and she could hear them speaking among themselves, their voices thick and sloppy because their mouths were full of meat.

"Have some more, Charlie?"

"No. Better not finish it."

"She *wants* us to finish it. She said so. Be doing her a favor."

"Okay then. Give me some more."

"That's a hell of a big club the guy must've used to hit poor Patrick," one of them was saying. "The doc says his skull was smashed all to pieces just like from a sledgehammer."

"That's why it ought to be easy to find."

"Exactly what I say."

"Whoever done it, they're not going to be carrying a thing like that around with them longer than they need."

One of them belched.

"Personally, I think it's right here on the premises."

"Probably right under our very noses. What you think, Jack?" And in the other room, Mary Maloney began to giggle.

Don't Look Behind You

Fredric Brown

Fredric Brown (1906-1972) was born in Cincinnati, Ohio. Both his parents died within a year of each other in 1920 and '21, leaving the young Brown to support himself. A graduate of Hanover College, Brown moved to Milwaukee in 1929 and worked as a proofreader for several publishers. He eventually accepted a position with the *Milwaukee Journal,* where he remained until 1947. That year Brown moved to New York and sold his first novel, *The Fabulous Clipjoint.* In 1948, the year he divorced his first wife, Brown received his first Edgar. He wrote *The Screaming Mimi,* arguably his greatest work and the basis of two films, in 1949. A year later Brown met and married Elizabeth Charlier and moved to Taos, New Mexico, for his health. Brown was particularly prolific over the next three years, writing several novels (*Night of the Jabberwock,* 1950; *Compliments of a Fiend,* 1950; *The Far Cry,* 1951; *The Case of the Dancing Sandwiches,* 1951; *We All Killed Grandma,* 1952), but declining health forced him to move again in 1954 to Arizona. He wrote several more novels, including the science fiction classic *Martians Go Home* (1955), *One for the Road* (1958), *Knock 3-1-2* (1959), and *The Late Lamented* (1959). By the 1960's, his health had continued to decline, and, while he sold frequently to television, Brown's output began to seriously decline. After a final novel, *Mrs. Murphy's Underpants* (1963), Brown only produced a handful of stories before his death of emphysema in 1972. His mystery stories are collected in three books: *Mostly Murder* (1953), *Nightmares and Geezenstacks* (1961), and *The Shaggy Dog and Other Murders* (1963).

Brown had a talent for experimenting with story form, as well as for infusing his tales with a taste of the macabre. "Don't Look Behind You" shows him at the top of his form, with a story in which the reader finds himself one of the characters.

JUST SIT BACK and relax, now. Try to enjoy this; it's going to be the last story you ever read, or nearly the last. After you finish it you can sit there and stall a while, you can find excuses to hang around your house, or your room, or your office, wherever you're reading this; but sooner or later you're going to have to get up and go out. That's

68

where I'm waiting for you: outside. Or maybe closer than that. Maybe in this room.

You think that's a joke of course. You think this is just a story in a book, and that I don't really mean you. Keep right on thinking so. But be fair; admit that I'm giving you fair warning.

Harley bet me I couldn't do it. He bet me a diamond he's told me about, a diamond as big as his head. So you see why I've got to kill you. And why I've got to tell you how and why and all about it first. That's part of the bet. It's just the kind of idea Harley would have.

I'll tell you about Harley first. He's tall and handsome, and suave and cosmopolitan. He looks something like Ronald Coleman, only he's taller. He dresses like a million dollars, but it wouldn't matter if he didn't; I mean that he'd look distinguished in overalls. There's a sort of magic about Harley, a mocking magic in the way he looks at you; it makes you think of palaces and far-off countries and bright music.

It was in Springfield, Ohio, that he met Justin Dean. Justin was a funny-looking little runt who was just a printer. He worked for the Atlas Printing & Engraving Company. He was a very ordinary little guy, just about as different as possible from Harley; you couldn't pick two men more different. He was only thirty-five, but he was mostly bald already, and he had to wear thick glasses because he'd worn out his eyes doing fine printing and engraving. He was a good printer and engraver: I'll say that for him.

I never asked Harley how he happened to come to Springfield, but the day he got there, after he'd checked in at the Castle Hotel, he stopped in at Atlas to have some calling cards made. It happened that Justin Dean was alone in the shop at the time, and he took Harley's order for the cards; Harley wanted engraved ones, the best. Harley always wants the best of everything.

Harley probably didn't even notice Justin; there was no reason why he should have. But Justin noticed Harley all right, and in him he saw everything that he himself would like to be, and never would be, because most of the things Harley has, you have to be born with.

And Justin made the plates for the cards himself and printed them himself, and he did a wonderful job—something he thought would be worthy of a man like Harley Prentice. That was the name engraved on the card, just that and nothing else, as all really important people have their cards engraved.

He did fine-line work on it, freehand cursive style, and used all the skill he had. It wasn't wasted, because the next day when Harley called to get the cards he held one and stared at it for a while, and then he looked at Justin, seeing him for the first time. He asked, "Who did this?"

And little Justin told him proudly who had done it, and Harley smiled at him and told him it was the work of an artist, and he asked Justin to have dinner with him that evening after work, in the Blue Room of the Castle Hotel.

That's how Harley and Justin got together, but Harley was careful. He waited until he'd known Justin a while before he asked him whether or not he could make plates for five and ten dollar bills. Harley had the contacts; he could market the bills in quantity with men who specialized in passing them, and—most important—he knew where he could get paper with the silk threads in it, paper that wasn't quite the genuine thing, but was close enough to pass inspection by anyone but an expert.

So Justin quit his job at Atlas and he and Harley went to New York, and they set up a little printing shop as a blind, on Amsterdam Avenue south of Sherman Square, and they worked at the bills. Justin worked hard, harder than he had ever worked in his life, because besides working on the plates for the bills, he helped meet expenses by handling what legitimate printing work came into the shop.

He worked day and night for almost a year, making plate after plate, and each one was a little better than the last, and finally he had plates that Harley said were good enough. That night they had dinner at the Waldorf-Astoria to celebrate and after dinner they went the rounds of the best night clubs, and it cost Harley a small fortune, but that didn't matter because they were going to get rich.

They drank champagne, and it was the first time Justin ever drank champagne and he got disgustingly drunk and must have made quite a fool of himself. Harley told him about it afterwards, but Harley wasn't mad at him. He took him back to his room at the hotel and put him to bed, and Justin was pretty sick for a couple of days. But that didn't matter, either, because they were going to get rich.

Then Justin started printing bills from the plates, and they got rich. After that, Justin didn't have to work so hard, either, because he turned down most jobs that came into the print shop, told them he was behind schedule and couldn't handle any more. He took just a little work, to keep up a front. And behind the front, he made five and ten dollar bills, and he and Harley got rich.

He got to know other people whom Harley knew. He met Bull Mallon, who handled the distribution end. Bull Mallon was built like a bull, that was why they called him that. He had a face that never smiled or changed expression at all except when he was holding burning matches to the soles of Justin's bare feet. But that wasn't then; that was later, when he wanted Justin to tell him where the plates were.

And he got to know Captain John Willys of the Police Department, who was a friend of Harley's, to whom Harley gave quite a bit of the money they made, but that didn't matter either, because there was plenty left and they all got rich. He met a friend of Harley's who was a big star of the stage, and one who owned a big New York newspaper. He got to know other people equally important, but in less respectable ways.

Harley, Justin knew, had a hand in lots of other enterprises besides the little mint on Amsterdam Avenue. Some of these ventures took him out of town, usually over weekends. And the weekend that Harley was murdered Justin never found out what really happened, except that Harley went away and didn't come back. Oh, he knew that he was murdered, all right, because the police found his body—with three bullet holes in his chest—in the most expensive suite of the best hotel in Albany. Even for a place to be found dead in Harley Prentice had chosen the best.

All Justin ever knew about it was that a long distance call came to him at the hotel where he was staying, the night that Harley was murdered—it must have been a matter of minutes, in fact, before the time the newspapers said Harley was killed.

It was Harley's voice on the phone, and his voice was debonair and unexcited as ever. But he said, "Justin? Get to the shop and get rid of the plates, the paper, everything. Right away. I'll explain when I see you." He waited only until Justin said, "Sure, Harley," and then he said, "Attaboy," and hung up.

Justin hurried around to the printing shop and got the plates and the paper and a few thousand dollars' worth of counterfeit bills that were on hand. He made the paper and bills into one bundle and the copper plates into another, smaller one, and he left the shop with no evidence that it had ever been a mint in miniature.

He was very careful and very clever in disposing of both bundles. He got rid of the big one first by checking in at a big hotel, not one he or Harley ever stayed at, under a false name, just to have a chance to put the big bundle in the incinerator there. It was paper and it would burn. And he made sure there was a fire in the incinerator before he dropped it down the chute.

The plates were different. They wouldn't burn, he knew, so he took a trip to Staten Island and back on the ferry and, somewhere out in the middle of the bay, he dropped the bundle over the side into the water.

Then, having done what Harley had told him to do, and having done it well and thoroughly, he went back to the hotel—his own hotel, not the one where he had dumped the paper and the bills—and went to sleep.

In the morning he read in the newspapers that Harley had been killed, and he was stunned. It didn't seem possible. He couldn't believe it; it was a joke someone was playing on him. Harley would come back to him, he knew. And he was right; Harley did, but that was later, in the swamp.

But anyway, Justin had to know, so he took the very next train for Albany. He must have been on the train when the police went to his hotel, and at the hotel they must have learned he'd asked at the desk about trains for Albany, because they were waiting for him when he got off the train there.

They took him to a station and they kept him there a long long time, days and days, asking him questions. They found out, after a while, that he couldn't have killed Harley because he'd been in New York City at the time Harley was killed in Albany but they knew also that he and Harley had been operating the little mint, and they thought that might be a lead to who killed Harley, and they were interested in the counterfeiting, too, maybe even more than in the murder. They asked Justin Dean questions, over and over and over, and he couldn't answer them, so he didn't. They kept him awake for days at a time, asking him questions over and over. Most of all they wanted to know where the plates were. He wished he could tell them that the plates were safe where nobody could ever get them again, but he couldn't tell them that without admitting that he and Harley had been counterfeiting, so he couldn't tell them.

They located the Amsterdam shop, but they didn't find any evidence there, and they really had no evidence to hold Justin on at all, but he didn't know that, and it never occurred to him to get a lawyer.

He kept wanting to see Harley, and they wouldn't let him; then, when they learned he really didn't believe Harley could be dead, they made him look at a dead man they said was Harley, and he guessed it was, although Harley looked different dead. He didn't look magnificent, dead. And Justin believed, then, but still didn't believe. And after that he just went silent and wouldn't say a word, even when they kept him awake for days and days with a bright light in his eyes, and kept slapping him to keep him awake. They didn't use clubs or rubber hoses, but they slapped him a million times and wouldn't let him sleep. And after a while he lost track of things and couldn't have answered their questions even if he'd wanted to.

For a while after that, he was in a bed in a white room, and all he remembers about that are nightmares he had, and calling for Harley and an awful confusion as to whether Harley was dead or not, and then things came back to him gradually and he knew he didn't want to stay in the white room; he wanted to get out so he could hunt for Harley. And if Harley was dead, he wanted to kill whoever had killed Harley, because Harley would have done tke same for him.

So he began pretending, and acting, very cleverly, the way the doctors and nurses seemed to want him to act, and after a while they gave him his clothes and let him go.

He was becoming cleverer now. He thought, What would Harley tell me to do? And he knew they'd try to follow him because they'd think he might lead them to the plates, which they didn't know were at the bottom of the bay, and he gave them the slip before he left Albany, and he went first to Boston, and from there by boat to New York, instead of going direct.

He went first to the print shop, and went in the back way after watching the alley for a long time to be sure the place wasn't guarded. It was a mess; they must have searched it very thoroughly for the plates.

Harley wasn't there, of course. Justin left and from a phone booth in a drugstore he telephoned their hotel and asked for Harley and was told Harley no longer lived there; and to be clever and not let them guess who he was, he asked for Justin Dean, and they said Justin Dean didn't live there any more either.

Then he moved to a different drugstore and from there he decided to call up some friends of Harley's, and he phoned Bull Mallon first and because Bull was a friend, he told him who he was and asked if he knew where Harley was.

Bull Mallon didn't pay any attention to that; he sounded excited, a little, and he asked, "Did the cops get the plates, Dean?" and Justin said they didn't, that he wouldn't tell them, and he asked again about Harley.

Bull asked, "Are you nuts, or kidding?" And Justin just asked him again, and Bull's voice changed and he said, "Where are you?" and Justin told him. Bull said, "Harley's here. He's staying under cover, but it's all right if you know, Dean. You wait right there at the drugstore, and we'll come and get you."

They came and got Justin, Bull Mallon and two other men in a car, and they told him Harley was hiding out way deep in New Jersey and that they were going to drive there now. So he went along and sat in the back seat between two men he didn't know, while Bull Mallon drove.

It was late afternoon then, when they picked him up, and Bull drove all evening and most of the night and he drove fast. so he must have gone farther than New Jersey, at least into Virginia or maybe farther, into the Carolinas.

The sky was getting faintly gray with first dawn when they stopped at a rustic cabin that looked like it had been used as a hunting lodge. It was miles from anywhere, there wasn't even a road leading to it, just a trail that was level enough for the car to be able to make it.

They took Justin into the cabin and tied him to a chair, and they told him Harley wasn't there, but Harley had told them that Justin would tell them where the plates were, and he couldn't leave until he did tell.

Justin didn't believe them; he knew then that they'd tricked him about Harley, but it didn't matter, as far as the plates were concerned. It didn't matter if he told them what he'd done with the plates, because they couldn't get them again, and they wouldn't tell the police. So he told them, quite willingly.

But they didn't believe him. They said he'd hidden the plates and was lying. They tortured him to make him tell. They beat him, and they cut him with knives, and they held burning matches and lighted cigars to the soles of his feet, and they pushed needles under his fingernails. Then they'd rest and ask him questions and if he could talk, he'd tell them the truth, and after a while they'd start to torture him again.

It went on for days and weeks—Justin doesn't know how long, but it was a long time. Once they went away for several days and left him tied up with nothing to eat or drink. They came back and started in all over again. And all the time he hoped Harley would come to help him, but Harley didn't come, not then.

After a while what was happening in the cabin ended, or anyway he didn't know any more about it. They must have thought he was dead; maybe they were right, or anyway not far from wrong.

The next thing he knows was the swamp. He was lying in shallow water at the edge of deeper water. His face was out of the water; it woke him when he turned a little and his face went under. They must have thought him dead and thrown him into the water, but he had floated into the shallow part before he had drowned, and a last flicker of consciousness had turned him over on his back with his face out.

I don't remember much about Justin in the swamp; it was a long time, but I just remember flashes of it. I couldn't move at first; I just lay there in the shallow water with my face out. It got dark and it got cold, I remember, and finally my arms would move a little and I got farther out of the water, lying in the mud with only my feet in the water. I slept or was unconscious again and when I woke up it was getting gray dawn, and that was when Harley came. I think I'd been calling him, and he must have heard.

He stood there, dressed as immaculately and perfectly as ever, right in the swamp, and he was laughing at me for being so weak and lying there like a log, half in the dirty water and half in the mud, and I got up and nothing hurt any more.

We shook hands and he said, "Come on, Justin, let's get you out of here," and I was so glad he'd come that I cried a little. He laughed at me for that and said I should lean on him and he'd help me walk, but I wouldn't do that, because I was coated with mud and filth of the swamp and he was so clean and perfect in a white linen suit, like an ad in a magazine. And all the way out of that swamp, all the days and nights we spent there, he never even got mud on his trouser cuffs, nor his hair mussed.

I told him just to lead the way, and he did, walking just ahead of me, sometimes turning around, laughing and talking to me and cheering me up. Sometimes I'd fall but I wouldn't let him come back and help me. But he'd wait patiently until I could get up. Sometimes I'd crawl instead when I couldn't stand up any more. Sometimes I'd have to swim streams that he'd leap lightly across.

And it was day and night and day and night, and sometimes I'd sleep, and things would crawl across me. And some of them I caught and ate, or maybe I dreamed that. I remember other things, in that swamp, like an organ that played a lot of the time, and sometimes angels in the air and devils in the water, but those were delirium, I guess.

Harley would say, "A little farther, Justin; we'll make it. And we'll get back at them, at all of them."

And we made it. We came to dry fields, cultivated fields with waist-high corn, but there weren't ears on the corn for me to eat. And then there was a stream, a clear stream that wasn't stinking water like the swamp, and Harley told me to wash myself and my clothes and I did, although I wanted to hurry on to where I could get food.

I still looked pretty bad; my clothes were clean of mud and filth but they were mere rags and wet, because I couldn't wait for them to dry, and I had a ragged beard and I was barefoot.

But we went on and came to a little farm building, just a two-room shack, and there was a smell of fresh bread just out of an oven, and I ran the last few yards to knock on the door. A woman, an ugly woman, opened the door and when she saw me she slammed it again before I could say a word.

Strength came to me from somewhere, maybe from Harley, although I can't remember him being there just then. There was a pile of kindling logs beside the door. I picked one of them up as though it were no heavier than a broomstick, and I broke down the door and killed the woman. She screamed a lot, but I killed her. Then I ate the hot fresh bread.

I watched from the window as I ate, and saw a man running across the field toward the house. I found a knife, and I killed him as he came in at the door. It was much better, killing with the knife; I liked it that way.

I ate more bread, and kept watching from all the windows, but no one else came. Then my stomach hurt from the hot bread I'd eaten and I had to lie down, doubled up, and when the hurting quit, I slept.

Harley woke me up, and it was dark. He said, "Let's get going; you should be far away from here before it's daylight."

I knew he was right, but I didn't hurry away. I was becoming, as you see, very clever now. I knew there were things to do first. I found matches and a lamp, and lighted the lamp. Then I hunted through the shack for everything I could use. I found clothes of the man, and they fitted me not too badly except that I had to turn up the cuffs of the trousers and the shirt. His shoes were big, but that was good because my feet were so swollen.

I found a razor and shaved; it took a long time because my hand wasn't steady, but I was very careful and didn't cut myself much.

I had to hunt hardest for their money, but I found it finally. It was sixty dollars.

And I took the knife, after I had sharpened it. It isn't fancy; just a bone-handled carving knife, but it's good steel. I'll show it to you, pretty soon now. It's had a lot of use.

Then we left and it was Harley who told me to stay away from the roads, and find railroad tracks. That was easy because we heard a train whistle far off in the night and knew which direction the tracks lay. From then on, with Harley helping, it's been easy.

You won't need the details from here. I mean, about the brakeman, and about the tramp we found asleep in the empty reefer, and about the near thing I had with the police in Richmond. I learned from that; I learned I mustn't talk to Harley when anybody else was around to hear. He hides himself from them; he's got a trick and they don't know he's there, and they think I'm funny in the head if I talk to him. But in Richmond I bought better clothes and got a haircut and a man I killed in an alley had forty dollars on him, so I had money again. I've done a lot of traveling since then. If you stop to think you'll know where I am right now.

I'm looking for Bull Mallon and the two men who helped him. Their names are Harry and Carl. I'm going to kill them when I find them. Harley keeps telling me that those fellows are big time and that I'm not ready for them yet. But I can be looking while I'm getting ready so I keep moving around. Sometimes I stay in one place long enough to hold a job as a printer for a while. I've learned a lot of things. I can hold a job and people don't think I'm too strange; they don't get scared when I look at them like they sometimes did a few months ago. And I've learned not to talk to Harley except in our own room and then only very quietly so people in the next room won't think I'm talking to myself .

And I've kept in practice with the knife. I've killed lots of people with it, mostly on the streets at night. Sometimes because they look like they might have money on them, but mostly just for practice and because I've come to like doing it. I'm really good with the knife by now. You'll hardly feel it.

But Harley tells me that kind of killing is easy and that it's something else to kill a person who's on guard, as Bull and Harry and Carl will be.

And that's the conversation that led to the bet I mentioned. I told Harley that I'd bet him that, right now, I could warn a man I was going to use the knife on him and even tell him why and approximately when, and that I could still kill him. And he bet me that I couldn't and he's going to lose that bet.

He's going to lose it because I'm warning you right now and you're not going to believe me. I'm betting that you're going to believe that this is just another story in a book. That you won't believe that this is the *only* copy of this book that contains this story and that this story is true. Even when I tell you how it was done, I don't think you'll really believe me.

You see I'm putting it over on Harley, winning the bet, by putting it over on you. He never thought, and you won't realize how easy it is for a good printer, who's been a counterfeiter too, to counterfeit one story in a book. Nothing like as hard as counterfeiting a five dollar bill.

I had to pick a book of short stories and I picked this one because I happened to notice that the last story in the book was titled *Don't Look Behind You* and that was going to be a good title for this. You'll see what I mean in a few minutes.

I'm lucky that the printing shop I'm working for now does book work and had a type face that matches the rest of this book. I had a little trouble matching the paper exactly, but I finally did and I've got it ready while I'm writing this. I'm writing this directly on a linotype, late at night in the shop where I'm working days. I even have the boss' permission, told him I was going to set up and print a story that a friend of mine had written, as a surprise for him, and that I'd melt the type metal back as soon as I'd printed one good copy.

When I finish writing this I'll make up the type in pages to match the rest of the book and I'll print it on the matching paper I have ready. I'll cut the new pages to fit and bind them in; you won't be able to tell the difference, even if a faint suspicion may cause you to look at it. Don't forget I made five and ten dollar bills you couldn't have told from the original, and this is kindergarten stuff compared to that job. And I've done enough bookbinding that I'll be able to take the last story out of the book and bind this one in instead of it and you won't be able to tell the difference no matter how closely you look. I'm going to do a perfect job of it if it takes me all night.

And tomorrow I'll go to some bookstore, or maybe a newsstand or even a drugstore that sells books and has other copies of this book, ordinary copies, and I'll plant this one there. I'll find myself a good place to watch from, and I'll be watching when you buy it.

The rest I can't tell you yet because it depends a lot on circumstances, whether you went right home with the book or what you did. I won't know till I follow you and keep watch till you read it—and I see that you're reading the last story in the book.

If you're home while you're reading this, maybe I'm in the house with you right now. Maybe I'm in this very room, hidden, waiting for you to finish the story. Maybe I'm watching through a window. Or maybe I'm sitting near you on the streetcar or train, if you're reading it there. Maybe I'm on the fire escape outside your hotel room. But wherever you're reading it, I'm near you, watching and waiting for you to finish. You can count on that.

You're pretty near the end now. You'll be finished in seconds and you'll close the book. still not believing. Or, if you haven't read the stories in order, maybe you'll turn back to start another story. If you do, you'll never finish it.

But don't look around; you'll be happier if you don't know, if you don't see the knife coming. When I kill people from behind they don't seem to mind so much.

Go on, just a few seconds or minutes, thinking this is just another story. Don't look behind you. Don't believe this—*until you feel the knife.*

Exactly What Happened

Jim Thompson

Jim Thompson (1906-1977) was born in Anadarko, Oklahoma. Thompson's family moved throughout Oklahoma and Texas before settling in Nebraska. He attended the University of Nebraska, and married his wife Alberta in 1931. Thompson held down various jobs to support his family, writing true crime stories for extra money. He accepted a position with the Oklahoma Writers' Project in the late 1930's. Thompson wrote his first novel, *Now and on Earth*, in 1942. While critically praised, the novel and its follow-up (*To Heed the Thunder,* 1946) were commercial failures. Thompson left the Writers' Project to edit *Saga* magazine during the 1940's, the first in a very long line of short-term editing assignments. He wrote his first mystery novel, *More Than Murder,* in 1949. Thompson wrote dozens of novels during short streaks of creativity; he wrote a dozen between 1952 and 1954. In the mid-50s, he wrote two scripts for Stanley Kubrick: *The Killing* (1956) and *Paths of Glory* (1957). Thompson survived on his writing, producing television scripts and novelizations in the 1960's. In 1976, he suffered a severe stroke that prevented him from writing. Depressed by this development, Thompson deliberately starved himself to death. His most well-known works include *The Killer Inside Me* (1952), *Cropper's Cabin* (1952), *The Criminal* (1953), *The Alcoholics* (1953), *Savage Night* (1953), *A Hell of a Woman* (1954), *After Dark, My Sweet* (1955), *The Kill-Off* (1957), *The Getaway* (1959), *The Grifters* (1963), *Pop. 1280* (1964), *Nothing But a Man* (1970), *Child of Rage* (1972) and *King Blood* (1973).

Thompson's strength comes from his highly realistic depiction of aberrant psychology and the world of the con-men and "grifters" he wrote about. "Exactly What Happened" depicts Thompson's world at its seediest, and packs a punch in spite of its somewhat conventional ending.

SEATED ON THE BED in his sleazy hotel room, Neil Keller allowed himself another short drink from the whiskey bottle and again picked up the hammer. It was a tiny instrument, with a head little larger than the head of a match. Keller raised it to his mouth, pushed back his upper lip with a finger, and gave one of his front teeth a firm tap.

The tooth moved under the blow. Wincing, Keller gave it a few more taps, then shifted to another tooth. It moved also—they were both loosening up nicely. Keller worked on them slowly but steadily, stopping only for an occasional painkilling drink.

Relatively speaking, there was not a great deal of pain—nothing at all compared with what it had been a month ago. It had been real hell then, back when he had begun the job of loosening two perfectly sound teeth—getting them to the point where they could be finally removed with only one more hour's steady effort.

Now, however, the agony was over, and he had nothing more unpleasant to look forward to than killing Jake Goss. One-Eyed Jake with the missing teeth, the mushy voice, the mole on his right cheek—a guy with a face you could never forget.

Jake had been pretty nice to Keller. Jake had kind of taken a fancy to him when Keller first holed up in this fleabag, and it was through Jake's recommendation that he'd got his job as night janitor in the Wexler Building—Jake was the night watchman.

He was stupid and boastful, this Jake Goss—a guy that had to spread around everything he knew. Still, he'd been pretty nice, so Keller sort of hated to kill him. And yet he couldn't help grinning a little when he thought about it.

It was so damned funny, you see. Really a riot. Keller was going to kill Jake, but it was Jake who would be tagged for murder! The murder of Neil Keller. He, Keller, would kill Jake and knock over Old Man Wexler for a hundred grand or better. But the cops—ha, ha—the cops would be looking for Jake.

Chuckling, Keller turned sideways on the bed and glanced down at the morning newspaper. It was open at the realty columns, where a story in small type announced the transfer by Otto J. Wexler of a certain piece of real estate—"assessed valuation $50,000."

Being assessed at $50,000, it would have sold for at least twice that much. Jake Goss had loftily explained this obvious fact to him one morning, while pointing out a similar item in the newspaper.

"See that the old man sold a house yesterday for ten thousand," he had said. "That means he's got maybe twenty grand in his safe tonight."

"Here you mean?" Keller had said, incredulously. "You mean he keeps that kind of dough up in his office—his apartment?"

"Yep. Getting his money out of real estate as fast as he can, and the kind of deals he's putting it into—not really illegal, y'know, but just a little shady—stuff that the banks won't touch, and with the kind of interest they can't charge. ''

Wexler was in the loan shark business in a big way, Jake explained, and he was expanding rapidly. "I know, see?" he went on, his one eye gleaming pridefully. "Me and Wexler are like that. Why, there ain't a morning passes that I don't drop in on him for a cuppa coffee. The old guy don't trust most people, so I guess he gets pretty lonesome. But—"

"Yeah, yeah, sure," Keller had cut in impatiently. "You have coffee with him, and he trusts you. But he wouldn't be sucker enough to keep any big dough *here*. He's kidding you about that."

"The hell he is! You mean, he'd be afraid of getting robbed? How's anyone going to rob him?"

Keller had hesitated. How? Well, now that he stopped to think about it, a robbery didn't look so simple. The old man's office-apartment was thoroughly burglar-alarmed. The building's doors were locked at night, and no one could get in or out unless Jake let them. Of course, one of the tenants could stick a gun in Jake's ribs, or—

Keller mentioned this possibility to the one-eyed man. Jake shook his head.

"So suppose some holdup artist did get in here. Suppose he got past them burglar alarms, and made the old man come across. What good would it do him? This building is right down in the middle of town. There's cops going by all night long. A guy wouldn't get ten feet from the door before they put the cuffs on him."

"Yeah," Keller nodded thoughtfully. "I guess that's right, isn't it?"

"Now, you or me," Jake said. "Suppose you or me tried to rob Wexler. He'd open the door for us, sure, so that would take care of one hurdle. And we wouldn't have any trouble getting out of the building or any trouble with the cops. But how far would we get? The robbery would be discovered in a few hours. They'd know that we did it, just because we've gone, and they'd have our descriptions down pat. Which is just the same as saying they'd have us cold. Oh, maybe we could take it on the lam for a little while, but sooner or later—"

"I guess you're right," Keller had nodded. "It just couldn't be done, Jake."

And he had laughed silently, contemptuously, as he spoke...

The two front teeth were out now. Keller stood in front of the lavatory mirror, snapping a black patch over one eye, applying an artgum mole to one cheek, stippling freckles across his nose, and thickening his brows with color pencils.

He put on his brown uniform cap. He slumped his shoulders, the way Jake slumped his. Then—well, nothing then. That was all there was to it. Except for the extraction of the teeth, the entire transformation had taken only a few minutes, yet it had made him into another man.

Naturally, he couldn't keep up the masquerade indefinitely. Given enough time, someone was bound to see through it. But no one would be given that much time. Not Wexler, after he'd been slugged and tied up. Not the cops, as Keller left the building.

Thus, they would swear that he was Jake, that it was Jake who had pulled the robbery and brazenly walked away with the loot.

They would have no suspicions—nor the opportunity to prove them—that he might not be Jake.

Keller studied his reflection in the mirror, mouthing silent words, grimacing experimentally. Those teeth—he would get the gaps filled later on. Meanwhile, as long as he was careful about smiling and talking, no one would even know that two teeth were missing.

He removed the eyepatch and mole, then scrubbed his face thoroughly. Wrapping the patch and color pencils in a handkerchief, he stuffed them into his pocket and left the hotel.

At the railroad station he retrieved a large briefcase from a rental locker. Proceeding to the men's room, he gave the attendant fifty cents and was admitted to a dressing cubicle. Some twenty minutes later he emerged, smartly attired, his work clothes stuffed into the briefcase, and taxied to a nearby hotel.

He had registered there several times before to establish his identity—or, rather, his false identity. So the doorman and bellboy greeted him as Mr. Jennings, and the clerk assured him that they were delighted to have Mr. Jennings back as a guest again.

"Going to have you with us for a while, sir?" he inquired, as he assigned a room to Keller. "Or is this another one of your flying trips?"

"Looks like a real quickie this time," Keller said briskly. "I have to close a deal tonight and head back to Chicago in the morning. Just hope I can squeeze in a few hours' sleep."

"Well, I hope so, too." The clerk frowned with professional warmth. "You drive yourself too hard, Mr. Jennings."

Arriving at his room, Keller dismissed the bellboy with a generous tip and received generous thanks in return. Then, as the youth departed beaming, Keller's own smile faded and he was filled with an uneasy sense of depression. It was a familiar feeling—one he experienced every time he came to this hotel.

Probably, he supposed, it derived from the way he was made welcome here, from the establishment's friendliness toward him. Its bought-and-paid-for, good-business kind of friendliness. For at such times it was borne home to him that he had never exactly been laved in the warmth of real friendship. Axiomatically, it was impossible.

Genuine friendship was a sharing arrangement. You knew a man's problems, his secret hopes and aspirations, and he knew yours. And you sympathized with and wished the best for one another.

That was real friendship—always a matter of give-and-take. So if you were strictly a taker, as Keller was, it obviously wasn't for him. He couldn't let a man know too much about him. Not only that, but he couldn't let himself know very much about the other man. If he did, you see, he might weaken. He might get to feel sorry for the man to the extent of letting him slip away.

Take Jake Goss, now—one-eyed, gap-toothed Jake. What was his background? Did he have a wife somewhere, or a sweetheart? How had he lost his eye and those teeth? Was his dullness, his absorption with gossip, only a protective reaction to lifelong failure? Was it his way of shedding the blame for his lack of achievement?

Jake was still a young man—little older, at least, than Keller. Yet he seemed quite content to go on forever in a cheap, monotonous, dead-end job.

Why? How could he have so little ambition? What had imprinted him so indelibly with the stamp of stupidity? What made the guy tick?

Sprawled on the bed, Keller let his eyes drift shut, dismissing the many questions.

He didn't know any of the answers—he didn't want to know them. For the sake of his future comfort and his present plans, it was better to leave Jake as he was—a human question-mark. A human zero who was soon to be erased.

Keller slept a few hours. Then, carrying his briefcase, he hurried out of the hotel and returned to the railroad station.

In the men's room he changed back into his work uniform. His business suit went into the briefcase, which he again placed in the locker. The suit would be rumpled, of course, but that was all right. When he went back to the hotel in the morning, he would look about as he should—as a man would look who had been up all night at an important conference.

Keller ate supper, then went to the Wexler Building. Mindful of his missing teeth, he greeted Jake cautiously, just a little nervously. But the one-eyed man obviously didn't notice. He was grumpy, in a bad mood about something or other. He didn't want to talk or be talked to, and he made it apparent.

That suited Keller perfectly, of course. Loading his pails and mops onto one of the elevators, he ascended to the top floor of the building and began his nightly work.

The hours passed slowly. At three in the morning he took over Jake's duties while Jake went out to eat. And at 3:30, on Jake's return, he himself went out for half an hour.

When he came back to the building Jake admitted him surlily, still grumpily silent. And Keller lowered his elevator to the basement.

The trip was routine at this hour of the morning. The incinerator, burdened with the night's accumulation of waste, was frequently in need of adjusting. So Keller adjusted it, opening its dampers to their widest. He listened to the responding roar of the flames and nodded with grim satisfaction.

That would take care of Jake—that and a few heavy blows from a steel poker. Between the two things, the poker and the fire, Jake would lose his one-eyed, missing-toothed identity. In effect, Jake would become Neil Keller.

Keller took out his wallet and stripped it of money. Then, with its identification cards intact, he tossed it into a dark corner and returned to the elevator.

Old man Wexler was an early riser. He was always up by six or before. At 6:30—never earlier—Jake Goss stopped by to share a cup of coffee with him. So at five minutes before six...

Keller parked the elevator on the second floor and took the make-up and eyepatch from his pocket. Working with practiced skill, he assumed the appearance of Jake Goss. He used extra care this morning, and the transformation was not merely good but was near-perfect—indeed, so perfect that even he was startled.

He stared at himself in the elevator mirror, fascinated by Jake's face, even a little frightened by it, actually believing—as the cops and Wexler were certain to—that he *was* Jake Goss.

It was 6:15 when he left the elevator and took to the stairs. At 6:20, having ascended two flights, he stood before the door of Wexler's apartment-office, sniffing the aroma of freshly brewed coffee, making one last swift check-through of his plans.

Let's see, he thought; *I give the old man a couple of medium-good pokes, just enough to make him behave without knocking him out. Then, as soon as he opens the safe, I bind and gag him, put him in the bedroom, and come back by the door to wait for Jake. And when Jake shows up at 6:30—*

But there was no use in going through that again. Besides, there wasn't time. Keller raised his hand and knocked.

The door opened abruptly.

Keller said, "Okay, Wexler! This is a—"

And that was all he said.

For suddenly his vocal cords, his face, his entire body seemed paralyzed. And he could only stand there helplessly and stare.

Not at Wexler, but at Keller. Yes, at Keller!

He, Neil Keller, was staring at Neil Keller.

Then something crashed down on his skull, and when he recovered consciousness he was in the basement. And the other Keller was standing over him, a heavy steel poker in his hands.

He didn't live very long after that—not long enough to solve the simple riddle of the other Keller. And, certainly, it was a simple enough riddle.

After all, if facial blemishes can be put *on* with make-up, they can be *concealed* with make-up—right? And if teeth can be *removed* they can also be put *in*—correct? And a glass eye is rather easily purchased—right?

Or, getting down to cases, if you can easily assume the appearance of another man, why can't he just as easily assume yours?

Well, you see how it was. But Neil Keller didn't. He didn't have the time.

In his last brief moments all he saw was himself. The one man he had not guarded against. The one man every man faces sooner or later. All he saw was that he was about to be murdered by himself—which, in a sense, was exactly what happened.

First Offense

Ed McBain

Ed McBain (b. 1928), the king of the police procedural, is the pseudonym of Evan Hunter. A native of New York City, his family moved to the Bronx in 1938, and he attended Evander Childs, Jr., High School. After he graduated from high school, Hunter attended the New York Art Student's League and Cooper Union Art School before joining the Navy in 1944. While serving his country, Hunter began to sell stories, and had published over a hundred by the time his first novel, *The Blackboard Jungle* (1954), was released. In 1949, he married Anita Melnick (whom he eventually divorced), and graduated Phi Beta Kappa from Hunter College one year later. Hunter produced one more novel under his name (*Second Ending*, 1956), before publishing the first of his 87th Precinct novels, *Cop Hater* (1957), under the pseudonym Ed McBain. Hunter has since interspersed novels written under his own name (*Strangers When We Meet*, 1958; *The Remarkable Harry*, 1960; *Buddwing*, 1964; *Last Summer*, 1968; *Every Little Crook and Nanny*, 1972; *Streets of Gold*, 1974; *Walk Proud*, 1979) with 87th Precinct novels (*King's Ransom*, 1959; *The Heckler*, 1960; *The Empty Hours*, 1962; *Ax*, 1964; *Doll*, 1965; *Fuzz*, 1968; *Hail, Hail, The Gang's All Here*, 1971; *Let's Hear It for the Deaf Man*, 1972; *So Long As You Both Shall Live*, 1976; *Lightning*, 1984; *Eight Black Horses*, 1985; *Widows*, 1990). In 1973, Hunter married his second wife, Mary Van Finley. Hunter has also written several screenplays, including *The Birds* (1962) and two based on his own novels: *Fuzz* (1972) and *Walk Proud* (1979). In 1981, Hunter began a second series under the McBain pseudonym, featuring lawyer Matthew Hope, with the novel *Rumplestiltskin*. He presently divides his time between Connecticut and New York.

McBain's fame rests on his sharp, no-nonsense prose and attention to detail. "First Offense," one of the author's favorites, is a powerful piece of work that packs an emotional punch.

HE SAT in the police van with the collar of his leather jacket turned up, the bright silver studs sharp against the otherwise unrelieved black. He was seventeen years old, and he wore his hair in a high black crown. He carried his head high and erect because he knew he had a good profile and he carried his mouth like a switch knife, ready to spring open at the slightest provocation. His hands were thrust deep into his jacket pockets, and his gray eyes reflected the walls of the van. There was excitement in his eyes, too, an almost holiday excitement. He tried to tell himself he was in trouble, but he couldn't quite believe it. His gradual descent to disbelief had been a spiral that had spun dizzily through the range of his emotions. Terror when the cop's flash had picked him out; blind panic when he'd started to run; rebellion when the cop's firm hand had closed around the leather sleeve of his jacket; sullen resignation when the cop had thrown him into the RMP car; and then cocky stubbornness when they'd booked him at the local precinct.

The desk sergeant had looked him over curiously, with a strange aloofness in his Irish eyes.

"What's the matter, Fatty?" he'd asked.

The sergeant stared at him implacably. "Put him away for the night," the sergeant said.

He'd slept overnight in the precinct cell block, and he'd awakened with this strange excitement pulsing through his narrow body, and it was the excitement that had caused his disbelief. Trouble, hell! He'd been in trouble before, but it had never felt like this. This was different. This was a ball, man. This was like being initiated into a secret society some place. His contempt for the police had grown when they refused him the opportunity to shave after breakfast. He was only seventeen but he had a fairly decent beard, and a man should be allowed to shave in the morning, what the hell! But even the beard had somehow lent to the unreality of the situation, made him appear—in his own eyes—somehow more desperate, more sinister-looking. He knew he was in trouble, but the trouble was glamorous, and he surrounded it with the gossamer lie of make-believe. He was living the story-book legend. He was big time now. They'd caught him and booked him, and he should have been scared but he was excited instead.

There was one other person in the van with him, a guy who'd spent the night in the cell block, too. The guy was an obvious bum, and his breath stank of cheap wine, but he was better than nobody to talk to.

"Hey!" he said.

The bum looked up. "You talking to me?"

"Yeah. Where we going?"

"The lineup, kid," the bum said. "This your first offense?"

"This's the first time I got caught," he answered cockily.

"All felonies go to the lineup," the bum told him. "And also some special types of misdemeanors. You commit a felony?"

"Yeah," he said, hoping he sounded nonchalant. What'd they have this bum in for anyway? Sleeping on a park bench?

"Well, that's why you're goin' to the lineup. They have guys from every detective squad in the city there, to look you over. So they'll remember you next time. They put you on a stage, and they read off the offense, and the Chief of Detectives starts firing questions at you. What's your name, kid?"

"What's it to you?"

"Don't get smart, punk, or I'll break your arm," the bum said.

He looked at the bum curiously. He was a pretty big guy, with a heavy growth of beard, and powerful shoulders. "My name's Stevie," he said.

"I'm Jim Skinner," the bum said. "When somebody's trying to give you advice, don't go hip on him."

"Yeah. Well, what's your advice?" he asked, not wanting to back down completely.

"When they get you up there, you don't have to answer anything. They'll throw questions, but you don't have to answer. Did you make a statement at the scene?"

"No," he answered.

"Good. Then don't make no statement now, either. They can't force you to. Just keep your mouth shut, and don't tell them nothing."

"I ain't afraid. They know all about it anyway," Stevie said.

The bum shrugged and gathered around him the sullen pearls of his scattered wisdom. Stevie sat in the van whistling, listening to the accompanying hum of the tires, hearing the secret hum of his blood beneath the other, louder sound. He sat at the core of a self-imposed importance, basking in its warm glow, whistling contentedly, secretly happy. Beside him, Skinner leaned back against the wall of the van.

When they arrived at the Center Street Headquarters, they put them in detention cells, awaiting the lineup which began at nine. At ten minutes to nine they led him out of his cell, and the cop who'd arrested him originally took him into the special prisoners' elevator.

"How's it feel being an elevator boy?" he asked the cop.

The cop didn't answer him. They went upstairs to the big room where the lineup was being held. A detective in front of them was pinning on his shield so he could get past the cop at the desk. They crossed the large gymnasium-like compartment, walking past the men sitting in folded chairs before the stage.

"Get a nice turnout, don't you?" Stevie said.

"You ever tried vaudeville?" the cop answered.

The blinds in the room had not been drawn yet, and Stevie could see everything clearly. The stage itself with the permanently fixed microphone hanging from a narrow metal tube above; the height markers— four feet, five feet, six feet—behind the mike on the wide white wall. The men in the seats, he knew, were all detectives and his sense of importance suddenly flared again when he realized these bulls had come from all over the city just to look at him. Behind the bulls was a raised platform with a sort of lecturer's stand on it. A microphone rested on the stand, and a chair was behind it, and he assumed this was where the chief bull would sit. There were uniformed cops stationed here and there around the room, and there was one man in civilian clothing who sat at a desk in front of the stage.

"Who's that?" Stevie asked the cop.

"Police stenographer," the cop answered. "He's going to take down your words for posterity."

They walked behind the stage, and Stevie watched as other felony offenders from all over the city joined them. There was one woman, but all the rest were men, and he studied their faces carefully, hoping to pick up some tricks from them, hoping to learn the subtlety of their expressions. They didn't look like much. He was better-looking than all of them, and the knowledge pleased him. He'd be the star of this little shindig. The cop who'd been with him moved over to talk to a big broad who was obviously a policewoman. Stevie looked around, spotted Skinner and walked over to him.

"What happens now?" he asked.

"They're gonna pull the shades in a few minutes," Skinner said. "Then they'll turn on the spots and start the lineup. The spots won't blind you, but you won't be able to see the faces of any of the bulls out there."

"Who wants to see them mugs?" Stevie asked.

Skinner shrugged. "When your case is called, your arresting officer goes back and stands near the Chief of Detectives, just in case the Chief needs more dope from him. The Chief'll read off your name and the borough where you was pinched. A number'll follow the borough. Like he'll say "Manhattan one" or "Manhattan two." That's just the number of the case from that borough. You're first, you get number one, you follow?"

"Yeah," Stevie said.

"He'll tell the bulls what they got you on, and then he'll say either "Statement" or "No statement". If you made a statement, chances are he won't ask many questions 'cause he won't want you to contradict anything damaging you already said. If there's no statement, he'll fire questions like a machine-gun. But you don't have to answer nothing."

"Then what?"

"When he's through, you go downstairs to get mugged and printed. Then they take you over to the Criminal Courts Building for arraignment."

"They're gonna take my picture, huh?" Stevie asked.

"Yeah."

"You think there'll be reporters here?"

"Huh?"

"Reporters."

"Oh. Maybe. All the wire services hang out in a room across the street from where the vans pulled up. They got their own police radio in there, and they get the straight dope as soon as it's happening, in case they want to roll with it. There may be some reporters." Skinner paused. "Why? What'd do you?"

"It ain't so much what I done," Stevie said. "I was just wonderin' if we'd make the papers."

Skinner stared at him curiously. "You're all charged up, ain't you, Stevie?"

"Hell, no. Don't you think I know I'm in trouble?"

"Maybe you don't know just how much trouble," Skinner said.

"What the hell are you talking about?"

"This ain't as exciting as you think, kid. Take my word for it."

"Sure, you know all about it."

"I been around a little," Skinner said drily.

"Sure, on park benches all over the country. I know I'm in trouble, don't worry."

"You kill anybody?"

"No," Stevie said.

"Assault?"

Stevie didn't answer.

"Whatever you done," Skinner advised, "and no matter how long you been doin' it before they caught you, make like it's your first time. Tell them you done it, and then say you don't know why you done it, but you'll never do it again. It might help you, kid. You might get off with a suspended sentence."

"Yeah?"

"Sure. And then keep your nose clean afterwards, and you'll be okay."

"Keep my nose clean! Don't make me laugh, pal."

Skinner clutched Stevie's arm in a tight grip. "Kid, don't be a damn fool. If you can get out, get out now! I coulda got out a hundred times, and I'm still with it, and it's no picnic. Get out before you get started."

Stevie shook off Skinner's hand. "Come on, willya?" he said, annoyed.

"Knock it off there," the cop said. "We're ready to start."

"Take a look at your neighbors, kid," Skinner whispered. "Take a hard look. And then get out of it while you still can."

Stevie grimaced and turned away from Skinner. Skinner whirled him around to face him again, and there was a pleading desperation on the unshaven face, a mute reaching in the red-rimmed eyes before he spoke again. "Kid," he said, "listen to me. Take my advice. I've been..."

"Knock it off!" the cop warned again.

He was suddenly aware of the fact that the shades had been drawn and the room was dim. It was very quiet out there, and he hoped they would take him first. The excitement had risen to an almost fever pitch inside him, and he couldn't wait to get on that stage. What the hell was Skinner talking about anyway? "Take a look at your neighbors, kid." The poor jerk probably had a wet brain. What the hell did the police bother with old drunks for, anyway?

A uniformed cop led one of the men from behind the stage, and Stevie moved a little to his left, so that he could see the stage, hoping none of the cops would shove him back where he wouldn't have a good view. His cop and the policewoman were still talking, paying no attention to him. He smiled, unaware that the smile developed as a smirk, and watched the first man mounting the steps to the stage.

The man's eyes were very small, and he kept blinking them, blinking them. He was bald at the back of his head, and he was wearing a Navy peacoat and dark tweed trousers, and his eyes were red-rimmed and sleepy-looking. He reached to the five-foot-six-inches marker on the wall behind him, and he stared out at the bulls, blinking.

"Assisi," the Chief of Detectives said, "Augustus, Manhattan one. Thirty-three years old. Picked up in a bar on 43rd and Broadway, carrying a *.45* Colt automatic. No statement. How about it, Gus?"

"How about what?" Assisi asked.

"Were you carrying a gun?"

"Yes, I was carrying a gun." Assisi seemed to realize his shoulders were slumped. He pulled them back suddenly, standing erect.

"Where, Gus?"

"In my pocket."

"What were you doing with the gun, Gus?"

"I was just carrying it."

"Why?"

"Listen, I'm not going to answer any questions," Assisi said. "You're gonna put me through a third-degree. I ain't answering nothing. I want a lawyer."

"You'll get plenty opportunity to have a lawyer," the Chief of Detectives said. "And nobody's giving you a third-degree. We just want to know what you were doing with a gun. You know that's against the law, don't you?"

"I've got a permit for the gun," Assisi said.

"We checked with Pistol Permits, and they say no. This is a Navy gun, isn't it?"

"Yeah."

"What?"

"I said yeah, it's a Navy gun."

"What were you doing with it? Why were you carrying it around?"

"I like guns."

"Why?"

"Why what? Why do I like guns? Because..."

"Why were you carrying it around?"

"I don't know."

"Well, you must have a reason for carrying a loaded *.45*. The gun *was* loaded, wasn't it?"

"Yeah, it was loaded."

"You have any other guns?"

"No."

"We found a .38 in your room. How about that one?"

"It's no good."

"What?"

"The .38."

"What do you mean, no good?"

"The firin' mechanism is busted."

"You want a gun that works, is that it?"

"I didn't say that."

"You said the .38's no good because it won't fire, didn't you?"

"Well, what good's a gun that won't fire?"

"Why do you need a gun that fires?"

"I was just carrying it. I didn't shoot anybody, did I?"

"No, you didn't. Were you planning on shooting somebody?"

"Sure," Assisi said. "That's just what I was planning."

"Who?"

"I don't know," Assisi said sarcastically. "Anybody. The first guy I saw, all right? Everybody, all right? I was planning on wholesale murder."

"Not murder, maybe, but a little larceny, huh?"

"Murder," Assisi insisted, in his stride now. "I was just going to shoot up the whole town. Okay? You happy now?"

"Where'd you get the gun?"

"In the Navy."

"Where?"

"From my ship."

"It's a stolen gun?"

"No, I found it."

"You stole government property, is that it?"

"I found it."

"When'd you get out of the Navy?"

"Three months ago."

"You worked since?"

"No."

"Where were you discharged?"

"Pensacola."

"Is that where you stole the gun?"

"I didn't steal it."

"Why'd you leave the Navy?"

Assisi hesitated for a long time.

"Why'd you leave the Navy?" the Chief of Detectives asked again

"They kicked me out!" Assisi snapped.

"Why?"

"I was undesirable!" he shouted.

"Why?"

Assisi did not answer.

"Why?"

There was silence in the darkened room. Stevie watched Assisi's face, the twitching mouth, the blinking eyelids.

"Next case," the Chief of Detectives said.

Stevie watched as Assisi walked across the stage and down the steps on the other side, where the uniformed cop met him. He'd handled himself well, Assisi had. They'd rattled him a little at the end there, but on the whole he'd done a good job. So the guy was lugging a gun around. So what? He was right, wasn't he? He didn't shoot nobody, so what was all the fuss about? Cops! They had nothing else to do, they went around hauling in guys who were carrying guns. Poor bastard was a veteran, too; that was really rubbing it in. But he did a good job up there, even though he was nervous, you could see he was very nervous.

A man and a woman walked past him and on to the stage. The man was very tall, topping the six-foot marker. The woman was shorter, a bleached blonde turning to fat.

"They picked them up together," Skinner whispered. "So they show them together. They figure a pair'll always work as a pair, usually."

"How'd you like that Assisi?" Stevie whispered back. "He really had them bulls on the run, didn't he?"

Skinner didn't answer. The Chief of Detectives cleared his throat. "MacGregor, Peter, aged forty-five, and Anderson, Marcia, aged forty-two, Bronx one. Got them in a parked car on the Grand Concourse. Back seat of the car was loaded with goods, including luggage, a typewriter, a portable sewing machine, and a fur coat. No statements. What about all that stuff, Pete?"

"It's mine."

"The fur coat, too?"

"No, that's Marcia's."

"You're not married, are you?"

"No."

"Living together?"

"Well, you know," Pete said.

"What about the stuff?" the Chief of Detectives said again.

"I told you," Peter said. "It's ours."

"What was it doing in the car?"

"Oh. Well, we were—uh..." The man paused for a long time. "We were going on a trip."

"Where to?"

"Where? Oh. To—uh..." Again he paused, frowning, and Stevie smiled, thinking what a clown this guy was. This guy was better than a sideshow at Coney. This guy couldn't tell a lie without having to think about it for an hour. And the dumpy broad with him was a hot sketch, too. This act alone was worth the price of admission.

"Uh..." Pete said, still fumbling for words. "Uh... we were going to—uh... Denver."

"What for?"

"Oh, just a little pleasure trip, you know," he said, attempting a smile.

"How much money were you carrying when we picked you up?"

"Forty dollars."

"You were going to Denver on forty dollars?"

"Well, it was fifty dollars. Yeah, it was more like fifty dollars."

"Come on, Pete, what were you doing with all that stuff in the car?"

"I told you. We were taking a trip."

"With a sewing-machine, huh? You do a lot of sewing, Pete?"

"Marcia does."

"That right, Marcia?"

The blonde spoke in a high, reedy voice. "Yeah, I do a lot of sewing."

"That fur coat, Marcia. Is it yours?"

"Sure."

"It has the initials G.D. on the lining. Those aren't your initials, are they, Marcia?"

"No."

"Whose are they?"

"Search me. We bought that coat in a hock shop."

"Where?"

"Myrtle Avenue, Brooklyn. You know where that is?"

"Yes, I know where it is. What about that luggage? It had initials on it, too. And they weren't yours or Pete's. How about it?"

"We got that in a hock shop, too."

"And the typewriter?"

"That's Pete's."

"Are you a typist, Pete?"

"Well. I fool around a little, you know."

"We're going to check all this stuff against our Stolen Goods list; you know that, don't you?"

"We got all that stuff in hock shops," Pete said. "If it's stolen, we don't know nothing about it."

"Were you going to Denver with him, Marcia?"

"Oh, sure."

"When did you both decide to go? A few minutes ago?"

"We decided last week sometime."

"Were you going to Denver by way of the Grand Concourse?"

"Huh?" Pete said.

"Your car was parked on the Grand Concourse. What were you doing there with a carload of stolen goods?"

"It wasn't stolen," Pete said.

"We were on our way to Yonkers," the woman said.

"I thought you were going to Denver."

"Yeah, but we had to get the car fixed first. There was something wrong with the..." She paused, turning to Pete. "What was it, Pete? That thing that was wrong?"

Pete waited a long time before answering. "Uh—the—uh... the flywheel, yeah. There's a garage up in Yonkers fixes them good, we heard. Flywheels, I mean."

"If you were going to Yonkers, why were you parked on the Concourse?"

"Well, we were having an argument."

"What kind of an argument?"

"Not an argument, really. Just a discussion, sort of."

"About what?"

"About what to eat."

"What!"

"About what to eat. I wanted to eat Chink's, but Marcia wanted a glass of milk and a piece of pie. So we were trying to decide whether we should go to the Chink's or the cafeteria. That's why we were parked on the Concourse."

"We found a wallet in your coat, Pete. It wasn't yours, was it?"

"No."

"Whose was it?"

"I don't know." He paused, then added hastily, "There wasn't no money in it."

"No, but there was identification. A Mr Simon Granger. Where'd you get it, Pete?"

"I found it in the subway. There wasn't no money in it."

"Did you find all that other stuff in the subway, too?"

"No, sir, I bought that." He paused. "I was going to return the wallet, but I forgot to stick it in the mail."

"Too busy planning for the Denver trip, huh?"

"Yeah, I guess so."

"When's the last time you earned an honest dollar, Pete?"

Pete grinned. "Oh, about two, three years ago, I guess."

"Here're their records," the Chief of Detectives said. "Marcia, 1938, Sullivan Law; 1939, Concealing Birth of Issue; 1940, Possession of Narcotics—you still on the stuff, Marcia?"

"No."

"1942, dis cond; 1943, Narcotics again; 1947—you had enough, Marcia?"

Marcia didn't answer.

"Pete," the Chief of Detectives said, "1940, Attempted Rape; 1941, Selective Service Act; 1942, dis cond; 1943, Attempted Burglary; 1945, Living on Proceeds of Prostitution; 1947, Assault and Battery, did two years at Ossining."

"I never done no time," Pete said.

"According to this, you did."

"I never done no time," he insisted.

"1950," the Chief of Detectives went on, "Carnal Abuse of a Child." He paused. "Want to tell us about that one, Pete?"

"I—uh..." Pete swallowed. "I got nothing to say."

"You're ashamed of *some* things, that it?"

Pete didn't answer.

"Get them out of here," the Chief of Detectives said.

"See how long he kept them up there?" Skinner whispered. "He knows what they are, wants every bull in the city to recognize them if they..."

"Come on," a detective said, taking Skinner's arm.

Stevie watched as Skinner climbed the steps to the stage. Those two had really been something, all right. And just looking at them, you'd never know they were such operators. You'd never know they...

"Skinner, James, Manhattan two. Aged fifty-one. Threw a garbage-can through the plate-glass window of a clothing shop on Third Avenue. Arresting officer found him inside the shop with a bundle of overcoats. No statement. That right, James?"

"I don't remember," Skinner said.

"Is it, or isn't it?"

"All I remember is waking up in jail this morning."

"You don't remember throwing that ash can through the window?"

"No, sir."

"You don't remember taking those overcoats?"

"No, sir."

"Well, you must have done it, don't you think? The off-duty detective found you inside the store with the coats in your arms."

"I got only his word for that, sir."

"Well, his word is pretty good. Especially since he found you inside the store with your arms full of merchandise."

"I don't remember, sir."

"You've been here before, haven't you?"

"I don't remember, sir."

"What do you do for a living, James?"

"I'm unemployed, sir."

"When's the last time you worked?"

"I don't remember, sir."

"You don't remember much of anything, do you?"

"I have a poor memory, sir."

"Maybe the record has a better memory than you, James," the Chief of Detectives said.

"Maybe so, sir. I couldn't say."

"I hardly know where to start, James. You haven't been exactly an ideal citizen."

"Haven't I, I, sir?"

"Here's as good a place as any. 1948, Assault and Robbery; 1949, Indecent Exposure; 1951, Burglary; 1952, Assault and Robbery again. You're quite a guy, aren't you, James?"

"If you say so, sir."

"I say so. Now how about that store?"

"I don't remember anything about a store, sir."

"Why'd you break into it?"

"I don't remember breaking into any store, sir."

"Hey, what's this?" the Chief of Detectives said suddenly.

"Sir?"

"Maybe we should've started back a little further, huh, James? Here, on your record. 1938, convicted of first-degree murder, sentenced to execution."

The assembled bulls began murmuring among themselves. Stevie leaned forward eagerly, anxious to get a better look at this bum who'd offered him advice.

"What happened there, James?"

"What happened where, sir?"

"You were sentenced to death? How come you're still with us?"

"The case was appealed."

"And never retried?"

"No, sir."

"You're pretty lucky, aren't you?"

"I'm pretty unlucky, sir, if you ask me."

"Is that right? You cheat the chair, and you call that unlucky. Well, the law won't slip up this time."

"I don't know anything about law, sir."

"You don't, huh?"

"No, sir. I only know that if you want to get a police station into action, all you have to do is buy a cheap bottle of wine and drink it quiet, minding your own business."

"And that's what you did, huh, James?"

"That's what I did, sir."

"And you don't remember breaking into that store?"

"I don't remember anything."

"All right, next case."

Skinner turned his head slowly, and his eyes met Stevie's squarely. Again there was the same mute pleading in his eyes, and then he turned his head away and shuffled off the stage and down the steps into the darkness.

The cop's hand closed around Stevie's biceps. For an instant he didn't know what was happening, and then he realized his case was the next one. He shook off the cop's hand, squared his shoulders, lifted his head and began climbing the steps.

He felt taller all at once. He felt like an actor coming on after his cue. There was an aura of unreality about the stage and the darkened room beyond it, the bulls sitting in that room.

The Chief of Detectives was reading off the information about him, but he didn't hear it. He kept looking at the lights, which were not really so bright, they didn't blind him at all. Didn't they have brighter lights? Couldn't they put more lights on him, so they could see him when he told his story?

He tried to make out the faces of the detectives, but he couldn't see them clearly, and he was aware of the Chief of Detectives' voice droning on and on, but he didn't hear what the man was saying, he heard only the hum of his voice. He glanced over his shoulder, trying to; see how tall he was against the markers, and then he stood erect, his shoulders back, moving closer to the hanging microphone, wanting to be sure his voice was heard when he began speaking.

"...no statement," the Chief of Detectives concluded. There was a long pause, and Stevie waited, holding his breath. "This your first offense, Steve?" the Chief of Detectives asked.

"Don't you know?" Stevie answered.

"I'm asking you."

"Yeah, it's my first offense."

"You want to tell us all about it?"

"There's nothing to tell. You know the whole story, anyway."

"Sure, but do you?"

"What are you talking about?"

"Tell us the story, Steve."

"Whatya makin' a big federal case out of a lousy stick-up for? Ain't you got nothing better to do with your time?"

"We've got plenty of time, Steve."

"Well, I'm in a hurry."

"You're not going any place, kid. Tell us about it."

"What's there to tell? There was a candy store stuck up, that's all."

"Did you stick it up?"

"That's for me to know and you to find out."

"We know you did."

"Then don't ask me stupid questions."

"Why'd you do it?"

"I ran out of butts."

"Come on, kid."

"I done it 'cause I wanted to."

"Why?"

"Look, you caught me cold, so let's get this over with, huh? Whatya wastin' time with me for?"

"We want to hear what you've got to say. Why'd you pick this particular candy store?"

"I just picked it. I put slips in a hat and picked this one out."

"You didn't really, did you, Steve?"

"No, I didn't really. I picked it 'cause there's an old crumb who runs it, and I figured it was a pushover."

"What time did you enter the store, Steve?"

"The old guy told you all this already, didn't he? Look, I know I'm up here so you can get a good look at me. All right, take your good look, and let's get it over with."

"What time, Steve?"

"I don't have to tell you nothing."

"Except that we know it already."

"Then why do you want to hear it again? Ten o'clock, all right? How does that fit?"

"A little early, isn't it?"

"How's eleven? Try that one for size."

"Let's make it twelve, and we'll be closer."

"Make it whatever you want to," Stevie said, pleased with the way he was handling this. They knew all about it, anyway, so he might as well have himself a ball, show them they couldn't shove him around.

"You went into the store at twelve; is that right?"

"If you say so, Chief."

"Did you have a gun?"

"No."

"What, then?"

"Nothing."

"Nothing at all?"

"Just me. I scared him with a dirty look, that's all."

"You had a switch knife, didn't you?"

"You found one on me, so why ask?"

"Did you use the knife?"

"No."

"You didn't tell the old man to open the cash register or you'd cut him up? Isn't that what you said?"

"I didn't make a tape recording of what I said."

"But you did threaten him with the knife. You did force him to open the cash register, holding the knife on him."

"I suppose so."

"How much money did you get?"

"You've got the dough. Why don't you count it?"

"We already have. Twelve dollars; is that right?"

"I didn't get a chance to count it. The Law showed."

"When did the Law show?"

"When I was leaving. Ask the cop who pinched me. He knows when."

"Something happened before you left, though."

"Nothing happened. I cleaned out the register and then blew. Period."

"Your knife had blood on it."

"Yeah? I was cleaning chickens last night."

"You stabbed the owner of that store, didn't you?"

"Me? I never stabbed nobody in my whole life."

"Why'd you stab him?"

"I didn't."

"Where'd you stab him?"

"I didn't stab him."

"Did he start yelling?"

"I don't know what you're talking about."

"You stabbed him, Steve. We know you did."

"You're full of crap."

"Don't get smart, Steve."

"Ain't you had your look yet? What the hell more do you want?"

"We want you to tell us why you stabbed the owner of that store."

"And I told you I didn't stab him."

"He was taken to the hospital last night with six knife-wounds in his chest and abdomen. Now how about that, Steve?"

"Save your questioning for the Detective Squad Room. I ain't saying another word."

"You had your money. Why'd you stab him?"

Stevie did not answer.

"Were you afraid?"

"Afraid of what?" Stevie answered defiantly.

"I don't know. Afraid he'd tell who held him up? Afraid he'd start yelling? What were you afraid of, kid?"

"I wasn't afraid of nothing. I told the old crumb to keep his mouth shut. He shoulda listened to me."

"He didn't keep his mouth shut?"

"Ask him."

"I'm asking you!"

"No, he didn't keep his mouth shut. He started yelling. Right after I'd cleaned out the drawer. The damn jerk, for a lousy twelve bucks he starts yelling."

"What'd you do?"

"I told him to shut up."

"And he didn't."

"No, he didn't. So I hit him, and he still kept yelling. So—I gave him the knife."

"Six times?"

"I don't know how many times. I just—gave it to him. He shouldn't have yelled. You ask him if I did any harm to him before that. Go ahead, ask him. He'll tell you. I didn't even touch the crumb before he started yelling. Go to the hospital and ask him if I touched him. Go ahead, ask him."

"We can't, Steve."

"Wh..."

"He died this morning."

"He..." For a moment, Stevie could not think clearly. Died? Is that what he'd said? The room was curiously still now. It had been silently attentive before, but this was something else, something different, and the stilmess suddenly chilled him, and he looked down at his shoes.

"I-I didn't mean him to pass away," he mumbled.

The police stenographer looked up. "To what?"

"To pass away," a uniformed cop repeated, whispering.

"What?" the stenographer asked again.

"He didn't mean him to pass away!" the cop shouted.

The cop's voice echoed in the silent room. The stenographer bent his head and began scribbling in his pad.

"Next case," the Chief of Detectives said.

Stevie walked off the stage, his mind curiously blank, his feet strangely leaden. He followed the cop to the door, and then walked with him to the elevator. They were both silent as the doors closed.

"You picked an important one for your first one," the cop said.

"He shouldn't have died on me," Stevie answered.

"You shouldn't have stabbed him," the cop said.

He tried to remember what Skinner had said to him before the lineup, but the noise of the elevator was loud in his ears, and he couldn't think clearly. He could only remember the word "neighbors" as the elevator dropped to the basement to join them.

A Needle for the Devil

Ruth Rendell

Ruth Rendell (b. 1930) was born in London. In 1946, she left
school to accept a position as a reporter and sub-editor of the *Essex
Express and Independent.* While at the paper, she met and married
Oswald Rendell. In 1963, an editor asked her to revise the light comic
novel she submitted. Rather than revise the manuscript, she presented
them with her first Inspector Wexford novel, *From Doon With Death*
(1964). She alternated between writing Wexford novels and novels of
suspense throughout the 1960's and '70's, producing such works as *To
Fear a Painted Devil* (1965), *A New Lease on Death* (1967), *The Secret
House of Death* (1968), *The Best Man to Die* (1969), and *Murder Being
Once Done* (1972). In 1974, she received the first of several awards when
Shake Hands Forever won the Current Crime Silver Cup. In 1976, she
won a Golden Dagger for *A Demon in My View.* Her first collection of
stories, *The Fallen Curtain and Other Stories,* won an Edgar. Most
recently, her novel *A Dark-Adapted Eye* won an Edgar in 1986. Her other
works include the novels *A Judgement in Stone* (1977), *Make Death Love
Me* (1979), *Master of the Moor* (1982), *The Killing Doll* (1984), *An
Unkindness of Ravens* (1985), and *The Bridesmaid* (1989), as well as the
short story collections *Means of Evil and Other Stories* (1979), *The Fever
Tree and Other Stories of Suspense* (1984), *The New Girlfriend and Other
Stories* (1986) and *Collected Stories* (1988).

Rendell's finest stories, like her novels *Live Flesh* (1986), and
Talking to Strange Men (1987), explore what makes a normal person
commit a criminal act. "A Needle for the Devil" carefully charts the
factors that drive its characters mad, and then propels its lead to a
logical—and gruesome—conclusion. "A Needle for the Devil" was
originally published in *Ellery Queen Mystery Magazine.*

THE DEVIL FINDS WORK for idle hands to do, as Mrs Gibson
used to say to her daughter, and Alice had found that in her case the
devil (or her own mysterious inner compulsions) led her to violence.
As a child she would strike people who annoyed her and when she was
fourteen she attacked her sister with a knife, though no harm was done.

But if her hands itched to injure, they were also gifted hands and as she was taught to occupy them with handicrafts, the impulse to violence grew less. Or was sublimated, as she learned to say when she began training to be a nurse.

Only her mother had opposed Alice's choice of a career. Perhaps it was only her mother who understood her. But her objections were overruled by Alice's father, her headmistress, the school careers officer, and Alice herself. And certainly Alice did well. There were no unfortunate incidents of the kind Mrs. Gibson had feared.

Naturally, in her new life, she had had to abandon her handicrafts. One cannot keep a loom or a potter's wheel in one's room in the nurses' residence. And there were many occasions when Alice would come off duty worn-out, not so much from lifting patients, making beds, and running to and fro, as from the exercise of an iron self-control. The impulse to hit, pinch, or otherwise manhandle a patient who had angered her had to be constantly suppressed.

Then the girl who shared her room came back from two days off duty wearing a knee-length white wool coat.

"I love your coat," said Alice. "It's gorgeous. It must have cost the earth."

"I made it," said Pamela.

"You *made* it? You mean you knitted it?"

"It wasn't very difficult and it only took three weeks."

Alice had never thought of knitting. Knitting was something one's grandmother did or one's aunts or pregnant women making layettes. But if Pamela could make the coat, which neither savored of aunts nor was layette-like, she was very sure she could. And it might solve that problem of hers which had lately become so pressing that she was afraid she might have to leave without finishing her training.

Knitting has the advantage over sewing or weaving that it requires basically only a ball of wool and a pair of needles. It can be done in one's lunch break, in a train, during night duty. It calms the nerves, occupies the hands, provides therapy—and supplies a wardrobe. Alice began knitting with enthusiasm and found that, because of its ubiquity and the way it can be taken up at any free moment, it answered her purpose better than any of her other crafts had done.

She progressed in her career, became a staff nurse, a sister, and by the time she was thirty had full charge of the men's medical ward at St.Gregory's Hospital for Officers. It was there, three or four years later, that she first set eyes on Rupert Clarigate who had been brought in after having a heart attack.

Rupert Clarigate was fifty-two at the time of his coronary. He was a bachelor who had retired from the army two years before with the rank of Lieutenant Colonel and had since been living very comfortably—too comfortably perhaps—on his handsome pension. Had he smoked less and walked more, eaten less lavishly of roast pheasant at his club and drunk less old Napoleon brandy afterwards he might not, according to his doctor, have been seized one night by a fierce pain down his left arm and up his left side and found himself a moment later lying on the floor, fighting for breath. His doctor was one of those who believe that a coronary patient should never be left unattended for the first few days after an attack. Hence, St.Gregory's and Sister Gibson. On his first morning in hospital he awoke to look into the sea-blue eyes of a slim young woman in a trim uniform whose blonde hair was half-covered by a starched white coif.

"Good morning, Colonel Clarigate," said Alice. "My goodness, but aren't you looking better this morning! It just shows what a good night's sleep can do."

Alice said this sort of thing to all her new patients but Rupert, who had never been in hospital before and had in fact been riotously healthy all his life till now, thought it was specially designed for him and that her tone was exceptionally sweet. He did not hear her, five minutes later, telling one of her students who had dropped a kidney dish that she was not only hopelessly unfitted to be a nurse but mentally retarded as well, because this diatribe was delivered in the cleansing department off the ward known as the sluice. He thought Alice must have a delightful disposition, always cheerful, always encouraging, endlessly patient, as well as being the sort of girl who looked as if she knew how to have a good time.

"Who's the lucky chap that's taking you out tonight, sister?" Rupert said as Alice put her head round the door before going off duty. "I envy him, I don't mind telling you."

"No chap, Colonel," said Alice. "I'm going to have a quiet evening doing my knitting in front of the TV."

Those statements were quite true. There was no chap. There had been in days gone by, several in fact, including one whom Alice would probably have married had she not once slapped his face (and thereby dislodged a filling from a molar) for teasing her. But she had been very young then and without her prop and resort. Since those days she had put her career before a possible husband and had become so used to the overtures and the flirtatious remarks of patients that she hardly took in what they said and scarcely thought of them as men.

Rupert Clarigate, however, was different. He was one of the hand-somest men she had ever seen and he had such a wonderful head of hair. For although his face was still youthful and unlined, his hair was snow-white; white and thick and ever so slightly wavy, and since he had left the army it had been allowed to grow just long enough to cover the tops of his ears. It was the first thing Alice had noticed about him. She had always felt a peculiar antipathy to baldness, and though accustomed to the most repulsive sights and to washing a wound or cleaning an abscess without a flicker of distaste, it was still as much as she could do to wash a man's bald pate or comb the hair which surrounded it. Rupert Clarigate looked as if he would never be bald, for not even a coin-sized bare spot showed amid the lush snowy mass.

Besides that, she liked his hearty jovial manner, the public school accent, the Sandhurst voice. The slightly lecherous admiration in his eyes, kept well under control, excited her. By the end of the first week of his stay she was in love, or would have said she was in love, having no criterion to judge by.

As for Colonel Clarigate, he had always intended to get married one day. A long-standing affair with another officer's wife had kept him single till he was thirty-five and after that was over he felt too set in his ways to embark on matrimony. Too selfish, the other officer's wife said. And it was true that Rupert could see no point in having a wife when he didn't want to stay in in the evenings, had no desire for children, disliked the idea of sharing his income and in any case had his officer's servant to wait on him and clean his quarters.

But he would marry one day—when he retired. Now retirement had come and he was living in the big inconvenient old house his parents had left him. There was no one to keep it clean. He ate rich food in expensive restaurants because there was no one at home to cook for him and he told himself he smoked too much because he was lonely. In fact, he had had his heart attack because he had no wife. Why should not pretty, efficient, kindly Sister Gibson be his wife?

Why not retire from nursing? thought Alice. Why should she not marry Colonel Clarigate and have a home of her own instead of a two-room flat that went with the job? Besides, she was in love with him and he had such beautiful thick hair.

He must be in love with Sister Gibson, thought Rupert, otherwise he would surely not feel so uneasy about her in the evenings when he was certain she must be out with some chap. This, he knew from his experience with the other officer's wife, was jealousy and a proof of love.

He left the hospital after three weeks and went to convalesce in the country. From there he wrote to Alice nearly every day. When he came home again he took her to the theatre to see a slapstick sexy comedy at which they both laughed very much, and then to the cinema to see a re-issue of *Carry On Nurse* which had them equally convulsed. On their third evening out together they became engaged.

"People may say it was sudden," said Alice, "but I feel we know each other through and through. After all there's no more intimate situation, is there, than that of nurse and patient?"

"I can think of one," said Rupert with a wink, and they both fell about laughing.

His fifty-third birthday occurred about a month after their engagement and Alice knitted him a pullover. It was rust red, bordered at the welt and on the neckline with fine stripes of cream and dark green and it suited him well, for Rupert, in spite of his high living, had never become fat. Alice insisted on looking after him. She took him out for sensible walks and gently discouraged him from smoking. The Clarigate house was not to her taste so he set about selling it and buying another. The prospect of furnishing this house which was in a seaside resort on the south coast—they could live anywhere they chose, Rupert said, there was no need to stay in London—filled Alice with excited anticipation, especially as Rupert was giving her a free hand with his savings.

The marriage took place in May, three months after their first meeting.

It was a quiet wedding, followed by a small luncheon party. Mrs Gibson, now a widow, was present and so was Alice's sister and that friend Pamela who had introduced her to the charms of knitting, and Pamela's husband Guy, a freelance writer and author of mystery novels. On Rupert's side were a cousin of his and his former commanding officer and Dr. Nicholson, that conscientious medical man who had been responsible for sending him to St.Gregory's. The newly married couple left at three to catch the plane that was to take them to Barbados for their honeymoon.

Alice had never before been away on a holiday without taking her knitting with her. In Palma de Mallorca she had knitted a Fair Isle cap and gloves for her niece, in Innsbruck she had begun an Aran for her brother-in-law and in the Isles of Greece she had finished a slipover for herself. But some instinct as to the rightness or suitability of certain actions told her that one does not take knitting on one's honeymoon, and indeed she found there would scarcely have been the opportunity to knit. One can hardly knit on a beach and they were mostly on the beach when they were not dining and dancing, for Rupert had been right when he assessed his wife as a girl who knew how to have a good time. Alice would have danced harder, eaten more heartily and stayed up even later were it not for her prudent care of her husband's health. While Rupert, vigorous and virile as he was, might in some ways seem as young as she, there was no getting away from the fact that he had had one coronary and might have another. She was glad to see that he had given up smoking and if, towards the end of their stay, she noticed an edge to his temper, she put this down to the heat.

Furnishing the new house took up all her time once they were returned. There were carpets to choose and order, plumbing and heating and electrical engineers to call, upholsterers and curtain makers to be urged on. Alice worked briskly, refusing to allow Rupert to help, but taking him out each evening with her for a therapeutic stroll along the sea front. He looked fitter than he had in all the five months she had known him and he could run upstairs now without shortness of breath.

It was on the morning after the day when the new carpets were fitted, after Alice had rearranged and polished the furniture, that she felt she could at last begin to relax. Rupert had gone to Dr. Nicholson's for his monthly check-up. She set out for the shopping center to buy herself some wool. On the previous evening, while they were out for their walk, Rupert had pointed out a man leaning over the sea wall who was wearing just the kind of sleeveless pullover he would fancy for himself. Alice had said nothing but had smiled and squeezed his arm.

During the years that had passed since Pamela walked in wearing that white coat, Alice had become an expert at her craft. She knew all there was to be known about it. She understood the finer points of grafting, of invisible casting off, of the weaving in of contrasts. She knew every kind of yarn available from top heavyweight natural wool to two-ply cotton and exactly which needles to use with each. Without reference to charts she could tell you that an English size fourteen needle is equivalent to the European two millimeter and the American double O. She could with ease adapt a pattern to a different size or, if necessary, work without a pattern at all. Once she had seen a jumper or cardigan she could copy it and turn out a precisely identical garment. And besides all this, the whole area of knitting was an emotive one to her. She could not help regarding it as having been a life saver and therefore it had become far more to her than some other woman's embroidery or crochet work. So it was natural that on entering a wool shop she should have a sensation of sick excitement as well as experiencing the deep pleasure felt, for example, by a scholar going into a library.

Woolcraft Limited she quickly judged a good shop of its kind and she spent a happy half-hour inside before finally choosing a pattern for a sleeveless pullover and six twenty-five gramme balls of a fine saxe blue wool and acrylic mixture.

There was no opportunity to begin that day. Rupert must have his lunch and then there would be an afternoon's gardening for both of them and in the evening they were going to a dinner-dance in the Pump Room. But on the following afternoon, while Rupert was down the garden trimming the privet hedge, Alice drew out her first ball of blue wool and began.

On moving into the house, she had appropriated the large bottom drawer of a chest in their living room for her knitting materials. In it were all her many leftover balls of wool and ends of wool from a multiplicity of garments made over the years, her gauge, her tape measure, her bodkins for sewing up and her sewing-up skeins and, ranged in front, all her pairs of needles, a pair of every possible size and each pair in its long plastic envelope. Alice had selected a pair of number fourteens, the very finest size for beginning on the welt of Rupert's pullover.

As she cast on the required number of one hundred and fifty stitches and felt the familiar thin metal pins against her hands and the soft, faintly fluffy yarn slip rhythmically between her fingers, a great calm descended upon Alice. It was like coming home after a long absence. It was like having a cigarette (she supposed) or a drink after a month's abstention. It was wonderful. It seemed to set the seal on her happiness. Here she was married, with a charming husband whom she loved, very well off, living in the home of her dreams, and now she was settled in her new life, once more taking up the hobby that afforded her so much pleasure. She had knitted about half an inch, for the work was slow with such fine materials, when she heard Rupert come in from the garden and rinse his hands under the kitchen tap. Presently he walked into the room where she was.

He stood a yard or two in from the doorway and stared at her. "What are you doing, sweetie?"

"Knitting," said Alice, smiling at him.

Rupert came and sat opposite her. He was fascinated. He knew there was such a thing as hand-knitting, or that there used to be, for he seemed to remember his mother mentioning it about forty years before, but he had never actually seen it being done. Alice's fingers flicked up and down, making precisely the same movement about a hundred times a minute. And they seemed to move independently of the rest of Alice, of her body which was gracefully relaxed, of her eyes which occasionally met his, and of her mind too, he suspected, which might be wandering off anywhere.

"I didn't know you knitted," he said after a while.

"Darling! Where do you think your red sweater came from? I told you I made it."

Rupert had not given much thought to the provenance of the red sweater. "I suppose I thought you must have done it on a machine," he said.

Alice laughed heartily at this. She continued to knit. Rupert read the evening paper which had just been delivered. After a time he said, "Can I talk to you while you're doing that?"

He sounded so like a little boy whose mother cannot be bothered with him that Alice's heart was touched. "Darling, of course you can. Talk away! I'm a very practiced knitter, you know. I can not only talk while I'm knitting, I can read, watch television—my goodness, I could knit in the dark!" And she fixed her eyes on him, smiling tenderly, while her fingers jerked up and down like pistons.

But Rupert didn't talk. He hardly said a word until they were out for their evening walk, and next day when she again took up the blue pullover she was once more conscious of his stare. After a while he lit a cigarette, his first for several weeks. Without a word he left the room and when she went into the kitchen to prepare their evening meal she found him sitting at the table, reading one of his favorite war memoirs.

It was not until Alice had had four sessions of work on the pullover and had completed six inches of the back, having changed by now to the slightly coarser needle, number twelve and made of red plastic, that Rupert made any further reference to her occupation.

"You know, sweetie," he said, "there's absolutely no reason why we shouldn't buy our clothes ready-made. We're not poor. I hope I haven't given you the impression that I'm a tight-fisted sort of chap. Any time you want the money to buy yourself a blouse or a dress or whatever that is, you've only to say the word."

"This isn't for me, Rupert, it's for you. You said you wanted a pullover like the one we saw on that man on the sea front."

"Did I? I suppose I must have if you say so but I don't recall it. Anyway, I can pop down to the men's outfitters and buy one if I feel inclined, can't I, eh? There's no need for you to wear yourself out making something I can buy in ten minutes."

"But I *like* knitting, darling. I love it. And I think home-knitted garments are much nicer than bought ones."

"Must make your fingers ache, I should think," said Rupert. "Talk about wearing one's fingers to the bone. I know the meaning of that phrase all right now, eh?"

"Don't be so silly," snapped Alice. "Of course it doesn't make my fingers ache. I enjoy it. And I think it's a great pity you've started smoking again."

Rupert smoked five cigarettes that day and ten the next and the day after that Pamela and Guy came to stay for a fortnight's holiday.

Rupert thought, and Alice agreed with him, that if you lived by the sea it was positively your duty to invite close friends for their summer holidays. Besides, Guy and Pamela, who hadn't a large income, had two children at expensive boarding schools and probably would otherwise have had no holiday at all. They arrived, while their children were away camping, for the middle two weeks of August.

Pamela had not knitted a row since her daughter was two but she liked to watch Alice at work. She said she found it soothing. And when she looked inside the knitting drawer in the chest and saw the leftover hanks of yarn in such delectable shades, pinks and lilacs and subtle greens and honey yellows and chocolate browns, she said it made her feel she must take it up again, for clothes cost so much and it would be a great saving.

Guy was not one of those writers who never speak of their work. He was always entertaining on the subject of the intricate and complex detective stories he yearly produced and would weave plots out of all kinds of common household incidents or create them from things he observed while they were out for a drive. Alice enjoyed hearing him evolve new murder methods and he played up to her with more and more ingenious and bizarre devices.

"Now take warfarin," he would say. "They use it to kill rats. It inhibits the clotting of the blood, so that when the rats fight among themselves and receive even a small wound they bleed to death."

"They give it to human beings too," said Alice, the nurse. "Or something very close to it. It stops clots forming in people who've had a thrombosis."

"Do they now? That's very interesting. If I were going to use that method in a book I'd have the murderer give his victim warfarin plus a strong sedative. Then a small cut, say to the wrist..."

Another time he was much intrigued by a book of Alice's on plants inadvisable for use in winemaking. Most illuminating for the thriller writer, he said.

"It says here that the skunk cabbage, whatever that may be, contains irritant crystals of calcium oxalate. If you eat the stuff the inside of your mouth swells up and you die because you can't breathe. Now your average pathologist might notice the swellings but I'd be willing to bet you anything he'd never suppose them the result of eating *lysichiton symplocarpus*. There's another undetectable murder method for you."

Alice was excited by his ingenuity and Pamela was used to it. Only Rupert, who had perhaps been nearer actual death than any of them, grew squeamish and was not sorry when the two weeks came to an end and Guy and Pamela were gone. Alice too felt a certain relief. It troubled her that her latent sadism, which she recognized for what it was, should be titillated by Guy's inventions. With thankfulness she returned to the gentle placebo of her knitting and took up the blue pullover again, all eight inches of it.

Rupert lit a cigarette.

"I say, I've been thinking, why don't I buy you a knitting machine?"

"I don't want a knitting machine, darling," said Alice.

"Had a look at one actually while I was out with old Guy one day. A bit pricey but I don't mind that, sweetie, if it makes you happy."

"I said I don't want a knitting machine. The point is that I like knitting by hand. I've already told you, it's my hobby, it's a great interest of mine. Why do I want a big cumbersome machine that takes up space and makes a noise when I've got my own two hands?"

He was silent. He watched her fingers working.

"As a matter of fact, it's the noise I don't like," he said.

"What noise?" said Alice, exasperated.

"That everlasting click-click-click."

"Oh, nonsense! You can't possibly hear anything right across the room."

"I can."

"You'll get used to it," said Alice.

But Rupert did not get used to it, and the next time Alice began her knitting he said: "It's not just the clicking, sweetie, it's the sight of your hands jerking about mechanically all the time. To be perfectly honest with you it gets on my nerves."

"Don't look then."

"I can't help it. There's an awful sort of fascination that draws my eyes."

Alice was beginning to feel nervous herself. A good deal of her pleasure was spoilt by those staring eyes and the knowledge of his dislike of what she did. It began to affect the texture of her work, making her take uneven stitches. She went on rather more slowly and after half an hour she let the nine-inch-long piece of blue fabric and the needles fall into her lap.

"Let's go out to dinner," said Rupert eagerly. "We'll go and have a couple of drinks down on the front and then we'll drive over to the Queen's for dinner."

"If you like," said Alice.

"And, sweetie, give up that silly old knitting, eh? For my sake? You wouldn't think twice about doing a little thing like that for me, would you?"

A little thing, he called it. Alice thought of it not twice but many times. She hardly thought of anything else and she lay awake for a large part of the night. But next day she did no knitting and she laid away what she had done in the drawer. Rupert was her husband, and marriage, as she had often heard people say, was a matter of give and take. This she would give to him, remembering all he had given her.

She missed her knitting bitterly. Those years of doing an active job, literally on her feet all day, and those leisure times when her hands had always been occupied, had unfitted her for reading or listening to music or watching television. With idle hands, it was hard for her to keep still. Incessantly, she fidgeted. And when Rupert, who had not once mentioned the sacrifice she had made for him, did at last refer to her knitting, she had an only just controllable urge to hit him.

They were passing, on an evening walk, that men's outfitters of which he had spoken when first he saw knitting in her hands, and there in the window was a heavyweight wool sweater in creamy white with on it an intricate Fair Isle pattern in red and grey.

"Bet you couldn't do that, eh, sweetie? It takes a machine to make a garment like that. I call that a grand job."

Alice's hands itched to slap his face. She not make that! Why, give her half a chance and she could make it in a week and turn out a far more beautiful piece of work than that object in the window. But her heart yearned after it, for all that. How easily, when she had been allowed to knit, could she have copied it! How marvelously would it have occupied her, working out those checks and chevrons on squared paper, weaving in the various threads with the yarn skilfully hooked round three fingers! She turned away. Was she never to be allowed to knit again? Must she wait until Rupert died before she could take up her needles?

It began to seem to Alice a monstrous cruelty, this thing which her husband had done to her. Why had she been so stupid as to marry someone she had known only three months? She thought she would enjoy punching him with her fists, pummelling his head, until he cried to her to stop and begged her to knit all she liked.

The change Rupert noticed in his wife he did not attribute to the loss of her hobby. He had forgotten about her knitting. He thought she had become irritable and nervous because she was anxious about his smoking—after all, none knew better than she that he shouldn't smoke—and he made a determined effort, his second since his marriage, to give it up.

After five days of total abstention it seemed to him as if every fiber of his body cried out for, yearned for, put out straining anguished stalks for, a cigarette. It was worst of all in the pub on the sea front where the atmosphere was laden with aromatic cigarette smoke, and there, while Alice was sitting at their table, he bought a surreptitious packet of twenty at the bar.

Back home, he took one out and lit it. His need for nicotine was so great that he had forgotten everything else. He had even forgotten that Alice was sitting opposite him. He took a wonderful long inhalation, the kind that makes the room rock and waves roar in one's head, a cool, aromatic, heady, glorious draw.

The next thing he knew the cigarette had been pulled out of his mouth and hurled into the fireplace and Alice was belaboring him with her fists while stamping on the remaining nineteen cigarettes in the packet.

"You mean selfish cruel beast! You can keep on with your filthy evil-smelling addiction that makes me sick to my stomach, you can keep that up, killing yourself, while I'm not allowed to do my poor harmless useful work. You selfish insensitive pig!"

It was their first quarrel and it went on for hours.

Next morning Rupert went into town and bought a hundred cigarettes and Alice locked herself in her bedroom and knitted. They were reconciled after two or three days. Rupert promised to undergo hypnosis for his smoking. Nothing was said at the time about Alice's knitting, but soon afterwards she explained quite calmly and rationally to Rupert that she needed to knit for her "nerves" and would have to devote specific time to it, such as an hour every evening during which she would go and sit in their little-used dining room.

Rupert said he would miss her. He hadn't got married for his wife to be in one room and he in another. But all right, he hadn't much option, he supposed, so long as it was only an hour.

It began as an hour. Alice found she didn't miss Rupert's company. It seemed to her that they had said to each other all they had to say and all they ever would have. If there had been any excitement in their marriage, there was none left now. Knitting itself was more interesting, though when this garment was completed she would make no more for Rupert. Let him go to his men's outfitters if that was what he wanted. She thought she might make herself a burgundy wool suit. And as she envisaged it, longing to begin, the allotted hour lengthened into an hour and a half, into two.

She had almost completed the back of the pullover after two and a half hours concentrated work, when Rupert burst into the room, a cigarette in his mouth and his breath smelling of whisky. He snatched the knitting out of her hands and pulled it off the red plastic needles and snapped each needle in half.

Alice screamed at him and seized his collar and began shaking him, but Rupert tore the pattern across and unravelled stitches as fast as he could go. Alice struck him repeatedly across the face. He dodged and hit her such a blow that she fell to the floor, and then he pulled out every one of those two or three hundred rows of knitting until all that remained was a loose and tangled pile of crinkled blue yarn.

Three days later she told him she wanted a divorce. Rupert said she couldn't want one as much as he did. In that case, said Alice, perhaps he would like to pack his things and leave the house as soon as possible.

"Me? Leave this house? You must be joking."

"Indeed I'm not joking. That's what a decent man would do."

"What, just walk out of a house I bought with my inheritance from my parents? Walk out on the furniture you bought with my life savings? You're not only a hysterical bitch, you're out of your mind. *You* can go. I'll pay my maintenance, the law forces me to do that, though it'll be the minimum I can get away with, I promise you."

"And you call yourself an officer and a gentleman!" said Alice. "What am I supposed to do? Go back to nursing? Go back to a poky flat? I'd rather die. Certainly I'm staying in this house."

They argued about it bitterly day after day. Rupert's need overcame the hypnosis and he chain-smoked. Alice was now afraid to knit in his presence, for he was physically stronger than she, even if she had had the heart to start the blue pullover once again. And whom would she give it to? She would not get out of the house, *her* house which Rupert had given her for which, in exchange, she had given him the most important thing she had.

"I gave up my knitting for you," she screamed at him, "and you can't even give me a house and a few sticks of furniture."

"You're mad," said Rupert. "You ought to be locked up."

Alice rushed at him and smacked his face. He caught her hands and threw her into a chair and slammed out of the room. He went down to the pub on the sea front and had two double whiskies and smoked a packet of cigarettes. When he got back Alice was in bed in the spare room. Just as he refused to leave the house, so Rupert had refused to get out of his own bedroom. He took two sleeping tablets and went to bed.

In the morning Alice went into the room where Rupert was and washed his scalp and combed his beautiful thick white hair. She changed the pillowcases, wiped a spot off Rupert's pajama jacket and then she phoned the doctor to say Rupert was dead. He must have passed away in his sleep. She had awakened to find him dead beside her.

"His heart, of course," said the doctor, and because Alice had been a nurse, "a massive myocardial infarction."

She nodded. "I suppose I should have expected it."

"Well, in these cases..."

"You never know, do you? I must be grateful for the few happy months we had together."

The doctor signed the death certificate. There was no question of an autopsy. Pamela and Guy came to the cremation and took Alice back home with them for four weeks. When Alice left to return to the house that was now entirely hers they promised to take her at her word and come to stay once again in the summer. Alice was very comfortably off, for by no means all Rupert's savings had been spent on the furniture, his life insurance had been considerable, and there was his army pension, reduced but still generous.

It was an amazingly young-looking Alice, her hair rinsed primrose, her figure the trimmest it had been in ten years, who met Guy and Pamela at the station. She was driving a new white Lancia coupé and wearing a very smart knitted suit in a subtle shade of burgundy.

"I love your suit," said Pamela.

"I made it."

"I really must take up knitting again. I used to be so good at it, didn't I? And think of the money one saves."

On the following evening, a Sunday, after they had spent most of the day on the beach, Pamela again reverted to the subject of knitting and said her fingers itched to start on something straightaway. Alice looked thoughtful. Then she opened the bottom drawer of the chest and took out the saxe blue wool.

"You could have this if you like, and this pattern. You could make it for Guy."

Pamela took the pattern which had apparently been torn in half and mended with sticking tape. She looked at the hanks of wool. "Has some of it been used?"

"I didn't like what I'd done so I undid it. The wool's been washed and carded to get the crinkles out."

"If you're thinking of making that for me," said Guy, "I'm all for it. Splendid idea."

"All right. Why not? Very fine needles it takes, doesn't it? Have you got a pair of fourteens, Alice?"

A shadow passed across Alice's face. She hesitated. Then she picked up the plastic envelopes one by one, but desultorily, until Pamela, fired now with enthusiasm, dropped on her knees beside her and began hunting through the drawer.

"Here we are. Number fourteen, two millimeters, US double O...There's only one needle here, Alice."

"Sorry about that, it must be lost." Alice took the single needle from her almost roughly and made as if to close the drawer.

"No, wait a minute, it's bound to be loose in there somewhere."

"I'm sure it isn't, it's lost. You won't have time to start tonight, anyway."

Guy said, "I don't see how you could lose one knitting needle."

"In a train," said Pamela, peering into each needle packet. "It could fall down the side of the seat and before you could get it out you'd be at your station."

"Alice never goes in trains."

"I suppose you could use it to unblock a drainpipe?"

"You'd use a big fat one for that. Now if this situation happened in one of my books I'd have it that the needle was a murder weapon. Inserted into the scalp of a person who was, say drugged or drunk, it would penetrate the covering of the brain and the brain itself, causing a subdural hemorrhage. You'd have to sharpen the point a bit, file it maybe, and then of course you'd throw it away afterwards. Hence, you see, only one number fourteen needle in the drawer. "

"And immediately they examined the body they'd find out," said his wife.

"Well, you know, I don't think they would. Did you know that almost all men over middle age have enough signs of coronary disease for a pathologist, unless he was exceptionally thorough, to assume that as the cause of death? Of course your victim would have to have a good head of hair to cover up the mark of entry..."

"For heaven's sake, let's change the subject," said Pamela, closing the drawer, for she had noticed that Alice, perhaps because of that tactless reference to coronaries, had gone very white and that the hands which held the wool were trembling.

But she managed a smile, "We'll buy you a pair of number fourteens tomorrow," she said, "and perhaps I'll start on something new as well. My mother always used to say that the devil finds work for idle hands to do."

Detection

The Murders in the Rue Morgue

Edgar Allan Poe

Edgar Allan Poe (1809-1849), the father of the modern detective
story, was born in Boston. When he was orphaned at the age of two, Poe
was reared by John Allan, a Virginia merchant. After the death of Allan's
wife, Poe ran away from home to Boston in 1827, where he published his
first poetry collection, *Tamerlane and Other Poems.* He enlisted in the
army later that year, and served for two years. Poe moved to Baltimore in
1829 and published a second collection, *Al Araaf Tamerlane and Minor
Poems.* The next year he attended—and was discharged from—West
Point. In 1831, after publishing a third volume (*Poems by Edgar A. Poe*),
Poe decided become a full-time writer. In 1833, his story "A MS. Found
in a Bottle" won a short-story competition. In 1835, Poe became editor of
The Southern Literary Messenger, the first in a long string of short-lived
editorial assignments. He married his cousin Virginia Clemm in 1836. In
1837, Poe moved first to Philadelphia, then to New York, contributing to
various magazines to earn a living. During his tenure with *Burton's
Gentlemen's Quarterly* (1839-1840), Poe wrote some of his best known
work, all of which were collected in *Tales of the Grotesque and Ara-
besque.* After his discharge from *Graham's* in 1842, Poe existed on the
revenue of his writing until 1845, when he accepted a position at *The
Broadway Journal.* There he accused Longfellow of plagiarism, and
gained the anger of the literary community. His standing was so bad that
his own magazine, *The New York Literati* (1846), was an abject failure.
When Virginia Poe died in 1847, Poe fell into alcoholism and depression.
He wrote sporadically until his death in Baltimore, under mysterious
circumstances, two years later.

"The Murders in the Rue Morgue" is a milestone in the annals of
mystery literature. Not only did it introduce the world's first series
detective, C. Auguste Dupin, it also introduced one of the mainstays of
the genre—the locked-room mystery.

RESIDING IN PARIS during the spring and part of the summer of
18—, I there became acquainted with a Monsieur C. Auguste Dupin.
This young gentleman was of an excellent—indeed of an illustrious
family, but, by a variety of untoward events, had been reduced to such

poverty that the energy of his character succumbed beneath it, and he ceased to bestir himself in the world, or to care for the retrieval of his fortunes. By courtesy of his creditors there still remained in his possession a small remnant of his patrimony; and, upon the income arising from this, he managed, by means of a rigorous economy, to procure the necessaries of life, without troubling himself about its superfluities. Books, indeed, were his sole luxuries, and in Paris these are easily obtained.

Our first meeting was at an obscure library in the Rue Montmartre, where the accident of our both being in search of the same very rare and very remarkable volume, brought us into closer communion. We saw each other again and again. I was deeply interested in the little family history which he detailed to me with all that candor which a Frenchman indulges whenever mere self is the theme. I was astonished, too, at the vast extent of his reading; and, above all, I felt my soul enkindled within me by the wild fervor, and the vivid freshness of his imagination. Seeking in Paris the objects I then sought, I felt that the society of such a man would be to me a treasure beyond price; and this feeling I frankly confided to him. It was at length arranged that we should live together during my stay in the city; and as my worldly circumstances were somewhat less embarrassed than his own, I was permitted to be at the expense of renting, and furnishing in a style which suited the rather fantastic gloom of our common temper, a time-eaten and grotesque mansion, long deserted through superstitions into which we did not inquire, and tottering to its fall in a retired and desolate portion of the Faubourg St. Germain.

Had the routine of our life at this place been known to the world, we should have been regarded as madmen—although, perhaps, as madmen of a harmless nature. Our seclusion was perfect. We admitted no visitors. Indeed the locality of our retirement had been carefully kept a secret from my own former associates; and it had been many years since Dupin had ceased to know or be known in Paris. We existed within ourselves alone.

It was a freak of fancy in my friend (for what else shall I call it?) to be enamored of the Night for her own sake; and into this *bizarrerie,* as into all his others, I quietly fell, giving myself up to his wild whims with a perfect abandon. The sable divinity would not herself dwell with us always; but we could counterfeit her presence. At the first dawn of the morning we closed all the massy shutters of our old building; lighted a couple of tapers which, strongly perfumed, threw out only the ghastliest and feeblest of rays. By the aid of these we then busied our souls in dreams—reading, writing, or conversing, until warned by the clock of the advent of the true Darkness. Then we sallied forth into the streets, arm in arm, continuing the topics of the day, or roaming far and wide until a late hour, seeking, amid the wild lights and shadows of the populous city, that infinity of mental excitement which quiet observation can afford.

At such times I could not help remarking and admiring (although from his rich ideality I had been prepared to expect it) a peculiar analytic ability in Dupin. He seemed, too, to take an eager delight in its exercise—if not exactly in its display—and did not hesitate to confess the pleasure thus derived. He boasted to me, with a low chuckling laugh, that most men, in respect to himself, wore windows in their bosoms, and was wont to follow up such assertions by direct and very startling proofs of his intimate knowledge of my own. His manner at these moments was frigid and abstract; his eyes were vacant in expression; while his voice, usually a rich tenor, rose into a treble which would have sounded petulantly but for the deliberateness and entire distinctness of the enunciation. Observing him in these moods, I often dwelt meditatively upon the old philosophy of the Bi-Part Soul, and amused myself with the fancy of a double Dupin—the creative and the resolvent.

Let it not be supposed, from what I have just said, that I am detailing any mystery, or penning any romance. What I have described in the Frenchman was merely the result of an excited, or perhaps of a diseased intelligence. But of the character of his remarks at the periods in question an example will best convey the idea.

We were strolling one night down a long dirty street, in the vicinity of the Palais Royal. Being both apparently occupied with thought, neither of us had spoken a syllable for fifteen minutes at least. All at once Dupin broke forth with these words—

"He is a very little fellow, that's true, and would do better for the *Théâtre des Variétés.*"

"There can be no doubt of that," I replied unwittingly, and not at first observing (so much had I been absorbed in reflection) the extraordinary manner in which the speaker had chimed in with my meditations. In an instant afterwards I recollected myself, and my astonishment was profound.

"Dupin," said I gravely, "this is beyond my comprehension. I do not hesitate to say that I am amazed, and can scarcely credit my senses. How was it possible you should know I was thinking of—?" Here I paused, to ascertain beyond a doubt whether he really knew of whom I thought.

"Of Chantilly," said he; "why do you pause? You were remarking to yourself that his diminutive figure unfitted him for tragedy."

This was precisely what had formed the subject of my reflections. Chantilly was a quondam cobbler of the Rue St. Denis, who, becoming stage-mad, had attempted the *rôle* of Xerxes, in Crébillon's tragedy so called, and been notoriously pasquinaded for his pains.

"Tell me, for Heaven's sake," I exclaimed, "the method—if method there is—by which you have been enabled to fathom my soul in this matter." In fact I was even more startled than I would have been willing to express.

"It was the fruiterer," replied my friend, "who brought you to the conclusion that the mender of soles was not of sufficient height for Xerxes *et id genus omne."*

"The fruiterer!—you astonish me—I know no fruiterer whomsoever."

"The man who ran up against you as we entered the street—it may have been fifteen minutes ago."

I now remembered that, in fact, a fruiterer, carrying upon his head a large basket of apples, had nearly thrown me down, by accident, as we passed from the Rue C— into the thoroughfare where we stood; but what this had to do with Chantilly I could not possibly understand.

There was not a particle of *charlatanerie* about Dupin. "I will explain," he said, "and that you may comprehend all clearly, we will first retrace the course of your meditations, from the moment in which I spoke to you until that of the *rencontre* with the fruiterer in question. The larger links of the chain run thus—Chantilly, Orion, Dr. Nichols, Epicurus, Stereotomy, the street stones, the fruiterer."

There are few persons who have not, at some period of their lives, amused themselves in retracing the steps by which particular conclusions of their own minds have been attained. The occupation is often full of interest; and he who attempts it for the first time is astonished by the apparently illimitable distance and incoherence between the starting-point and the goal. What then must have been my amazement when I heard the Frenchman speak what he had just spoken, and when I could not help acknowledging that he had spoken the truth! He continued—

"We had been talking of horses, if I remember aright, just before leaving the Rue C—. This was the last subject we discussed. As we crossed into the street, a fruiterer, with a large basket upon his head, brushing quickly past us, thrust you upon a pile of paving-stones collected at a spot where the causeway is undergoing repair. You stepped upon one of the loose fragments, slipped, slightly strained your ankle, appeared vexed or sulky, muttered a few words, turned to look at the pile, and then proceeded in silence. I was not particularly attentive to what you did; but observation has become with me, of late, a species of necessity.

"You kept your eyes on the ground—glancing, with a petulant expression, at the holes and ruts in the pavement (so that I saw you were still thinking of the stones), until we reached the little alley called Lamartine, which has been paved, by way of experiment, with the overlapping and riveted blocks. Here your countenance brightened up, and perceiving your lips move, I could not doubt that you murmured the word 'stereotomy,' a term very affectedly applied to this species of pavement. I knew that you could not say to yourself 'stereotomy' without being brought to think of atomies, and thus of the theories of Epicurus; and since, when we discussed this subject not very long ago, I mentioned to you how singularly, yet with how little notice, the vague guesses of that noble Greek had met with confirmation in the late nebular cosmogony, I felt that you could not avoid casting your eyes upward to the great nebula Orion, and I certainly expected that you would do so. You did look up; and I was now assured that I had correctly followed your steps. But in that bitter tirade upon Chantilly, which appeared in yesterday's *Musée,* the satirist making some disgraceful allusions to the cobbler's change of name upon assuming the buskin, quoted a Latin line about which we have often conversed. I mean the line

'Perdidit antiquum litera prima sonum.'

I had told you that this was in reference to Orion, formerly written Urion; and, from certain pungencies connected with this explanation, I was aware that you could not have forgotten it. It was clear, therefore, that you would not fail to combine the two ideas of Orion and Chantilly. That you did combine them I saw by the character of the smile which passed over your lips. You thought of the poor cobbler's immolation. So far you had been stooping in your gait; but now I saw you draw yourself up to your full height. I was then sure that you reflected upon the diminutive figure of Chantilly. At this point I interrupted your meditations to remark that as, in fact, he *was* a very little fellow, that Chantilly, he would do better at the *Théâtre des Variétés.*"

Not long after this, we were looking over an evening edition of the *Gazette des Tribunaux* when the following paragraphs arrested our attention:

"EXTRAORDINARY MURDERS.—This morning about three o'clock, the inhabitants of the Quartier St. Roch were aroused from sleep by a succession of terrific shrieks, issuing, apparently, from the fourth story of a house in the Rue Morgue, known to be in the sole occupancy of one Madame L'Espanaye, and her daughter, Mademoiselle Camille L'Espanaye. After some delay, occasioned by a fruitless attempt to procure admission in the usual manner, the gateway was broken in with a crowbar, and eight or ten of the neighbors entered, accompanied by two gendarmes. By this time the cries had ceased; but, as the party rushed up the first flight of stairs, two or more rough voices in angry contention were distinguished, and seemed to proceed from the upper part of the house. As the second landing was reached, these sounds also had ceased, and everything remained perfectly quiet. The party spread themselves, and hurried from room to room. Upon arriving at a large back chamber in the fourth story (the door of which, being found locked with the key inside, was forced open), a spectacle presented itself which struck every one present not less with horror than with astonishment.

"The apartment was in the wildest disorder—the furniture broken and thrown about in all directions. There was only one bedstead; and from this the bed had been removed and thrown into the middle of the floor. On a chair lay a razor, besmeared with blood. On the hearth were two or three long and thick tresses of gray human hair, also dabbled in blood, and seeming to have been pulled out by the roots. Upon the floor were found four napoleons, an earring of topaz, three large silver spoons, three smaller of *métal d'Alger,* and two bags, containing nearly four thousand francs in gold. The drawers of a bureau, which stood in one corner, were open, and had been apparently rifled, although many articles still remained in them. A small iron safe was discovered under the *bed* (not under the bedstead). It was open, with the key still in the door. It had no contents beyond a few old letters, and other papers of little consequence.

"Of Madame L'Espanaye no traces were here seen; but an unusual quantity of soot being observed in the fireplace, a search was made in the chimney, and (horrible to relate!) the corpse of the daughter, head downward, was dragged therefrom; it having been thus forced up the narrow aperture for a considerable distance. The body was quite warm. Upon examining it, many excoriations were perceived, no doubt occasioned by the violence with which it had been thrust up and disengaged. Upon the face were many severe scratches, and, upon the throat, dark bruises, and deep indentations of finger nails, as if the deceased had been throttled to death.

"After a thorough investigation of every portion of the house, without further discovery, the party made its way into a small paved yard in the rear of the building, where lay the corpse of the old lady, with her throat so entirely cut that, upon an attempt to raise her, the head fell off. The body as well as the head was fearfully mutilated—the former so much so as scarcely to retain any semblance of humanity.

"To this horrible mystery there is not as yet, we believe, the slightest clew."

The next day's paper had these additional particulars:

"THE TRAGEDY IN THE RUE MORGUE.—Many individuals have been examined in relation to this most extraordinary and frightful affair" (the word *"affaire"* has not yet in France that levity of import which it conveys with us), "but nothing whatever has transpired to throw light upon it. We give below all the material testimony elicited.

"Pauline Dubourg, laundress, deposes that she has known both the deceased for three years, having washed for them during that period. The old lady and her daughter seemed on good terms—very affectionate towards each other. They were excellent pay. Could not speak in regard to their mode or means of living. Believed that Madame L. told fortunes for a living. Was reputed to have money put by. Never met any persons in the house when she called for the clothes or took them home. Was sure that they had no servant in employ. There appeared to be no furniture in any part of the building, except in the fourth story.

"*Pierre Moreau,* tobacconist, deposes that he has been in the habit of selling small quantities of tobacco and snuff to Madame L'Espanaye for nearly four years. Was born in the neighborhood, and has always resided there. The deceased and her daughter had occupied the house in which the corpses were found for more than six years. It was formerly occupied by a jeweler, who under-let the upper rooms to various persons. The house was the property of Madame L. She became dissatisfied with the abuse of the premises by her tenant, and moved into them herself, refusing to let any portion. The old lady was childish. Witness had seen the daughter some five or six times during the six years. The two lived an exceedingly retired life—were reputed to have money. Had heard it said among the neighbors that Madame L. told fortunes—did not believe it. Had never seen any person enter the door except the old lady and her daughter, a porter once or twice, and a physician some eight or ten times.

"Many other persons, neighbors, gave evidence to the same effect. No one was spoken of as frequenting the house. It was not known whether there were any living connections of Madame L. and her daughter. The shutters of the front windows were seldom opened. Those in the rear were always closed, with the exception of the large back room, fourth story. The house was a good house—not very old.

"*Isidore Muset,* gendarme, deposes that he was called to the house about three o'clock in the morning, and found some twenty or thirty persons at the gateway, endeavoring to gain admittance. Forced it open at length, with a bayonet—not with a crowbar. Had but little difficulty in getting it open, on account of its being a double or folding gate, and bolted neither at bottom nor top. The shrieks were continued until the gate was forced, and then suddenly ceased. They seemed to be screams of some person (or persons) in great agony, were loud and drawn out, not short and quick. Witness led the way upstairs. Upon reaching the first landing, heard two voices in loud and angry contention—the one a gruff voice, the other much shriller—a very strange voice. Could distinguish some words of the former, which was that of a Frenchman. Was positive that it was not a woman's voice. Could distinguish the words 'sacré' and 'diable.' The shrill voice was that of a foreigner. Could not be sure whether it was the voice of a man or of a woman. Could not make out what was said, but believed the language to be Spanish. The state of the room and of the bodies was described by this witness as we described them yesterday.

"*Henri Duval,* a neighbor, and by trade a silversmith, deposes that he was one of the party who first entered the house. Corroborates the testimony of Muset in general. As soon as they forced an entrance, they reclosed the door, to keep out the crowd, which collected very fast, notwithstanding the lateness of the hour. The shrill voice, this witness thinks, was that of an Italian. Was certain it was not French. Could not be sure that it was a man's voice. It might have been a woman's. Was not acquainted with the Italian language. Could not distinguish the words but was convinced by the intonation that the speaker was an Italian. Knew Madame L. and her daughter. Had conversed with both frequently. Was sure that the shrill voice was not that of either of the deceased.

"— *Odenheimer,* restaurateur. This witness volunteered his testimony. Not speaking French, was examined through an interpreter. Is a native of Amsterdam. Was passing the house at the time of the shrieks. They lasted for several minutes—probably ten. They were long and loud—very awful and distressing. Was one of those who entered the building. Corroborated the previous evidence in every respect but one. Was sure that the shrill voice was that of a man—of a Frenchman. Could not distinguish the words uttered. They were loud and quick—unequal—spoken apparently in fear as well as in anger. The voice was harsh—not so much shrill as harsh. Could not call it a shrill voice. The gruff voice said repeatedly '*Sacré,*' '*diable,*' and once '*mon Dieu.*'

"*Jules Mignaud*, banker, of the firm of Mignaud et Fils, Rue Deloraine. Is the elder Mignaud. Madame L'Espanaye had some property. Had opened an account with his banking house in the spring of the year— (eight years previously). Made frequent deposits in small sums. Had checked for nothing until the third day before her death, when she took out in person the sum of 4000 francs. This sum was paid in gold, and a clerk sent home with the money.

"*Adolphe Le Bon,* clerk to Mignaud et Fils, deposes that on the day in question, about noon, he accompanied Madame L'Espanaye to her residence with the 4000 francs put up in two bags. Upon the door being opened, Mademoiselle L. appeared and took from his hands one of the bags, while the old lady relieved him of the other. He then bowed and departed. Did not see any person in the street at the time. It is a by-street—very lonely.

"*William Bird,* tailor, deposes that he was one of the party who entered the house. Is an Englishman. Has lived in Paris two years. Was one of the first to ascend the stairs. Heard the voices in contention. The gruff voice was that of a Frenchman. Could make out several words, but cannot now remember all. Heard distinctly '*sacré*' and '*mon Dieu.*' There was a sound at the moment as if of several persons struggling—a scraping and scuffling sound. The shrill voice was very loud—louder than the gruff one. Appeared to be that of a German. Might have been a woman's voice. Does not understand German.

"Four of the above-named witnesses, being recalled, deposed that the door of the chamber in which was found the body of Mademoiselle L. was locked on the inside when the party reached it. Everything was perfectly silent—no groans or noises of any kind. Upon forcing the door no person was seen. The windows, both of the back and front room, were down and firmly fastened from within. A door between the two rooms was closed, but not locked. The door leading from the front room into the passage was locked, with the key on the inside. A small room in the front of the house, on the fourth story, at the head of the passage, was open, the door being ajar. This room was crowded with old beds, boxes, and so forth. These were carefully removed and searched. There was not an inch of any portion of the house which was not carefully searched. Sweeps were sent up and down the chimneys. The house was a four-story one, with garrets *(mansardes).* A trap-door on the roof was nailed down very securely—did not appear to have been opened for years. The time elapsing between the hearing of the voices in contention and the breaking open of the room door was variously stated by the witnesses. Some made it as short as three minutes—some as long as five. The door was opened with difficulty.

"*Alfonzo Garcio,* undertaker, deposes that he resides in the Rue Morgue. Is a native of Spain. Was one of the party who entered the house. Did not proceed upstairs. Is nervous, and was apprehensive of the consequences of agitation. Heard the voices in contention. The gruff voice was that of a Frenchman. Could not distinguish what was said. The shrill voice was that of an Englishman—is sure of this. Does not understand the English language, but judges by the intonation.

"*Alberto Montani,* confectioner, deposes that he was among the first to ascend the stairs. Heard the voices in question. The gruff voice was that of a Frenchman. Distinguished several words. The speaker appeared to be expostulating. Could not make out the words of the shrill voice. Spoke quick and unevenly. Thinks it the voice of a Russian. Corroborates the general testimony. Is an Italian. Never conversed with a native of Russia.

"Several witnesses, recalled, here testified that the chimneys of all the rooms on the fourth story were too narrow to admit the passage of a human being. By 'sweeps' were meant cylindrical sweeping-brushes, such as are employed by those who clean chimneys. These brushes were passed up and down every flue in the house. There is no back passage by which any one could have descended while the party proceeded upstairs. The body of Mademoiselle L'Espanaye was so firmly wedged in the chimney that it could not be got down until four or five of the party united their strength.

"*Paul Dumas,* physician, deposes that he was called to view the bodies about daybreak. They were both then lying on the sacking of the bedstead in the chamber where Mademoiselle L. was found. The corpse of the young lady was much bruised and excoriated. The fact that it had been thrust up the chimney would sufficiently account for these appearances. The throat was greatly chafed. There were several deep scratches just below the chin, together with a series of livid spots which were evidently the impression of fingers. The face was fearfully discolored, and the eyeballs protruded. The tongue had been partially bitten through. A large bruise was discovered upon the pit of the stomach, produced, apparently, by the pressure of a knee. In the opinion of M. Dumas, Mademoiselle L'Espanaye had been throttled to death by some person or persons unknown. The corpse of the mother was horribly mutilated. All the bones of the right leg and arm were more or less shattered. The left tibia much splintered, as well as all the ribs of the left side. Whole body dreadfully bruised and discolored. It was not possible to say how the injuries had been inflicted. A heavy club of wood, or a broad bar of iron—a chair—any large, heavy, and obtuse weapon would have produced such results, if wielded by the hands of a very powerful man. No woman could have inflicted the blows with any weapon. The head of the deceased, when seen by witness, was entirely separated from the body, and was also greatly shattered. The throat had evidently been cut with some very sharp instrument—probably with a razor.

"*Alexandre Etienne*, surgeon, was called with M. Dumas, to view the bodies. Corroborated the testimony and the opinions of M. Dumas.

"Nothing further of importance was elicited, although several other persons were examined. A murder so mysterious, and so perplexing in all its particulars, was never before committed in Paris—if indeed a murder has been committed at all. The police are entirely at fault—an unusual occurrence in affairs of this nature. There is not, however, the shadow of a clew apparent."

The evening edition of the paper stated that the greatest excitement still continued in the Quartier St. Roch—that the premises in question had been carefully researched, and fresh examinations of witnesses instituted, but all to no purpose. A postscript, however, mentioned that Adolphe Le Bon had been arrested and imprisoned—although nothing appeared to criminate him, beyond the facts already detailed.

Dupin seemed singularly interested in the progress of this affair—at least so I judged from his manner, for he had made no comments. It was only after the announcement that Le Bon had been imprisoned, that he asked me my opinion respecting the murders.

I could merely agree with all Paris in considering them an insoluble mystery. I saw no means by which it would be possible to trace the murderer.

"We must not judge of the means," said Dupin, "by this shell of an examination. The Parisian police, so much extolled for acumen, are cunning, but no more. There is no method in their proceedings, beyond the method of the moment. They make a vast parade of measures; but, not unfrequently, these are so ill adapted to the objects proposed, as to put us in mind of Monsieur Jourdain's calling for his *robe de chambre—pour mieux entendre la musique.* The results attained by them are not unfrequently surprising, but for the most part are brought about by simple diligence and activity. When these qualities are unavailing, their schemes fail. Vidocq, for example, was a good guesser, and a persevering man. But, without educated thought, he erred continually by the very intensity of his investigations. He impaired his vision by holding the object too close. He might see, perhaps, one or two points with unusual clearness, but in so doing, he necessarily lost sight of the matter as a whole. Thus there is such a thing as being too profound. Truth is not always in a well. In fact, as regards the more important knowledge, I do believe that she is invariably superficial. The depth lies in the valleys where we seek her, and not upon the mountain top where she is found. The modes and sources of this kind of error are well typified in the contemplation of the heavenly bodies. To look at a star by glances—to view it in a sidelong way, by turning toward it the exterior portions of the retina (more susceptible of feeble impressions of light than the interior), is to behold the star distinctly—is to have the best appreciation of its luster—a luster which grows dim just in proportion as we turn our vision *fully* upon it. A greater number of rays actually fall upon the eye in the latter case, but, in the former, there is the more refined capacity for comprehension. By undue profundity we perplex and enfeeble thought; and it is possible to make even Venus herself vanish from the firmament by a scrutiny too sustained, too concentrated, or too direct.

"As for these murders, let us enter into some examinations for ourselves, before we make up an opinion respecting them. An inquiry will afford us amusement" (I thought this an odd term, so applied, but said nothing), "and besides, Le Bon once rendered me a service for which I am not ungrateful. We will go and see the premises with our own eyes. I know G—, the Prefect of Police, and shall have no difficulty in obtaining the necessary permission."

The permission was obtained, and we proceeded at once to the Rue Morgue. This is one of those miserable thoroughfares which intervene between the Rue Richelieu and the Rue St. Roch. It was late in the afternoon when we reached it, as this quarter is at a great distance from that in which we resided. The house was readily found; for there were still many persons gazing up at the closed shutters, with an objectless curiosity, from the opposite side of the way. It was an ordinary Parisian house, with a gate-way, on one side of which was a glazed watch-box, with a sliding-panel in the window, indicating a *loge de concierge*. Before going in we walked up the street, turned down an alley, and then, again turning, passed in the rear of the building—Dupin, meanwhile, examining the whole neighborhood, as well as the house, with a minuteness of attention for which I could see no possible object.

Retracing our steps, we came again to the front of the dwelling, rang, and having shown our credentials, were admitted by the agents in

Edgar Allan Poe

charge. We went upstairs,—into the chamber where the body of Mademoiselle L'Espanaye had been found, and where both the deceased still lay. The disorders of the room had, as usual, been suffered to exist. I saw nothing beyond what had been stated in the *Gazette des Tribunaux.* Dupin scrutinized everything—not excepting the bodies of the victims. We then went into the other rooms, and into the yard, a gendarme accompanying us throughout. The examination occupied us until dark, when we took our departure. On our way home my companion stepped in for a moment at the office of one of the daily papers.

I have said that the whims of my friend were manifold, and that *je les ménagais*—for this phrase there is no English equivalent. It was his humor, now, to decline all conversation on the subject of the murders, until about noon the next day. He then asked me, suddenly, if I had observed anything *peculiar* at the scene of the atrocity.

There was something in his manner of emphasizing the word "peculiar," which caused me to shudder, without knowing why.

"No, nothing *peculiar,*" I said; "nothing more, at least, than we both saw stated in the paper."

"The *Gazette,*" he replied, "has not entered, I fear, into the unusual horror of the thing. But dismiss the idle opinions of this print. It appears to me that this mystery is considered insoluble, for the very reason which should cause it to be regarded as easy of solution —I mean for the *outré* character of its features. The police are confounded by the seeming absence of motive—not for the murder itself—but for the atrocity of the murder. They are puzzled, too, by the seeming impossibility of reconciling the voices heard in contention, with the facts that no one was discovered upstairs but the assassinated Mademoiselle L'Espanaye, and that there were no means of egress without the notice of the party ascending. The wild disorder of the room; the corpse thrust, with the head downward, up the chimney; the frightful mutilation of the body of the old lady; these considerations, with those just mentioned, and others which I need not mention, have sufficed to paralyze the powers, by putting completely at fault the boasted acumen of the government agents. They have fallen into the gross but common error of confounding the unusual with the abstruse. But it is by these deviations from the plane of the ordinary that reason feels its way, if at all, in its search for the true. In investigations such as we are now pursuing, it should not be so much asked 'what has occurred?' as 'what has occurred that has never occurred before?' In fact, the facility with which I shall arrive, or have arrived, at the solution of this mystery, is in the direct ratio of its apparent insolubility in the eyes of the police."

I stared at the speaker in mute astonishment.

"I am now awaiting," continued he, looking toward the door of our apartment—"I am now awaiting a person who, although perhaps not the perpetrator of these butcheries, must have been in some measure implicated in their perpetration. Of the worst portion of the crimes committed, it is probable that he is innocent. I hope that I am right in this supposition; for upon it I build my expectation of reading the entire riddle. I look for the man here—in this room every moment. It is true that he may not arrive; but the probability is that he will. Should he come, it will be necessary to detain him. Here are pistols; and we both know how to use them when occasion demands their use."

I took the pistols, scarcely knowing what I did, or believing what I heard, while Dupin went on, very much as if in a soliloquy. I have already spoken of his abstract manner at such times. His discourse was addressed to myself; but his voice, although by no means loud, had that intonation which is commonly employed in speaking to some one at a great distance. His eyes, vacant in expression, regarded only the wall.

"That the voices heard in contention," he said, "by the party upon the stairs, were not the voices of the women themselves, was fully proved by the evidence. This relieves us of all doubt upon the question whether the old lady could have first destroyed the daughter, and afterwards have committed suicide. I speak of this point chiefly for the sake of method; for the strength of Madame L'Espanaye would have been utterly unequal to the task of thrusting her daughter's corpse up the chimney as it was found; and the nature of the wounds upon her own person entirely precludes the idea of self-destruction. Murder, then, has been committed by some third party; and the voices of this third party were those heard in contention. Let me now advert—not to the whole testimony respecting these voices—but to what was *peculiar* in that testimony. Did you observe anything peculiar about it?"

I remarked that, while all the witnesses agreed in supposing the gruff voice to be that of a Frenchman, there was much disagreement in regard to the shrill, or, as one individual termed it, the harsh voice.

"That was the evidence itself," said Dupin, "but it was not the peculiarity of the evidence. You have observed nothing distinctive. Yet there *was* something to be observed. The witnesses, as you remark, agreed about the gruff voice; they were here unanimous. But in regard to the shrill voice, the peculiarity is—not that they disagreed—but, that, while an Italian, an Englishman, a Spaniard, a Hollander, and a Frenchman attempted to describe it, each one spoke of it as that *of a foreigner*. Each is sure that it was not the voice of one of his own countrymen. Each likens it—not to the voice of an individual of any nation with whose language he is conversant —but the converse. The Frenchman supposes it the voice of a Spaniard, and 'might have distinguished some words *had he been acquainted with the Spanish.*' The Dutchman maintains it to have been that of a Frenchman; but we find it stated that, '*not understanding French, this witness was examined through an interpreter.*' The Englishman thinks it the voice of a German, and '*does not understand German.*' The Spaniard 'is sure' that it was that of an Englishman, but 'judges by the intonation' altogether, '*as he has no knowledge of the English.*' The Italian believes it the voice of a Russian, but '*has never conversed with a native of Russia.*' A second Frenchman differs, moreover, with the first, and is positive that the voice was that of an Italian; but, *not being cognizant of that tongue,* is, like the Spaniard, 'convinced by the intonation.' Now, how strangely unusual must that voice have really been, about which such testimony as this *could* have been elicited!—in whose *tones,* even, denizens of the five great divisions of Europe could recognize nothing familiar! You will say that it might have been the voice of an Asiatic—of an African. Neither Asiatics nor Africans abound in Paris; but, without denying the inference, I will now merely call your attention to three points. The voice is termed by one witness 'harsh rather than shrill.' It is represented by two others to have been 'quick and *unequal.*' No words—no sounds resembling words—were by any witness mentioned as distinguishable.

"I know not," continued Dupin, "what impression I may have made, so far, upon your own understanding; but I do not hesitate to say that legitimate deductions even from this portion of the testimony—the portion respecting the gruff and shrill voices—are in themselves sufficient to engender a suspicion which should give direction to all further progress in the investigation of the mystery. I said 'legitimate deductions'; but my meaning is not thus fully expressed. I designed to imply that the deductions are the *sole* proper ones, and that the suspicion arises *inevitably* from them as the single result. What the suspicion is, however, I will not say just yet. I merely wish you to bear in mind that, with myself, it was sufficiently forcible to give a definite form—a certain tendency—to my inquiries in the chamber.

"Let us now transport ourselves, in fancy, to this chamber. What shall we first seek here? The means of egress employed by the murderers. It is not too much to say that neither of us believe in preternatural events. Madame and Mademoiselle L'Espanaye were not destroyed by spirits. The doers of the deed were material, and escaped materially.

Then how? Fortunately, there is but one mode of reasoning upon the point, and that mode *must* lead us to a definite decision. Let us examine, each by each, the possible means of egress. It is clear that the assassins were in the room where Mademoiselle L'Espanaye was found, or at least in the room adjoining, when the party ascended the stairs. It is, then, only from these two apartments that we have to seek issues. The police have laid bare the floors, the ceilings, and the masonry of the walls, in every direction. No *secret* issues could have escaped their vigilance. But, not trusting to *their* eyes, I examined with my own. There were, then, *no* secret issues. Both doors leading from the rooms into the passage were securely locked, with the keys inside. Let us turn to the chimneys. These, although of ordinary width for some eight or ten feet above the hearths, will not admit, throughout their extent, the body of a large cat. The impossibility of egress, by means already stated, being thus absolute, we are reduced to the windows. Through those of the front room no one could have escaped without notice from the crowd in the street. The murderers *must* have passed, then, through those of the back room. Now, brought to this conclusion in so unequivocal a manner as we are, it is not our part, as reasoners, to reject it on account of apparent impossibilities. It is only left for us to prove that these apparent 'impossibilities' are, in reality, not such.

"There are two windows in the chamber. One of them is unobstructed by furniture, and is wholly visible. The lower portion of the other is hidden from view by the head of the unwieldy bedstead which is thrust close up against it. The former was found securely fastened from within. It resisted the utmost force of those who endeavored to raise it. A large gimlet hole had been pierced in its frame to the left, and a very stout nail was found fitted therein, nearly to the head. Upon examining the other window, a similar nail was seen similarly fitted in it; and a vigorous attempt to raise this sash, failed also. The police were now entirely satisfied that egress had not been in these directions. And, *therefore,* it was thought a matter of supererogation to withdraw the nails and open the windows.

"My own examination was somewhat more particular, and was so for the reason I have just given—because here it was, I knew, that all apparent impossibilities *must* be proved to be not such in reality.

"I proceeded to think thus—a *posteriori.* The murderers *did* escape from one of these windows. This being so, they could not have refastened the sashes from the inside, as they were found fastened—the consideration which put a stop, through its obviousness, to the scrutiny of the police in this quarter. Yet the sashes *were* fastened. They must, then, have the power of fastening themselves. There was no escape from this conclusion. I stepped to the unobstructed casement, withdrew the nail with some difficulty, and attempted to raise the sash. It resisted all my efforts, as I had anticipated. A concealed spring must, I now knew, exist; and this corroboration of my idea convinced me that my premises, at least, were correct, however mysterious still appeared the circumstances attending the nails. A careful search soon brought to light the hidden spring. I pressed it, and, satisfied with the discovery, forbore to upraise the sash.

"I now replaced the nail and regarded it attentively. A person passing out through this window might have reclosed it, and the spring would have caught; but the nail could not have been replaced. The conclusion was plain, and again narrowed in the field of my investigations. The assassins *must* have escaped through the other window. Supposing, then, the springs upon each sash to be the same, as was probable, there *must* be found a difference between the nails, or at least between the modes of their fixture. Getting upon the sacking of the bedstead, I looked over the head-board minutely at the second casement. Passing my hand down behind the board, I readily discovered and pressed the spring, which was, as I had supposed, identical in character with its neighbor. I now looked at the nail. It was as stout as the other, and apparently fitted in the same manner, driven in nearly up to the head.

"You will say that I was puzzled; but, if you think so, you must have misunderstood the nature of the inductions. To use a sporting phrase, I had not been once 'at fault.' The scent had never for an instant been lost. There was no flaw in any link of the chain. I had traced the secret to its ultimate result—and that result was *the nail*. It had, I say, in every respect, the appearance of its fellow in the other window; but this fact was an absolute nullity (conclusive as it might seem to be) when compared with the consideration that here, at this point, terminated the clew. 'There *must* be something wrong,' I said, 'about the nail.' I touched it; and the head, with about a quarter of an inch of the shank, came off in my fingers. The rest of the shank was in the gimlet hole, where it had been broken off. The fracture was an old one (for its edges were incrusted with rust), and had apparently been accomplished by the blow of a hammer, which had partially embedded, in the top of the bottom sash, the head portion of the nail. I now carefully replaced this head portion in the indentation whence I had taken it, and the resemblance to a perfect nail was complete—the fissure was invisible.

Pressing the spring, I gently raised the sash for a few inches; the head went up with it, remaining firm in its bed. I closed the window, and the semblance of the whole nail was again perfect.

"The riddle, so far, was now unriddled. The assassin had escaped through the window which looked upon the bed. Dropping of its own accord upon his exit (or perhaps purposely closed), it had become fastened by the spring; and it was the retention of this spring which had been mistaken by the police for that of the nail—further inquiry being thus considered unnecessary.

"The next question is that of the mode of descent. Upon this point I had been satisfied in my walk with you around the building. About five feet and a half from the casement in question there runs a lightning-rod. From this rod it would have been impossible for any one to reach the window itself, to say nothing of entering it. I observed, however, that the shutters of the fourth story were of the peculiar kind called by Parisian carpenters *ferrades*—a kind rarely employed at the present day, but frequently seen upon very old mansions at Lyons and Bordeaux. They are in the form of an ordinary door (a single, not a folding door), except that the lower half is latticed or worked in open trellis, thus according an excellent hold for the hands. In the present instance these shutters are fully three feet and a half broad. When we saw them from the rear of the house, they were both about half open—that is to say, they stood off at right angles from the wall. It is probable that the police, as well as myself, examined the back of the tenement; but, if so, in looking at these *ferrades* in the line of their breadth (as they must have done), they did not perceive this great breadth itself, or at all events, failed to take it into due consideration. In fact, having once satisfied themselves that no egress could have been made in this quarter, they would naturally bestow here a very cursory examination. It was clear to me, however, that the shutter belonging to the window at the head of the bed, would, if swung fully back to the wall, reach to within two feet of the lightning-rod. It was also evident that, by exertion of a very unusual degree of activity and courage, an entrance into the window, from the rod, might have been thus effected. By reaching to the distance of two feet and a half (we now suppose the shutter open to its whole extent) a robber might have taken a firm grasp upon the trellis-work. Letting go, then, his hold upon the rod, placing his feet securely against the wall, and springing boldly from it, he might have swung the shutter so as to close it, and, if we imagine the window open at the time, might even have swung himself into the room.

"I wish you to bear especially in mind that I have spoken of a *very* unusual degree of activity as requisite to success in so hazardous and so difficult a feat. It is my design to show you, first, that the thing might possibly have been accomplished; but, secondly and *chiefly,* I wish to impress upon your understanding the *very extraordinary*—the almost preternatural character of that agility which could have accomplished it.

"You will say, no doubt, using the language of the law, that 'to make out my case,' I should rather undervalue, than insist upon a full estimation of the activity required in this matter. This may be the practice in law, but it is not the usage of reason. My ultimate object is only the truth. My immediate purpose is to lead you to place in juxtaposition that *very unusual* activity of which I have just spoken, with that *very peculiar* shrill (or harsh) and *unequal* voice, about whose nationality no two persons could be found to agree, and in whose utterance no syllabification could be detected."

At these words a vague and half-formed conception of the meaning of Dupin flitted over my mind. I seemed to be upon the verge of comprehension, without power to comprehend, as men, at times, find themselves upon the brink of remembrance, without being able in the end to remember. My friend went on with his discourse.

"You will see," he said, "that I have shifted the question from the mode of egress to that of ingress. It was my design to convey the idea that both were effected in the same manner, at the same point. Let us now revert to the interior of the room. Let us survey the appearances here. The drawers of the bureau, it is said, had been rifled, although many articles of apparel still remain within them. The conclusion here is absurd. It is a mere guess—a very silly one—and no more. How are we to know that the articles found in the drawers were not all these drawers had originally contained? Madame L'Espanaye and her daughter lived an exceedingly retired life—saw no company—seldom went out—had little use for numerous changes of habiliment. Those found were at least of as good quality as any likely to be possessed by these ladies. If a thief had taken any, why did he not take the best— why did he not take all? In a word, why did he abandon four thousand francs in gold to encumber himself with a bundle of linen? The gold *was* abandoned. Nearly the whole sum mentioned by Monsieur Mignaud, the banker, was discovered, in bags, upon the floor. I wish you, therefore, to discard from your thoughts the blundering idea of motive, engendered in the brains of the police by that portion of the evidence which speaks of money delivered at the door of the house. Coincidences ten times as remarkable as this (the delivery of the money and murder committed within three days upon the party receiving it) happen to all of us every hour of our lives, without attracting even momentary notice. Coincidences, in general, are great stumbling-blocks in the way of that class of thinkers who have been educated to know nothing of the theory of probabilities—that theory to which the most glorious objects of human research are indebted for the most glorious of illustration. In the present instance, had the gold been gone, the fact of its delivery three days before would have formed something more than a coincidence. It would have been corroborative of this idea of motive. But, under the real circumstances of the case, if we are to suppose gold the motive of this outrage, we must also imagine the perpetrator so vacillating an idiot as to have abandoned his gold and his motive together.

"Keeping now steadily in mind the points to which I have drawn your attention—that peculiar voice, that unusual agility, and that star-tling absence of motive in a murder so singularly atrocious as this—let us glance at the butchery itself. Here is a woman strangled to death by manual strength, and thrust up a chimney, head downward. Ordinary assassins employ no such modes of murder as this. Least of all, do they thus dispose of the murdered. In the manner of thrusting the corpse up the chimney, you will admit that there was something *excessively outré*—something altogether irreconcilable with our common notions of human action, even when we suppose the actors the most depraved of men. Think, too, how great must have been that strength which could have thrust the body up such an aperture so forcibly that the united vigor of several persons was found barely sufficient to drag it *down!*

"Turn, now, to other indications of the employment of a vigor most marvelous. On the hearth were thick tresses—very thick tresses—of gray human hair. These had been torn out by the roots. You are aware of the great force necessary in tearing thus from the head even twenty or thirty hairs together. You saw the locks in question as well as myself. Their roots (a hideous sight!) were clotted with fragments of the flesh of the scalp—sure token of the prodigious power which had been exerted in uprooting perhaps half a million of hairs at a time. The throat of the old lady was not merely cut, but the head absolutely severed from the body: the instrument was a mere razor. I wish you also to look at the *brutal* ferocity of these deeds. Of the bruises upon the body of Madame L'Espanaye I do not speak. Monsieur Dumas, and his worthy co-adjutor Monsieur Etienne, have pronounced that they

were inflicted by some obtuse instrument; and so far these gentlemen
are very correct. The obtuse instrument was clearly the stone pavement
in the yard, upon which the victim had fallen from the window which
looked in upon the bed. This idea, however simple it may now seem,
escaped the police for the same reason that the breadth of the shutters
escaped them—because, by the affair of the nails, their perception had
been hermetically sealed against the possibility of the windows having
ever been opened at all.

"If now, in addition to all these things, you have properly reflected
upon the odd disorder of the chamber, we have gone so far as to
combine the ideas of an agility astounding, a strength superhuman, a
ferocity brutal, a butchery without motive, a *grotesquerie* in horror
absolutely alien from humanity, and a voice foreign in tone to the ears
of men of many nations, and devoid of all distinct or intelligible
syllabification. What result, then, has ensued? What impression have
I made upon your fancy?"

I felt a creeping of the flesh as Dupin asked me the question. "A
madman," I said, "has done this deed—some raving maniac escaped
from a neighboring *Maison de Santé.*"

"In some respects," he replied, "your idea is not irrelevant. But the
voices of madmen, even in their wildest paroxysms, are never found to
tally with that peculiar voice heard upon the stairs. Madmen are of
some nation, and their language, however incoherent in its words, has
always the coherence of syllabification. Besides, the hair of a madman
is not such as I now hold in my hand. I disentangled this little tuft from
the rigidly clutched fingers of Madame L'Espanaye. Tell me what you
can make of it."

"Dupin," I said, completely unnerved, "this hair is most unusual—
this is no *human* hair."

"I have not asserted that it is," said he; "but, before we decide this
point, I wish you to glance at the little sketch I have here traced upon
this paper. It is a *fac-simile* drawing of what has been described in one
portion of the testimony as 'dark bruises, and deep indentations of
finger nails,' upon the throat of Mademoiselle L'Espanaye, and in
another (by Messrs. Dumas and Etienne), as a 'series of livid spots,
evidently the impression of fingers.'

"You will perceive," continued my friend, spreading out the paper
upon the table before me, "that this drawing gives the idea of a firm
and fixed hold. There is no *slipping* apparent. Each finger has re-
tained—possibly until the death of the victim—the fearful grasp by
which it originally embedded itself. Attempt, now, to place all your

fingers, at the same time, in the respective impressions as you see them.''

I made the attempt in vain.

"We are possibly not giving this matter a fair trial,'' he said. "The paper is spread out upon a plane surface; but the human throat is cylindrical. Here is a billet of wood, the circumference of which is about that of the throat. Wrap the drawing round it, and try the experiment again.''

I did so; but the difiiculty was even more obvious than before. "This,'' I said, "is the mark of no human hand.''

"Read now,'' replied Dupin, "this passage from Cuvier.''

It was a minute anatomical and generally descriptive account of the large fulvous Ourang-Outang of the East Indian Islands. The gigantic stature, the prodigious strength and activity, the wild ferocity, and the imitative propensities of these mammalia are sufficiently well known to all. I understood the full horrors of the murder at once.

"The description of the digits,'' said I, as I made an end of reading, "is in exact accordance with this drawing. I see that no animal but an Ourang-Outang, of the species here mentioned, could have impressed the indentations as you have traced them. This tuft of tawny hair, too, is identical in character with that of the beast of Cuvier. But I cannot possibly comprehend the particulars of this frightful mystery. Besides, there were *two* voices heard in contention and one of them was unquestionably the voice of a Frenchman.''

"True; and you will remember an expression attributed almost unanimously by the evidence, to this voice—the expression, *'Mon Dieu!'* This, under the circumstances, has been justly characterized by one of the witnesses (Montani, the confectioner) as an expression of remonstrance, or expostulation. Upon these two words, therefore, I have mainly built my hopes of a full solution of the riddle. A Frenchman was cognizant of the murder. It is possible—indeed it is far more than probable—that he was innocent of all participation in the bloody transactions which took place. The Ourang-Outang may have escaped from him. He may have traced it to the chamber; but, under the agitating circumstances which ensued, he could never have recaptured it. It is still at large. I will not pursue these guesses—for I have no right to call them more—since the shades of reflection upon which they are based are scarcely of sufficient depth to be appreciable to my own intellect, and since I could not pretend to make them intelligible to the understanding of another. We will call them guesses, then, and speak of them as such. If the Frenchman in question is indeed, as I suppose, innocent of this atrocity, this advertisement, which I left last night upon our return home, at the office of *Le Monde* (a paper devoted to the shipping interest, and much sought by sailors), will bring him to our residence.

He handed me a paper, and I read thus:

"CAUGHT—*In the Bois de Boulogne, early in the morning of the —inst.* [the morning of the murder] *a very large, tawny Ourang-Outang of the Bornese species. The owner (who is ascertained to be a sailor, belonging to a Maltese vessel) may have the animal again, upon identifying it satisfactorily,* and paying *a few charges rising from its capture and keeping. Call at No.—, Rue—, Faubourg St. Germain—au troisieme."*

"How was it possible," I asked, "that you should know the man to be a sailor, and belonging to a Maltese vessel?"

"I do *not* know it," said Dupin. "I am not *sure* of it. Here, however, is a small piece of ribbon, which from its form, and from its greasy appearance, has evidently been used in tying the hair in one of those long *queues* of which sailors are so fond. Moreover, this knot is one which few besides sailors can tie, and is peculiar to the Maltese. I picked the ribbon up at the foot of the lightning-rod. It could not have belonged to either of the deceased. Now if, after all I am wrong in my induction from this ribbon, that the Frenchman was a sailor belonging to a Maltese vessel, still I can have done no harm in saying what I did in the advertisement. If I am in error, he will merely suppose that I have been misled by some circumstance into which he will not take the trouble to inquire. But if I am right, a great point is gained. Cognizant although innocent of the murder, the Frenchman will naturally hesitate about replying to the advertisement—about demanding the Ourang-Outang. He will reason thus: 'I am innocent; I am poor; my Ourang-Outang is of great value—to one in my circumstances a fortune of itself—why should I lose it through idle apprehensions of danger? Here it is within my grasp. It was found in the Bois de Boulogne—at a vast distance from the scene of that butchery. How can it ever be suspected that a brute beast should have done the deed? The police are at fault, they have failed to procure the slightest clew. Should they even trace the animal, it would be impossible to prove me cognizant of the murder, or to implicate me in guilt on account of that cognizance. Above all, *I am known.* The advertiser designates me as the possessor of the beast. I am not sure to what limit his knowledge may extend. Should I avoid claiming a property of so great value, which it is known that I possess, I will render the animal at least liable to suspicion. It is not my policy to attract attention either to myself or to the beast. I will answer the advertisement, get the Ourang-Outang, and keep it close until this matter has blown over.'"

At this moment we heard a step upon the stairs.

"Be ready," said Dupin, "with your pistols, but neither use them nor show them until at a signal from myself."

The front door of the house had been left open, and the visitor had entered, without ringing, and advanced several steps upon the staircase. Now, however, he seemed to hesitate. Presently we heard him descending. Dupin was moving quickly to the door, when we again heard him coming up. He did not turn back a second time, but stepped up with decision, and rapped at the door of our chamber.

"Come in," said Dupin, in a cheerful and hearty tone.

A man entered. He was a sailor, evidently—a tall, stout, and muscular looking person, with a certain dare-devil expression of countenance not altogether unprepossessing. His face, greatly sunburnt, was more than half hidden by whisker and mustachio. He had with him a huge oaken cudgel, but appeared to be otherwise unarmed. He bowed awkwardly, and bade us "good evening," in French accents, which, although somewhat Neufchâtelish, were still sufficiently indicative of a Parisian origin.

"Sit down, my friend," said Dupin. "I suppose you have called about the Ourang-Outang. Upon my word, I almost envy you the possession of him; a remarkably fine, and no doubt a very valuable animal. How old do you suppose him to be?"

The sailor drew a long breath, with the air of a man relieved of some intolerable burden, and then replied, in an assured tone.

"I have no way of telling—but he can't be more than four or five years old. Have you got him here?"

"Oh, no; we had no conveniences for keeping him here. He is at a livery stable in the Rue Dubourg, just by. You can get him in the morning. Of course, you are prepared to identify the property?"

"To be sure I am, sir."

"I shall be sorry to part with him," said Dupin.

"I don't mean that you should be at all this trouble for nothing, sir," said the man. "Couldn't expect it. Am very willing to pay a reward for the finding of the animal—that is to say, anything in reason."

"Well," replied my friend, "that is all very fair, to be sure. Let me think! What should I have? Oh! I will tell you. My reward shall be this. You shall give me all the information in your power about these murders in the Rue Morgue."

Dupin said the last words in a very low tone, and very quietly. Just as quietly, too, he walked toward the door, locked it, and put the key in his pocket. He then drew a pistol from his bosom, and placed it, without the least flurry, upon the table.

The sailor's face flushed up as if he were struggling with suffocation. He started to his feet and grasped his cudgel; but the next moment he fell back into his seat, trembling violently, and with the countenance of death itself. He spoke not a word. I pitied him from the bottom of my heart.

"My friend," said Dupin, in a kind tone, "you are alarming yourself unnecessarily—you are indeed. We mean you no harm whatever. I pledge you the honor of a gentleman, and of a Frenchman, that we intend you no injury. I perfectly well know that you are innocent of the atrocities in the Rue Morgue. It will not do, however, to deny that you are in some measure implicated in them. From what I have already said, you must know that I have had means of information about this matter—means of which you could never have dreamed. Now the thing stands thus. You have done nothing which you could have avoided—nothing, certainly, which renders you culpable. You were not even guilty of robbery, when you might have robbed with impunity. You have nothing to conceal. You have no reason for concealment. On the other hand, you are bound by every principle of honor to confess all you know. An innocent man is now imprisoned, charged with that crime of which you can point out the perpetrator."

The sailor had recovered his presence of mind, in a great measure, while Dupin uttered these words; but his original boldness of bearing was all gone.

"So help me God," said he, after a brief pause, "I *will* tell you all I know about this affair; but I do not expect you to believe one half I say—I would be a fool indeed if I did. Still, I *am* innocent, and I will make a clean breast if I die for it."

What he stated was in substance this. He had lately made a voyage to the Indian Archipelago. A party, of which he formed one, landed at Borneo, and passed into the interior on an excursion of pleasure. Himself and a companion had captured the Ourang-Outang. This companion dying, the animal fell into his own exclusive possession. After great trouble, occasioned by the intractable ferocity of his captive during the home voyage, he at length succeeded in lodging it safely at his own residence in Paris, where, not to attract toward himself the unpleasant curiosity of his neighbors, he kept it carefully secluded, until such time as it should recover from a wound in the foot, received from a splinter on board ship. His ultimate design was to sell it.

Returning home from some sailors' frolic on the night, or rather in the morning of the murder, he found the beast occupying his own bedroom, into which it had broken from a closet adjoining, where it had been, as was thought, securely confined. Razor in hand, and fully lathered, it was sitting before a looking-glass, attempting the operation of shaving, in which it had no doubt previously watched its master through the key-hole of the closet. Terrified at the sight of so dangerous a weapon in the possession of an animal so ferocious, and so well able to use it, the man, for some moments, was at a loss what to do. He had been accustomed, however, to quiet the creature, even in its fiercest moods, by the use of a whip, and to this he now resorted. Upon sight of it, the Ourang-Outang sprang at once through the door of the chamber, down the stairs, and thence, through a window, unfortunately open, into the.street.

The Frenchman followed in despair; the ape, razor still in hand, occasionally stopping to look back and gesticulate at its pursuer, until the latter had nearly come up with it. It then again made off. In this manner the chase continued for a long time. The streets were profoundly quiet, as it was nearly three o'clock in the morning. In passing down an alley in the rear of the Rue Morgue, the fugitive's attention was arrested by a light gleaming from the open window of Madame L'Espanaye's chamber, in the fourth story of her house. Rushing to the building, it perceived the lightning-rod, clambered up with inconceivable agility, grasped the shutter, which was thrown fully back against the wall, and, by its means, swung itself directly upon the headboard of the bed. The whole feat did not occupy a minute. The shutter was kicked open again by the Ourang-Outang as it entered the room.

The sailor, in the meantime, was both rejoiced and perplexed. He had strong hopes of now recapturing the brute, as it could scarcely escape from the trap into which it had ventured, except by the rod, where it might be intercepted as it came down. On the other hand, there was much cause for anxiety as to what it might do in the house. This latter reflection urged the man still to follow the fugitive. A lightning-rod is ascended without difficulty, especially by a sailor; but, when he had arrived as high as the window, which lay far to his left, his career was stopped; the most that he could accomplish was to reach over so as to obtain a glimpse of the interior of the room. At this glimpse he nearly fell from his hold; through excess of horror. Now it was that those hideous shrieks arose upon the night, which had startled from slumber the inmates of the Rue Morgue. Madame L'Espanaye and her daughter, habited in their night clothes, had apparently been occupied in arranging some papers in the iron chest already mentioned, which had been wheeled into the middle of the room. It was open, and its contents lay beside it on the floor. The victims must have been sitting with their backs toward the window; and, from the time elapsing between the ingress of the beast and the screams, it seems probable that it was not immediately perceived. The flapping-to of the shutter would naturally have been attributed to the wind.

As the sailor looked in, the gigantic animal had seized Madame L'Espanaye by the hair (which was loose, as she had been combing it), and was flourishing the razor about her face, in imitation of the motions of a barber. The daughter lay prostrate and motionless; she had swooned. The screams and struggles of the old lady (during which the hair was torn from her head) had the effect of changing the probably pacific purposes of the Ourang-Outang into those of wrath. With one determined sweep of its muscular arm it nearly severed her head from her body. The sight of blood inflamed its anger into frenzy. Gnashing its teeth and flashing fire from its eyes, it flew upon the body of the girl, and embedded its fearful talons in her throat, retaining its grasp until she expired. Its wandering and wild glances fell at this moment upon the head of the bed, over which the face of its master, rigid with horror, was just discernible. The fury of the beast, who no doubt bore still in mind the dreaded whip, was instantly converted into fear. Conscious of having deserved punishment, it seemed desirous of concealing its bloody deeds, and skipped about the chamber in an agony of nervous agitation; throwing down and breaking the furniture as it moved, and dragging the bed from the bedstead. In conclusion, it seized first the corpse of the daughter, and thrust it up the chimney, as it was found; then that of the old lady, which it immediately hurled through the window headlong.

As the ape approached the casement with its mutilated burden, the sailor shrank aghast to the rod, and rather gliding than clambering down it, hurried at once home—dreading the consequences of the butchery, and gladly abandoning, in his terror, all solicitude about the fate of the Ourang-Outang. The words heard by the party upon the staircase were the Frenchman's exclamations of horror and affright, commingled with the fiendish jabberings of the brute.

I have scarcely anything to add. The Ourang-Outang must have escaped from the chamber, by the rod, just before the breaking of the door. It must have closed the window as it passed through it. It was subsequently caught by the owner himself, who obtained for it a very large sum at the *Jardin des Plantes*. Le Bon was instantly released upon our narration of the circumstances (with some comments from Dupin) at the bureau of the Prefect of Police. This functionary, however, well disposed to my friend, could not altogether conceal his chagrin at the turn which affairs had taken, and was fain to indulge in a sarcasm or two, about the propriety of every person minding his own business.

"Let him talk," said Dupin, who had not thought it necessary to reply. "Let him discourse; it will ease his conscience. I am satisfied with having defeated him in his own castle. Nevertheless, that he failed in the solution of this mystery is by no means that matter for wonder which he supposes it; for in truth, our friend the Prefect is somewhat too cunning to be profound. In his wisdom is no *stamen*. It is all head and no body, like the pictures of the goddess Laverna—or, at best, all head and shoulders, like a codfish. But he is a good creature after all. I like him especially for one master-stroke of cant, by which he has attained his reputation for ingenuity. I mean the way he has '*de nier ce qui est, et d'expliquer ce qui n'est pas.*'"

The Adventure of the Norwood Builder

Arthur Conan Doyle

Arthur Conan Doyle (1859-1930) was born in Edinburgh, Scotland. He studied medicine at the University of Edinburgh from 1877-1881. In 1879, Doyle sold his first story, "The Mystery of Sassassa Valley." After receiving his M.D. certificate in 1885, he married Louise Hawkins. Upon his return from the Boer Wars, Doyle wrote his first novel—and the first Sherlock Holmes adventure—*A Study in Scarlet* (1887). After the success of his second Holmes novel, *The Sign of Four* (1890), Doyle abandoned his practice to become a writer. He became involved in politics, running for Parliament twice. He wrote two collections of Holmes stories, *Adventures of Sherlock Holmes* (1892) and *Memoirs of Sherlock Holmes* (1893). In 1897, he met Jean Leckie, whom he married after his first wife's death in 1907. Doyle attempted to write historical romances such as *Rodney Stone* (1896), but their lack of popularity prompted Doyle to revive Holmes in *The Hound The Baskervilles* in 1902. Three years later saw the release of *The Return of Sherlock Holmes*. Doyle continued to write non-Holmes novels such as *Sir Nigel* (1906), but only the Professor Challenger novels (*The Lost World*, 1912; *The Poison Belt*, 1913) met with success. In 1914, he revived Holmes with *The Valley of Fear* (1914), and attempted to kill him off in *His Last Bow* (1917). When his son died fighting in World War I, Doyle became obsessed with spiritualism. In 1926, he published both the last Professor Challenger book, *The Land of Mists,* and *the History of Spiritualism.* Doyle wrote a final Holmes collection, *The Casebook of Sherlock Holmes,* in 1927. Three years later, Doyle died of heart failure in Sussex.

"The Adventure of the Norwood Builder" is not as famous as such tales as "The Speckled Band," but is a clever tale of disappearance and deception that makes excellent use of the patented Holmes deductive skills.

"FROM THE POINT of view of the criminal expert," said Mr. Sherlock Holmes, "London has become a singularly uninteresting city since the death of the late lamented Professor Moriarty."

"I can hardly think that you would find many decent citizens to agree with you," I answered.

"Well, well, I must not be selfish," said he, with a smile, as he pushed back his chair from the breakfast-table. "The community is certainly the gainer, and no one the loser, save the poor out-of-work specialist, whose occupation has gone. With that man in the field, one's morning paper presented infinite possibilities. Often it was only the smallest trace, Watson, the faintest indication, and yet it was enough to tell me that the great malignant brain was there, as the gentlest tremors of the edges of the web remind one of the foul spider which lurks in the center. Petty thefts, wanton assaults, purposeless outrage—to the man who held the clue all could be worked into one connected whole. To the scientific student of the higher criminal world, no capital in Europe offered the advantages which London then possessed. But now—" He shrugged his shoulders in humorous deprecation of the state of things which he had himself done so much to produce.

At the time of which I speak, Holmes had been back for some months, and I at his request had sold my practice and returned to share the old quarters in Baker Street. A young doctor, named Verner, had purchased my small Kensington practice, and given with astonishingly little demur the highest price that I ventured to ask—an incident which only explained itself some years later, when I found that Verner was a distant relation of Holmes, and that it was my friend who had really found the money.

Our months of partnership had not been so uneventful as he had stated, for I find, on looking over my notes, that this period includes the case of the papers of ex-President Murillo, and also the shocking affair of the Dutch steamship *Friesland,* which so nearly cost us both our lives. His cold and proud nature was always averse, however, from anything in the shape of public applause, and he bound me in the most stringent terms to say no further word of himself, his methods, or his successes—a prohibition which, as I have explained, has only now been removed.

Mr. Sherlock Holmes was leaning back in his chair after his whimsical protest, and was unfolding his morning paper in a leisurely fashion, when our attention was arrested by a tremendous ring at the bell, followed immediately by a hollow drumming sound, as if someone were beating on the outer door with his fist. As it opened there came a tumultuous rush into the hall, rapid feet clattered up the stair, and an instant later a wild-eyed and frantic young man, pale, dishev-

elled, and palpitating, burst into the room. He looked from one to the
other of us, and under our gaze of inquiry he became conscious that
some apology was needed for this unceremonious entry.

"I'm sorry, Mr. Holmes," he cried. "You mustn't blame me. I am
nearly mad. Mr. Holmes, I am the unhappy John Hector McFarlane."

He made the announcement as if the name alone would explain both
his visit and its manner, but I could see, by my companion's unrespon-
sive face, that it meant no more to him than to me.

"Have a cigarette, Mr. McFarlane," said he, pushing his case across.
"I am sure that, with your symptoms, my friend Dr. Watson here
would prescribe a sedative. The weather has been so very warm these
last few days. Now, if you feel a little more composed, I should be glad
if you would sit down in that chair, and tell us very slowly and quietly
who you are, and what it is that you want. You mentioned your name,
as if I should recognize it, but I assure you that, beyond the obvious
facts that you are a bachelor, a solicitor, a Freemason, and an asth-
matic, I know nothing whatever about you."

Familiar as I was with my friend's methods, it was not difficult for
me to follow his deductions, and to observe the untidiness of attire, the
sheaf of legal papers, the watch-charm, and the breathing which had
prompted them. Our client, however, stared in amazement.

"Yes, I am all that, Mr. Holmes; and, in addition, I am the most
unfortunate man at this moment in London. For heaven's sake, don't
abandon me, Mr. Holmes! If they come to arrest me before I have
finished my story, make them give me time, so that I may tell you the
whole truth. I could go to jail happy if I knew that you were working
for me outside."

"Arrest you!" said Holmes. "This is really most grati—most interesting. On what charge do you expect to be arrested?"

"Upon the charge of murdering Mr. Jonas Oldacre, of Lower Norwood."

My companion's expressive face showed a sympathy which was not,
I am afraid, entirely unmixed with satisfaction.

"Dear me," said he, "it was only this moment at breakfast that I was
saying to my friend, Dr. Watson, that sensational cases had disappeared out of our papers."

Our visitor stretched forward a quivering hand and picked up the
Daily Telegraph, which still lay upon Holmes's knee.

"If you had looked at it, sir, you would have seen at a glance what
the errand is on which I have come to you this morning. I feel as if my
name and my misfortune must be in every man's mouth." He turned it

over to expose the central page. "Here it is, and with your permission I will read it to you. Listen to this, Mr. Holmes. The headlines are: 'Mysterious Affair at Lower Norwood. Disappearance of a Well Known Builder. Suspicion of Murder and Arson. A Clue to the Criminal.' That is the clue which they are already following, Mr. Holmes, and I know that it leads infallibly to me. I have been followed from London Bridge Station, and I am sure that they are only waiting for the warrant to arrest me. It will break my mother's heart—it will break her heart!" He wrung his hands in an agony of apprehension, and swayed backward and forward in his chair.

I looked with interest upon this man, who was accused of being the perpetrator of a crime of violence. He was flaxen-haired and handsome, in a washed-out negative fashion, with frightened blue eyes, and a clean-shaven face, with a weak, sensitive mouth. His age may have been about twenty-seven, his dress and bearing that of a gentleman. From the pocket of his light summer overcoat protruded the bundle of endorsed papers which proclaimed his profession.

"We must use what time we have," said Holmes. "Watson, would you have the kindness to take the paper and to read the paragraph in question?"

Underneath the vigorous headlines which our client had quoted, I read the following suggestive narrative:

"Late last night, or early this morning, an incident occurred at Lower Norwood which points, it is feared, to a serious crime. Mr. Jonas Oldacre is a well known resident of that suburb, where he has carried on his business as a builder for many years. Mr. Oldacre is a bachelor, fifty-two years of age, and lives in Deep Dene House, at the Sydenham end of the road of that name. He has had the reputation of being a man of eccentric habits, secretive and retiring. For some years he has practically withdrawn from the business, in which he is said to have massed considerable wealth. A small timber-yard still exists, however, at the back of the house, and last night, about twelve o'clock, an alarm was given that one of the stacks was on fire. The engines were soon upon the spot, but the dry wood burned with great fury, and it was impossible to arrest the conflagration until the stack had been entirely consumed. Up to this point the incident bore the appearance of an ordinary accident, but fresh indications seem to point to serious crime. Surprise was expressed at the absence of the master of the establishment from the scene of the fire, and an inquiry followed, which showed that he had disappeared from the house. An examination of his room revealed that the bed had not been slept in, that a safe which stood in it was open, that a number of important papers were scattered about the room, and finally, that there were signs of a murderous struggle, slight traces of blood being found within the room, and an oaken walking-stick, which also showed stains of blood upon the handle. It is known that Mr. Jonas Oldacre had received a late visitor in his bedroom upon that night, and the stick found has been identified as the property of this person, who is a young London solicitor named John Hector McFarlane, junior partner of Graham and McFarlane, of 426 Gresham Buildings, E. C. The police believe that they have evidence in their possession which supplies a very convincing motive for the crime, and altogether it cannot be doubted that sensational developments will follow.

"LATER.—It is rumored as we go to press that Mr. John Hector McFarlane has actually been arrested on the charge of the murder of Mr. Jonas Oldacre. It is at least certain that a warrant has been issued. There have been further and sinister developments in the investigation at Norwood. Besides the signs of a struggle in the room of the unfortunate builder it is now known that the French windows of his bedroom (which is on the ground floor) were found to be open, that there were marks as if some bulky object had been dragged across to the wood-pile, and, finally, it is asserted that charred remains have been found among the charcoal ashes of the fire. The police theory is that a most sensational crime has been committed, that the victim was clubbed to death in his own bedroom, his papers rifled, and his dead body dragged across to the wood-stack, which was then ignited so as to hide all traces of the crime. The conduct of the criminal investigation has been left in the experienced hands of Inspector Lestrade, of Scotland Yard, who is following up the clues with his accustomed energy and sagacity."

Sherlock Holmes listened with closed eyes and fingertips together to this remarkable account.

"The case has certainly some points of interest," said he, in his languid fashion. "May I ask, in the first place, Mr. McFarlane, how it is that you are still at liberty since there appears to be enough evidence to justify your arrest?"

"I live at Torrington Lodge, Blackheath, with my parents, Mr. Holmes, but last night, having to do business very late with Mr. Jonas Oldacre, I stayed at an hotel in Norwood, and came to my business from there. I knew nothing of this affair until I was in the train, when I read what you have just heard. I at once saw the horrible danger of my position, and I hurried to put the case into your hands. I have no doubt that I should have been arrested either at my city office or at my home. A man followed me from London Bridge Station, and I have no doubt—Great heaven! what is that?"

It was a clang of the bell, followed instantly by heavy steps upon the stair. A moment later, our old friend Lestrade appeared in the doorway. Over his shoulder I caught a glimpse of one or two uniformed police-men outside.

"Mr. John Hector McFarlane?" said Lestrade.

Our unfortunate client rose with a ghastly face.

"I arrest you for the wilful murder of Mr. Jonas Oldacre, of Lower Norwood."

McFarlane turned to us with a gesture of despair, and sank into his chair once more like one who is crushed.

"One moment, Lestrade," said Holmes. "Half an hour more or less can make no difference to you, and the gentleman was about to give us an account of this very interesting affair, which might aid us in clearing it up."

"I think there will be no difficulty in clearing it up," said Lestrade, grimly.

"None the less, with your permission, I should be much interested to hear his account."

"Well, Mr. Holmes, it is difficult for me to refuse you anything, for you have been of use to the force once or twice in the past, and we owe you a good turn at Scotland Yard," said Lestrade. "At the same time I must remain with my prisoner, and I am bound to warn him that anything he may say will appear in evidence against him."

"I wish nothing better," said our client. "All I ask is that you should hear and recognize the absolute truth."

Lestrade looked at his watch. "I'll give you half an hour," said he.

"I must explain first," said McFarlane, "that I knew nothing of Mr. Jonas Oldacre. His name was familiar to me, for many years ago my parents were acquainted with him, but they drifted apart. I was very much surprised, therefore, when yesterday, about three o'clock in the afternoon, he walked into my office in the city. But I was still more astonished when he told me the object of his visit. He had in his hand several sheets of a notebook, covered with scribbled writing—here they are—and he laid them on my table.

"'Here is my will,' said he. 'I want you, Mr. McFarlane, to cast it into proper legal shape. I will sit here while you do so.'

"I set myself to copy it, and you can imagine my astonishment when I found that, with some reservations, he had left all his property to me. He was a strange little ferret-like man, with white eyelashes, and when I looked up at him I found his keen gray eyes fixed upon me with an amused expression. I could hardly believe my own senses as I read the terms of the will; but he explained that he was a bachelor with hardly any living relation, that he had known my parents in his youth, and that he had always heard of me as a very deserving young man, and was assured that his money would be in worthy hands. Of course, I could only stammer out my thanks. The will was duly finished, signed, and witnessed by my clerk. This is it on the blue paper, and these slips, as I have explained, are the rough draft. Mr. Jonas Oldacre then informed me that there were a number of documents—building leases, title-deeds, mortgages, scrip, and so forth—which it was necessary that I should see and understand. He said that his mind would not be easy until the whole thing was settled, and he begged me to come out to his house at Norwood that night, bringing the will with me, and to arrange matters. 'Remember, my boy, not one word to your parents about the affair until everything is settled. We will keep it as a little surprise for them.' He was very insistent upon this point, and made me promise it faithfully.

"You can imagine, Mr. Holmes, that I was not in a humor to refuse him anything that he might ask. He was my benefactor, and all my desire was to carry out his wishes in every particular. I sent a telegram home, therefore, to say that I had important business on hand, and that it was impossible for me to say how late I might be. Mr. Oldacre had told me that he would like me to have supper with him at nine, as he might not be home before that hour. I had some difficulty in finding his house, however, and it was nearly half-past before I reached it. I found him—"

"One moment!" said Holmes. "Who opened the door?"

"A middle-aged woman, who was, I suppose, his housekeeper."

"And it was she, I presume, who mentioned your name?"

"Exactly," said McFarlane.

"Pray proceed."

McFarlane wiped his damp brow, and then continued his narrative:

"I was shown by this woman into a sitting-room, where a frugal supper was laid out. Afterwards, Mr. Jonas Oldacre led me into his bedroom, in which there stood a heavy safe. This he opened and took out a mass of documents, which we went over together. It was between eleven and twelve when we finished. He remarked that we must not disturb the housekeeper. He showed me out through his own French window, which had been open all this time."

"Was the blind down?" asked Holmes.

"I will not be sure, but I believe that it was only half down. Yes, I remember how he pulled it up in order to swing open the window. I could not find my stick, and he said, 'Never mind, my boy, I shall see a good deal of you now, I hope, and I will keep your stick until you come back to claim it.' I left him there, the safe open, and the papers made up in packets upon the table. It was so late that I could not get back to Blackheath, so I spent the night at the Anerley Arms, and I knew nothing more until I read of this horrible affair in the morning."

"Anything more that you would like to ask, Mr. Holmes?" said Lestrade, whose eyebrows had gone up once or twice during this remarkable explanation.

"Not until I have been to Blackheath."

"You mean to Norwood," said Lestrade.

"Oh, yes, no doubt that is what I must have meant," said Holmes, with his enigmatical smile. Lestrade had learned by more experiences than he would care to acknowledge that that razor-like brain could cut through that which was impenetrable to him. I saw him look curiously at my companion.

"I think I should like to have a word with you presently, Mr. Sherlock Holmes," said he. "Now, Mr. McFarlane, two of my constables are at the door, and there is a four-wheeler waiting." The wretched young man arose, and with a last beseeching glance at us walked from the room. The officers conducted him to the cab, but Lestrade remained.

Holmes had picked up the pages which formed the rough draft of the will, and was looking at them with the keenest interest upon his face.

"There are some points about that document, Lestrade, are there not?" said he pushing them over.

The official looked at them with a puzzled expression.

"I can read the first few lines, and these in the middle of the second page, and one or two at the end. Those are as clear as print," said he, "but the writing in between is very bad, and there are three places where I cannot read it at all."

"What do you make of that?" said Holmes.

"Well, what do *you* make of it?"

"That it was written in a train. The good writing represents stations, the bad writing movement, and the very bad writing passing over points. A scientific expert would pronounce at once that this was drawn up on a suburban line, since nowhere save in the immediate vicinity of a great city could there be so quick a succession of points. Granting that his whole journey was occupied in drawing up the will, then the train was an express, only stopping once between Norwood and London Bridge."

Lestrade began to laugh.

"You are too many for me when you begin to get on your theories, Mr. Holmes," said he. "How does this bear on the case?"

"Well, it corroborates the young man's story to the extent that the will was drawn up by Jonas Oldacre in his journey yesterday. It is curious—is it not?—that a man should draw up so important a document in so haphazard a fashion. It suggests that he did not think it was going to be of much practical importance. If a man drew up a will which he did not intend ever to be effective, he might do it so."

"Well, he drew up his own death warrant at the same time," said Lestrade.

"Oh, you think so?"

"Don't you?"

"Well, it is quite possible, but the case is not clear to me yet."

"Not clear? Well, if that isn't clear, what *could* be clear? Here is a young man who learns suddenly that, if a certain older man dies, he will succeed to a fortune. What does he do? He says nothing to anyone, but he arranges that he shall go out on some pretext to see his client that night. He waits until the only other person in the house is in bed, and then in the solitude of a man's room he murders him, burns his body in the wood-pile, and departs to a neighboring hotel. The bloodstains in the room and also on the stick are very slight. It is probable that he imagined his crime to be a bloodless one, and hoped that if the body were consumed it would hide all traces of the method of his death—traces which, for some reason, must have pointed to him. Is not all this obvious?"

"It strikes me, my good Lestrade, as being just a trifle too obvious," said Holmes. "You do not add imagination to your other great qualities, but if you could for one moment put yourself in the place of this young man, would you choose the very night after the will had been made to commit your crime? Would it not seem dangerous to you to make so very close a relation between the two incidents? Again, would you choose an occasion when you are known to be in the house, when a servant has let you in? And, finally, would you take the great pains to conceal the body, and yet leave your own stick as a sign that you were the criminal? Confess, Lestrade, that all this is very unlikely."

"As to the stick, Mr. Holmes, you know as well as I do that a criminal is often flurried, and does such things, which a cool man would avoid. He was very likely afraid to go back to the room. Give me another theory that would fit the facts."

"I could very easily give you half a dozen," said Holmes. "Here, for example, is a very possible and even probable one. I make you a free present of it. The older man is showing documents which are of evident value. A passing tramp sees them through the window, the blind of which is only half down. Exit the solicitor. Enter the tramp! He seizes a stick, which he observes there, kills Oldacre, and departs after burning the body."

"Why should the tramp burn the body?"

"For the matter of that, why should McFarlane?"

"To hide some evidence."

"Possibly the tramp wanted to hide that any murder at all had been committed."

"And why did the tramp take nothing?"

"Because they were papers that he could not negotiate."

Lestrade shook his head, though it seemed to me that his manner was less absolutely assured than before.

"Well, Mr. Sherlock Holmes, you may look for your tramp, and while you are finding him we will hold on to our man. The future will show which is right. Just notice this point, Mr. Holmes: that so far as we know, none of the papers were removed, and that the prisoner is the one man in the world who had no reason for removing them, since he was heir-at-law, and would come into them in any case."

My friend seemed struck by this remark.

"I don't mean to deny that the evidence is in some ways very strongly in favor of your theory," said he. "I only wish to point out that there are other theories possible. As you say, the future will decide. Good-morning! I dare say that in the course of the day I shall drop in at Norwood and see how you are getting on."

When the detective departed, my friend rose and made his preparations for the day's work with the alert air of a man who has a congenial task before him.

"My first movement, Watson," said he, as he bustled into his frockcoat, "must, as I said, be in the direction of Blackheath."

"And why not Norwood?"

"Because we have in this case one singular incident coming close to the heels of another singular incident. The police are making the mistake of concentrating their attention upon the second, because it happens to be the one which is actually criminal. But it is evident to me that the logical way to approach the case is to begin by trying to throw some light upon the first incident—the curious will, so suddenly made, and to so unexpected an heir. It may do something to simplify what followed. No, my dear fellow, I don't think you can help me. There is no prospect of danger, or I should not dream of stirring out without you. I trust that when I see you in the evening, I will be able to report that I have been able to do something for this unfortunate youngster, who has thrown himself upon my protection."

It was late when my friend returned, and I could see, by a glance at his haggard and anxious face, that the high hopes with which he had started had not been fulfilled. For an hour he droned away upon his violin, endeavoring to soothe his own ruffled spirits. At last he flung down the instrument, and plunged into a detailed account of his misadventures.

"It's all going wrong, Watson—all as wrong as it can go. I kept a bold face before Lestrade, but, upon my soul, I believe that for once the fellow is on the right track and we are on the wrong. All my instincts are one way, and all the facts are the other, and I much fear that British juries have not yet attained that pitch of intelligence when they will give the preference to my theories over Lestrade's facts."

"Did you go to Blackheath?"

"Yes, Watson, I went there, and I found very quickly that the late lamented Oldacre was a pretty considerable blackguard. The father was away in search of his son. The mother was at home—a little, fluffy, blue-eyed person, in a tremor of fear and indignation. Of course, she would not admit even the possibility of his guilt. But she would not express either surprise or regret over the fate of Oldacre. On the contrary, she spoke of him with such bitterness that she was unconsciously considerably strengthening the case of the police for, of course, if her son had heard her speak of the man in this fashion, it would predispose him towards hatred and violence. 'He was more like a malignant and cunning ape than a human being,' said she, 'and he always was, ever since he was a young man.'

"'You knew him at that time?' said I.

"'Yes, I knew him well, in fact, he was an old suitor of mine. Thank heaven that I had the sense to turn away from him and to marry a better, if poorer, man. I was engaged to him, Mr. Holmes, when I heard a shocking story of how he had turned a cat loose in an aviary, and I was so horrified at his brutal cruelty that I would have nothing more to do with him.' She rummaged in a bureau, and presently she produced a photograph of a woman shamefully defaced and mutilated with a knife. 'That is my own photograph,' she said. 'He sent it to me in that state, with his curse, upon my wedding morning.'

"'Well,' said I, 'at least he has forgiven you now, since he has left all his property to your son.'

"'Neither my son nor I want anything from Jonas Oldacre, dead or alive!' she cried, with a proper spirit. 'There is a God in heaven, Mr. Holmes, and that same God who has punished that wicked man will show, in His own good time, that my son's hands are guiltless of his blood.'

"Well, I tried one or two leads, but could get at nothing which would help our hypothesis, and several points which would make against it. I gave it up at last, and off I went to Norwood.

"This place, Deep Dene House, is a big modern villa of staring brick, standing back in its own grounds, with a laurel-clumped lawn in front of it. To the right and some distance back from the road was the timber-yard which had been the scene of the fire. Here's a rough plan on a leaf of my notebook. This window on the left is the one which opens into Oldacre's room. You can look into it from the road, you see. That is about the only bit of consolation I have had to-day. Lestrade was not there, but his head constable did the honors. They had just found a great treasure-trove. They had spent the morning raking among the ashes of the burned wood-pile, and besides the charred organic remains they had secured several discolored metal discs. I examined them with care, and there was no doubt that they were trouser buttons. I even distinguished that one of them was marked with the name of 'Hyams,' who was Oldacre's tailor. I then worked the lawn very carefully for signs and traces, but this drought has made everything as hard as iron. Nothing was to be seen save that some body or bundle had been dragged through a low privet hedge which is in a line with the wood-pile. All that, of course, fits in with the offficial theory. I crawled about the lawn with an August sun on my back, but I got up at the end of an hour no wiser than before.

"Well, after this fiasco I went into the bedroom and examined that also. The blood-stains were very slight, mere smears and discolorations, but undoubtedly fresh. The stick had been removed, but there also the marks were slight. There is no doubt about the stick belonging to our client. He admits it. Footmarks of both men could be made out on the carpet, but none of any third person, which again is a trick for the other side. They were piling up their score all the time and we were at a standstill.

"Only one little gleam of hope did I get—and yet it amounted to nothing. I examined the contents of the safe, most of which had been taken out and left on the table. The papers had been made up into sealed envelopes, one or two of which had been opened by the police. They were not, so far as I could judge, of any great value, nor did the bank-book show that Mr. Oldacre was in such very affluent circumstances. But it seemed to me that all the papers were not there. There were allusions to some deeds—possibly the more valuable—which I could not find. This, of course, if we could definitely prove it, would turn Lestrade's argument against himself; for who would steal a thing if he knew that he would shortly inherit it?

"Finally, having drawn every other cover and picked up no scent, I tried my luck with the housekeeper. Mrs. Lexington is her name—a little, dark silent person, with suspicious and sidelong eyes. She could tell us something if she would—I am convinced of it. But she was as close as wax. Yes, she had let Mr. McFarlane in at half-past nine. She wished her hand had withered before she had done so. She had gone to bed at half-past ten. Her room was at the other end of the house and she could hear nothing of what passed. Mr. McFarlane had left his hat, and to the best of her belief his stick, in the hall. She had been awakened by the alarm of fire. Her poor, dear master had certainly been murdered. Had he any enemies? Well, every man had enemies, but Mr. Oldacre kept himself very much to himself, and only met people in the way of business. She had seen the buttons, and was sure that they belonged to the clothes which he had worn last night. The wood-pile was very dry, for it had not rained for a month. It burned like tinder, and by the time she reached the spot, nothing could be seen but flames. She and all the firemen smelled the burned flesh from inside it. She knew nothing of the papers, nor of Mr. Oldacre's private affairs.

"So, my dear Watson, there's my report of a failure. And yet—and yet—" he clenched his thin hands in a paroxysm of conviction—"I *know* it's all wrong. I feel it in my bones. There is something that has not come out, and that housekeeper knows it. There was a sort of sulky defiance in her eyes, which only goes with guilty knowledge. However, there's no good talking any more about it, Watson; but unless some lucky chance comes our way I fear that the Norwood Disappearance Case will not figure in that chronicle of our successes which I foresee that a patient public will sooner or later have to endure."

"Surely," said I, "the man's appearance would go far with any jury?"

"That is a dangerous argument, my dear Watson. You remember that terrible murderer, Bert Stevens, who wanted us to get him off in '87? Was there ever a more mild-mannered, Sunday-school young man?"

"It is true."

"Unless we succeed in establishing an alternative theory, this man is lost. You can hardly find a flaw in the case which can now be presented against him, and all further investigation has served to strengthen it. By the way, there is one curious little point about those papers which may serve us as the starting-point for an inquiry. On looking over the bank-book I found that the low state of the balance was principally due to large checks which have been made out during the last year to Mr. Cornelius. I confess that I should be interested to know who this Mr. Cornelius may be with whom a retired builder has had such very large transactions. Is it possible that he has had a hand in the affair? Cornelius might be a broker, but we have found no scrip to correspond with these large payments. Failing any other indication, my researches must now take the direction of an inquiry at the bank for the gentleman who has cashed these checks. But I fear, my dear fellow, that our case will end ingloriously by Lestrade hanging our client, which will certainly be a triumph for Scotland Yard."

I do not know how far Sherlock Holmes took any sleep that night, but when I came down to breakfast I found him pale and harassed, his bright eyes the brighter for the dark shadows round them. The carpet round his chair was littered with cigarette-ends and with the early editions of the morning papers. An open telegram lay upon the table.

"What do you think of this, Watson?" he asked, tossing it across.

It was from Norwood, and ran as follows:

Important fresh evidence to hand. McFarlane's guilt definitely established. Advise you to abandon case.

LESTRADE.

"This sounds serious," said I.

"It is Lestrade's little cock-a-doodle of victory," Holmes answered, with a bitter smile. "And yet it may be premature to abandon the case. After all, important fresh evidence is a two-edged thing, and may possibly cut in a very different direction to that which Lestrade imagines. Take your breakfast Watson, and we will go out together and see what we can do. I feel as if I shall need your company and your moral support to-day."

My friend had no breakfast himself, for it was one of his peculiarities that in his more intense moments he would permit himself no food, and I have known him presume upon his iron strength until he has fainted from pure inanition. "At present I cannot spare energy and nerve force for digestion," he would say in answer to my medical remonstrances. I was not surprised, therefore, when this morning he left his untouched meal behind him, and started with me for Norwood. A crowd of morbid sightseers were still gathered round Deep Dene House, which was just such a suburban villa as I had pictured. Within the gates Lestrade met us, his face flushed with victory, his manner grossly triumphant.

"Well, Mr. Holmes, have you proved us to be wrong yet? Have you found your tramp?" he cried.

"I have formed no conclusion whatever," my companion answered.

"But we formed ours yesterday, and now it proves to be correct, so you must acknowledge that we have been a little in front of you this time, Mr. Holmes."

"You certainly have the air of something unusual having occurred," said Holmes.

Lestrade laughed loudly.

"You don't like being beaten any more than the rest of us do," said he. "A man can't expect always to have it his own way, can he, Dr. Watson? Step this way, if you please, gentlemen, and I think I can convince you once for all that it was John McFarlane who did this crime."

He led us through the passage and out into a dark hall beyond.

"This is where young McFarlane must have come out to get his hat after the crime was done," said he. "Now look at this." With dramatic suddenness he struck a match, and by its light exposed a stain of blood upon the whitewashed wall. As he held the match nearer, I saw that it was more than a stain. It was the well-marked print of a thumb.

"Look at that with your magnifying glass, Mr. Holmes."

"Yes, I am doing so."

"You are aware that no two thumb-marks are alike?"

"I have heard something of the kind."

"Well, then, will you please compare that print with this wax impression of young McFarlane's right thumb, taken by my orders this morning?"

As he held the waxen print close to the blood-stain, it did not take a magnifying glass to see that the two were undoubtedly from the same thumb. It was evident to me that our unfortunate client was lost.

"That is final," said Lestrade.

"Yes, that is final," I involuntarily echoed.

"It is final," said Holmes.

Something in his tone caught my ear, and I turned to look at him. An extraordinary change had come over his face. It was writhing with inward merriment. His two eyes were shining like stars. It seemed to me that he was making desperate efforts to restrain a convulsive attack of laughter.

"Dear me! Dear me!" he said at last. "Well, now, who would have thought it? And how deceptive appearances may be, to be sure! Such a nice young man to look at! It is a lesson to us not to trust our own judgment, is it not, Lestrade?"

"Yes, some of us are a little too much inclined to be cock-sure, Mr. Holmes," said Lestrade. The man's insolence was maddening, but we could not resent it.

"What a providential thing that this young man should press his right thumb against the wall in taking his hat from the peg! Such a very natural action, too, if you come to think if it." Holmes was outwardly calm, but his whole body gave a wriggle of suppressed excitement as he spoke.

"By the way, Lestrade, who made this remarkable discovery?"

"It was the housekeeper, Mrs. Lexington, who drew the night constable's attention to it."

"Where was the night constable?"

"He remained on guard in the bedroom where the crime was committed, so as to see that nothing was touched."

"But why didn't the police see this mark yesterday?"

"Well, we had no particular reason to make a careful examination of the hall. Besides, it's not in a very prominent place, as you see."

"No, no—of course not. I suppose there is no doubt that the mark was there yesterday?"

Lestrade looked at Holmes as if he thought he was going out of his mind. I confess that I was myself surprised both at his hilarious manner and at his rather wild observation.

"I don't know whether you think that McFarlane came out of jail in the dead of the night in order to strengthen the evidence against himself," said Lestrade. "I leave it to any expert in the world whether that is not the mark of his thumb."

"It is unquestionably the mark of his thumb."

"There, that's enough," said Lestrade. "I am a practical man, Mr. Holmes, and when I have got my evidence I come to my conclusions. If you have anything to say, you will find me writing my report in the sitting-room."

Holmes had recovered his equanimity, though I still seemed to detect gleams of amusement in his expression.

"Dear me, this is a very sad development, Watson, is it not?" said he. "And yet there are singular points about it which hold out some hopes for our client."

"I am delighted to hear it," said I, heartily. "I was afraid it was all up with him."

"I would hardly go so far as to say that, my dear Watson. The fact is that there is one really serious flaw in this evidence to which our friend attaches so much importance."

"Indeed, Holmes! What is it?"

"Only this: that I *know* that that mark was not there when I examined the hall yesterday. And now, Watson, let us have a little stroll round in the sunshine."

With a confused brain, but with a heart into which some warmth of hope was returning, I accompanied my friend in a walk round the garden. Holmes took each face of the house in turn, and examined it with great interest. He then led the way inside, and went over the whole building from basement to attic. Most of the rooms were unfurnished, but none the less Holmes inspected them all minutely. Finally, on the top corridor, which ran outside three untenanted bedrooms, he again was seized with a spasm of merriment.

"There are really some very unique features about this case, Watson," said he. "I think it is time now that we took our friend Lestrade into our confidence. He has had his little smile at our expense, and perhaps we may do as much by him, if my reading of this problem proves to be correct. Yes, yes, I think I see how we should approach it."

The Scotland Yard inspector was still writing in the parlor when Holmes interrupted him.

"I understood that you were writing a report of this case," said he.

"So I am."

"Don't you think it may be a little premature? I can't help thinking that your evidence is not complete."

Lestrade knew my friend too well to disregard his words. He laid down his pen and looked curiously at him.

"What do you mean, Mr. Holmes?"

"Only that there is an important witness whom you have not seen."

"Can you produce him?"

"I think I can."

"Then do so."

"I will do my best. How many constables have you?"

"There are three within call."

"Excellent!" said Holmes. "May I ask if they are all large, able-bodied men with powerful voices?"

"I have no doubt they are, though I fail to see what their voices have to do with it."

"Perhaps I can help you to see that and one or two other things as well," said Holmes. "Kindly summon your men, and I will try."

Five minutes later, three policemen had assembled in the hall.

"In the outhouse you will find a considerable quantity of straw," said Holmes. "I will ask you to carry in two bundles of it. I think it will be of the greatest assistance in producing the witness whom I require. Thank you very much. I believe you have some matches in your pocket, Watson. Now, Mr. Lestrade, I will ask you all to accompany me to the top landing."

As I have said, there was a broad corridor there, which ran outside three empty bedrooms. At one end of the corridor we were all marshalled by Sherlock Holmes the constables grinning and Lestrade staring at my friend with amazement, expectation, and derision chasing each other across his features. Holmes stood before us with the air of a conjurer who is performing a trick.

"Would you kindly send one of your constables for two buckets of water? Put the straw on the floor here, free from the wall on either side. Now I think that we are all ready."

Lestrade's face had begun to grow red and angry.

"I don't know whether you are playing a game with us, Mr. Sherlock Holmes," said he. "If you know anything, you can surely say it without all this tomfoolery."

"I assure you, my good Lestrade, that I have an excellent reason for everything that I do. You may possibly remember that you chaffed me a little, some hours ago, when the sun seemed on your side of the hedge, so you must not grudge me a little pomp and ceremony now. Might I ask you, Watson, to open that window, and then to put a match to the edge of the straw?"

I did so, and driven by the draught, a coil of gray smoke swirled down the corridor, while the dry straw crackled and flamed.

"Now we must see if we can find this witness for you, Lestrade. Might I ask you all to join in the cry of 'Fire!'? Now then; one, two, three——"

"Fire!" we all yelled.

"Thank you. I will trouble you once again."

"Fire!"

"Just once more, gentlemen, and all together."

"Fire!" The shout must have rung over Norwood.

It had hardly died away when an amazing thing happened. A door suddenly flew open out of what appeared to be solid wall at the end of the corridor, and a little, wizened man darted out of it, like a rabbit out of its burrow.

"Capital!" said Holmes, calmly. "Watson, a bucket of water over the straw. That will do! Lestrade, allow me to present you with your principal missing witness, Mr. Jonas Oldacre."

The detective stared at the newcomer with blank amazement. The latter was blinking in the bright light of the corridor, and peering at us and at the smouldering fire. It was an odious face—crafty, vicious, malignant, with shifty, light-gray eyes and white lashes.

"What's this, then?" said Lestrade, at last. "What have you been doing all this time, eh?"

Oldacre gave an uneasy laugh, shrinking back from the furious red face of the angry detective.

"I have done no harm."

"No harm? You have done your best to get an innocent man hanged. If it wasn't for this gentleman here, I am not sure that you would not have succeeded."

The wretched creature began to whimper.

"I am sure, sir, it was only my practical joke."

"Oh! a joke, was it? You won't find the laugh on your side, I promise you. Take him down, and keep him in the sitting-room until I come. Mr. Holmes," he continued, when they had gone, "I could not speak before the constables, but I don't mind saying, in the presence of Dr. Watson, that this is the brightest thing that you have done yet, though it is a mystery to me how you did it. You have saved an innocent man's life, and you have prevented a very grave scandal, which would have ruined my reputation in the Force."

Holmes smiled, and clapped Lestrade upon the shoulder.

"Instead of being ruined, my good sir, you will find that your reputation has been enormously enhanced. Just make a few alterations in that report which you were writing, and they will understand how hard it is to throw dust in the eyes of Inspector Lestrade."

"And you don't want your name to appear?"

"Not at all. The work is its own reward. Perhaps I shall get the credit also at some distant day, when I permit my zealous historian to lay out his foolscap once more—eh, Watson? Well, now, let us see where this rat has been lurking."

A lath-and-plaster partition had been run across the passage six feet from the end, with a door cunningly concealed in it. It was lit within by slits under the eaves. A few articles of furniture and a supply of food and water were within, together with a number of books and papers.

"There's the advantage of being a builder," said Holmes, as we came out. "He was able to fix up his own little hiding-place without any confederate—save, of course, that precious housekeeper of his, whom I should lose no time in adding to your bag, Lestrade."

"I'll take your advice. But how did you know of this place, Mr. Holmes?"

"I made up my mind that the fellow was in hiding in the house. When I paced one corridor and found it six feet shorter than the corresponding one below, it was pretty clear where he was. I thought he had not the nerve to lie quiet before an alarm of fire. We could, of course, have gone in and taken him, but it amused me to make him reveal himself. Besides, I owed you a little mystification, Lestrade, for your chaff in the morning."

"Well, sir, you certainly got equal with me on that. But how in the world did you know that he was in the house at all?"

"The thumb-mark, Lestrade. You said it was final and so it was, in a very different sense. I knew it had not been there the day before. I pay a good deal of attention to matters of detail, as you may have observed, and I had examined the hall, and was sure that the wall was clear. Therefore, it had been put on during the night."

"But how?"

"Very simply. When those packets were sealed up, Jonas Oldacre got McFarlane to secure one of the seals by putting his thumb upon the soft wax. It would be done so quickly and so naturally, that I daresay the young man himself has no recollection of it. Very likely it just so happened, and Oldacre had himself no notion of the use he would put it to. Brooding over the case in that den of his, it suddenly struck him what absolutely damning evidence he could make against McFarlane by using that thumb-mark. It was the simplest thing in the world for him to take a wax impression from the seal, to moisten it in as much blood as he could get from a pin-prick, and to put the mark upon the wall during the night, either with his own hand or with that of his housekeeper. If you examine among those documents which he took with him into his retreat, I will lay you a wager that you find the seal with the thumb-mark upon it."

"Wonderful!" said Lestrade. "Wonderful! It's all as clear as crystal, as you put it. But what is the object of this deep deception, Mr. Holmes?"

It was amusing to me to see how the detective's overbearing manner had changed suddenly to that of a child asking questions of its teacher.

"Well, I don't think that is very hard to explain. A very deep, malicious, vindictive person is the gentleman who is now waiting us downstairs. You know that he was once refused by McFarlane's mother? You don't! I told you that you should go to Blackheath first and Norwood afterwards. Well, this injury, as he would consider it, has rankled in his wicked, scheming brain, and all his life he has longed for vengeance, but never seen his chance. During the last year or two, things have gone against him—secret speculation, I think—and he finds himself in a bad way. He determines to swindle his creditors, and for this purpose he pays large checks to a certain Mr. Cornelius, who is, I imagine, himself under another name. I have not traced these checks yet, but I have no doubt that they were banked under that name at some provincial town where Oldacre from time to time led a double existence. He intended to change his name altogether, draw this money, and vanish, starting life again elsewhere."

"Well, that's likely enough."

"It would strike him that in disappearing he might throw all pursuit off his track, and at the same time have an ample and crushing revenge upon his old sweetheart, if he could give the impression that he had been murdered by her only child. It was a masterpiece of villainy and he carried it out like a master. The idea of the will, which would give an obvious motive for the crime, the secret visit unknown to his own parents, the retention of the stick, the blood, and the animal remains and buttons in the wood-pile, all were admirable. It was a net from which it seemed to me, a few hours ago, that there was no possible escape. But he had not that supreme gift of the artist, the knowledge of when to stop. He wished to improve that which was already perfect—to draw the rope tighter yet round the neck of his unfortunate victim—and so he ruined all. Let us descend, Lestrade. There are just one or two questions that I would ask him."

The malignant creature was seated in his own parlor, with a policeman upon each side of him.

"It was a joke, my good sir—a practical joke, nothing more," he whined incessantly. "I assure you, sir, that I simply concealed myself in order to see the effect of my disappearance, and I am sure that you would not be so unjust as to imagine that I would have allowed any harm to befall poor young Mr. McFarlane."

"That's for a jury to decide," said Lestrade. "Anyhow, we shall have you on a charge of conspiracy, if not for attempted murder."

"And you'll probably find that your creditors will impound the banking account of Mr. Cornelius," said Holmes.

The little man started, and turned his malignant eyes upon my friend.

"I have to thank you for a good deal," said he. "Perhaps I'll pay my debt some day."

Holmes smiled indulgently.

"I fancy that, for some few years, you will find your time very fully occupied, said he. "By the way, what was it you put into the wood-pile besides your old trousers? A dead dog, or rabbits, or what? You won't tell? Dear me, how very unkind of you! Well, well, I daresay that a couple of rabbits would account both for the blood and for the charred ashes. If ever you write an account, Watson, you can make rabbits serve your turn."

The Dublin Mystery

Baroness Orczy

Baroness Emmuska Orczy (1865-1947) was born in Tarna-Örs,
Hungary. Her father, the composer Felix Orczy, had to flee to Budapest
because of a peasant uprising. The Orczy family ended up moving constantly, finally settling in London. Orczy was originally trained in music
until family friend Franz Liszt suggested her talent lay elsewhere. She
attended the Heatherly School of the Arts, where she met her husband,
Montagu Barstow. In 1895, Orczy and her husband translated a number
of Hungarian fairy tales for English publication. Orczy began submitting
stories at the turn of the century, and was originally published in *Pear-
son's*. A series of stories featuring the Old Man in the Corner ran in *Royal
Magazine* in 1901-05. While popular enough to spawn two novels (*The
Case of Miss Elliot*, 1905; *Unravelled Knots*, 1925), her greatest success
came with the release of *The Scarlet Pimpernel* in 1905. Orczy continued
to live in London, producing works such as *A Son of the People* (1906),
The Elusive Pimpernel (1908), *The Nest of the Sparrowhawk* (1909), *Lady
Molly of Scotland Yard* (1910), and *Eldorado* (1913), before moving to
Monte Carlo with the onset of World War I. She lived there until the death
of her husband in 1943. Moving back to London, her literary output
decreased until her death four years later. Other works of note include *The
Laughing Cavalier* (1914), *Leatherface* (1916), *Lord Tony's Wife* (1917),
The First Sir Percy (1920), *Pimpernel and Rosemary* (1924), *A Joyous
Adventure* (1932), *The Way of the Scarlet Pimpernel* (1933), *Sir Percy
Leads the Band* (1936), *The Divine Folly* (1937), *Mam'zelle Guillotine*
(1940), *Pride of Race* (1942), and her autobiography, *The Chains in the
Links of Life* (1947).

"The Dublin Mystery," with its forged will and double murder, is
typical of the Baroness' fast-paced, inventive style.

"I ALWAYS THOUGHT that the history of that forged will was
about as interesting as any I had read," said the man in the corner that
day. He had been silent for some time and was meditatively sorting and
looking through a packet of small photographs in his pocket-book.

174

Polly guessed that some of these would presently be placed before her for inspection—and she had not long to wait.

"That is old Brooks," he said, pointing to one of the photographs, "Millionaire Brooks, as he was called, and these are his two sons, Percival and Murray. It was a curious case, wasn't it? Personally I don't wonder that the police were completely at sea. If a member of that highly estimable force happened to be as clever as the clever author of that forged will, we should have very few undetected crimes in this country."

"That is why I always try to persuade you to give our poor ignorant police the benefit of your great insight and wisdom," said Polly, with a smile.

"I know," he said blandly, "you have been most kind in that way, but I am only an amateur. Crime interests me only when it resembles a clever game of chess, with many intricate moves which all tend to one solution, the checkmating of the antagonist—the detective forces of the country. Now, confess that, in the Dublin mystery, the clever police there were absolutely checkmated."

"Absolutely."

"Just as the public was. There were actually two crimes committed in one city which have completely baffled detection: the murder of Patrick Wethered the lawyer, and the forged will of Millionaire Brooks. There are not many millionaires in Ireland; no wonder old Brooks was a notability in his way, since his business—bacon curing, I believe it was—is said to be worth over £2,000,000 of solid money.

"His younger son, Murray, was a refined, highly educated man, and was, moreover, the apple of his father's eye, as he was the spoilt darling of Dublin society; good-looking, a splendid dancer, and a perfect rider, he was the acknowledged 'catch' of the matrimonial market of Ireland, and many a very aristocratic house was opened hospitably to the favorite son of the millionaire.

"Of course, Percival Brooks, the eldest son, would inherit the bulk of the old man's property and also probably the larger share in the business; he, too, was good-looking, more so than his brother; he, too, rode, danced, and talked well, but it was many years ago that mammas with marriageable daughters had given up all hopes of Percival Brooks as a probable son-in-law. That young man's infatuation for Maisie Fortescue, a lady of undoubted charm but very doubtful antecedents, who had astonished the London and Dublin music-halls with her extravagant dances, was too well known and too old-established to encourage any hopes in other quarters.

"Whether Percival Brooks would ever marry Maisie Fortescue was thought to be very doubtful. Old Brooks had the full disposal of all his wealth, and it would have fared ill with Percival if he introduced an undesirable wife into the magnificent Fitzwilliam Place establishment.

"That is how matters stood," continued the man in the corner, "when Dublin society one morning learnt, with deep regret and dismay, that old Brooks had died very suddenly at his residence after only a few hours' illness. At first it was generally understood that he had had an apoplectic stroke; anyway, he had been at business hale and hearty as ever the day before his death, which occurred late on the evening of February 1st.

"It was the morning papers of February 2nd which told the sad news to their readers, and it was those selfsame papers which on that eventful morning contained another even more startling piece of news, that proved the prelude to a series of sensations such as tranquil, placid Dublin had not experienced for many years. This was, that on that very afternoon which saw the death of Dublin's greatest millionaire, Mr. Patrick Wethered, his solicitor, was murdered in Phoenix Park at five o'clock in the afternoon while actually walking to his own house from his visit to his client in Fitzwilliam Place.

"Patrick Wethered was as well known as the proverbial town pump; his mysterious and tragic death filled all Dublin with dismay. The lawyer, who was a man sixty years of age, had been struck on the back of the head by a heavy stick, garrotted, and subsequently robbed, for neither money, watch, or pocket-book were found upon his person, whilst the police soon gathered from Patrick Wethered's household that he had left home at two o'clock that afternoon, carrying both watch and pocket-book, and undoubtedly money as well.

"An inquest was held, and a verdict of willful murder was found against some person or persons unknown.

"But Dublin had not exhausted its stock of sensations yet. Millionaire Brooks had been buried with due pomp and magnificence, and his will had been proved (his business and personalty being estimated at £2,500,000) by Percival Gordon Brooks, his eldest son and sole executor. The younger son, Murray, who had devoted the best years of his life to being a friend and companion to his father, while Percival ran after ballet-dancers and music-hall stars—Murray, who had avowedly been the apple of his father's eye in consequence —was left with a miserly pittance of £300 a year, and no share whatever in the gigantic business of Brooks & Sons, bacon curers, of Dublin.

"Something had evidently happened within the precincts of the Brooks' town mansion, which the public and Dublin society tried in vain to fathom. Elderly mammas and blushing *débutantes* were already thinking of the best means whereby next season they might more easily show the cold shoulder to young Murray Brooks, who had so suddenly become a hopeless 'detrimental' in the marriage market, when all these sensations terminated in one gigantic, overwhelming bit of scandal, which for the next three months furnished food for gossip in every drawing-room in Dublin.

"Mr. Murray Brooks, namely, had entered a claim for probate of a will, made by his father in 1891, declaring that the later will, made the very day of his father's death and proved by his brother as sole executor, was null and void, that will being a forgery.

"The facts that transpired in connection with this extraordinary case were sufficiently mysterious to puzzle everybody. As I told you before, all Mr. Brooks' friends never quite grasped the idea that the old man should so completely have cut off his favorite son with the proverbial shilling.

"You see, Percival had always been a thorn in the old man's flesh. Horse-racing, gambling, theaters, and music-halls were, in the old pork-butcher's eyes, so many deadly sins which his son committed every day of his life, and all the Fitzwilliam Place household could testify to the many and bitter quarrels which had arisen between father and son over the latter's gambling or racing debts. Many people asserted that Brooks would sooner have left his money to charitable institutions than seen it squandered upon the brightest stars that adorned the music-hall stage.

"The case came up for hearing early in the autumn. In the meanwhile Percival Brooks had given up his race-course associates, settled down in the Fitzwilliam Place mansion, and conducted his father's business, without a manager, but with all the energy and forethought which he had previously devoted to more unworthy causes.

"Murray had elected not to stay on in the old house; no doubt associations were of too painful and recent a nature; he was boarding with the family of a Mr. Wilson Hibbert, who was the late Patrick Wethered's, the murdered lawyer's, partner. They were quiet, homely people, who lived in a very pokey little house in Kilkenny Street, and poor Murray must, in spite of his grief, have felt very bitterly the change from his luxurious quarters in his father's mansion to his present tiny room and homely meals.

"Percival Brooks, who was now drawing an income of over a hundred thousand a year, was very severely criticized for adhering so strictly to the letter of his father's will, and only paying his brother that paltry £300 a year, which was very literally but the crumbs off his own magnificent dinner table.

"The issue of that contested will case was therefore awaited with eager interest. In the meanwhile the police, who had at first seemed fairly loquacious on the subject of the murder of Mr. Patrick Wethered, suddenly became strangely reticent, and by their very reticence aroused a certain amount of uneasiness in the public mind, until one day the *Irish Times* published the following extraordinary, enigmatic paragraph:

> "'We hear on authority which cannot be questioned, that certain extraordinary developments are expected in connection with the brutal murder of our distinguished townsman Mr. Wethered; the police, in fact, are vainly trying to keep it secret that they hold a clew which is as important as it is sensational and that they only await the impending issue of a well-known litigation in the probate court to effect an arrest.'

"The Dublin public flocked to the court to hear the arguments in the great will case. I myself journeyed down to Dublin. As soon as I succeeded in fighting my way to the densely crowded court, I took stock of the various actors in the drama, which I as a spectator was prepared to enjoy. There were Percival Brooks and Murray his brother, the two litigants, both good-looking and well-dressed, and both striving, by keeping up a running conversation with their lawyers, to appear unconcerned and confident of the issue. With Percival Brooks was Henry Oranmore, the eminent Irish K.C., whilst Walter Hibbert, a rising young barrister, the son of Wilson Hibbert, appeared for Murray.

"The will of which the latter claimed probate was one dated 1891, and had been made by Mr. Brooks during a severe illness which threatened to end his days. This will had been deposited in the hands of Messrs. Wethered and Hibbert, solicitors to the deceased, and by it Mr. Brooks left his personalty equally divided between his two sons, but had left his business entirely to his youngest son, with a charge of £2000 a year upon it, payable to Percival. You see that Murray Brooks therefore had a very deep interest in that second will being found null and void.

"Old Mr. Hibbert had very ably instructed his son, and Walter Hibbert's opening speech was exceedingly clever. He would show, he said, on behalf of his client, that the will dated February 1st, 1908, could never have been made by the late Mr. Brooks, as it was absolutely contrary to his avowed intentions, and that if the late Mr. Brooks did on the day in question make any fresh will at all, it certainly was *not* the one proved by Mr. Percival Brooks, for that was absolutely a forgery from beginning to end. Mr. Walter Hibbert proposed to call several witnesses in support of both these points.

"On the other hand, Mr. Henry Oranmore, K.C., very ably and courteously replied that he too had several witnesses to prove that Mr. Brooks certainly did make a will on the day in question, and that, whatever his intentions may have been in the past, he must have modified them on the day of his death, for the will proved by Mr. Percival Brooks was found after his death under his pillow, duly signed and witnessed and in every way legal.

"Then the battle began in sober earnest. There were a great many witnesses to be called on both sides, their evidence being of more or less importance—chiefly less. But the interest centered round the prosaic figure of John O'Neill, the butler of Fitzwilliam Place, who had been in Mr. Brooks' family for thirty years.

"'I was clearing away my breakfast things,' said John, 'when I heard the master's voice in the study close by. Oh, my, he was that angry! I could hear the words "disgrace," and "villain," and "liar" and "ballet-dancer," and one or two other ugly words as applied to some female lady, which I would not like to repeat. At first I did not take much notice, as I was quite used to hearing my poor dear master having words with Mr. Percival. So I went downstairs carrying my breakfast things; but I had just started cleaning my silver when the study bell goes ringing violently, and I hear Mr. Percival's voice shouting in the hall: "John! quick! Send for Dr. Mulligan at once. Your master is not well! Send one of the men, and you come up and help me to get Mr. Brooks to bed."

"'I sent one of the grooms for the doctor,' continued John, who seemed still affected at the recollection of his poor master, to whom he had evidently been very much attached, 'and I went up to see Mr. Brooks. I found him lying on the study floor, his head supported in Mr. Percival's arms. "My father has fallen in a faint," said the young master; "help me to get him up to his room before Dr. Mulligan comes."

"'Mr. Percival looked very white and upset, which was only natural; and when we had got my poor master to bed, I asked if I should not go and break the news to Mr. Murray, who had gone to business an hour ago. However, before Mr. Percival had time to give me an order the doctor came. I thought I had seen death plainly writ in my master's face, and when I showed the doctor out an hour later, and he told me that he would be back directly, I knew that the end was near.

"'Mr. Brooks rang for me a minute or two later. He told me to send at once for Mr. Wethered, or else for Mr. Hibbert, if Mr. Wethered could not come. "I haven't many hours to live, John," he says to me—"my heart is broke, the doctor says my heart is broke. A man shouldn't marry and have children, John, for they will sooner or later break his heart." I was so upset I couldn't speak; but I sent round at once for Mr. Wethered, who came himself just about three o'clock that afternoon.

"'After he had been with my master about an hour I was called in, and Mr. Wethered said to me that Mr. Brooks wished me and one other of us servants to witness that he had signed a paper which was on a table by his bedside. I called Pat Mooney, the head footman, and before us both Mr. Brooks put his name at the bottom of that paper. Then Mr. Wethered give me the pen and told me to write my name as a witness, and that Pat Mooney was to do the same. After that we were both told that we could go.'

"The old butler went on to explain that he was present in his late master's room on the following day when the undertakers, who had come to lay the dead man out, found a paper underneath his pillow. John O'Neill, who recognized the paper as the one to which he had appended his signature the day before, took it to Mr. Percival, and gave it into his hands.

"In answer to Mr. Walter Hibbert, John asserted positively that he took the paper from the undertaker's hand and went straight with it to Mr. Percival's room.

"'He was alone,' said John; 'I gave him the paper. He just glanced at it, and I thought he looked rather astonished, but he said nothing, and I at once left the room.'

"'When you say that you recognized the paper as the one which you had seen your master sign the day before, how did you actually recognize that it was the same paper?' asked Mr. Hibbert amidst breathless interest on the part of the spectators. I narrowly observed the witness's face.

"'It looked exactly the same paper to me, sir,' replied John, somewhat vaguely.

"'Did you look at the contents, then?'

"'No, sir; certainly not.'

"'Had you done so the day before?'

"'No, sir, only at my master's signature.'

"'Then you only thought by the *outside* look of the paper that it was the same?'

"'It looked the same thing, sir,' persisted John obstinately.

"You see," continued the man in the corner, leaning eagerly forward across the narrow marble table, "the contention of Murray Brooks' adviser was that Mr. Brooks, having made a will and hidden it—for some reason or other under his pillow—that will had fallen, through the means related by John O'Neill, into the hands of Mr. Percival Brooks, who had destroyed it and substituted a forged one in its place, which adjudged the whole of Mr. Brooks' millions to himself. It was a terrible and daring accusation directed against a gentleman who, in spite of his many wild oats sowed in early youth, was a prominent and important figure in Irish high life.

"All those present were aghast at what they heard, and the whispered comments I could hear around me showed that public opinion, at least, did not uphold Mr. Murray Brooks' daring accusation against his brother.

"But John O'Neill had not finished his evidence, and Mr. Walter Hibbert had a bit of sensation still up his sleeve. He had, namely, produced a paper, the will proved by Mr. Percival Brooks, and had asked John O'Neill if once again he recognized the paper.

"'Certainly, sir,' said John unhesitatingly, 'that is the one the undertaker found under my poor dead master's pillow, and which I took to Mr. Percival's room immediately.'

"Then the paper was unfolded and placed before the witness.

"'Now, Mr. O'Neill, will you tell me if that is your signature?'

"John looked at it for a moment; then he said: 'Excuse me, sir,' and produced a pair of spectacles which he carefully adjusted before he again examined the paper. Then he thoughtfully shook his head.

"'It don't look much like my writing, sir,' he said at last. 'That is to say,' he added, by way of elucidating the matter, 'it does look like my writing, but then I don't think it is.'

"There was at that moment a look in Mr. Percival Brooks' face,"
continued the man in the corner quietly, "which then and there gave
me the whole history of that quarrel, that illness of Mr. Brooks, of the
will, aye! and of the murder of Patrick Wethered too.

"All I wondered at was how every one of those learned counsel on
both sides did not get the clew just the same as I did, but went on
arguing, speechifying, cross-examining for nearly a week, until they
arrived at the one conclusion which was inevitable from the very first,
namely, that the will *was* a forgery—a gross, clumsy, idiotic forgery,
since both John O'Neill and Pat Mooney, the two witnesses, absolutely
repudiated the signatures as their own. The only successful bit of
calligraphy the forger had done was the signature of old Mr. Brooks.

"It was a very curious fact, and one which had undoubtedly aided
the forger in accomplishing his work quickly, that Mr. Wethered the
lawyer, having, no doubt, realized that Mr. Brooks had not many
moments in life to spare, had not drawn up the usual engrossed,
magnificent document dear to the lawyer heart, but had used for his
client's will one of those regular printed forms which can be purchased
at any stationer's.

"Mr. Percival Brooks, of course, flatly denied the serious allegation
brought against him. He admitted that the butler had brought him the
document the morning after his father's death, and that he certainly, on
glancing at it, had been very much astonished to see that that document
was his father's will. Against that he declared that its contents did not
astonish him in the slightest degree, that he himself knew of the
testator's intentions, but that he certainly thought his father had entrusted the will to the care of Mr. Wethered, who did all his business
for him.

"'I only very cursorily glanced at the signature,' he concluded,
speaking in a perfectly calm, clear voice; 'you must understand that the
thought of forgery was very far from my mind, and that my father's
signature is exceedingly well imitated, if, indeed, it is not his own,
which I am not at all prepared to believe. As for the two witnesses'
signatures, I don't think I had ever seen them before. I took the
document to Messrs. Barkston and Maud, who had often done business
for me before, and they assured me that the will was in perfect form
and order.'

"Asked why he had not entrusted the will to his father's solicitors,
he replied:

"'For the very simple reason that exactly half an hour before the will
was placed in my hands, I had read that Mr. Patrick Wethered had been

murdered the night before. Mr. Hibbert, the junior partner, was not personally known to me.'

"After that, for form's sake, a good deal of expert evidence was heard on the subject of the dead man's signature. But that was quite unanimous, and merely went to corroborate what had already been established beyond a doubt, namely, that the will dated February 1st, 1908, was a forgery, and probate of the will dated 1891 was therefore granted to Mr. Murray Brooks, the sole executor mentioned therein.

"Two days later the police applied for a warrant for the arrest of Mr. Percival Brooks on a charge of forgery.

"The Crown prosecuted, and Mr. Brooks had again the support of Mr. Oranmore, the eminent K.C. Perfectly calm, like a man conscious of his own innocence and unable to grasp the idea that justice does sometimes miscarry, Mr. Brooks, the son of the millionaire, himself still the possessor of a very large fortune under the former will, stood up in the dock on that memorable day in October, 1908, which still no doubt lives in the memory of his many friends.

"All the evidence with regard to Mr. Brooks' last moments and the forged will was gone through over again. That will, it was the contention of the Crown, had been forged so entirely in favor of the accused, cutting out every one else, that obviously no one but the beneficiary under that false will would have had any motive in forging it.

"Very pale, and with a frown between his deep-set, handsome Irish eyes, Percival Brooks listened to this large volume of evidence piled up against him by the Crown.

"At times he held brief consultations with Mr. Oranmore, who seemed as cool as a cucumber. Have you ever seen Oranmore in court? He is a character worthy of Dickens. His pronounced brogue, his fat, podgy, clean-shaven face, his not always immaculately clean large hands, have often delighted the caricaturist. As it very soon transpired during that memorable magisterial inquiry, he relied for a verdict in favor of his client upon two main points, and he had concentrated all his skill upon making these two points as telling as he possibly could.

"The first point was the question of time. John O'Neill, cross-examined by Oranmore, stated without hesitation that he had given the will to Mr. Percival at eleven o'clock in the morning. And now the eminent K.C. brought forward and placed in the witness-box the very lawyers into whose hands the accused had then immediately placed the will. Now, Mr. Barkston, a very well-known solicitor of King Street, declared positively that Mr. Percival Brooks was in his office at a quarter before twelve; two of his clerks testified to the same time exactly, and it was *impossible,* contended Mr. Oranmore, that within three-quarters of an hour Mr. Brooks could have gone to a stationer's, bought a will form, copied Mr. Wethered's writing, his father's signature, and that of John O'Neill and Pat Mooney.

"Such a thing might have been planned, arranged, practiced, and ultimately, after a great deal of trouble, successfully carried out, but human intelligence could not grasp the other as a possibility.

"Still the judge wavered. The eminent K.C. had shaken but not shattered his belief in the prisoner's guilt. But there was one point more, and this Oranmore, with the skill of a dramatist, had reserved for the fall of the curtain.

"He noted every sign in the judge's face, he guessed that his client was not yet absolutely safe, then only did he produce his last two witnesses.

"One of them was Mary Sullivan, one of the housemaids in the Fitzwilliam mansion. She had been sent up by the cook at a quarter past four o'clock on the afternoon of February 1st with some hot water, which the nurse had ordered, for the master's room. Just as she was about to knock at the door Mr. Wethered was coming out of the room. Mary stopped with the tray in her hand, and at the door Mr. Wethered turned and said quite loudly: 'Now, don't fret, don't be anxious; do try and be calm. Your will is safe in my pocket, nothing can change it or alter one word of it but yourself.'

"It was, of course, a very ticklish point in law whether the housemaid's evidence could be accepted. You see, she was quoting the words of a man since dead, spoken to another man also dead. There is no doubt that had there been very strong evidence on the other side against Percival Brooks, Mary Sullivan's would have counted for nothing; but, as I told you before, the judge's belief in the prisoner's guilt was already very seriously shaken, and now the final blow aimed at it by Mr. Oranmore shattered his last lingering doubts.

"Dr. Mulligan, namely, had been placed by Mr. Oranmore into the witness-box. He was a medical man of unimpeachable authority, in fact, absolutely at the head of his profession in Dublin. What he said practically corroborated Mary Sullivan's testimony. He had gone in to see Mr. Brooks at half-past four, and understood from him that his lawyer had just left him.

"Mr. Brooks certainly, though terribly weak, was calm and more composed. He was dying from a sudden heart attack, and Dr. Mulligan foresaw the almost immediate end. But he was still conscious and managed to murmur feebly: 'I feel much easier in my mind now,

doctor—I have made my will—Wethered has been—he's got it in his
pocket—it is safe there—safe from that—' But the words died on his
lips, and after that he spoke but little. He saw his two sons before he
died, but hardly knew them or even looked at them.

"You see," concluded the man in the corner, "you see that the
prosecution was bound to collapse. Oranmore did not give it a leg to
stand on. The will was forged, it is true, forged in the favor of Percival
Brooks and of no one else, forged for him and for his benefit. Whether
he knew and connived at the forgery was never proved or, as far as I
know, even hinted, but it was impossible to go against all the evidence,
which pointed that, as far as the act itself was concerned, he at least
was innocent. You see, Dr. Mulligan's evidence was not to be shaken.
Mary Sullivan's was equally strong.

"There were two witnesses swearing positively that old Brooks' will
was in Mr. Wethered's keeping when that gentleman left the Fitzwilliam mansion at a quarter past four. At five o'clock in the afternoon the
lawyer was found dead in Phoenix Park. Between a quarter past four
and eight o'clock in the evening Percival Brooks never left the
house—that was subsequently proved by Oranmore up to the hilt and
beyond a doubt. Since the will found under old Brooks' pillow was a
forged will, where then was thc will he did make, and which Wethered
carried away with him in his pocket?"

"Stolen, of course," said Polly, "by those who murdered and robbed
him; it may have been of no value to them, but they naturally would
destroy it, lest it might prove a clew against them."

"Then you think it was mere coincidence?" he asked excitedly.

"What?"

"That Wethered was murdered and robbed at the very moment that
he carried the will in his pocket, whilst another was being forged in its
place?"

"It certainly would be very curious, if it *were* a coincidence," she
said musingly.

"Very," he repeated with biting sarcasm, whilst nervously his bony
fingers played with the inevitable bit of string. "Very curious indeed.
Just think of the whole thing. There was the old man with all his
wealth, and two sons, one to whom he is devoted, and the other with
whom he does nothing but quarrel. One day there is another of these
quarrels, but more violent, more terrible than any that have previously
occurred, with the result that the father, heart-broken by it all, has an
attack of apoplexy and practically dies of a broken heart. After that he

alters his will and subsequently a will is proved which turns out to be a forgery.

"Now everybody—police, press, and public alike—at once jump to the conclusion that, as Percival Brooks benefits by that forged will, Percival Brooks must be the forger."

"Seek for him whom the crime benefits, is your own axiom." argued the girl.

"I beg your pardon?"

"Perclval Brooks benefited to the tune of £2,000,000."

"I beg your pardon. He did nothing of the sort. He was left with less than half the share that his younger brother inherited."

"Now, yes; but that was a former will and—"

"And that forged will was so clumsily executed, the signature so carelessly imitated, that the forgery was bound to come to light. Did *that* never strike you?"

"Yes, but—"

"There is no but," he interrupted. "It was all as clear as daylight to me from the very first. The quarrel with the old man, which broke his heart, was not with his eldest son, with whom he was used to quarreling, but with the second son whom he idolized, in whom he believed. Don't you remember how John O'Neill heard the words 'liar' and 'deceit'? Percival Brooks had never deceived his father. His sins were all on the surface. Murray had led a quiet life, had pandered to his father, and fawned upon him, until, like most hypocrites, he at last got found out. Who knows what ugly gambling debt or debt of honor, suddenly revealed to old Brooks, was the cause of that last and deadly quarrel?

"You remember that it was Percival who remained beside his father and carried him up to his room. Where was Murray throughout that long and painful day, when his father lay dying—he, the idolized son, the apple of the old man's eye? You never hear his name mentioned as being present there all that day. But he knew that he had offended his father mortally, and that his father meant to cut him off with a shilling. He knew that Mr. Wethered had been sent for, that Wethered left the house soon after four o'clock.

"And here the cleverness of the man comes in. Having lain in wait for Wethered and knocked him on the back of the head with a stick, he could not very well make that will disappear altogether. There remained the faint chance of some other witnesses knowing that Mr. Brooks had made a fresh will, Mr. Wethered's partner, his clerk, or one of the confidential servants in the house. Therefore a will must be discovered after the old man's death.

"Now, Murray Brooks was not an expert forger; it takes years of training to become that. A forged will executed by himself would be sure to be found out—yes, that's it, sure to be found out. The forgery will be palpable—let it be palpable, and then it will be found out, branded as such, and the original will of 1891, so favorable to the young blackguard's interests, would be held as valid. Was it devilry or merely additional caution which prompted Murray to pen that forged will so glaringly in Percival's favor? It is impossible to say.

"Anyhow, it was the cleverest touch in that marvelously devised crime. To plan that evil deed was great, to execute it was easy enough. He had several hours' leisure in which to do it. Then at night it was simplicity itself to slip the document under the dead man's pillow. Sacrilege causes no shudder to such natures as Murray Brooks. The rest of the drama you know already—"

"But Percival Brooks?"

"The jury returned a verdict of 'Not guilty.' There was no evidence against him."

"But the money? Surely the scoundrel does not have the enjoyment of it still?"

"No; he enjoyed it for a time, but he died about three months ago, and forgot to take the precaution of making a will, so his brother Percival has got the business after all. If you ever go to Dublin, I should order some of Brooks' bacon if I were you. It is very good."

The Eye of Apollo

G.K. Chesterton

G.K. Chesterton (1874-1936) was born in London. His father, an estate agent, was a voracious hobbyist and instilled in Chesterton a love of "romantic things." When he was 13, Chesterton went to St. Paul's Prep School, where he first gained a reputation as an eccentric. From 1894-1895, he attended the Slade School of Art. After he left school, Chesterton worked with Fisher Unwin as an editor and blurb writer, contributing poetry and commentaries to newspapers like the *Daily Mail* in his free time. By 1901, when his first book, *The Defendant,* was published, he was a widely-read and respected columnist/reviewer. He married Frances Blogg in 1901, and published his first novel, *The Napoleon of Notting Hill,* in 1904. Chesterton continued to write essays and criticism such as *Heretics* (1905) and *Charles Dickens* (1906), as well as novels like *The Club of Queer Trades* (1905). In 1908, Chesterton wrote the first of his books on Catholic beliefs, *Orthodoxy,* as well as his novel *The Man Who Was Thursday.* Catholicism fascinated Chesterton (he converted to the Roman Catholic faith in 1922), and he devoted more and more of his writing to the subject, the most famous of which are the stories of Father Brown. The first Father Brown collection, *The Innocence of Father Brown,* was released in 1911. He wrote four other collections (*The Wisdom of Father Brown,* 1914; *The Incredulity of Father Brown,* 1926; *The Secret of Father Brown,* 1927; *The Scandal of Father Brown,* 1935), as well as plays (*Magic,* 1913; *The Judgement of Dr. Johnson,* 1927), essay collections (*The Crimes of England,* 1915; *Eugenics and Other Evils,* 1922), literary criticism (*Victorian Age in Literature,* 1913; *William Cobbett,* 1925; *Robert Louis Stevenson,* 1927), religious works (*St. Francis of Assisi,* 1923; *The Everlasting Man,* 1925; *St. Thomas Aquinas,* 1933), and his posthumously published autobiography (1936) before his death.

"The Eye of Apollo" is the type of story Chesterton is famous for. The ingenuity of its "impossible" crime and eye for characterization makes it a perennial favorite that holds up to repeated readings.

THAT SINGULAR smoky sparkle, at once a confusion and a transparency, which is the strange secret of the Thames, was changing more and more from its grey to its glittering extreme as the sun climbed to the zenith over Westminster, and two men crossed Westminster Bridge. One man was very tall and the other very short; they might even have been fantastically compared to the arrogant clock-tower of Parliament and the humbler humped shoulders of the Abbey, for the short man was in clerical dress. The official description of the tall man was M. Hercule Flambeau, private detective, and he was going to his new offices in a new pile of flats facing the Abbey entrance. The official description of the short man was the Reverend J. Brown, attached to St. Francis Xavier's Church, Camberwell, and he was coming from a Camberwell deathbed to see the new offices of his friend.

The building was American in its sky-scraping altitude, and American also in the oiled elaboration of its machinery of telephones and lifts. But it was barely finished and still understaffed; only three tenants had moved in; the office just above Flambeau was occupied, as also was the office just below him; the two floors above that and the three floors below were entirely bare. But the first glance at the new tower of flats caught something much more arresting. Save for a few relics of scaffolding, the one glaring object was erected outside the office just above Flambeau's. It was an enormous gilt effigy of the human eye, surrounded with rays of gold, and taking up as much room as two or three of the office windows.

"What on earth is that?" asked Father Brown, and stood still.

"Oh, a new religion," said Flambeau, laughing; "one of those new religions that forgive your sins by saying you never had any. Rather like Christian Science, I should think. The fact is that a fellow calling himself Kalon (I don't know what his name is, except that it can't be that) has taken the flat just above me. I have two lady typewriters underneath me, and this enthusiastic old humbug on top. He calls himself the New Priest of Apollo, and he worships the sun."

"Let him look out," said Father Brown. "The sun was the cruellest of all the gods. But what does that monstrous eye mean?"

"As I understand it, it is a theory of theirs," answered Flambeau, "that a man can endure anything if his mind is quite steady. Their two great symbols are the sun and the open eye; for they say that if a man were really healthy he could stare at the sun."

"If a man were really healthy," said Father Brown, "he would not bother to stare at it."

"Well, that's all I can tell you about the new religion," went on Flambeau carelessly. "It claims, of course, that it can cure all physical diseases."

"Can it cure the one spiritual disease?" asked Father Brown, with a serious curiosity.

"And what is the one spiritual disease?" asked Flambeau, smiling.

"Oh, thinking one is quite well," said his friend.

Flambeau was more interested in the quiet little office below him than in the flamboyant temple above. He was a lucid Southerner, incapable of conceiving himself as anything but a Catholic or an atheist; and new religions of a bright and pallid sort were not much in his line. But humanity was always in his line, especially when it was good-looking; moreover, the ladies downstairs were characters in their way. The office was kept by two sisters, both slight and dark, one of them tall and striking. She had a dark, eager and aquiline profile, and was one of those women whom one always thinks of in profile, as of the clean-cut edge of some weapon. She seemed to cleave her way through life. She had eyes of startling brilliancy, but it was the brilliancy of steel rather than of diamonds; and her straight, slim figure was a shade too stiff for its grace. Her younger sister was like her shortened shadow, a little greyer, paler, and more insignificant. They both wore a business-like black, with little masculine cuffs and collars. There are thousands of such curt, strenuous ladies in the offices of London, but the interest of these lay rather in their real than their apparent position.

For Pauline Stacey, the elder, was actually the heiress of a crest and half a county, as well as great wealth; she had been brought up in castles and gardens, before a frigid fierceness (peculiar to the modern woman) had driven her to what she considered a harsher and a higher existence. She had not, indeed, surrendered her money; in that there would have been a romantic or monkish abandon quite alien to her masterful utilitarianism. She held her wealth, she would say, for use upon practical social objects. Part of it she had put into her business, the nucleus of a model typewriting emporium; part of it was distributed in various leagues and causes for the advancement of such work among women. How far Joan, her sister and partner, shared this slightly prosaic idealism no one could be very sure. But she followed her leader with a dog-like affection which was somehow more attractive, with its touch of tragedy, than the hard, high spirits of the elder. For Pauline Stacey had nothing to say to tragedy; she was understood to deny its existence.

Her rigid rapidity and cold impatience had amused Flambeau very much on the first occasion of his entering the flats. He had lingered outside the lift in the entrance hall waiting for the lift-boy, who generally conducts strangers to the various floors. But this bright-eyed falcon of a girl had openly refused to endure such official delay. She said sharply that she knew all about the lift, and was not dependent on boys—or men either. Though her flat was only three floors above, she managed in the few seconds of ascent to give Flambeau a great many of her fundamental views in an off-hand manner; they were to the general effect that she was a modern working woman and loved modern working machinery. Her bright black eyes blazed with abstract anger against those who rebuke mechanic science and ask for the return of romance. Everyone, she said, ought to be able to manage machines, just as she could manage the lift. She seemed almost to resent the fact of Flambeau opening the lift-door for her; and that gentleman went up to his own apartments smiling with somewhat mingled feelings at the memory of such spit-fire self-dependence.

She certainly had a temper, of a snappy, practical sort; the gestures of her thin, elegant hands were abrupt or even destructive. Once Flambeau entered her office on some typewriting business, and found she had just flung a pair of spectacles belonging to her sister into the middle of the floor and stamped on them. She was already in the rapids of an ethical tirade about the "sickly medical notions" and the morbid admission of weakness implied in such an apparatus. She dared her sister to bring such artificial, unhealthy rubbish into the place again. She asked if she was expected to wear wooden legs or false hair or glass eyes; and as she spoke her eyes sparkled like the terrible crystal.

Flambeau, quite bewildered with this fanaticism, could not refrain from asking Miss Pauline (with direct French logic) why a pair of spectacles was a more morbid sign of weakness than a lift, and why, if science might help us in the one effort, it might not help us in the other.

"That is *so* different," said Pauline Stacey, loftily. "Batteries and motors and all those things are marks of the force of man—yes, Mr. Flambeau, and the force of woman too! We shall take our turn at these great engines that devour distance and defy time. That is high and splendid—that is really science. But these nasty props and plasters the doctors sell—why, they are just badges of poltroonery. Doctors stick on legs and arms as if we were born cripples and sick slaves. But I was free-born, Mr. Flambeau! People only think they need these things because they have been trained in fear instead of being trained in power and courage, just as the silly nurses tell children not to stare at the sun, and so they can't do it without blinking. But why among the stars should there be one star I may not see? The sun is not my master, and I will open my eyes and stare at him whenever I choose."

"Your eyes," said Flambeau, with a foreign bow, "will dazzle the sun." He took pleasure in complimenting this strange stiff beauty, partly because it threw her a little off her balance. But as he went upstairs to his floor he drew a deep breath and whistled, saying, to himself: "So she has got into the hands of that conjurer upstairs with his golden eye." For, little as he knew or cared about the new religlon of Kalon, he had heard of his special notion about sun-gazing.

He soon discovered that the spiritual bond between the floors above and below him was close and increasing. The man who called himself Kalon was a magnificent creature, worthy, in a physical sense, to be the pontiff of Apollo. He was nearly as tall even as Flambeau, and very much better looking, with a golden beard, strong blue eyes, and a mane flung back like a lion's. In structure he was the blonde beast of Nietzsche, but all this animal beauty was heightened, brightened and softened by genuine intellect and spirituality. If he looked like one of the great Saxon kings, he looked like one of the kings that were also saints. And this despite the cockney incongruity of his surroundings; the fact that he had an office half-way up a building in Victoria Street; that the clerk (a commonplace youth in cuffs and collars) sat in the outer room, between him and the corridor; that his name was on a brass plate, and the gilt emblem of his creed hung above his street, like the advertisement of an oculist. All this vulgarity could not take away from the man called Kalon the vivid oppression and inspiration that came from his soul and body. When all was said, a man in the presence of this quack did feel in the presence of a great man. Even in the loose jacket-suit of linen that he wore as a workshop dress in his office he was a fascinating and formidable figure; and when robed in the white vestments and crowned with the golden circlet, in which he daily saluted the sun, he really looked so splendid that the laughter of the street people sometimes died suddenly on their lips. For three times in the day the new sun-worshipper went out on his little balcony, in the face of all Westminster, to say some litany to his shining lord: once at daybreak, once at sunset, and once at the shock of noon. And it was while the shock of noon still shook faintly from the towers of Parliament and parish church that Father Brown, the friend of Flambeau, first looked up and saw the white priest of Apollo.

Flambeau had seen quite enough of these daily salutations of Phoebus, and plunged into the porch of the tall building without even looking for his clerical friend to follow. But Father Brown, whether from a professional interest in ritual or a strong individual interest in tomfoolery, stopped and stared up at the balcony of the sun-worshipper, just as he might have stopped and stared up at a Punch and Judy. Kalon the Prophet was already erect, with argent garments and uplifted hands, and the sound of his strangely penetrating voice could be heard all the way down the busy street uttering his solar litany. He was already in the middle of it; his eyes were fixed upon the flaming disc. It is doubtful if he saw anything or anyone on this earth; it is substantially certain that he did not see a stunted, round-faced priest who, in the crowd below, looked up at him with blinking eyes. That was perhaps the most startling difference between even these two far divided men. Father Brown could not look at anything without blinking; but the priest of Apollo could look on the blaze at noon without a quiver of the eyelid.

"O sun," cried the prophet, "O star that art too great to be allowed among the stars! O fountain that flowest quietly in that secret spot that is called space. White Father of all white unwearied things, white flames and white flowers and white peaks. Father, who art more innocent than all thy most innocent and quiet children; primal purity, into the peace of which—"

A rush and crash like the reversed rush of a rocket was cloven with a strident and incessant yelling. Five people rushed into the gate of the mansions as three people rushed out, and for an instant they all deafened each other. The sense of some utterly abrupt horror seemed for a moment to fill half the street with bad news—bad news that was all the worse because no one knew what it was. Two figures remained still after the crash of commotion: the fair priest of Apollo on the balcony above, and the ugly priest of Christ below him.

At last the tall figure and titanic energy of Flambeau appeared in the doorway of the mansions and dominated the little mob. Talking at the top of his voice like a fog-horn, he told somebody or anybody to go for a surgeon; and as he turned back into the dark and thronged entrance his friend Father Brown slipped in insignificantly after him. Even as he ducked and dived through the crowd he could still hear the magnificent melody and monotony of the solar priest still calling on the happy god who is the friend of fountains and flowers.

Father Brown found Flambeau and some six other people standing round the enclosed space into which the lift commonly descended. But the lift had not descended. Something else had descended; something that ought to have come by a lift.

For the last four minutes Flambeau had looked down on it; had seen the brained and bleeding figure of that beautiful woman who denied the existence of tragedy. He had never had the slightest doubt that it was Pauline Stacey; and, though he had sent for a doctor, he had not the slightest doubt that she was dead.

He could not remember for certain whether he had liked her or disliked her; there was so much both to like and dislike. But she had been a person to him, and the unbearable pathos of details and habit stabbed him with all the small daggers of bereavement. He remembered her pretty face and priggish speeches with a sudden secret vividness which is all the bitterness of death. In an instant like a bolt from the blue, like a thunderbolt from nowhere, that beautiful and defiant body had been dashed down the open well of the lift to death at the bottom. Was it suicide? With so insolent an optimist it seemed impossible. Was it murder? But who was there in those hardly inhabited flats to murder anybody? In a rush of raucous words, which he meant to be strong and suddenly found weak, he asked where was that fellow Kalon. A voice, habitually heavy, quiet and full, assured him that Kalon for the last fifteen minutes had been away up on his balcony worshipping his god. When Flambeau heard the voice, and felt the hand of Father Brown, he turned his swarthy face and said abruptly:

"Then, if he has been up there all the time, who can have done it?"

"Perhaps," said the other, "we might go upstairs and find out. We have half an hour before the police will move."

Leaving the body of the slain heiress in charge of the surgeons, Flambeau dashed up the stairs to the typewriting office, found it utterly empty, and then dashed up to his own. Having entered that, he abruptly returned with a new and white face to his friend.

"Her sister," he said, with an unpleasant seriousness, "her sister seems to have gone out for a walk."

Father Brown nodded. "Or, she may have gone up to the office of that sun man," he said. "If I were you I should just verify that, and then let us all talk it over in your office. No," he added suddenly, as if remembering something, "shall I ever get over that stupidity of mine? Of course, in their office downstairs."

Flambeau stared; but he followed the little father downstairs to the empty flat of the Staceys, where that impenetrable pastor took a large red-leather chair in the very entrance, from which he could see the stairs and landings, and waited. He did not wait very long. In about four minutes three figures descended the stairs, alike only in their solemnity. The first was Joan Stacey, the sister of the dead woman—

evidently she *had* been upstairs in the temporary temple of Apollo; the second was the priest of Apollo himself, his litany finished, sweeping down the empty stairs in utter magnificence—something in his white robes, beard and parted hair had the look of Doré's Christ leaving the Pretorium; the third was Flambeau, black browed and somewhat bewildered.

Miss Joan Stacey, dark, with a drawn face and hair prematurely touched with grey, walked straight to her own desk and set out her papers with a practical flap. The mere action rallied everyone else to sanity. If Miss Joan Stacey was a criminal, she was a cool one. Father Brown regarded her for some time with an odd little smile, and then, without taking his eyes off her, addressed himself to somebody else.

"Prophet," he said, presumably addressing Kalon, "I wish you would tell me a lot about your religion."

"I shall be proud to do it," said Kalon, inclining his still crowned head, "but I am not sure that I understand."

"Why, it's like this," said Father Brown, in his frankly doubtful way: "We are taught that if a man has really bad first principles, that must be partly his fault. But, for all that, we can make some difference between a man who insults his quite clear conscience and a man with a conscience more or less clouded with sophistries. Now, do you really think that murder is wrong at all?"

"Is this an accusation?" asked Kalon very quietly.

"No," answered Brown, equally gently, "it is the speech for the defense."

In the long and startled stillness of the room the prophet of Apollo slowly rose; and really it was like the rising of the sun. He filled that room with his light and life in such a manner that a man felt he could as easily have filled Salisbury Plain. His robed form seemed to hang the whole room with classic draperies; his epic gesture seemed to extend it into grander perspectives, till the little black figure of the modern cleric seemed to be a fault and an intrusion, a round, black blot upon some splendor of Hellas.

"We meet at last, Caiaphas," said the prophet. "Your church and mine are the only realities on this earth. I adore the sun, and you the darkening of the sun; you are the priest of the dying and I of the living God. Your present work of suspicion and slander is worthy of your coat and creed. All your church is but a black police; you are only spies and detectives seeking to tear from men confessions of guilt, whether by treachery or torture. You would convict men of crime, I would convict them of innocence. You would convince them of sin, I would convince them of virtue.

"Reader of the books of evil, one more word before I blow away your baseless nightmares for ever. Not even faintly could you understand how little I care whether you can convict me or no. The things you call disgrace and horrible hanging are to me no more than an ogre in a child's toy-book to a man once grown up. You said you were offering the speech for the defense. I care so little for the cloudland of this life that I will offer you the speech for the prosecution. There is but one thing that can be said against me in this matter, and I will say it myself. The woman that is dead was my love and my bride, not after such manner as your tin chapels call lawful, but by a law purer and sterner than you will ever understand. She and I walked another world from yours, and trod palaces of crystal while you were plodding through tunnels and corridors of brick. Well, I know that policemen, theological and otherwise, always fancy that where there has been love there must soon be hatred; so there you have the first point made for the prosecution. But the second point is stronger; I do not grudge it you. Not only is it true that Pauline loved me, but it is also true that this very morning, before she died, she wrote at that table a will leaving me and my new church half a million. Come, where are the handcuffs? Do you suppose I care what foolish things you do with me? Penal servitude will only be like waiting for her at a wayside station. The gallows will only be going to her in a headlong car."

He spoke with the brain-shaking authority of an orator, and Flambeau and Joan Stacey stared at him in amazed admiration. Father Brown's face seemed to express nothing but extreme distress; he looked at the ground with one wrinkle of pain across his forehead. The prophet of the sun leaned easily against the mantelpiece and resumed:

"In a few words I have put before you the whole case against me—the only possible case against me. In fewer words still I will blow it to pieces, so that not a trace of it remains. As to whether I have committed this crime, the truth is in one sentence: I could not have committed this crime. Pauline Stacey fell from this floor to the—ground at five minutes past twelve. A hundred people will go into the witness-box and say that I was standing out upon the balcony of my own rooms above from just before the stroke of noon to a quarter-past—the usual period of my public prayers. My clerk (a respectable youth from Clapham, with no sort of connection with me) will swear that he sat in my outer office all the morning, and that no communication passed through. He will swear that I arrived a full ten minutes before the hour, fifteen minutes before any whisper of the accident, and that I did not leave the office or the balcony all that time. No one ever had so complete an alibi; I could subpoena half Westminster. I think you had better put the handcuffs away again. The case is at an end.

"But last of all, that no breath of this idiotic suspicion remain in the air, I will tell you all you want to know. I believe I do know how my unhappy friend came by her death. You can, if you choose, blame me for it, or my faith and philosophy at least; but you certainly cannot lock me up. It is well known to all students of the higher truths that certain adepts and *illuminati* have in history attained the power of levitation— that is, of being self-sustained upon the empty air. It is but a part of that general conquest of matter which is the main element in our occult wisdom. Poor Pauline was of an impulsive and ambitious temper. I think, to tell the truth, she thought herself somewhat deeper in the mysteries than she was; and she has often said to me, as we went down in the lift together, that if one's will were strong enough, one could float down as harmlessly as a feather. I solemnly believe that in some ecstasy of noble thoughts she attempted the miracle. Her will, or faith, must have failed her at the crucial instant, and the lower law of matter had its horrible revenge. There is the whole story, gentlemen, very sad and, as you think, very presumptuous and wicked, but certainly not criminal or in any way connected with me. In the short-hand of the police-courts, you had better call it suicide. I shall always call it heroic failure for the advance of science and the slow scaling of heaven."

It was the first time Flambeau had ever seen Father Brown vanquished. He still sat looking at the ground, with a painful and corrugated brow, as if in shame. It was impossible to avoid the feeling which the prophet's winged words had fanned, that here was a sullen, professional suspecter of men overwhelmed by a prouder and purer spirit of natural liberty and health. At last he said, blinking as if in bodily distress: "Well, if that is so, sir, you need do no more than take the testamentary paper you spoke of and go. I wonder where the poor lady left it."

"It will be over there on her desk by the door, I think," said Kalon, with that massive innocence of manner that seemed to acquit him wholly. "She told me specially she would write it this morning, and I actually saw her writing as I went up in the lift to my own room."

"Was her door open then?" asked the priest, with his eye on the corner of the matting.

"Yes," said Kalon calmly.

"Ah! it has been open ever since," said the other, and resumed his silent study of the mat.

"There is a paper over here," said the grim Miss Joan, in a somewhat singular voice. She had passed over to her sister's desk by the doorway, and was holding a sheet of blue foolscap in her hand. There was a sour smile on her face that seemed unfit for such a scene or occasion, and Flambeau looked at her with a darkening brow.

Kalon the prophet stood away from the paper with that loyal unconsciousness that had carried him through. But Flambeau took it out of the lady's hand, and read it with the utmost amazement. It did, indeed, begin in the formal manner of a will, but after the words "I give and bequeath all of which I die possessed" the writing abruptly stopped with a set of scratches, and there was no trace of the name of any legatee. Flambeau, in wonder, handed this truncated testament to his clerical friend, who glanced at it and silently gave it to the priest of the sun.

An instant afterwards that pontiff, in his splendid sweeping draperies, had crossed the room in two great strides, and was towering over Joan Stacey, his blue eyes standing from his head.

"What monkey tricks have you been playing here? " he cried. "That's not all Pauline wrote."

They were startled to hear him speak in quite a new voice, with a Yankee shrillness in it; all his grandeur and good English had fallen from him like a cloak.

"That is the only thing on her desk," said Joan, and confronted him steadily with the same smile of evil favor.

Of a sudden the man broke out into blasphemies and cataracts of incredulous words. There was something shocking about the dropping of his mask; it was like a man's real face falling off.

"See here!" he cried in broad American, when he was breathless with cursing, "I may be an adventurer, but I guess you're a murderess. Yes, gentlemen, here's your death explained, and without any levitation. The poor girl is writing a will in my favor; her cursed sister comes in, struggles for the pen, drags her to the well, and throws her down before she can finish it. Sakes! I reckon we want the handcuffs after all."

"As you have truly remarked," replied Joan, with ugly calm, "your clerk is a very respectable young man, who knows the nature of an oath; and he will swear in any court that I was up in your office arranging some typewriting work for five minutes before and five

minutes after my sister fell. Mr. Flambeau will tell you that he found
me there."

There was a silence.

"Why, then," cried Flambeau, "Pauline was alone when she fell,
and it was suicide!"

"She was alone when she fell," said Father Brown, "but it was not
suicide."

"Then how did she die?" asked Flambeau impatiently.

"She was murdered."

"But she was alone," objected the detective.

"She was murdered when she was all alone," answered the priest.

All the rest stared at him, but he remained sitting in the same old
dejected attitude, with a wrinkle in his round forehead and an appearance of impersonal shame and sorrow; his voice was colorless and sad.

"What I want to know," cried Kalon, with an oath, "is when the
police are coming for this bloody and wicked sister. She's killed her
flesh and blood; she's robbed me of half a million that was just as
sacredly mine as—"

"Come, come, prophet," interrupted Flambeau, with a kind of sneer;
"remember that all this world is a cloudland."

The hierophant of the sun-god made an effort to climb back on his
pedestal. "It is not the mere money," he cried, "though that would
equip the cause throughout the world. It is also my beloved one's
wishes. To Pauline all this was holy. In Pauline's eyes—"

Father Brown suddenly sprang erect, so that his chair fell over flat
behind him. He was deathly pale, yet he seemed fired with a hope; his
eyes shone.

"That's it!" he cried in a clear voice. "That's the way to begin. In
Pauline's eyes—"

The tall prophet retreated before the tiny priest in an almost mad
disorder. "What do you mean? How dare you?" he cried repeatedly.

"In Pauline's eyes," repeated the priest, his own shining more and
more. "Go on—in God's name, go on. The foulest crime the fiends
ever prompted feels lighter after confession, and I implore you to
confess. Go on, go on—in Pauline's eyes—"

"Let me go, you devil!" thundered Kalon, struggling like a giant in
bonds. "Who are you, you cursed spy, to weave your spiders' webs
round me, and peep and peer? Let me go."

"Shall I stop him?" asked Flambeau, bounding towards the exit, for
Kalon had already thrown the door wide open.

"No; let him pass," said Father Brown, with a strange deep sigh that seemed to come from the depths of the universe. "Let Cain pass by, for he belongs to God."

There was a long-drawn silence in the room when he had left it, which was to Flambeau's fierce wits one long agony of interrogation. Miss Joan Stacey very coolly tidied up the papers on her desk.

"Father," said Flambeau at last, "it is my duty, not my curiosity only—it is my duty to find out, if I can, who committed the crime."

"Which crime?" asked Father Brown.

"The one we are dealing with, of course," replied his impatient friend.

"We are dealing with two crimes," said Brown, "crimes of very different weight—and by very different criminals."

Miss Joan Stacey, having collected and put away her papers, proceeded to lock up her drawer. Father Brown went on, noticing her as little as she noticed him.

"The two crimes," he observed, "were committed against the same weakness of the same person, in a struggle for her money. The author of the larger crime found himself thwarted by the smaller crime; the author of the smaller crime got the money."

"Oh, don't go on like a lecturer," groaned Flambeau; "put it in a few words."

"I can put it in one word," answered his friend.

Miss Joan Stacey skewered her business-like black hat on to her head with a business-like black frown before a little mirror, and, as the conversation proceeded, took her handbag and umbrella in an unhurried style, and left the room.

"The truth is one word, and a short one," said Father Brown. "Pauline Stacey was blind."

"Blind!" repeated Flambeau, and rose slowly to his whole huge stature.

"She was subject to it by blood," Brown proceeded. "Her sister would have started eyeglasses if Pauline would have let her; but it was her special philosophy or fad that one must not encourage such diseases by yielding to them. She would not admit the cloud; or she tried to dispel it by will. So her eyes got worse and worse with straining; but the worst strain was to come. It came with this precious prophet, or whatever he calls himself, who taught her to stare at the hot sun with the naked eye. It was called accepting Apollo. Oh, if these new pagans would only be old pagans, they would be a little wiser! The old pagans knew that mere naked Nature-worship must have a cruel side. They knew that the eye of Apollo can blast and blind.''

There was a pause, and the priest went on in a gentle and even broken voice. "Whether or no that devil deliberately made her blind, there is no doubt that he deliberately killed her through her blindness. The very simplicity of the crime is sickening. You know he and she went up and down in those lifts without official help; you know also how smoothly and silently the lifts slide. Kalon brought the lift to the girl's landing, and saw her, through the open door, writing in her slow, sightless way the will she had promised him. He called out to her cheerily that he had the lift ready for her, and she was to come out when she was ready. Then he pressed a button and shot soundlessly up to his own floor, walked through his own office, out on to his own balcony, and was safely praying before the crowded street when the poor girl, having finished her work, ran gaily out to where lover and lift were to receive her, and stepped—''

"Don't!'' cried Flambeau.

"He ought to have got half a million by pressing that button,'' continued the little father, in the colorless voice in which he talked of such horrors. "But that went smash. It went smash because there happened to be another person who also wanted the money, and who also knew the secret about poor Pauline's sight. There was one thing about that will that I think nobody noticed: although it was unfinished and without signature, the other Miss Stacey and some servant of hers had already signed it as witnesses. Joan had signed first, saying Pauline could finish it later, with a typical feminine contempt for legal forms. Therefore, Joan wanted her sister to sign the will without real witnesses. Why? I thought of the blindness, and felt sure she had wanted Pauline to sign in solitude because she had wanted her not to sign at all.

"People like the Staceys always use fountain pens; but this was specially natural to Pauline. By habit and her strong will and memory she could still write almost as well as if she saw; but she could not tell when her pen needed dipping. Therefore, her fountain pens were carefully filled by her sister—all except this fountain pen. This was carefully *not* filled by her sister; the remains of the ink held out for a few lines and then failed altogether. And the prophet lost five hundred thousand pounds and committed one of the most brutal and brilliant murders in human history for nothing.''

Flambeau went to the open door and heard the official police ascending the stairs. He turned and said: "You must have followed everything devilish close to have traced the crime to Kalon in ten minutes."

Father Brown gave a sort of start.

"Oh! to him," he said. "No; I had to follow rather close to find out about Miss Joan and the fountain pen. But I knew Kalon was the criminal before I came into the front door."

"You must be joking!" cried Flambeau.

"I'm quite serious," answered the priest. "I tell you I knew he had done it, even before I knew what he had done."

"But why?"

"These pagan stoics," said Brown reflectively, "always fail by their strength. There came a crash and a scream down the street, and the priest of Apollo did not start or look round. I did not know what it was. But I knew that he was expecting it."

The Superfluous Finger

Jacques Futrelle

Jacques Futrelle (1875-1912) was born in Pike County, Georgia. Very little is known of his early life, other than the fact that he read Vidocq's autobiography, as well as a large amount of Poe and Doyle. In 1880, Futrelle began working at a newspaper in Richmond, Virginia. He married L. May Peel in 1895. After managing a theater for two years, Futrelle moved to Boston to join the staff of the *Boston-American* in 1904. In 1905, Futrelle's first Thinking Machine adventure, "The Problem of Cell 13," was serialized in the paper. When the editorial staff invited readers to send in their own solutions, over two hundred and fifty answers were received. Futrelle wrote a handful of Thinking Machine novels and collections, including *The Chase of the Golden Plate* (1906), *The Thinking Machine* (1907), and *The Thinking Machine on The Case* (1908), but his greatest fame was in writing light romances such as *Elusive Isabel* and *The Diamond Master* (both 1909). After the publication of *My Lady's Garter* (1912), Futrelle died on board the Titanic a hero, helping with the evacuation of the other passengers.

"The Superfluous Finger" is full of devilish plotting and wry observations, proof that Futrelle and the Thinking Machine are unjustifiably neglected.

SHE DREW OFF her left glove, a delicate, crinkled suede affair, and offered her bare hand to the surgeon.

An artist would have called it beautiful, perfect, even; the surgeon, professionally enough. set it down as an excellent structural specimen. From the polished pink nails of the tapering fingers to the firm, well moulded wrist, it was distinctly the hand of a woman of ease—one that had never known labor, a pampered hand Dr. Prescott told himself.

"The forefinger," she exclaimed calmly. "I should like to have it amputated at the first joint, please."

"Amputated?" gasped Dr. Prescott. He stared into the pretty face of his caller. It was flushed softly, and the red lips were parted in a slight smile. It seemed quite an ordinary affair to her. The surgeon bent over the hand with quick interest. "Amputated!" he repeated.

"I came to you." she went on with a nod, "because I have been informed that you are one of the most skilful men of your profession, and the cost of the operation is quite immaterial."

Dr. Prescott pressed the pink nail of the forefinger then permitted the blood to rush back into it. Several times he did this, then he turned the hand over and scrutinized it closely inside from the delicately lined palm to the tips of the fingers. When he looked up at last there was an expression of frank bewilderment on his face.

"What's the matter with it?" he asked.

"Nothing." the woman replied pleasantly. "I merely want it off from the first joint."

The surgeon leaned back in his chair with a frown of perplexity on his brow, and his visitor was subjected to a sharp, professional stare. She bore it unflinchingly and even smiled a little at his obvious perturbation.

"Why do you want it off?" he demanded.

The woman shrugged her shoulders a little impatiently.

"I can't tell you that," she replied. "It really is not necessary that you should know. You are a surgeon, I want an operation performed. That is all."

There was a long pause; the mutual stare didn't waver.

"You must understand, Miss—Miss—er——" began Dr. Prescott at last. "By the way, you have not introduced yourself?" She was silent. "May I ask your name?"

"My name is of no consequence," she replied calmly. "I might, of course, give you a name, but it would not be mine, therefore any name would be superfluous."

Again the surgeon stared.

"When do you want the operation performed?" he inquired.

"Now," she replied. "I am ready."

"You must understand," he said severely, "that surgery is a profession for the relief of human suffering, not for mutilation—willful mutilation I might say."

"I understand that perfectly," she said. "But where a person submits of her own desire to—to mutilation as you call it, I can see no valid objection on your part."

"It would be criminal to remove a finger where there is no necessity for it," continued the surgeon bluntly. "No good end could be served."

A trace of disappointment showed in the young woman's face, and again she shrugged her shoulders.

"The question after all," she said finally, "is not one of ethics but is simply whether or not you *will* perform the operation. Would you do it for, say, a thousand dollars?"

"Not for five thousand dollars," blurted the surgeon.

"Well, for ten thousand then?" she asked, quite casually.

All sorts of questions were pounding in Dr. Prescott's mind. Why did a young and beautiful woman desire—why was she anxious even—to sacrifice a perfectly healthy finger? What possible purpose would it serve to mar a hand which was as nearly perfect as any he had ever seen? Was it some insane caprice? Staring deeply into her steady, quiet eyes he could only be convinced of her sanity. Then what?

"No, madam," he said at last, vehemently, "I would not perform the operation for any sum you might mention, unless I was first convinced that the removal of that finger was absolutely necessary. That, I think, is all."

He arose as if to end the consultation. The woman remained seated and continued thoughtful for a minute.

"As I understand it," she said, "you *would* perform the operation if I could convince you that it was absolutely necessary?"

"Certainly," he replied promptly, almost eagerly. His curiosity was aroused. "Then it would come within the range of my professional duties."

"Won't you take my word that it is necessary, and that it is impossible for me to explain why?"

"No. I must know why."

The woman arose and stood facing him. The disappointment had gone from her face now.

"Very well," she remarked steadily. "You *will* perform the operation if it is necessary, therefore if I should shoot the finger off, perhaps—?"

"Shoot it off?" exclaimed Dr. Prescott in amazement. "Shoot it off?"

"That is what I said," she replied calmly. "If I should shoot the finger off you would consent to dress the wound? You would make any necessary amputation?"

She held up the finger under discussion and looked at it curiously. Dr. Prescott himself stared at it with a sudden new interest.

"Shoot it off?" he repeated. "Why you must be mad to contemplate such a thing," he exploded, and his face flushed in sheer anger. "I—I will have nothing whatever to do with the affair, madam. Good day."

"I should have to be very careful, of course," she mused, "but I think perhaps one shot would be sufficient; then I should come to you and demand that you dress it?"

There was a question in the tone. Dr. Prescott stared at her for a full minute, then walked over and opened the door.

"In my profession, madam," he said coldly, "there is too much possibility of doing good and relieving actual suffering for me to consider this matter or discuss it further with you. There are three persons now waiting in the ante-room who *need* my services. I shall be compelled to ask you to excuse me."

"But you will dress the wound?" the woman insisted, undaunted by his forbidding tone and manner.

"I shall have nothing whatever to do with it," declared the surgeon, positively, finally. "If you need the services of any medical man permit me to suggest that it is an alienist and not a surgeon."

The woman didn't appear to take offense.

"Someone would have to dress it," she continued insistently. "I should much prefer that it be a man of undisputed skill—you I mean; therefore I shall call again. Good day."

There was a rustle of silken skirts and she was gone. Dr. Prescott stood for an instant gazing after her in frank wonder and annoyance in his eyes, his attitude, then he went back and sat down at the desk. The crinkled suede glove still lay where she had left it. He examined it gingerly then with a final shake of his head dismissed the affair and turned to other things.

Early next afternoon Dr. Prescott was sitting in his office writing when the door from the ante-room where patients awaited his leisure was thrown open and the young man in attendance rushed in.

"A lady has fainted, sir," he said hurriedly. "She seems to be hurt."

Dr. Prescott arose quickly and strode out. There, lying helplessly back in her chair with white face and closed eyes, was his visitor of the day before. He stepped toward her quickly, then hesitated as he recalled their conversation. Finally, however, professional instinct, the desire to relieve suffering, and perhaps curiosity, too, caused him to go to her. The left hand was wrapped in an improvised bandage through which there was a trickle of blood. He glared at it with incredulous eyes.

"Hanged if she didn't do it," he blurted angrily.

The fainting spell, Dr. Prescott saw, was due only to loss of blood and physical pain, and he busied himself trying to restore her to consciousness. Meanwhile he gave some hurried instructions to the young man who was in attendance in the ante-room.

"Call up Professor Van Dusen on the 'phone," he directed, "and ask him if he can assist me in a minor operation. Tell him it's rather a curious case and I am sure it will interest him."

It was in this manner that the problem of the superfluous finger first came to the attention of The Thinking Machine. He arrived just as the mysterious woman was opening her eyes to consciousness from the fainting spell. She stared at him glassily, unrecognizingly; then her glance wandered to Dr. Prescott. She smiled.

"I knew you'd have to do it," she murmured weakly.

After the ether had been administered for the operation, a simple and an easy one, Dr. Prescott stated the circumstances of the case to The Thinking Machine. The scientist stood with his long, slender fingers resting lightly on the young woman's pulse, listening in silence.

"What do you make of it?" demanded the surgeon.

The Thinking Machine didn't say. At the moment he was leaning over the unconscious woman, squinting at her forehead. With his disengaged hand he stroked the delicately pencilled eye-brows several times the wrong way, and again at close range squinted at them. Dr. Prescott saw and seeing, understood.

"No, it isn't that," he said and he shuddered a little. "I thought of it myself. Her bodily condition is excellent, splendid."

It was some time later when the young woman was sleeping lightly, placidly under the influence of a soothing potion, that The Thinking Machine spoke of the peculiar events which had preceded the operation. Then he was sitting in Dr. Prescott's private office. He had picked up a woman's glove from the desk.

"This is the glove she left when she first called, isn't it?" he inquired.

"Yes."

"Did you happen to see her remove it?"

"Yes."

The Thinking Machine curiously examined the dainty, perfumed trifle, then, arising suddenly, went into the adjoining room where the woman lay asleep. He stood for an instant gazing down admiringly at the exquisite, slender figure; then, bending over, he looked closely at her left hand. When at last he straightened up, it seemed that some unspoken question in his mind had been answered. He rejoined Dr. Prescott.

"It's difficult to say what motive is back of her desire to have the finger amputated," he said musingly. "I could perhaps venture a conjecture but if the matter is of no importance to you beyond mere curiosity I should not like to do so. Within a few months from now, I daresay, important developments will result and I should like to find out something more about her. That I can do when she returns to wherever she is stopping in the city. I'll 'phone to Mr. Hatch and have him ascertain for me where she goes, her name and other things which may throw a light on the matter."

"He will follow her?"

"Yes, precisely. Now we only seem to know two facts in connection with her. First, she is English."

"Yes," Dr. Prescott agreed. "Her accent, her appearance, everything about her suggests that."

"And the second fact is of no consequence at the moment," resumed The Thinking Machine. "Let me use your 'phone please."

Hutchinson Hatch, reporter, was talking.

"When the young woman left Dr. Prescott's, she took the cab which had been ordered for her and told the driver to go ahead until she stopped him. I got a good look at her, by the way. I managed to pass just as she entered the cab and walking on down got into another cab, which was waiting for me. Her cab drove for three or four blocks aimlessly, and finally stopped. The driver stooped down as if to listen to someone inside, and my cab passed. Then the other cab turned across a side street and after going eight or ten blocks, pulled up in front of an apartment house. The young woman got out and went inside. Her cab went away. Inside I found out that she was Mrs. Frederick Chevedon Morey. She came there last Tuesday—this is Friday—with her husband, and they engaged—"

"Yes, I knew she had a husband," interrupted The Thinking Machine.

"——engaged apartments for three months. When I had learned this much I remembered your instructions as to steamers from Europe landing on the day they took apartments or possibly a day or so before. I was just going out when Mrs. Morey stepped out of the elevator and preceded me to the door. She had changed her clothing and wore a different hat.

"It didn't seem to be necessary then to find out where she was going, for I knew I could find her when I wanted to, so I went down and made inquiries at the steamship offices. I found, after a great deal of work, that none of the three steamers which arrived the day the apartments were rented had brought a Mr. and Mrs. Morey, but a steamer on the day before had brought a Mr. and Mrs. David Girardeau from Liverpool. Mrs. Girardeau answered Mrs. Morey's description to the minutest detail, even to the gown she wore when she left the steamer. It was the same gown she wore when she left Dr. Prescott's after the operation."

That was all. The Thinking Machine sat with his enormous yellow head pillowed against a high-backed chair and his long slender fingers pressed tip to tip. He asked no questions and made no comment for a long time, then:

"About how many minutes was it from the time she entered the house until she came out again?"

"Not more than ten or fifteen," was the reply. "I was still talking casually to the people down stairs trying to find out something about her."

"What do they pay for their apartment?" asked the scientist, irrelevantly.

"Three hundred dollars a month."

The Thinking Machine's squint eyes were fixed immovably on a small discolored spot on the ceiling of his laboratory.

"Whatever else may develop in this matter, Mr. Hatch," he said after a time, "we must admit that we have met a woman with extraordinary courage—nerve, I daresay you'd call it. When Mrs. Morey left Dr. Prescott's operating room, she was so ill and weak from the shock that she could hardly stand, and now you tell me she changed her dress and went out immediately after she returned home."

"Well, of course——" Hatch said, apologetically.

"In that event," resumed the scientist, "we must assume also that the matter is one of the utmost importance to her, and yet the nature of the case had led me to believe that it might be months, perhaps, before there would be any particular development in it."

"What? How?" asked the reporter.

"The final development doesn't seem, from what I know, to belong on this side of the ocean at all," explained The Thinking Machine. "I imagine it is a case for Scotland Yard. The problem of course is: What made it necessary for her to get rid of that finger? If we admit her sanity, we can count the possible answers to this question on one hand, and at least three of these answers take the case back to England," He paused. "By the way, was Mrs. Morey's hand bound up in the same way when you saw her the second time?"

"Her left hand was in a muff," explained the reporter. "I couldn't see, but it seems to me that she wouldn't have had time to change the manner of its dressing."

"It's extraordinary," commented the scientist. He arose and paced back and forth across the room. "Extraordinary," he repeated. "One can't help but admire the fortitude of women under certain circumstances, Mr. Hatch. I think perhaps this particular case had better be called to the attention of Scotland Yard, but first I think it would be best for you to call on the Moreys tomorrow—you can find some pretext—and see what you can learn about them. You are an ingenious young man—I'll leave it all to you."

Hatch did call at the Morey apartments on the morrow, but under circumstances which were not at all what he expected. He went there with Detective Mallory, and Detective Mallory went there in a cab at full speed because the manager of the apartment house had 'phoned that Mrs. Frederick Chevedon Morey had been found murdered in her apartments. The detective ran up two flights of stairs and blundered, heavy-footed into the rooms, and there he paused in the presence of death.

The body of the woman lay on the floor and some one had mercifully covered it with a cloth from the bed. Detective Mallory drew the covering down from over the face and Hatch stared with a feeling of awe at the beautiful countenance which had, on the day before, been so radiant with life. Now it was distorted into an expression of awful agony and the limbs were drawn up convulsively. The mark of the murderer was at the white, exquisitely rounded throat—great black bruises where powerful, merciless fingers had sunk deeply into the soft flesh.

A physician in the house had preceded the police. After one glance at the woman and a swift, comprehensive look about the room Detective Mallory turned to him inquiringly.

"She has been dead for several hours," the doctor volunteered, "possibly since early last night. It appears that some virulent, burning poison was administered and then she was choked. I gather this from an examination of her mouth."

These things were readily to be seen; also it was plainly evident for many reasons that the finger marks at the throat were those of a man, but each step beyond these obvious facts only served further to bewilder the investigators. First was the statement of the night elevator boy.

"Mr. and Mrs. Morey left here last night about eleven o'clock," he said. "I know because I telephoned for a cab, and later brought them down from the third floor. They went into the manager's office leaving two suit cases in the hall. When they came out I took the suit cases to a cab that was waiting. They got in it and drove away."

"When did they return?" inquired the detective.

"They didn't return, sir," responded the boy. "I was on duty until six o'clock this morning. It just happened that no one came in after they went out until I was off duty at six."

The detective turned to the physician again.

"Then she couldn't have been dead since early last night," he said.

"She has been dead for several hours—at least twelve, possibly longer," said the physician firmly. "There's no possible argument about that."

The detective stared at him scornfully for an instant, then looked at the manager of the house.

"What was said when Mr. and Mrs. Morey entered your office last night?" he asked. "Were you there?"

"I was there, yes," was the reply. "Mr. Morey explained that they had been called away for a few days unexpectedly and left the keys of the apartment with me. That was all that was said: I saw the elevator boy take the suit cases out for them as they went to the cab."

"How did it come then, if you knew they were away that some one entered here this morning, and so found the body?"

"I discovered the body myself," replied the manager. "There was some electric wiring to be done in here and I thought their absence would be a good time for it. I came up to see about it and saw—that."

He glanced at the covered body with a little shiver and a grimace. Detective Mallory was deeply thoughtful for several minutes.

"The woman is here and she's dead," he said finally. "If she is here, she came back here, dead or alive last night between the time she went out with her husband and the time her body was found this morning. Now that's an absolute fact. But *how* did she come here?"

Of the three employees of the apartment house only the elevator boy on duty had not spoken. Now he spoke because the detective glared at him fiercely.

"I didn't see either Mr. or Mrs. Morey come in this morning," he explained hastily. "Nobody came in at all except the postman and some delivery wagon drivers up to the time the body was found."

Again Detective Mallory turned on the manager.

"Does any window of this apartment open on a fire escape?" he demanded.

"Yes—this way."

They passed through the short hallway to the back. Both the windows were locked on the inside, so it appeared that even if the woman had been brought into the room that way, the windows would not have been fastened unless her murderer went out of the house the front way. When Detective Mallory reached this stage of the investigation, he sat down and stared from one to the other of the silent little party as if he considered the entire matter some affair which they had perpetrated to annoy him.

Hutchinson Hatch started to say something, then thought better of it and turning, went to the telephone below. Within a few minutes The Thinking Machine stepped out of a cab in front and paused in the lower hall long enough to listen to the facts developed. There was a perfect network of wrinkles in the dome-like brow when the reporter concluded.

"It's merely a transfer of the final development in the affair from England to this country," he said enigmatically. "Please 'phone for Dr. Prescott to come here immediately."

He went on to the Morey apartments. With only a curt nod for Detective Mallory, the only one of the small party who knew him, he proceeded to the body of the dead woman and squinted down without a trace of emotion into the white pallid face. After a moment he dropped on his knees beside the inert body and examined the mouth and the finger marks about the white throat.

"Carbolic acid and strangulation," he remarked tersely to Detective Mallory who was leaning over watching him with something of hopeful eagerness in his stolid face. The Thinking Machine glanced past him to the manager of the house. "Mr. Morey is a powerful, athletic man in appearance?" he asked.

"Oh, no," was the reply. "He's short and slight, only a little larger than you are."

The scientist squinted aggressively at the manager as if the description were not quite what he expected. Then the slightly puzzled expression passed.

"Oh, I see," he remarked. "Played the piano," This was not a question; it was a statement.

"Yes, a great deal," was the reply, "so much so in fact that twice we had complaints from other persons in the house despite the fact that they had been here only a few days."

"Of course," mused the scientist abstractedly. "Of course. Perhaps Mrs. Morey did not play at all?"

"I believe she told me she did not."

The Thinking Machine drew down the thin cloth which had been thrown over the body and glanced at the left hand.

"Dear me! Dear me!" he exclaimed suddenly, and he arose. "Dear me!" he repeated. "That's the—" He turned to the manager and the two elevator boys. "This is Mrs. Morey beyond any question?"

The answer was a chorus of affirmation accompanied by some startling facial expressions.

"Did Mr. and Mrs. Morey employ any servants?"

"No," was the reply. "They had their meals in the café below most of the time. There is no housekeeping in these apartments at all."

"How many persons live in the building?"

"A hundred, I should say."

"There is a great deal of passing to and fro, then?"

"Certainly. It was rather unusual that so few persons passed in and out last night and this morning, and certainly Mrs. Morey and her husband were not among them, if that's what you're trying to find out."

The Thinking Machine glanced at the physician who was standing by silently.

"How long do you make it that she's been dead?" he asked.

"At least twelve hours," replied the physician. "Possibly longer."

"Yes, nearer fourteen, I imagine."

Abruptly he left the group and walked through the apartment and back again slowly. As he re-entered the room where the body lay, the door from the hall opened and Dr. Prescott entered, followed by Hutchinson Hatch. The Thinking Machine led the surgeon straight to the body and drew the cloth down from the face. Dr. Prescott started back with an exclamation of astonishment, recognition.

"There's no doubt about it at all in your mind?" inquired the scientist.

"Not the slightest," replied Dr. Prescott positively. "It's the same woman."

"Yet, look here!"

With a quick movement The Thinking Machine drew down the cloth
still more. Dr. Prescott together with those who had no idea of what to
expect, peered down at the body. After one glance the surgeon dropped
on his knees and examined closely the dead left hand. The forefinger
was off at the first joint. Dr. Prescott stared, stared incredulously. After
a moment his eyes left the maimed hand and settled again on her face.

"I have never seen—never dreamed—of such a startling—" he
began.

"That settles it all, of course," interrupted The Thinking Machine.
"It solves and proves the problem at once. Now, Mr. Mallory, if we
can go to your office or some place where we will be undisturbed I
will—"

"But who killed her?" demanded the detective abruptly.

"Let us find a quiet place," said The Thinking Machine in his usual
irritable manner.

Detective Mallory, Dr. Prescott, The Thinking Machine, Hutchinson
Hatch and the apartment house physician were seated in the front room
of the Morey apartments with all doors closed against prying, inquisi-
tive eyes. At the scientist's request Dr. Prescott repeated the circumstances leading up to the removal of a woman's left forefinger, and
there The Thinking Machine took up the story.

"Suppose, Mr. Mallory," and the scientist turned to the detective, "a
woman should walk into *your* office and say she must have a finger cut
off, what would you think?"

"I'd think she was crazy," was the prompt reply.

"Naturally, in your position," The Thinking Machine went on, "you
are acquainted with many strange happenings. Wouldn't this one
instantly suggest something to you? Something that was to happen
months off?"

Detective Mallory considered it wisely, but was silent.

"Well, here," declared The Thinking Machine. "A woman whom
we now know to be Mrs. Morey wanted her finger cut off. It instantly
suggested three, four, five, a dozen possibilities. Of course, only one,
or possibly two in combination, could be true. Therefore which one?
A little logic now to prove that two and two always make four—not
some times but *all* the time.

"Naturally the first supposition was insanity. We pass that as absurd on its face. Then disease—a taint of leprosy perhaps which had been visible on the left forefinger. I tested for that, and that was eliminated. Three strong reasons for desiring the finger off, either of which is strongly probable, remained. The fact that the woman was unmistakably English was obvious. From the mark of a wedding ring on her glove and a corresponding mark on her finger—she wore no such ring—we could safely surmise that she was married. These were the two first facts I learned. Substantiative evidence that she was married and not a widow came partly from her extreme youth and the lack of mourning in her attire.

"Then Mr. Hatch followed her, learned her name, where she lived and later the fact that she had arrived with her husband on a steamer a day or so before they took apartments here. This was proof that she was English, and proof that she had a husband. They came over on the steamer as Mr. and Mrs. David Girardeau—here they were Mr. and Mrs. Frederick Chevedon Morey. Why this difference in name? The circumstance in itself pointed to irregularity—crime committed or contemplated. Other things made me think it was merely contemplated and that it could be prevented; for then absence of every fact gave me no intimation that there would be murder. Then came the murder presumably of—Mrs. Morey?"

"Isn't it Mrs. Morey?" demanded the detective.

"Mr. Hatch recognized the woman as the one he had followed, I recognized her as the one on which there had been an operation, Dr. Prescott also recognized her," continued The Thinking Machine. "To convince myself, after I had found the manner of death, that it was the woman, I looked at her left hand. I found that the forefinger was gone—it had been removed by a skilled surgeon at the first joint. And this fact instantly showed me that the dead woman was not Mrs. Morey at all but somebody else; and incidentally cleared up the entire affair."

"How?" demanded the detective. "I thought you just said that you had helped cut off her forefinger?"

"Dr. Prescott and I cut off that finger yesterday," replied The Thinking Machine calmly. "The finger of the dead woman had been cut off months, perhaps years, ago."

There was blank amazement on Detective Mallory's face, and Hatch was staring straight into the squint eyes of the scientist. Vaguely, as through a mist, he was beginning to account for many things which had been hitherto inexplicable.

"The perfectly healed wound on the hand eliminated every possibility but one," The Thinking Machine resumed. "Previously I had been informed that Mrs. Morey did not—or said she did not—play the piano. I had seen the bare possibility of an immense insurance on her hands, and some trick to defraud the insurance company by marring one. Of course, against this was the fact that she had offered to pay a large sum for the operation; that their expenses here must have been enormous, so I was beginning to doubt the tenability of this supposition. The fact that the dead woman's finger was off removed that possibility completely, as it also removed the possibility of a crime of some sort in which there might have been left behind a tell-tale print of that forefinger. If there had been a serious crime with the trace of the finger as evidence, its removal would have been necessary to her.

"Then the one thing remained—that is that Mrs. Morey or whatever her name is—was in a conspiracy with her husband to get possession of certain properties, perhaps a title—remember she is English—by sacrificing that finger so that identification might be in accordance with the description of an heir whom she was to impersonate. We may well believe that she was provided with the necessary documentary evidence, and we know conclusively—we don't conjecture but we *know*—that the dead woman in there is the woman whose rights were to have been stolen by the so-called Mrs. Morey."

"But that is Mrs. Morey, isn't it?" demanded the detective again.

"No," was the sharp retort. "The perfect resemblance to Mrs. Morey and the finger removed long ago makes that clear. There is, I imagine, a relationship between them—perhaps they are cousins. I can hardly believe they are twins because the necessity, then of one impersonating the other to obtain either money or a title, would not have existed so palpably, although it is possible that Mrs. Morey, if disinherited or disowned, would have resorted to such a course."

There was silence for several minutes. Each member of the little group was turning over the stated facts mentally.

"But how did she come here—like this?" Hatch inquired.

"You remember, Mr. Hatch, when you followed Mrs. Morey here you told me she dressed again and went out?" asked the scientist in turn. "It was not Mrs. Morey you saw then—she was ill and I knew it from the operation—it was Miss Rossmore. The manager says a hundred persons live in this house—that there is a great deal of passing in and out. Can't you see that when there is such a startling resemblance Miss Rossmore could pass in and out at will and always be mistaken for Mrs. Morey? That no one would ever notice the difference?"

"But who killed her?" asked Detective Mallory, curiously. "How? Why?"

"Morey killed her," said The Thinking Machine flatly. "How did he kill her? We can fairly presume that first he tricked her into drinking the acid, then perhaps she was screaming with the pain of it, and he choked her to death. I imagined first he was a large, powerful man, because his grip on her throat was so powerful that he ruptured the jugular inside; but instead of that he plays the piano a great deal, which would give him the hand-power to choke her. And why? We can suppose only that it was because she had in some way learned of their purpose. That would have established the motive. The crowning delicacy of the affair was Morey's act in leaving his keys with the manager here. He did not anticipate that the apartments would be entered for several days—after they were safely away—while there was a chance that if neither of them had been seen here and their disappearance was unexplained the rooms would have been opened to ascertain why. That is all, I think."

"Except to catch Morey and his wife," said the detective grimly.

"Easily done," said The Thinking Machine. "I imagine, if this murder is kept out of the newspapers for a couple of hours you can find them about to sail for Europe. Suppose you try the line they came over on?"

It was just three hours later that the accused man and wife were taken prisoner. They had just engaged passage on the steamer which sailed at half past four o'clock.

Their trial was a famous one and resulted in conviction after an astonishing story of an attempt to seize an estate and title belonging rightfully to a Miss Evelyn Rossmore who had mysteriously disappeared years before, and was identified with the dead woman.

The Four Suspects

Agatha Christie

Agatha Christie (1890-1976), the Grand Dame of Mystery Fiction, was born in Torquay, England. Christie was cared for by her two grandmothers, one of whom was the inspiration for Miss Marple. While she had no formal education, Christie was a voracious reader. In 1914, she married Archie Christie. During the war, Christie worked as a nurse and pharmacist, jobs which inspired her first novel, *The Mysterious Affair at Styles* (1920). In 1926, after the release of *The Murder of Roger Ayckroyd,* her husband divorced her—increasing sales greatly. In 1929, Christie travelled Iraq and met archeologist Max Mallowan, the man she married a year later. In 1930, her first Miss Marple novel, *Murder at the Vicarage,* was published. Christie divided her time between the Mideast and England, producing such classics as *The Tuesday Club Murders* (1932), *Murder on the Orient Express* (1934), *The ABC Murders* (1936), *Death on the Nile* (1937), *Ten Little Indians* (1939), *Evil Under The Sun* (1941), and *Sparkling Cyanide* (1945). In 1947, Christie wrote a radio play for the Queen Mother, *Three Blind Mice;* it would later be rewritten as *The Mousetrap* (1953), one of the longest running plays in history. In 1954, she was awarded Grandmaster status by the Mystery Writers of America. This was the first of several honors for Christie, including a 1955 Drama Desk award for her play *Witness for the Prosecution,* and an honorary degree from the University of Exeter in 1961. Her later novels include *The Mirror Crack'd from Side to Side* (1962) and *Halloween Party* (1969). In 1971, just as she was named a Dame of the British Empire, Christie broke her hip. While she never recovered from this injury, Christie still wrote such novels as *Elephants Can Remember* (1972) and *Curtain* (1975), which depicted the death of Hercule Poirot. After imagining the death of her famous detective, Christie died in 1976.

"The Four Suspects," featuring the formal detective story's First Lady, Miss Jane Marple, is an excellent example of the type of wit and observation that has made Agatha Christie such a popular author.

THE CONVERSATION HOVERED round undiscovered and unpunished crimes. Everyone in turn vouchsafed an opinion: Colonel Bantry, his plump amiable wife, Jane Helier, Dr. Lloyd, and even old

Miss Marple. The one person who did not speak was the one best fitted in most people's opinion to do so. Sir Henry Clithering, ex-Commissioner of Scotland Yard, sat silent, twisting his moustache—or rather stroking it—and half smiling, as though at some inward thought that amused him.

"Sir Henry," said Mrs. Bantry at last, "if you don't say something, I shall scream. Are there a lot of crimes that go unpunished, or are there not?"

"You're thinking of newspaper headlines, Mrs. Bantry. SCOTLAND YARD AT FAULT AGAIN. And a list of unsolved mysteries to follow."

"Which really, I suppose, form a very small percentage of the whole?" said Dr. Lloyd.

"Yes, that is so. The hundreds of crimes that are solved and the perpetrators punished are seldom heralded and sung. But that isn't quite the point at issue, is it? When you talk of undiscovered crimes and unsolved crimes, you are talking of two different things. In the first category come all the crimes that Scotland Yard never hears about, the crimes that no one even knows have been committed."

"But I suppose there aren't very many of those?" said Mrs. Bantry.

"Aren't there?"

"Sir Henry! You don't mean there are?"

"I should think," said Miss Marple thoughtfully, "that there must be a very large number."

The charming old lady, with her old-world, unruffled air, made her statement in a tone of the utmost placidity.

"My dear Miss Marple," said Colonel Bantry.

"Of course," said Miss Marple, "a lot of people are stupid. And stupid people get found out, whatever they do. But there are quite a number of people who aren't stupid, and one shudders to think of what they might accomplish unless they had very strongly rooted principles."

"Yes," said Sir Henry, "there are a lot of people who aren't stupid. How often does some crime come to light simply by reason of a bit of unmitigated bungling, and each time one asks oneself the question: If this hadn't been bungled, would anyone ever have known?"

"But that's very serious, Clithering," said Colonel Bantry. "Very serious, indeed."

"Is it?"

"What do you mean, is it? Of course it's serious."

"You say crime goes unpunished, but does it? Unpunished by the law perhaps, but cause and effect works outside the law. To say that every crime brings its own punishment is by way of being a platitude, and yet in my opinion nothing can be truer."

"Perhaps, perhaps," said Colonel Bantry. "But that doesn't alter the seriousness—the—er—seriousness—" He paused, rather at a loss.

Sir Henry Clithering smiled.

"Ninety-nine people out of a hundred are doubtless of your way of thinking," he said. "But you know, it isn't really guilt that is important—it's innocence. That's the thing that nobody will realize."

"I don't understand," said Jane Helier.

"I do," said Miss Marple. "When Mrs. Trent found half a crown missing from her bag, the person it affected most was the daily woman, Mrs. Arthur. Of course the Trents thought it was her, but being kindly people and knowing she had a large family and a husband who drinks, well—they naturally didn't want to go to extremes. But they felt differently toward her, and they didn't leave her in charge of the house when they went away, which made a great difference to her; and other people began to get a feeling about her too. And then it suddenly came out that it was the governess. Mrs. Trent saw her through a door reflected in a mirror. The purest chance—though I prefer to call it Providence. And that, I think, is what Sir Henry means. Most people would be only interested in who took the money, and it turned out to be the most unlikely person—just like in detective stories! But the real person it was life and death to was poor Mrs. Arthur, who had done nothing. That's what you mean, isn't it, Sir Henry?"

"Yes, Miss Marple, you've hit off my meaning exactly. Your charwoman person was lucky in the instance you relate. Her innocence was shown. But some people may go through a lifetime crushed by the weight of a suspicion that is really unjustified."

"Are you thinking of some particular instance, Sir Henry?" asked Mrs. Bantry shrewdly.

"As a matter of fact, Mrs. Bantry, I am. A very curious case. A case where we believe murder to have been committed, but with no possible chance of ever proving it."

"Poison, I suppose," breathed Jane. "Something untraceable."

Dr. Lloyd moved restlessly and Sir Henry shook his head.

"No, dear lady. Not the secret arrow poison of the South American Indians! I wish it were something of that kind. We have to deal with something much more prosaic—so prosaic, in fact, that there is no hope of bringing the deed home to its perpetrator. An old gentleman who fell downstairs and broke his neck; one of those regrettable accidents which happen every day."

"But what happened really?"

"Who can say?" Sir Henry shrugged his shoulders. "A push from behind? A piece of cotton or string tied across the top of the stairs and carefully removed afterward? That we shall never know."

"But you do think that it—well, wasn't an accident? Now why?" asked the doctor.

"That's rather a long story, but—well, yes, we're pretty sure. As I said, there's no chance of being able to bring the deed home to anyone—the evidence would be too flimsy. But there's the other aspect of the case—the one I was speaking about. You see, there were four people who might have done the trick. One's guilty, but the other three are innocent. And unless the truth is found out, those three are going to remain under the terrible shadow of doubt."

"I think," said Mrs. Bantry, "that you'd better tell us your long story."

"I needn't make it so very long after all," said Sir Henry. "I can at any rate condense the beginning. That deals with a German secret society—the *Schwartze Hand*—something after the lines of the Camorra or what is most people's idea of the Camorra. A scheme of blackmail and terrorization. The thing started quite suddenly after the war and spread to an amazing extent. Numberless people were victimized by it. The authorities were not successful in coping with it, for its secrets were jealously guarded, and it was almost impossible to find anyone who could be induced to betray them.

"Nothing much was ever known about it in England, but in Germany it was having a most paralyzing effect. It was finally broken up and dispersed through the efforts of one man, a Dr. Rosen, who had at one time been very prominent in Secret Service work. He became a member, penetrated its inmost circle, and was, as I say, instrumental in bringing about its downfall.

"But he was, in consequence, a marked man, and it was deemed wise that he should leave Germany—at any rate for a time. He came to England, and we had letters about him from the police in Berlin. He came and had a personal interview with me. His point of view was both dispassionate and resigned. He had no doubts of what the future held for him.

"'They will get me, Sir Henry,' he said. 'Not a doubt of it.' He was a big man with a fine head and a very deep voice, with only a slight guttural intonation to tell of his nationality. 'That is a foregone conclusion. It does not matter, I am prepared. I faced the risk when I undertook this business. I have done what I set out to do. The organization can never be gotten together again. But there are many members of it at liberty, and they will take the only revenge they can—my life. It is simply a question of time, but I am anxious that that time should be as long as possible. You see, I am collecting and editing some very interesting material—the result of my life's work. I should like, if possible, to be able to complete my task.'

"He spoke very simply, with a certain grandeur which I could not but admire. I told him we would take all precautions, but he waved my words aside.

"'Some day, sooner or later, they will get me,' he repeated. 'When that day comes, do not distress yourself. You will, I have no doubt, have done all that is possible.'

"He then proceeded to outline his plans, which were simple enough. He proposed to take a small cottage in the country where he could live quietly and go on with his work. In the end he selected a village in Somerset—King's Gnaton, which was seven miles from a railway station and singularly untouched by civilization. He bought a very charming cottage, had various improvements and alterations made, and settled down there most contentedly. His household consisted of his niece, Greta; a secretary; an old German servant who had served him faithfully for nearly forty years; and an outside handy man and gardener who was a native of King's Gnaton."

"The four suspects," said Dr. Lloyd softly.

"Exactly. The four suspects. There is not much more to tell. Life went on peacefully at King's Gnaton for five months and then the blow fell. Dr. Rosen fell down the stairs one morning and was found dead about half an hour later. At the time the accident must have taken place, Gertrud was in her kitchen with the door closed and heard nothing—so she says. Fräulein Greta was in the garden, planting some bulbs— again, so she says. The gardener, Dobbs, was in the small potting shed having his elevenses— so he says; and the secretary was out for a walk, and once more there is only his own word for it. No one had an alibi—no one can corroborate anyone else's story. But one thing is certain. No one from outside could have done it, for a stranger in the little village of King's Gnaton would be noticed without fail. Both the back and the front doors were locked, each member of the household having his own key. So you see it narrows down to those four. And yet each one seems to be above suspicion. Greta, his own brother's child. Gertrud, with forty years of faithful service. Dobbs, who has never been out of King's Gnaton. And Charles Templeton, the secretary—"

"Yes," said Colonel Bantry, "what about him? He seems the suspicious person to my mind. What do you know about him?"

"It is what I knew about him that put him completely out of court—at any rate, at the time," said Sir Henry gravely. "You see, Charles Templeton was one of my own men."

"Oh!" said Colonel Bantry, considerably taken aback.

"Yes. I wanted to have someone on the spot, and at the same time I didn't want to cause talk in the village. Rosen really needed a secretary. I put Templeton on the job. He's a gentleman, he speaks German fluently, and he's altogether a very able fellow."

"But, then, which do you suspect?" asked Mrs. Bantry in a bewildered tone. "They all seem so—well, impossible."

"Yes, so it appears. But you can look at the thing from another angle. Fräulein Greta was his niece and a very lovely girl, but the war has shown us time and again that brother can turn against sister, or father against son, and so on, and the loveliest and gentlest of young girls did some of the most amazing things. The same thing applies to Gertrud, and who knows what other forces might be at work in her case? A quarrel, perhaps, with her master, a growing resentment all the more lasting because of the long faithful years behind her. Elderly women of that class can be amazingly bitter sometimes. And Dobbs? Was he right outside it because he had no connection with the family? Money will do much. In some way Dobbs might have been approached and bought.

"For one thing seems certain: Some message or some order must have come from outside. Otherwise, why five months' immunity? No, the agents of the society must have been at work. Not yet sure of Rosen's perfidy, they delayed till the betrayal had been traced to him beyond any possible doubt. And then, all doubts set aside, they must have sent their message to the spy within the gates—the message that said, 'Kill.'"

"How nasty!" said Jane Helier, and shuddered.

"But how did the message come? That was the point I tried to elucidate—the one hope of solving my problem. One of those four people must have been approached or communicated with in some way. There would be no delay—I knew that; as soon as the command came, it would be carried out. That was a peculiarity of the *Schwartze Hand.*

"I went into the question, went into it in a way that will probably strike you as being ridiculously meticulous. Who had come to the cottage that morning? I eliminated nobody. Here is the list."

He took an envelope from his pocket and selected a paper from its contents.

"The butcher, bringing some neck of mutton. Investigated and found correct.

"The grocer's assistant, bringing a packet of corn flour, two pounds of sugar, a pound of butter, and a pound of coffee. Also investigated and found correct.

"The postman, bringing two circulars for Fräulein Rosen, a local letter for Gertrud, three letters for Dr. Rosen, one with a foreign stamp, and two letters for Mr. Templeton, one also with a foreign stamp."

Sir Henry paused and then took a sheaf of documents from the envelope.

"It may interest you to see these for yourself. They were handed me by the various people concerned or collected from the wastepaper basket. I need hardly say they've been tested by experts for invisible ink, et cetera. No excitement of that kind is possible."

Everyone crowded round to look. The catalogues were respectively from a nurseryman and from a prominent London fur establishment. The two bills addressed to Dr. Rosen were a local one for seeds for the garden and one from a London stationery firm. The letter addressed to him ran as follows:

My Dear Rosen—Just back from Dr. Helmuth Spath's. I saw Edgar Jackson the other day. He and Amos Perry have just come back from Tsingtau. In all Honesty I can't say I envy them the trip. Let me have news of you soon. As I said before: Beware of a certain person. You know who I mean, though you don't agree.—Yours,

Georgina.

"Mr. Templeton's mail consisted of this bill which, as you see, is an account rendered from his tailor, and a letter from a friend in Germany," went on Sir Henry. "The latter, unfortunately, he tore up while out on his walk. Finally we have the letter received by Gertrud."

Dear Mrs. Swartz—We're hoping as how you be able to come to the social on friday evening. The vicar says has he hopes you will—one and all being welcome. The resipy for the ham was very good, and I thanks you for it. Hoping as this finds you well and that we shall see you friday I remain

Yours faithfully,
Emma Greene.

Dr. Lloyd smiled a little over this and so did Mrs. Bantry. "I think the last letter can be put out of court," said Dr. Lloyd.

"I thought the same," said Sir Henry, "but I took the precaution of verifying that there was a Mrs. Greene and a church social. One can't be too careful, you know."

"That's what our friend Miss Marple always says," said Dr. Lloyd, smiling. "You're lost in a daydream, Miss Marple. What are you thinking out?"

Miss Marple gave a start.

"So stupid of me," she said. "I was just wondering why the word Honesty in Dr. Rosen's letter was spelled with a capital H."

Mrs. Bantry picked it up.

"So it is," she said. "Oh!"

"Yes, dear," said Miss Marple. "I thought you'd notice!"

"There's a definite warning in that letter," said Colonel Bantry. "That's the first thing caught my attention. I notice more than you'd think. Yes, a definite warning—against whom?"

"There's rather a curious point about that letter," said Sir Henry. "According to Templeton, Dr. Rosen opened the letter at breakfast and tossed it across to him, saying he didn't know who the fellow was from Adam."

"But it wasn't a fellow," said Jane Helier. "It was signed 'Georgina.'"

"It's difficult to say which it is," said Dr. Lloyd. "It might be Georgey, but it certainly looks more like Georgina. Only it strikes me that the writing is a man's."

"You know, that's interesting," said Colonel Bantry. "His tossing it across the table like that and pretending he knew nothing about it. Wanted to watch somebody's face. Whose face—the girl's? Or the man's?"

"Or even the cook's?" suggested Mrs. Bantry. "She might have been in the room bringing in the breakfast. But what I don't see is...it's most peculiar—"

She frowned over the letter. Miss Marple drew closer to her. Miss Marple's finger went out and touched the sheet of paper. They murmured together.

"But why did the secretary tear up the other letter?" asked Jane Helier suddenly. "It seems—oh, I don't know—it seems queer. Why should he have letters from Germany? Although, of course, if he's above suspicion, as you say—"

"But Sir Henry didn't say that," said Miss Marple quickly, looking up from her murmured conference with Mrs. Bantry. "He said four suspects. So that shows that he includes Mr. Templeton. I'm right, am I not, Sir Henry?"

"Yes, Miss Marple. I have learned one thing through bitter experience. Never say to yourself that anyone is above suspicion. I gave you reasons just now why three of these people might after all be guilty, unlikely as it seemed. I did not at that time apply the same process to Charles Templeton. But I came to it at last through pursuing the rule I have just mentioned. And I was forced to recognize this: That every army and every navy and every police force has a certain number of traitors within its ranks, much as we hate to admit the idea. And I examined dispassionately the case against Charles Templeton.

"I asked myself very much the same questions as Miss Helier has just asked. Why should he, alone of all the house, not be able to produce the letter he had received—a letter, moreover, with a German stamp on it. Why should he have letters from Germany?

"The last question was an innocent one, and I actually put it to him. His reply came simply enough. His mother's sister was married to a German. The letter had been from a German girl cousin. So I learned something I did not know before—that Charles Templeton had relations with people in Germany. And that put him definitely on the list of suspects—very much so. He is my own man—a lad I have always liked and trusted; but in common justice and fairness I must admit that he heads that list.

"But there it is—I do not know! I do not know...And in all probability I never shall know. It is not a question of punishing a murderer. It is a question that to me seems a hundred times more important. It is the blighting, perhaps, of an honorable man's whole career ...because of suspicion—a suspicion that I dare not disregard."

Miss Marple coughed and said gently:

"Then, Sir Henry, if I understand you rightly, it is this young Mr. Templeton only who is so much on your mind?"

"Yes, in a sense. It should, in theory, be the same for all four, but that is not actually the case. Dobbs, for instance—suspicion may attach to him in my mind, but it will not actually affect his career. Nobody in the village has ever had any idea that old Dr. Rosen's death was anything but an accident. Gertrud is slightly more affected. It must make, for instance, a difference in Fräulein Rosen's attitude toward her. But that, possibly, is not of great importance to her.

"As for Greta Rosen—well, here we come to the crux of the matter. Greta is a very pretty girl and Charles Templeton is a good-looking young man, and for five months they were thrown together with no outer distractions. The inevitable happened. They fell in love with each other—even if they did not come to the point of admitting the fact in words.

"And then the catastrophe happens. It is three months ago now, and a day or two after I returned, Greta Rosen came to see me. She had sold the cottage and was returning to Germany, having finally settled up her uncle's affairs. She came to me personally, although she knew I had retired, because it was really about a personal matter she wanted to see me. She beat about the bush a little, but at last it all came out. What did I think? That letter with the German stamp—she had worried about it and worried about it—the one Charles had torn up. Was it all right? Surely it must be all right. Of course she believed his story, but—oh, if she only knew! If she knew—for certain.

"You see? The same feeling: the wish to trust—but the horrible lurking suspicion, thrust resolutely to the back of the mind, but persisting nevertheless. I spoke to her with absolute frankness and asked her to do the same. I asked her whether she had been on the point of caring for Charles and he for her.

"'I think so,' she said. 'Oh yes, I know it was so. We were so happy. Every day passed so contentedly. We knew—we both knew. There was no hurry—there was all the time in the world. Some day he would tell me he loved me, and I should tell him that I, too—Ah! But you can guess! And now it is all changed. A black cloud has come between us—we are constrained, when we meet we do not know what to say. It is, perhaps, the same with him as with me...We are each saying to ourselves, "If I were sure!" That is why, Sir Henry, I beg of you to say to me, "You may be sure, whoever killed your uncle, it was not Charles Templeton!" Say it to me! Oh, say it to me! I beg—I beg!'

"I couldn't say it to her. They'll drift farther and farther apart, those two—with suspicion like a ghost between them—a ghost that can't be laid."

He leaned back in his chair; his face looked tired and grey. He shook his head once or twice despondently.

"And there's nothing more can be done, unless—" He sat up straight again and a tiny whimsical smile crossed his face. "—unless Miss Marple can help us. Can't you, Miss Marple? I've a feeling that letter might be in your line, you know. The one about the church social. Doesn't it remind you of something or someone that makes everything perfectly plain? Can't you do something to help two helpless young people who want to be happy?"

Behind the whimsicality there was something earnest in his appeal. He had come to think very highly of the mental powers of this frail, old-fashioned maiden lady. He looked across at her with something very like hope in his eyes.

Miss Marple coughed and smoothed her lace.

"It does remind me a little of Annie Poultny," she admitted. "Of course the letter is perfectly plain—both to Mrs. Bantry and myself. I don't mean the church-social letter, but the other one. You living so much in London and not being a gardener, Sir Henry, would not have been likely to notice."

"Eh?" said Sir Henry. "Notice what?"

Mrs. Bantry reached out a hand and selected a catalogue. She opened it and read aloud with gusto:

"'Dr. Helmuth Spath. Pure lilac, a wonderfully fine flower, carried on exceptionally long and stiff stem. Splendid for cutting and garden decoration. A novelty of striking beauty.

"'Edgar Jackson. Beautifully shaped chrysanthemum-like flower of a distinct brick-red color.

"'Amos Perry. Brilliant red, highly decorative.

"'Tsingtau. Brilliant orange-red, showy garden plant and lasting cut flower.

"'Honesty—'"

"With a capital H, you remember," murmured Miss Marple.

"'Honesty. Rose and white shades, enormous perfect-shaped flower.'"

Mrs. Bantry flung down the catalogue and said with immense explosive force:

"Dahlias!"

"And their initial letters spell 'Death,'" explained Miss Marple.

"But the letter came to Dr. Rosen himself," objected Sir Henry.

"That was the clever part of it," said Miss Marple. "That and the warning in it. What would he do, getting a letter from someone he didn't know, full of names he didn't know. Why, of course, toss it over to his secretary."

"Then, after all—"

"Oh no!" said Miss Marple. "Not the secretary. Why, that's what makes it so perfectly clear that it wasn't him. He'd never have let that letter be found if so. And equally he'd never have destroyed a letter to himself with a German stamp on it. Really, his innocence is—if you'll allow me to use the world—just shining."

"Then who—"

"Well, it seems almost certain—as certain as anything can be in this world. There was another person at the breakfast table, and she would quite naturally under the circumstances—put out her hand for the letter and read it. And that would be that. You remember that she got a gardening catalogue by the same post—"

"Greta Rosen," said Sir Henry slowly. "Then her visit to me—"

"Gentlemen never see through these things," said Miss Marple. "And I'm afraid they often think we old women are—well, cats, to see things the way we do. But there it is. One does know a great deal about one's own sex, unfortunately. I've no doubt there was a barrier between them. The young man felt a sudden inexplicable repulsion. He suspected, purely through instinct, and couldn't hide the suspicion. And I really think that the girl's visit to you was just pure spite. She was safe enough really, but she just went out of her way to fix your suspicions definitely on poor Mr. Templeton. You weren't nearly so sure about him until after her visit."

"I'm sure it was nothing that she said—" began Sir Henry.

"Gentlemen," said Miss Marple calmly, "never see through these things."

"And that girl—" He stopped. "She commits a cold-blooded murder and gets off scot-free!"

"Oh no, Sir Henry," said Miss Marple. "Not scot-free. Neither you nor I believe that. Remember what you said not long ago. No. Greta Rosen will not escape punishment. To begin with, she must be in with a very queer set of people—blackmailers and terrorists—associates who will do her no good and will probably bring her to a miserable end. As you say, one mustn't waste thoughts on the guilty—it's the innocent who matter. Mr. Templeton, who I daresay will marry that German cousin, his tearing up her letter looks—well, it looks suspicious—using the word in quite a different sense from the one we've been using all the evening. A little as though he were afraid of the other girl noticing or asking to see it? Yes, I think there must have been some little romance there. And then there's Dobbs—though, as you say, I daresay it won't much matter to him. His elevenses are probably all he thinks about. And then there's that poor old Gertrud—the one who reminded me of Annie Poultny. Poor Annie Poultny. Fifty years' faithful service and suspected of making away with Miss Lamb's will, though nothing could be proved. Almost broke the poor creature's faithful heart. And then after she was dead it came to light in the secret drawer of the tea caddy where old Miss Lamb had put it herself for safety. But too late then for poor Annie.

"That's what worries me so about that poor old German woman. When one is old, one becomes embittered very easily. I felt much more sorry for her than for Mr. Templeton, who is young and good-looking and evidently a favorite with the ladies. You will write to her, won't you, Sir Henry, and just tell her that her innocence is established beyond doubt? Her dear old master dead, and she no doubt brooding and feeling herself suspected of...Oh! It won't bear thinking about!"

"I will write, Miss Marple," said Sir Henry. He looked at her curiously. "You know, I shall never quite understand you. Your outlook is always a different one from what I expect."

"My outlook, I'm afraid, is a very petty one," said Miss Marple humbly. "I hardly ever go out of St. Mary Mead."

"And yet you have solved what may be called an international mystery," said Sir Henry. "For you have solved it. I am convinced of that."

Miss Marple blushed, then bridled a little.

"I was, I think, well educated for the standard of my day. My sister and I had a German governess—a Fräulein. A very sentimental creature. She taught us the language of flowers—a forgotten study nowadays, but most charming. A yellow tulip, for instance, means 'Hopeless Love,' while a China aster means 'I Die of Jealousy at Your Feet.' That letter was signed Georgina, which I seem to remember as dahlia in German, and that of course made the whole thing perfectly clear. I wish I could remember the meaning of dahlia, but alas, that eludes me. My memory is not what it was."

"At any rate, it didn't mean 'Death.'"

"No, indeed. Horrible, is it not? There are very sad things in the world."

"There are," said Mrs. Bantry with a sigh. "It's lucky one has flowers and one's friends."

"She puts us last, you observe," said Dr. Lloyd.

"A man used to send me purple orchids every night to the theater," said Jane dreamily.

"'I Await Your Favors'—that's what that means," said Miss Marple brightly.

Sir Henry gave a peculiar sort of cough and turned his head away.

Miss Marple gave a sudden exclamation.

"I've remembered. Dahlias mean 'Treachery and Misrepresentation.'"

"Wonderful," said Sir Henry. "Absolutely wonderful."

And he sighed.

The Entertaining Episode of the Article in Question

Dorothy L. Sayers

> **Dorothy L. Sayers** (1893-1957) grew up in England's Fen country.
> Sayers was originally tutored at home before being sent to the Godolphin
> School at Salisbury in 1908. She obtained both a B.A. and an M.A. from
> Oxford in 1915—one of the first women to graduate from that college.
> She held down various jobs as an editor before accepting a position at
> Benson's advertising agency in 1922. Her first Wimsey novel, *Whose
> Body?*, was released in 1923. In 1926, *Clouds of Witness* was released.
> Sayers married Captain Oswald Atherton Fleming that year. She pro-
> duced two more novels, *Unnatural Death* (1927) and *The Unpleasantness
> at the Bellona Club* (1928), before moving to Witham in 1929. After
> editing the first *Omnibus of Crime* that year, Sayers produced *Strong
> Poison* (1930) and helped found The Detection Club. 1931 saw the release
> of *The Five Red Herrings*. She produced five more Wimsey novels (*Have
> His Carcase*, 1932; *Murder Must Advertise*, 1933; *The Nine Tailors*,
> 1934; *Gaudy Night*, 1935; *Busman's Honeymoon*, 1937), but began to
> devote more time to religious writings and essays. Among these are *The
> Zeal of Thy House* (1937), *The Greatest Drama Ever Staged* (1938), *He
> That Should Come* (1939), *Begin Here: A War-Time Essay* (1940), *The
> Other Six Deadly Sins* (1943), *Unpopular Opinions* (1947) and *The Lost
> Tools of Learning* (1948). In 1949, she published the first third of her
> translation of Dante's *Divine Comedy*. In 1950, her husband died, and
> shortly afterwards Sayers became the churchwarden of St. Thomas
> Church in London. Sayers died in 1957, a few days before Christmas,
> from an alleged stroke.
>   The Lord Wimsey series is known for its light, breezy style. This
> story originally appeared in the only collection of Wimsey stories, *Lord
> Peter Views the Body*.

THE UNPROFESSIONAL detective career of Lord Peter Wimsey
was regulated (though the word has no particular propriety in this
connection) by a persistent and undignified inquisitiveness. The habit
of asking silly questions—natural, though irritating, in the immature

male—remained with him long after his immaculate man, Bunter, had become attached to his service to shave the bristles from his chin and see to the due purchase and housing of Napoleon brandies and Villar y Villar cigars. At the age of thirty-two his sister Mary christened him Elephant's Child. It was his idiotic enquiries (before his brother, the Duke of Denver, who grew scarlet with mortification) as to what the Woolsack was really stuffed with that led the then Lord Chancellor idly to investigate the article in question, and to discover, tucked deep within its recesses, that famous diamond necklace of the Marchioness of Writtle, which had disappeared on the day Parliament was opened and been safely secreted by one of the cleaners. It was by a continual and personal badgering of the Chief Engineer at 2LO on the question of "Why is Oscillation and How is it Done?" that his lordship incidentally unmasked the great Proffsky gang of Anarchist conspirators, who were accustomed to converse in code by a methodical system of howls, superimposed (to the great annoyance of listeners in British and European stations) upon the London wave-length and duly relayed by 5XX over a radius of some five or six hundred miles. He annoyed persons of more leisure than decorum by suddenly taking into his head to descend to the Underground by way of the stairs, though the only exciting things he ever actually found there were the blood-stained boots of the Sloane Square murderer; on the other hand when the drains were taken up at Glegg's Folly, it was by hanging about and hindering the plumbers at their job that he accidentally made the discovery which hanged that detestable poisoner, William Girdlestone Chitty.

Accordingly, it was with no surprise at all that the reliable Bunter, one April morning, received the announcement of an abrupt change of plan.

They had arrived at the Gare St. Lazare in good time to register the luggage. Their three months' trip to Italy had been purely for enjoyment, and had been followed by a pleasant fortnight in Paris. They were now intending to pay a short visit to the Duc de Sainte-Croix in Rouen on their way back to England. Lord Peter paced the Salle des Pas Perdus for some time, buying an illustrated paper or two and eyeing the crowd. He bent an appreciative eye on a slim, shingled creature with the face of a Paris *gamin,* but was forced to admit to himself that her ankles were a trifle on the thick side; he assisted an elderly lady who was explaining to the bookstall clerk that she wanted a map of Paris and not a *carte postale,* consumed a quick cognac at one of the little green tables at the far end, and then decided he had better go down and see how Bunter was getting on.

In half an hour Bunter and his porter had worked themselves up to the second place in the enormous queue—for, as usual, one of the weighing-machines was out of order. In front of them stood an agitated little group—the young woman Lord Peter had noticed in the Salle des Pas Perdus, a sallow-faced man of about thirty, their porter, and the registration official, who was peering eagerly through his little *guichet*.

"Mais je te répète que je ne les ai pas," said the sallow man heatedly. "Voyons, voyons. C'est bien toi qui les as pris, n'est-ce-pas? Eh bien, alors, comment veux-tu que je les aie, moi?"

"Mais non, mais non, je te les ai bien donnés là-haut, avant d'aller chercher les journaux."

"Je t'assure que non. Enfin, c'est évident! J'ai cherché partout, que diable! Tu ne m'as rien donné, du tout, du tout."

"Mais puisque je t'ai dit d'aller faire enrégistrer les bagages! Ne faut-il pas que je t'aie bien remis les billets? Me prends-tu pour un imbécile? Va! On n'est pas dépourvu de sens! Mais regarde l'heure! Le train part à II h. 20 m. Cherche un peu, au moins."

"Mais puisque j'ai cherché partout—le gilet, rien! Le jacquet rien, rien! Le pardessus—rien! rien! rien! C'est toi—"

Here the porter, urged by the frantic cries and stamping of the queue, and the repeated insults of Lord Peter's porter, flung himself into the discussion.

"P't-être qu' m'sieur a bouté les billets dans son pantalon," he suggested.

"Triple idiot!" snapped the traveller, "je vous le demande—est-ce qu'on a jamais entendu parler de mettre des billets dans son pantalon? Jamais—"

The French porter is a Republican, and, moreover, extremely ill-paid. The large tolerance of his English colleague is not for him.

"Ah!" said he, dropping two heavy bags and looking round for moral support. "Vous dîtes? En voilà du joli! Allons; mon p'tit, ce n'est pas parcequ'on porte un fauxcol qu'on a le droit d'insulter les gens."

The discussion might have become a full-blown row, had not the young man suddenly discovered the missing tickets—incidentally, they were in his trousers-pocket after all—and continued the registration of his luggage, to the undisguised satisfaction of the crowd.

"Bunter," said his lordship, who had turned his back on the group and was lighting a cigerette, "I am going to change the tickets. We shall go straight to London. Have you got that snapshot affair of yours with you?"

"Yes, my lord."

"The one you can work from your pocket without anyone noticing?"

"Yes, my lord."

"Get me a picture of those two."

"Yes, my lord."

"I will see to the luggage. Wire to the Duc that I am unexpectedly called home."

"Very good, my lord."

Lord Peter did not allude to the matter again till Bunter was putting his trousers in the press in their cabin on board the *Normannia*. Beyond ascertaining that the young man and woman who had aroused his curiosity were on the boat as second-class passengers, he had sedulously avoided contact with them.

"Did you get that photograph?"

"I hope so, my lord. As your lordship knows, the aim from the breast-pocket tends to be unreliable. I have made three attempts, and trust that one at least may prove to be not unsuccessful."

"How soon can you develop them?"

"At once, if your lordship pleases. I have all the materials in my suit case."

"What fun!" said Lord Peter, eagerly tying himself into a pair of mauve silk pajamas. "May I hold the bottles and things?"

Mr. Bunter poured 3 ounces of water into an 8-ounce measure, and handed his master a glass rod and a minute packet.

"If your lordship would be so good as to stir the contents of the white packet slowly into the water," he said, bolting the door, "and, when dissolved, add the contents of the blue packet."

"Just like a Seidlitz powder," said his lordship happily. "Does it fizz?"

"Not much, my lord," replied the expert, shaking a quantity of hypo crystals into the hand-basin.

"That's a pity," said Lord Peter. "I say, Bunter, it's no end of a bore to dissolve."

"Yes, my lord," returned Bunter sedately. "I have always found that part of the process exceptionally tedious, my lord."

Lord Peter jabbed viciously with the glass rod.

"Just you wait," he said, in a vindictive tone, "till we get to Waterloo."

Three days later Lord Peter Wimsey sat in his book-lined sitting-room at 110A Piccadilly. The tall bunches of daffodils on the table smiled in the spring sunshine, and nodded to the breeze which danced in from the open window. The door opened, and his lordship glanced up from a handsome edition of the Contes de la Fontaine, whose handsome hand-colored Fragonard plates he was examining with the aid of a lens.

"Morning, Bunter. Anything doing?"

"I have ascertained, my lord, that the young person in question has entered the service of the elder Duchess of Medway. Her name is Célestine Berger."

"You are less accurate than usual, Bunter. Nobody off the stage is called Célestine. You should say 'under the name of Célestine Berger.' And the man?"

"He is domiciled at this address in Guilford Street, Bloomsbury, my lord."

"Excellent, my Bunter. Now give me *Who's Who*. Was it a very tiresome job?"

"Not exceptionally so, my lord."

"One of these days I suppose I shall give you something to do which you *will* jib at," said his lordship, "and you will leave me and I shall cut my throat. Thanks. Run away and play. I shall lunch at the club."

The book which Bunter had handed his employer indeed bore the words *Who's Who* engrossed upon its cover, but it was to be found in no public library and in no bookseller's shop. It was a bulky manuscript, closely filled, in part with the small print-like handwriting of Mr. Bunter, in part with Lord Peter's neat and altogether illegible hand. It contained biographies of the most unexpected people, and the most unexpected facts about the most obvious people. Lord Peter turned to a very long entry under the name of the Dowager Duchess of Medway. It appeared to make satisfactory reading, for after a time he smiled, closed the book, and went to the telephone.

"Yes—this is the Duchess of Medway. Who is it?"

The deep, harsh old voice pleased Lord Peter. He could see the imperious face and upright figure of what had been the most famous beauty in the London of the 'sixties.

"It's Peter Wimsey, duchess."

"Indeed, and how do you do, young man? Back from your Continental jaunting?"

"Just home—and longing to lay my devotion at the feet of the most fascinating lady in England."

"God bless my soul, child, what do you want?" demanded the duchess. "Boys like you don't flatter an old woman for nothing."

"I want to tell you my sins, duchess."

"You should have lived in the great days," said the voice appreciatively. "Your talents are wasted on the young fry."

"That is why I want to talk to you, duchess."

"Well, my dear, if you've committed any sins worth hearing I shall enjoy your visit."

"You are as exquisite in kindness as in charm. I am coming this afternoon."

"I will be home to you and no one else. There."

"Dear lady, I kiss your hands," said Lord Peter, and he heard a deep chuckle as the duchess rang off.

"You may say what you like, duchess," said Lord Peter from his reverential position on the fender-stool, "but you are the youngest grandmother in London, not excepting my own mother."

"Dear Honoria is the merest child," said the duchess. "I have twenty years more experience of life, and have arrived at the age when we boast of them. I have every intention of being a great-grandmother before I die. Sylvia is being married in a fortnight's time, to that stupid son of Attenbury's."

"Abcock?"

"Yes. He keeps the worst hunters I ever saw, and doesn't know still champagne from sauterne. But Sylvia is stupid, too, poor child, so I dare say they will get on charmingly. In my day one had to have either brains or beauty to get on—preferably both. Nowadays nothing seems to be required but a total lack of figure. But all the sense went out of society with the House of Lords' veto. I except you, Peter. You have talents. It is a pity you do not employ them in politics."

"Dear lady, God forbid."

"Perhaps you are right, as things are. There were giants in my day. Dear Dizzy. I remember so well, when his wife died, how hard we all tried to get him—Medway had died the year before—but he was wrapped up in that stupid Bradford woman, who had never even read a line of one of his books, and couldn't have understood 'em if she had. And now we have Abcock standing for Midhurst, and married to Sylvia!"

"You haven't invited me to the wedding, duchess dear. I'm so hurt," sighed his lordship.

"Bless you, child, *I* didn't send out the invitations, but I suppose your brother and that tiresome wife of his will be there. You must come, of course, if you want to. I had no idea you had a passion for weddings."

"Hadn't you?" said Peter. "I have a passion for this one. I want to see Lady Sylvia wearing white satin and the family lace and diamonds, and to sentimentalize over the days when my fox-terrier bit the stuffing out of her doll."

"Very well, my dear, you shall. Come early and give me your support. As for the diamonds, if it weren't a family tradition, Sylvia shouldn't wear them. She has the impudence to complain of them."

"I thought they were some of the finest in existence."

"So they are. But she says the settings are ugly and old-fashioned, and she doesn't like diamonds, and they won't go with her dress. Such nonsense. Whoever heard of a girl not liking diamonds? She wants to be something romantic and moonshiny in pearls. I have no patience with her."

"I'll promise to admire them," said Peter—"use the privilege of early acquaintance and tell her she's an ass and so on. I'd love to have a view of them. When do they come out of cold storage?"

"Mr. Whitehead will bring them up from the Bank the night before," said the duchess, "and they'll go into the safe in my room. Come round at twelve o'clock and you shall have a private view of them."

"That would be delightful. Mind they don't disappear in the night, won't you?"

"Oh, my dear, the house is going to be over-run with policemen. Such a nuisance. I suppose it can't be helped."

"Oh, I think it's a good thing," said Peter. "I have rather an unwholesome weakness for policemen."

On the morning of the wedding-day, Lord Peter emerged from Bunter's hands a marvel of sleek brilliance. His primrose-colored hair was so exquisite a work of art that to eclipse it with his glossy hat was like shutting up the sun in a shrine of polished jet; his spats, light trousers, and exquisitely polished shoes formed a tone-symphony in monochrome. It was only by the most impassioned pleading that he persuaded his tyrant to allow him to place two small photographs and a thin, foreign letter in his breast-pocket. Mr. Bunter, likewise immaculately attired, stepped into the taxi after him. At noon precisely they were deposited beneath the striped awning which adorned the door of the Duchess of Medway's house in Park Lane. Bunter promptly disappeared in the direction of the back entrance, while his lordship mounted the step and asked to see the dowager.

The majority of the guests had not yet arrived, but the house was full of agitated people, flitting hither and thither, with flowers and prayer-books, while a clatter of dishes and cutlery from the dining-room proclaimed the laying of a sumptuous breakfast. Lord Peter was shown into the morning-room while the footman went to announce him, and here he found a very close friend and devoted colleague, Detective-Inspector Parker, mounting guard in plain clothes over a costly collection of white elephants. Lord Peter greeted him with an affectionate hand-grip.

"All serene so far?" he inquired.

"Perfectly O.K."

"You got my note?"

"Sure thing. I've got three of our men shadowing your friend in Guilford Street. The girl is very much in evidence here. Does the old lady's wig and that sort of thing. Bit of a coming-on disposition, isn't she?"

"You surprise me," said Lord Peter. "No"—as his friend grinned sardonically—"you really do. Not seriously? That would throw all my calculations out."

"Oh, no! Saucy with her eyes and her tongue, that's all."

"Do her job well?"

"I've heard no complaints. What put you on to this?"

"Pure accident. Of course I may be quite mistaken."

"Did you receive any information from Paris?"

"I wish you wouldn't use that phrase," said Lord Peter peevishly. "It's so of the Yard—yardy. One of these days it'll give you away."

"Sorry," said Parker. "Second nature, I suppose."

"Those are the things to beware of," returned his lordship, with an earnestness that seemed a little out of place. "One can keep guard on everything but just those second-nature tricks." He moved across to the window, which overlooked the tradesmen's entrance. "Hullo!" he said, "here's our bird."

Parker joined him, and saw the neat, shingled head of the French girl from the Gare St. Lazare, topped by a neat black bandeau and bow. A man with a basket full of white narcissi had rung the bell, and appeared to be trying to make a sale. Parker gently opened the window, and they heard Célestine say with a marked French accent, "No, nossing to-day, sank you." The man insisted in the monotonous whine of his type, thrusting a big bunch of the white flowers upon her, but she pushed them back into the basket with an angry exclamation and flirted away, tossing her head and slapping the door smartly to. The man moved off muttering. As he did so a thin, unhealthy-looking lounger in a check cap detached himself from a lamp-post opposite and mouched along the street after him, at the same time casting a glance up at the window. Mr. Parker looked at Lord Peter, nodded, and made a slight sign with his hand. At once the man in the check cap removed his cigarette from his mouth, extinguished it, and, tucking the stub behind his ear, moved off without a second glance.

"Very interesting," said Lord Peter, when both were out of sight. "Hark!"

There was a sound of running feet overhead—a cry—and a general commotion. The two men dashed to the door as the bride, rushing frantically downstairs with her bevy of bridesmaids after her, proclaimed in a hysterical shriek: "The diamonds! They're stolen! They're gone!"

Instantly the house was in an uproar. The servants and the caterers' men crowded into the hall; the bride's father burst out from his room in a magnificent white waistcoat and no coat; the Duchess of Medway descended upon Mr. Parker, demanding that something should be done; while the butler, who never to the day of his death got over the disgrace, ran out of the pantry with a corkscrew in one hand and a priceless bottle of crusted port in the other, which he shook with all the vehemence of a town-crier ringing a bell. The only dignified entry was made by the dowager duchess, who came down like a ship in sail, dragging Célestine with her, and admonishing her not to be so silly.

"Be quiet, girl," said the dowager. "Anyone would think you were going to be murdered."

"Allow me, your grace," said Mr. Bunter, appearing suddenly from nowhere in his usual unperturbed manner, and taking the agitated Célestine by the arm. "Young woman, calm yourself "

"But what is to be *done*?" cried the bride's mother. "How did it happen?"

It was at this moment that Detective-Inspector Parker took the floor. It was the most impressive and dramatic moment in his whole career. His magnificent calm rebukcd the clamorous nobility surrounding him.

"Your grace," he said, "there is no cause for alarm. Our measures have been taken. We have the criminals and the gems, thanks to Lord Peter Wimsey, from whom we received inf—"

"Charles!" said Lord Peter in an awful voice.

"Warning of the attempt. One of our men is just bringing in the male criminal at the front door, taken red-handed with your grace's diamonds in his possession." (All gazed round, and perceived indeed the check-capped lounger and a uniformed constable entering with the flower-seller between them.) "The female criminal, who picked the lock of your grace's safe, is—here! No, you don't," he added, as Célestine, amid a torrent of apache language which nobody, fortunately, had French enough to understand, attempted to whip out a revolver from the bosom of her demure black dress. "Célestine Berger," he continued, pocketing the weapon, "I arrest you in the name of the law, and I warn you that anything you say will be taken down and used as evidence against you."

"Heaven help us," said Lord Peter; "the roof would fly off the court. And you've got the name wrong, Charles. Ladies and gentlemen, allow me to introduce to you Jacques Lerouge, knows as Sans-culotte—the youngest and cleverest thief, safe-breaker, and female impersonator that ever occupied a dossier in the Palais de Justice."

There was a gasp. Jacques Sans-culotte gave vent to a low oath and cocked a *gamin* grimace at Peter.

"C'est parfait," said he; "toutes mes félicitations, milord, what you call a fair cop, hein? And now I know him," he added, grinning at Bunter, "the so-patient Englishman who stand behind us in the queue at St. Lazare. But tell me, please, how you know me, that I may correct it, *next time.*"

"I have mentioned to you before, Charles," said Lord Peter, "the unwisdom of falling into habits of speech. They give you away. Now, in France, every male child is brought up to use masculine adjectives about himself. He says: Que je suis beau! But a little girl has it rammed home to her that she is female; she must say: Que je suis belle! It must make it beastly hard to be a female impersonator. When I am at a station and I hear an excited young woman say to her companion, "Me prends-tu pour *un* imbécile—the masculine article arouses curiosity. And that's that!" he concluded briskly. "The rest was merely a matter of getting Bunter to take a photograph and communicating with our friends of the Sûreté and Scotland Yard."

Jacques Sans-culotte bowed again.

"Once more I congratulate milord. He is the only Englishman I have ever met who is capable of appreciating our beautiful language. I will pay great attention in future to the article in question."

With an awful look, the Dowager Duchess of Medway advanced upon Lord Peter.

"Peter," she said, "do you mean to say you *knew* about this, and that for the last three weeks you have allowed me to be dressed and undressed and put to bed by a *young man?*"

His lordship had the grace to blush.

"Duchess," he said humbly, "on my honor I didn't know absolutely for certain till this morning. And the police were so anxious to have these people caught red-handed. What can I do to show my penitence? Shall I cut the privileged beast in pieces?"

The grim old mouth relaxed a little.

"After all," said the dowager duchess, with the delightful consciousness that she was going to shock her daughter-in-law, "there are very few women of my age who could make the same boast. It seems that we die as we have lived, my dear."

For indeed the Dowager Duchess of Medway had been notable in her day.

Death and Company

Dashiell Hammett

Dashiell Hammett (1894-1961), the first great writer of the hard-boiled detective tale, was born in Maryland. In 1901, Hammett's family moved to Baltimore. When he was fourteen, Hammett left school and wandered from job to job until he became an operative for the Pinkerton Detective Agency in 1915. He served in the U.S. Army Ambulance Corps from 1918-19. Hammett moved to San Francisco during his tenure at Pinkerton and resigned in 1922 after a serious illness. Hammett barely made a living by writing short stories, ad copy, and reviews. In 1923, he began to sell stories to *Black Mask* magazine. His first two novels, *The Dain Curse* and *Red Harvest,* were serialized in *Black Mask* in 1929. After the publication of *The Maltese Falcon* the following year, Hammett moved to Los Angeles to write screenplays. In 1931, he produced *The Glass Key.* He produced one more novel, *The Thin Man,* in 1934. Hammett was increasingly involved in left-wing politics in the late 1930's, and was named chairman of the Committee on Election Rights in 1940. He served in the Aleutians during World War II and was named President of the Civil Rights Congress in 1946. At this time, Hammett accepted a teaching position at the Jefferson School of Social Research in New York, a position he held until 1955. In 1951, he served a six month jail term for refusing to testify on the Civil Right Congress's bail fund. Hammett was called before the McCarthy commission in 1953. His health declined in later years, and attempts to write another novel failed. Hammett died of lung cancer in 1961.

"Death and Company" is the last short story to feature The Continental Op, Hammett's first series character. It displays Hammett's mastery of street language and plotting.

THE OLD MAN introduced me to the other man in his office—his name was Chappell—and said: "Sit down."

I sat down.

Chappell was a man of forty-five or so, solidly built and dark-complexioned, but shaky and washed out by worry or grief or fear. His eyes were red-rimmed and their lower lids sagged, as did his lower lip. His hand, when I shook it, had been flabby and damp.

The Old Man picked up a piece of paper from his desk and held it out to me. I took it. It was a letter crudely printed in ink, all capital letters.

MARTIN CHAPPELL

DEAR SIR—

IF YOU EVER WANT TO SEE YOUR WIFE ALIVE AGAIN YOU WILL DO JUST WHAT YOU ARE TOLD AND THAT IS TO GO TO THE LOT ON THE CORNER OF TURK AND LARKIN ST. AT EXACTLY 12 TO-NIGHT AND PUT $5000 IN $100 BILLS UNDER THE PILE OF BRICKS BEHIND THE BILL BOARD. IF YOU DO NOT DO THIS OR IF YOU GO TO THE POLICE OR IF YOU TRY ANY TRICKS YOU WILL GET A LETTER TO-MORROW TELLING YOU WHERE TO FIND HER CORPSE. WE MEAN BUSINESS.

DEATH & CO.

I put the letter back on the Old Man's desk.

He said: "Mrs. Chappell went to a matinée yesterday afternoon. She never returned home. Mr. Chappell received this in the mail this morning."

"She go alone?" I asked.

"I don't know," Chappell said. His voice was very tired. "She told me she was going when I left for the office in the morning, but she didn't say which show she was going to or if she was going with anybody."

"Who'd she usually go with?"

He shook his head hopelessly. "I can give you the names and addresses of all her closest friends, but I'm afraid that won't help. When she hadn't come home late last night I telephoned all of them— everybody I could think of—and none of them had seen her."

"Any idea who could have done this?" I asked.

Again he shook his head hopelessly.

"Any enemies? Anybody with a grudge against you, or against her? Think, even if it's an old grudge or seems pretty slight. There's something like that behind most kidnapings."

"I know of none," he said wearily. "I've tried to think of anybody I know or ever knew who might have done it, but I can't."

"What business are you in?"

He looked puzzled, but replied: "I've an advertising agency."

"How about discharged employees?"

"No, the only one I've ever discharged was John Hacker and he has a better job now with one of my competitors and we're on perfectly good terms."

I looked at the Old Man. He was listening attentively, but in his usual aloof manner, as if he had no personal interest in the job. I cleared my throat and said to Chappell: "Look here. I want to ask some questions that you'll probably think—well—brutal, but they're necessary. Right?"

He winced as if he knew what was coming, but nodded and said: "Right."

"Has Mrs. Chappell ever stayed away over night before?"

"No, not without my knowing where she was." His lips jerked a little. "I think I know what you are going to ask. I'd like—I'd rather not hear. I mean I know it's necessary, but, if I can, I think I'd rather try to tell without your asking."

"I'd like that better too," I agreed. "I hope you don't think I'm getting any fun out of this."

"I know," he said. He took a deep breath and spoke rapidly, hurrying to get it over: "I've never had any reason to believe that she went anywhere that she didn't tell me about or had any friends she didn't tell me about. Is that"—his voice was pleading—"what you wanted to know?"

"Yes, thanks." I turned to the Old Man again. The only way to get anything out of him was to ask for it, so I said: "Well?"

He smiled courteously, like a well-satisfied blank wall, and murmured: "You have the essential facts now, I think. What do you advise?"

"Pay the money of course first," I replied, and then complained: "It's a damned shame that's the only way to handle a kidnaping. These Death and Co. birds are pretty dumb, picking that spot for the pay-off. It would be duck soup to nab them there." I stopped complaining and asked Chappell: "You can manage the money all right?"

"Yes."

I addressed the Old Man: "Now about the police?"

Chappell began: "No, not the police! Won't they—"

I interrupted him: "We've got to tell them, in case something goes wrong and to have them all set for action as soon as Mrs. Chappell is safely home again. We can persuade them to keep their hands off till then." I asked the Old Man: "Don't you think so?"

He nodded and reached for his telephone. "I think so. I'll have Lieutenant Fielding and perhaps someone from the District Attorney's office come up here and we'll lay the whole thing before them."

Fielding and an Assistant District Attorney named McPhee came up. At first they were all for making the Turk-and-Larkin-Street-brick-pile a midnight target for half the San Francisco police force, but we finally persuaded them to listen to reason. We dug up the history of kidnaping from Ross to Parker and waved it in their faces and showed them that the statistics were on our side: more success and less grief had come from paying what was asked and going hunting afterwards than from trying to nail the kidnapers before the kidnaped were released.

At half past eleven o'clock that night Chappell left his house, alone, with five thousand dollars wrapped in a sheet of brown paper in his pocket. At twenty minutes past twelve he returned.

His face was yellowish and wet with perspiration and he was trembling.

"I put it there," he said difficultly. "I didn't see anybody."

I poured out a glass of his whisky and gave it to him.

He walked the floor most of the night. I dozed on a sofa. Half a dozen times at least I heard him go to the street door to open it and look out. Detective-sergeants Muir and Callahan went to bed. They and I had planted ourselves there to get any information Mrs. Chappell could give us as soon as possible.

She did not come home.

At nine in the morning Callahan was called to the telephone. He came away from it scowling.

"Nobody's come for the dough yet," he told us.

Chappell's drawn face became wide-eyed and open-mouthed with horror. "You had the place watched?" he cried.

"Sure," Callahan said, "but in an all right way. We just had a couple of men stuck up in an apartment down the block with field-glasses. Nobody could tumble to that."

Chappell turned to me, horror deepening in his face. "What?"

The door-bell rang.

Chappell ran to the door and presently came back excitedly tearing a special-delivery-stamped envelope open. Inside was another of the crudely printed letters.

MARTIN CHAPPELL

DEAR SIR—

WE GOT THE MONEY ALL RIGHT BUT HAVE GOT TO HAVE MORE TO-NIGHT THE SAME AMOUNT AT THE SAME TIME AND EVERY-THING ELSE THE SAME. THIS TIME WE WILL HONESTLY SEND YOUR WIFE HOME ALIVE IF YOU DO AS YOU ARE TOLD. IF YOU DO NOT OR SAY A WORD TO THE POLICE YOU KNOW WHAT TO EXPECT AND YOU BET YOU WILL GET IT.

DEATH & CO.

Callahan said: "What the hell?"

Muir growled: "Them—at the window must be blind."

I looked at the postmark on the envelope. It was earlier that morning. I asked Chappell: "Well, what are you going to do?"

He swallowed and said: "I'll give them every cent I've got if it will bring Louise home safe."

At half past eleven o'clock that night Chappell left his house with another five thousand dollars. When he returned the first thing he said was: "The money I took last night is really gone."

This night was much like the previous one except that he had less hopes of seeing Mrs. Chappell in the morning. Nobody said so, but all of us expected another letter in the morning asking for still another five thousand dollars.

Another special-delivery letter did come, but it read:

MARTIN CHAPPELL

DEAR SIR—

WE WARNED YOU TO KEEP THE POLICE OUT OF IT AND YOU DISOBEYED. TAKE YOUR POLICE TO APT. 313 AT 895 POST ST. AND

YOU WILL FIND THE CORPSE WE PROMISED YOU IF YOU DIS-
OBEYED.

DEATH & CO.

Callahan cursed and jumped for the telephone.

I put an arm around Chappell as he swayed, but he shook himself together and turned fiercely on me.

"You've killed her!" he cried.

"Hell with that," Muir barked. "Let's get going."

Muir, Chappell, and I went out to Chappell's car, which had stood two nights in front of the house. Callahan ran out to join us as we were moving away.

The Post Street address was only a ten-minute ride from Chappell's house the way we did it. It took a couple of more minutes to find the manager of the apartment house and to take her keys away from her. Then we went up and entered apartment

A tall slender woman with curly red hair lay dead on the living-room floor. There was no question of her being dead: she had been dead long enough for discoloration to have got well under way. She was lying on her back. The tan flannel bathrobe—apparently a man's—she had on had fallen open to show pinkish lingerie. She had on stockings and one slipper. The other slipper lay near her.

Her face and throat and what was visible of her body were covered with bruises. Her eyes were wide open and bulging, her tongue out: she had been beaten and then throttled.

More police detectives joined us and some policemen in uniform. We went into our routine.

The manager of the house told us the apartment had been occupied by a man named Harrison M. Rockfield. She described him: about thirty-five years old, six feet tall, blond hair, gray or blue eyes, slender, perhaps a hundred and sixty pounds, very agreeable personality, dressed well. She said he had been living there alone for three months. She knew nothing about his friends, she said, and had not seen Mrs. Chappell before. She had not seen Rockfield for two or three days but had thought nothing of it as she often went a week or so without seeing some tenants.

We found a plentiful supply of clothing in the apartment, some of which the manager positively identified as Rockfield's. The police department experts found a lot of masculine fingerprints that we hoped were his.

We couldn't find anybody in adjoining apartments who had heard the racket that must have been made by the murder.

We decided that Mrs. Chappell had probably been killed as soon as she was brought to the apartment—no later than the night of her disappearance, anyhow.

"But why?" Chappell demanded dumbfoundedly.

"Playing safe. You wouldn't know till after you'd come across. She wasn't feeble. It would be hard to keep her quiet in a place like this."

A detective came in with the package of hundred-dollar bills Chappell had placed under the brick-pile the previous night.

I went down to headquarters with Callahan to question the men stationed at a nearby apartment-window to watch the vacant lot. They swore up and down that nobody—"not as much as a rat"—could have approached the brick-pile without being seen by them. Callahan's answer to that was a bellowed "The hell they couldn't—they did!"

I was called to the telephone. Chappell was on the wire. His voice was hoarse.

"The telephone was ringing when I got home," he said, "and it was him."

"Who ?"

"Death and Co., he said. That's what he said, and he told me that it was my turn next. That's all he said. 'This is Death and Co., and it's your turn next.'"

"I'll be right out," I said. "Wait for me."

I told Callahan and the others what Chappell had told me.

Callahan scowled. "—," he said, "I guess we're up against another of those—damned nuts!"

Chappell was in a bad way when I arrived at his house. He was shivering as if with a chill and his eyes were almost idiotic in their fright.

"It's—it's not only that—that I'm afraid," he tried to explain. "I am—but it's—I'm not that afraid—but—but with Louise—and—it's the shock and all. I—"

"I know," I soothed him. "I know. And you haven't slept for a couple of days. Who's your doctor? I'm going to phone him."

He protested feebly, but finally gave me his doctor's name.

The telephone rang as I was going towards it. The call was for me, from Callahan.

"We've pegged the fingerprints," he said triumphantly. "They're Dick Moley's. Know him?"

"Sure," I said, "as well as you do."

Moley was a gambler, gunman, and grifter-in-general with a police record as long as his arm.

Callahan was saying cheerfully: "That's going to mean a fight when we find him, because you know how tough that—is. And he'll laugh while he's being tough."

"I know," I said.

I told Chappell what Callahan had told me. Rage came into his face and voice when he heard the name of the man accused of killing his wife.

"Ever hear of him?" I asked.

He shook his head and went on cursing Moley in a choked, husky voice.

I said: "Stop that. That's no good. I know where to find Moley."

His eyes opened wide. "Where?" he gasped.

"Want to go with me?"

"Do I?" he shouted. Weariness and sickness had dropped from him.

"Get your hat," I said, "and we'll go."

He ran upstairs for his hat and down with it.

He had a lot of questions as we went out and got into his car. I answered most of them with: "Wait, you'll see."

But in the car he went suddenly limp and slid down in his seat.

"What's the matter?" I asked.

"I can't," he mumbled. "I've got to—help me into the house—the doctor."

"Right," I said, and practically carried him into the house.

I spread him on a sofa, had a maid bring him water, and called his doctor's number. The doctor was not in.

When I asked him if there was any other particular doctor he wanted he said weakly: "No, I'm all right. Go after that—that man."

"All right," I said.

I went outside, got a taxicab, and sat in it.

Twenty minutes later a man went up Chappell's front steps and rang the bell. The man was Dick Moley, alias Harrison M. Rockfield.

He took me by surprise. I had been expecting Chappell to come out, not anyone to go in. He had vanished indoors and the door was shut by the time I got there.

I rang the bell savagely.

A heavy pistol roared inside, twice.

I smashed the glass out of the door with my gun and put my left hand in, feeling for the latch.

The heavy pistol roared again and a bullet hurled splinters of glass into my cheek, but I found the latch and worked it.

I kicked the door back and fired once straight ahead at random. Something moved in the dark hallway then and without waiting to see what it was I fired again, and when something fell I fired at the sound.

A voice said: "Cut it out. That's enough. I've lost my gun."

It wasn't Chappell's voice. I was disappointed.

Near the foot of the stairs I found a light-switch and turned it on. Dick Moley was sitting on the floor at the other end of the hallway holding one leg.

"That damned fool maid got scared and locked this door," he complained, "or I'd've made it out back."

I went nearer and picked up his gun. "Get you anywhere but the leg?" I asked.

"No. I'd've been all right if I hadn't dropped the gun when it upset me."

"You've got a lot of ifs," I said. "I'll give you another one. You've got nothing to worry about but that bullet-hole if you didn't kill Chappell."

He laughed. "If he's not dead he must feel funny with those two .44's in his head."

"That was—damned dumb of you," I growled.

He didn't believe me. He said: "It was the best job I ever pulled."

"Yeah? Well, suppose I told you that I was only waiting for another move of his to pinch him for killing his wife?"

He opened his eyes at that.

"Yeah," I said, "and you have to walk in and mess things up. I hope to—they hang you for it." I knelt down beside him and began to slit his pants-leg with my pocket-knife.

"What'd you do? Go in hiding after you found her dead in your rooms because you knew a guy with your record would be out of luck, and then lose your head when you saw in the extras this afternoon what kind of a job he'd put up on you?"

"Yes," he said slowly, "though I'm not sure I lost my head. I've got a hunch I came pretty near giving the — — — — what he deserved."

"That's a swell hunch," I told him. "We were ready to grab him. The whole thing had looked phoney. Nobody had come for the money the first night, but it wasn't there the next day, so he said. Well, we only had his word for it that he had actually put it there and hadn't found it the next night. The next night, after he had been told the place was watched he left the money there, and then he wrote the note saying Death & Company knew he'd gone to the police. That wasn't public news, either. And then her being killed before anybody knew she was kidnaped. And then tying it to you when it was too dizzy—no, you are dizzy, or you wouldn't have pulled this one. Anyhow we had enough to figure he was wrong, and if you'd let him alone we'd have pulled him, put it in the papers, and waited for you to come forth and give us what we needed to clear you and swing him." I was twisting my neck-tie around his leg above the bullet-hole. "But that's too sensible for you. How long you been playing around with her?"

"A couple of months," he said, "only I wasn't playing. I meant it."

"How'd he happen to catch her there alone?"

He shook his head. "He must've followed her there that afternoon when she was supposed to be going to the theater. Maybe he waited outside until he saw me go out. I had to go downtown, but I wasn't gone an hour. She was already cold when I came back." He frowned. "I don't think she'd've answered the door-bell, though maybe—or maybe he'd had a duplicate made of the key she had."

Some policemen came in: the frightened maid had had sense enough to use the telephone.

"Do you think he planned it that way from the beginning?" Moley asked.

I didn't. I thought he had killed his wife in a jealous rage and later thought of the Death and Co. business.

The Inner Circle

Ellery Queen

Ellery Queen is the pseudonym of cousins Manfred B. Lee (1905-1971) and Frederic Dannay (1905-1982). Native New Yorkers, Dannay's family moved to Elmyria when he was small. Lee stayed in New York, and attended New York University. In 1926, Dannay married his first of three wives, Mary Beck. Two years later, the cousins collaborated on an entry for the *McClure's* Mystery Writing contest—since each manuscript had to be submitted under a pseudonym, they decided to use their detective's name. The manuscript became the first Ellery Queen mystery, *The Roman Hat Mystery*. Other novels and stories were released, as well as a second series under the pseudonym Barnaby Ross (At one time, Lee and Dannay lectured around the country as "Queen" and "Ross"). In 1933, they attempted to start up their own magazine, *Mystery League,* but it folded after four issues. In the mid-1930's, they moved to Hollywood to write screenplays. Lee and Dannay moved back to New York to work on several projects, including the Ellery Queen radio show (1939-1948), the collection *The New Adventures of Ellery Queen* (1940), several anthologies (*101 Year's Entertainment,* 1941; *Sporting Blood,* 1942; *The Misadventures of Sherlock Holmes,* 1944), novels (*Calamity Town,* 1942; *There Was an Old Woman,* 1943; *Ten Day's Wonder,* 1948; *Cat of Many Tails,* 1949), and editing *Ellery Queen Mystery Magazine* (founded in 1944). In 1950, they were asked to contribute to a national Sunday supplement, and the short mysteries printed there were collected in *QBI—Queen's Bureau of Investigations* (1955). The Queen novels became more infrequent as the cousins grew apart in the 1950's: novels such as *The Origin of Evil* (1951), *The Scarlet Letter* (1953), *The Finishing Stroke* (1958), and *The Player on the Other Side* (1963), were more allegorical and complex in nature. Lee suffered a series of heart attacks in the late 1960's, and died in 1971—a few weeks before the release of the last Queen novel, *A Fine and Private Place.* Dannay retired the pseudonym and devoted his time to editing *Ellery Queen Mystery Magazine.* In 1975 he married his third wife, Rose Koppell. His health began to fail in 1980, and Dannay died of heart failure two years later.

The Ellery Queen stories are the ultimate extension of the "Mystery as Intellectual Puzzle," with crimes being solved on the basis of verbal clues and riddles. "The Inner Circle" demonstrates this while also delivering a deliciously complicated problem of identity.

IF YOU ARE an Eastern alumnus who has not been to New York
since last year's All-University Dinner, you will be astounded to learn
that the famous pickled-pine door directly opposite the elevators on the
thirteenth floor of your Alumni Club in Murray Hill is now inscribed:
LINEN ROOM.

Visit The Alumni Club on your next trip to Manhattan and see for
yourself. On the door now consigned to napery, in the area where the
stainless steel medallion of Janus glistened for so long, you will detect
a ghostly circumference some nine inches in diameter—all that is left
of the Januarians. Your first thought will of course be that they have
removed to more splendid quarters. Undeceive yourself. You may
search from cellar to sundeck and you will find no crumb's trace of
either Janus or his disciples.

Hasten to the Steward for an explanaton and he will give you one as
plausable as it will be false.

And you will do no better elsewhere.

The fact is, only a very few share the secret of The Januarians'
obliteration, and these have taken a vow of silence. And why? Because
Eastern is a young—a very young—temple of learning; and there are
calamities only age can weather. There is more to it than even that. The
cataclysm of events struck at the handiwork of the Architects themselves, that legendary band who builded the tabernacle and created the
holy canons. So Eastern's shame is kept steadfastly covered with
silence; and if we uncover its bloody stones here, it is only because the
very first word on the great seal of Eastern University is: *Veritas.*

To a Harvard man, "Harvard '13" means little more than "Harvard
'06" or "Harvard '79," unless "Harvard '13" happens to be his own
graduating class. But to an Eastern man, of whatever vintage "Eastern
'13" is *sui generis.* Their names bite deep into the strong marble of
The Alumni Club lobby. A member of the Class is traditionally The
Honorable Mr. Honorary President of The Eastern Alumni Associa-
tion. To the last man they carry gold, lifetime, non-cancelable passes
to Eastern football games. At the All-University Dinner, Eastern '13
shares the Cancellor's parsley-decked table. The twined-elbow Rite of
the Original Libation, drunk in foaming beer (the second most sacred
canon), is dedicated to that Class and no other.

One may well ask why this exaltaton of Eastern '13 as against, for
example, Eastern '98? The answer is that there was no Eastern '12, and
Eastern '98 never existed. For Eastern U. was not incorporated under
the laws of the State of New York until A.D. 1909, from which it

solemnly follows that Eastern '13 was the university's very first graduating class.

It was Charlie Mason who said they must be gods, and it was Charlie Mason who gave them Janus. Charlie was destined to forge a chain of one hundred and twenty-three movie houses which bring Abbott and Costello to millions; but in those days Charlie was a lean weaver of dreams, the Class Poet, an antiquarian with a passion for classical allusion. Eastern '13 met on the eve of graduation in the Private Party Room of McElvy's Brauhaus in Riverdale, and the air was boiling with pipe smoke, malt fumes, and motions when Charlie rose to make his historic speech.

"Mr. Chairman," he said to Bill Updike, who occupied the Temporary Chair. "Fellows," he said to the nine others. And he paused.

Then he said: *"We are the First Alumni."*

He paused again.

"The eyes of the future are on us." (Stan Jones was taking notes, as Recording Secretary of the Evening, and we have Charlie's address verbatim. You have seen it in The Alumni club lobby, under glass. Brace yourself: It, too, has vanished.)

"What we do here tonight, therefore, will initiate a whole codex of Eastern tradition."

And now, the Record records, there was nothing to be heard in that smoky room but the whizz of the electric fan over the lithograph of Woodrow Wilson.

"I have no hesitation in saying—out loud!—that we men in this room, tonight...that we're...Significant. Not as individuals! But as the Class of '13." And then Charlie drew himself up and said quietly: *"They will remember us and we must give them something to remember"* (the third sacred canon).

"Such as?" said Morry Green, who was to die in a French ditch five years later.

"A sign," said Charlie. "A symbol, Morry—a symbol of our First-ness."

Eddie Temple, who was graduating eleventh in the Class, exhibited his tongue and blew a coarse, fluttery blast.

"That may be the sign *you* want to be remembered by, Ed," began Charlie crossly...

"Shut up, Temple!" growled Van Hamisher.

"Read that bird out of the party!" yelled Ziss Brown, who was suspected of holding radical views because his father had stumped for Teddy Roosevelt in '12.

"Sounds good," said Bill Updike, scowling, "Go on, Charlie."

"What sign?" demanded Rod Black.

"Anything specific in mind?" called Johnnie Cudwise.

Charlie said one word.

"Janus."

And he paused.

"Janus," they muttered, considering him.

"Yes, Janus," said Charlie. "The god of good beginnings—"

"Well, we're beginning," said Morry Green.

"Guaranteed to result in good endings—"

"It certainly applies," nodded Bill Updike.

"Yeah," said Bob Smith. "Eastern's sure on its way to big things."

"Janus of the two faces," cried Charlie Mason mystically. "I wish to point out that he looks in opposite directions!"

"Say, that's right—"

"The past and the future—"

"Smart stuff—"

"Go on, Charlie!"

"Janus," cried Charlie—"Janus, who was invoked by the Romans before any other god at the beginning of an important undertaking!"

"Wow!"

"This is certainly important!"

"The beginning of the day, month, and year were sacred to him! *Janus was the god of doorways!"*

"JANUS!" they shouted, leaping to their feet; and they raised their tankards and drank deep.

And so from that night forward the annual meeting of the Class of '13 was held on Janus's Day, the first day of January; and the Class of '13 adopted, by unanimous vote, the praenomen of The Januarians. Thus the double-visaged god became patron of Eastern's posterity, and that is why until recently Eastern official stationery was impressed with his two-bearded profiles. It is also why the phrase "to be two-faced," when uttered by Columbia or N.Y.U. men, usually means "to be a student at, or a graduate of, Eastern U."—a development unfortunately not contemplated by Charlie Mason on that historic eve; at least, not consciously.

But let us leave the profounder explorations to psychiatry. Here it is sufficient to record that some time more than thirty years later the phrase suddenly took on a grim verisimilitude; and the Januarians thereupon laid it, so to speak, on the doorstep of one well acquainted with such changelings of chance.

For it was during Christmas week of last year that Bill Updike came—stealthily—to see Ellery. He did not come as young Billy who had presided at the beery board in the Private Party Room of McElvy's Brauhaus on that June night in 1913. He came, bald, portly, and opulently engraved upon a card: Mr. William Updike, President of The Brokers National Bank of New York, residence Dike Hollow, Scarsdale; and he looked exactly as worried as bankers are supposed to look and rarely do.

"Business, business," said Nikki Porter, shaking her yuletide permanent. "It's Christmas week, Mr. Updike. I'm sure Mr. Queen wouldn't consider taking—"

But at that moment Mr. Queen emerged from his sanctum to give his secretary the lie.

"Nikki holds to the old-fashioned idea about holidays, Mr. Updike," said Ellery, shaking Bill's hand. "Ah, the Januarians. Isn't your annual meeting a few days from now—on New Year's Day?"

"How did you know—?" began the bank president.

"I could reply, in the manner of the Old Master," said Ellery with a chuckle, "that I've made an intensive study of lapel buttons, but truth compels me to admit that one of my best friends is Eastern '28 and he's described that little emblem on your coat so often I couldn't help but recognize it at once." The banker figured the disk on his lapel nervously. It was of platinum, ringed with tiny garnets, and the gleaming circle enclosed the two faces of Janus. "What's the matter—is someone robbing your bank?"

"It's worse than that."

"Worse...?"

"Murder."

Nikkie glared at Mr. Updike. Any hope of keeping Ellery's nose off the grindstone until January second was now merely a memory. But out of duty she began: "Ellery..."

"At least," said Bill Updike tensely, "I *think* it's murder."

Nikki gave up. Ellery's nose was noticeably honed.

"Who..."

"It's sort of complicated," muttered the banker, and he began to fidget before Ellery's fire. "I suppose you know, Queen, that The Januarians began with only eleven men."

Ellery nodded. "The total graduating class of Eastern '13."

"It seems silly now, with Eastern's classes of three and four thousand, but in those days we thought it was all pretty important—"

"Manifest destiny."

"We were young. Anyway, World War I came along and we lost two of our boys right away—Morry Green and Buster Selby. So at our New Year's Day meeting in 1920 we were only nine. Then in the market collapse of '29 Vern Hamisher blew the top of his head off, and in 1930 John Cudwise, who was serving his first term in Congress, was killed in a plane crash on his way to Washington—you probably remember. So we've been just seven for many years now."

"And awfully close friends you must be," said Nikki, curiosity conquering pique.

"Well..." began Updike, and he stopped, to begin over again. "For a long time now we've all thought it was sort of juvenile, but we've kept coming back to these damned New Year's Day meetings out of habit or—or something. No, that's not true. It isn't just habit. It's because...it's *expected* of us." He flushed. "I don't know—they've—well—deified us." He looked bellicose, and Nikkie swallowed a giggle hastily. "It's got on our nerves. I mean—well, damn it all, we're not exactly the 'close' friends you'd think!" He stopped again, then resumed in a sort of desperation: "See here, Queen. I've got to confess something. There's been a clique of us within The Januarians for years. We've called ourselves...The Inner Circle."

"The what?" gasped Nikki.

The banker mopped his neck, avoiding their eyes. The Inner Circle, he explained, had begun with one of those dully devious phenomena of modern life known as a "business opportunity"—a business opportunity which Mr. Updike, a considerably younger Mr. Updike, had found himself unable to grasp for lack of some essential element, unnamed. Whatever it was that Mr. Updike had required, four other men could supply it; whereupon, in the flush of an earlier camaraderie, Updike had taken four of his six fellow-deities into his confidence, and the result of this was a partnership of five of the existing seven Januarians.

"There were certain business reasons why we didn't want our er...names associated with the ah...enterprise. So we organized a dummy corporation and agreed to keep our names out of it and the whole thing absolutely secret, even from our—from the remaining two Januarians. It's a secret from them to this day."

"Club within a club," said Nikki. "I think that's cute."

"All five of you in this—hrm!—Inner Circle," inquired Ellery politely, "are alive?"

"We were last New Year's Day. But since the last meeting of The Januarians..." the banker glanced at Ellery's harmless windows furtively, "three of us have died. *Three of The Inner Circle.*"

"And you suspect that they were murdered?"

"Yes. Yes, I do!"

"For what motive?"

The banker launched into a very involved and—to Nikki, who was thinking wistfully of New Year's Eve—tiresome explanation. It had something to do with some special fund or other, which seemed to have no connection with the commercial aspects of The Inner Circle's activities—a substantial fund by this time, since each year the five partners put a fixed percentage of their incomes from the dummy corporation into it. Nikki dreamed of balloons and noisemakers. "—now equals a reserve of around $200,000 worth of negotiable securities." Nikki stopped dreaming with a bump.

"What's the purpose of this fund, Mr. Updike?" Ellery was saying sharply. "What happens to it? When?"

"Well, er...that's just it, Queen," said the Banker. "Oh, I know what you'll think..."

"Don't tell me," said Ellery in a terrible voice, "it's a form of tontine insurance plan, Updike—*last survivor takes all?*"

"Yes," whispered William Updike, looking for the moment like Billy Updike.

"I knew it!" Ellery jumped out of his fireside chair. "Haven't I told you repeatedly, Nikki, there's no fool like a banker? The financial mentality rarely rises above the age of eight, when life's biggest thrill is to pay five pins for admission to a magic-lantern show in Stinky's cellar. This hard-eyed man of money, whose business it is to deal in safe investments, becomes party to a melodramatic scheme whereby the only way you can recoup your ante is to slit the throats of your four partners. Inner Circles! Januarians!" Ellery threw himself back in his chair. "Where's this silly invitation to murder cached, Updike?"

"In a safe-deposit box at The Brokers National," muttered the banker.

"Your own bank. Very cosy for *you,*" said Ellery.

"No, no, Mr. Queen, all five of us have keys to the box—"

"What happened to the keys of the three Inner Circleites who died last year?"

"By agreement, dead members' keys are destroyed in the presence of the survivors—"

"Then there are only two keys to that safe-deposit box now in existence; yours and the key in the possession of the only other living Inner Circular?"

"Yes—"

"And you're afraid said sole-surviving associate murdered the deceased trio of your absurd quintet and has his beady eye on you, Updike?—so that as the last man alive of The Inner Circle he would fall heir to the entire $200,000 boodle?"

"What else can I think?" cried the banker.

"The obvious," retorted Ellery, "which is that your three pals traveled the natural route of all flesh. Is the $200,000 still in the box?"

"Yes. I looked just before coming here today."

"You want me to investigate."

"Yes, yes—"

"Very well. What's the name of this surviving fellow-conspirator of yours in The Inner Circle?"

"No," said Bill Updike.

"I beg pardon?"

"Suppose I'm wrong? If they *were* ordinary deaths, I'd have dragged someone I've known a hell of a long time into a mess. No, you investigate first, Mr. Queen. Find evidence of murder, and I'll go all the way."

"You won't tell me his name?"

"No."

The ghost of New Year's Eve stirred. But then Ellery grinned, and it settled back in the grave. Nikki sighed and reached for her notebook.

"All right, Mr. Updike. Who were the three Inner Circlovians who died this year?"

"Robert Carlton Smith, J. Stanford Jones, and Ziss Brown—Peter Zissing Brown."

"Their occupations?"

"Bob Smith was head of the Kradle Kap Baby Foods Korporation. Stan Jones was top man of Jones-Jones-Mallison-Jones, the ad agency. Ziss Brown was retired."

"From what?"

Updike said stiffly: "Brassières."

"I suppose they do pall. Leave me the addresses of the executors, please, and any other data you think might be helpful."

When the banker had gone, Ellery reached for the telephone.

"Oh dear," said Nikki. "You're not calling...Club Bongo?"

"What?"

"You know? New Year's Eve?"

"Heavens, no. My pal Eastern '28. Cully?... The same to you. Cully, who are the four Januarians? Nikki, take this down...William Updike—yes?...Charles Mason? Oh, yes, the god who fashioned Olympus...Rodney Black, Junior—um-hm...and Edward I. Temple? Thanks, Cully. And now forget I called." Ellery hung up. "Black, Mason, and Temple, Nikki. The only Januarians alive outside of Updike. Consequently one of those three is Updike's last associate in The Inner Circle."

"And the question is which one."

"Bright girls. But first let's dig into the deaths of Smith, Jones, and Brown. Who knows? Maybe Updike's got something."

It took exactly forty-eight hours to determine that Updike had nothing at all. The deaths of Januarians-Inner Circlers Smith, Jones, and Brown were impeccable.

"Give it to him, Velie," said Inspector Queen at Headquarters the second morning after the banker's visit to the Queen apartment.

Sergeant Velie cleared his massive throat. "The Kradle Kap Baby Foods character—"

"Robert Carlton Smith."

"Rheumatic heart for years. Died in an oxygen tent after the third heart attack in eighteen hours, with three fancy medics in attendance and a secretary who was there to take down his last words."

"Which were probably, 'Free Enterprise,'" said the Inspector. "Go on, Sergeant!"

"J. Stanford Jones, the huckster. Gassed in World War 1, in recent years developed t.b. And that's what he died of. Want the sanitarium affidavits, Maestro? I had photostats telephotoed from Arizona."

"Thorough little man, aren't you?" growled Ellery. "And Peter Zissing Brown, retired from brassières?"

"Kidneys and gall-bladder. Brown died on the operatin' table."

"Wait till you see what I'm wearing tonight." said Nikki. "Apricot taffeta—"

"Nikki, get Updike on the phone," said Ellery absently. "Brokers National."

"He's not there, Ellery," said Nikki, when she had put down the Inspector's phone. "Hasn't come into his bank this morning. It has the darlingest bouffant skirt—"

"Try his home."

"Dike Hollow, Scarsdale, wasn't it? With the new back, and a neckline that—Hello?" And after a while the three men heard Nikki say in a strange voice: *"What?"* and then: "Oh," faintly. She thrust the phone at Ellery. "You'd better take it."

"What's the matter? Hello? Ellery Queen. Updike there?"

A bass voice said, "Well—no, Mr. Queen. He's been in an accident."

"Accident! Who's this speaking?"

"Captain Rosewater of the Highway Police. Mr. Updike ran his car into a ravine near his home here some time last night. We just found him."

"I hope he's all right!"

"He's dead."

"Four!" Ellery was mumbling as Sergeant Velie drove the Inspector's car up into Westchester. "Four in one year!"

"Coincidence," said Nikki desperately, thinking of the festivities on the agenda for that evening.

"All I know is that forty-eight hours after Updike asks me to find out if his three cronies of The Inner Circle who died this year hadn't been murdered, he himself is found lying in a gulley with four thousand pounds of used car on top of him."

"Accidents," began Sergeant Velie, "will hap—"

"I want to see that 'accident'!"

A State trooper flagged them on the Parkway near a cutoff and sent them down the side road. This road, it appeared, was a shortcut to Dike Hollow which Updike habitually used in driving home from the City; his house lay some two miles from the Parkway. They found the evidence of his last drive about midway. The narrow blacktop road twisted sharply to the left at this point, but Bill Updike had failed to twist with it. He had driven straight ahead and through a matchstick guardrail into the ravine. As it plunged over, the car had struck the bole of a big old oak. The shock catapulted the banker through his windshield and he had landed at the bottom of the ravine just before his vehicle.

"We're still trying to figure out a way of lifting that junk off him," said Captain Rosewater when they joined him forty feet below the road.

The ravine narrowed in a V here and the car lay in its crotch upside down. Men were swarming around it with crowbars, chains, and acetylene torches. "We've uncovered enough to show us he's mashed flat."

"His face, too, Captain?" asked Ellery suddenly.

"No, his face wasn't touched. We're trying to get the rest of him presentable enough so we can let his widow identify him." The trooper nodded toward a flat rock twenty yards down the ravine on which sat a small woman in a mink coat. She wore no hat and her smart gray hair was whipping in the Christmas wind. A woman in a cloth coat, wearing a nurse's cap, stood over her.

Ellery said, "Excuse me," and strode away. When Nikki caught up with him he was already talking to Mrs. Updike. She was drawn up on the rock like a caterpillar.

"He had a directors' meeting at the bank last night. I phoned one of his associates about 2 A.M. He said the meeting had broken up at eleven and Bill had left to drive home." Her glance strayed up the ravine. "At four-thirty this morning I phoned the police."

"Did you know your husband had come to see me, Mrs. Updike—two mornings ago?"

"Who are you?"

"Ellery Queen."

"No." She did not seem surprised, or frightened, or anything.

"Did you know Robert Carlton Smith, J. Stanford Jones, Peter Zissing Brown?"

"Bill's classmates? They passed away. This year," she added suddenly."This year," she repeated. And then she laughed. "I thought the gods were immortal."

"Did you know that your husband, Smith, Jones, and Brown were an 'inner circle' in the Januarians?"

"Inner Circle." She frowned. "Oh, yes, Bill mentioned it occasionally. No, I didn't know they were in it."

Ellery leaned forward in the wind

"Was Edward I. Temple in it, Mrs. Updike? Rodney Black, Junior? Charlie Mason?

"I don't know. Why are you questioning me? Why—?" Her voice was rising now, and Ellery murmured something placative as Captain Rosewater hurried up and said: "Mrs. Updike. If you'd be good enough..."

She jumped off the rock. *"Now?"*

"Please."

The trooper captain took one arm, the nurse the other, and between them they half-carried William Updike's widow up the ravine toward the overturned car.

Nikki found it necessary to spend some moments with her handkerchief.

When she looked up, Ellery had disappeared.

She found him with his father and Sergeant Velie on the road above the ravine. They were standing before a large maple looking at a road-sign. Studded lettering on the yellow sign spelled out *Sharp Curve Ahead,* and there was an elbow-like illustration.

"No lights on this road," the Inspector was saying as Nikki hurried up, "so he must have had his brights on—"

"And they'd sure enough light up this reflector sign. I don't get it, Inspector," complained Sergeant Velie. "Unless his lights just weren't workin'."

"More likely fell asleep over the wheel, Velie."

"No," said Ellery.

"What, Ellery?"

"Updike's lights were all right, and he didn't doze off."

"I don't impress when I'm c-cold," Nikki said, shivering. "But just the same, how do you know, Ellery?"

Ellery pointed to two neat holes in the maple bark, very close to the edge of the sign.

"Woodpeckers?" said Nikki. But the air was gray and sharp as steel, and it was hard to forget Mrs. Updike's look.

"This bird, I'm afraid," drawled Ellery, "had no feathers. Velie, borrow something we can pry this sign off with."

When Velie returned with some tools, he was mopping his face. "She just identified him," he said. "Gettin' warmer, ain't it?"

"What d'ye expect to find, Ellery?" demanded the Inspector.

"Two full sets of rivet-holes."

Sergeant Velie said: "Bong," as the road-sign came away from the tree.

"I'll be damned," said Inspector Queen softly. "Somebody removed these rivets last night, and after Updike crashed into the ravine—"

"Riveted the warning sign back on," cried Nikki, "only he got careless and didn't use the same holes!"

"Murder," said Ellery. "Smith, Jones, and Brown died of natural causes. But three of the five co-owners of that fund dying in a single year—"

"Gave Number 5 an idea!"

"If Updike died, too, the $200,000 in securities would... Ellery!" roared his father. "Where are you running to?"

"There's a poetic beauty about this case," Ellery was saying restlessly to Nikki as they waited in the underground vaults of The Brokers National Bank. "Janus was the god of entrances. Keys were among his trapping of office. In fact, he was sometimes known as *Patulcius*— 'opener'. Opener! I knew at once we were too late."

"You knew, you knew," said Nikki peevishly. "And New Year's Eve only hours away! You can be wrong."

"Not this time. Why else was Updike murdered last night in such a way as to make it appear an accident? Our mysterious Januarian hotfooted it down here first thing this morning and cleaned out that safe-deposit box belonging to The Inner Circle. The securities are gone, Nikki."

Within an hour, Ellery's prophecy was historical fact.

The box was opened with Bill Updike's key. It was empty.

And of *Patulcius*, no trace. It quite upset the Inspector. For it appeared that The Inner Circle had contrived a remarkable arrangement for access to their safe-deposit box. It was gained, not by the customary signature on an admissoin slip, but through the presentation of a talisman. This talisman was quite unlike the lapel button of the Januarians. It was a golden key, and on the key was incised the two-faced god, within concentric circles. The outer circle was of Januarian garnets, the inner of diamonds. A control had been deposited in the files of the vault company. Anyone presenting a replica of it was to be admitted to the The Inner Circle's repository by order of no less a personage, the vault manager informed them, than the late President Updike himself—who, Inspector Queen remarked with bitterness, had been more suited by temperment to preside over the Delancey Street Junior Spies.

"Anybody remember admitting a man this morning who flashed one of these doojiggers?"

An employee was found who duly remembered, but when he described the vault visitor as great-coated and mufflered to the eyes, wearing dark glasses, walking with a great limp, and speaking in a laryngitical whisper, Ellery said wearily: "Tomorrow's the annual meeting of The Januarians, dad, and *Patulcius* won't dare not to show up. We'd better try to clean it up there."

These, then were the curious events preceding the final meeting of The Januarians in the thirteenth-floor sanctuary of The Eastern Alumni Club, beyond the door bearing the stainless steel medallion of the god Janus.

We have no apocryphal writings to reveal what self-adoring mysteries were performed in that room on other New Year's Days; but on January the first of this year, The Januarians held a most unorthodox service, in that two lay figures—the Queens, *pater et filius*—moved in and administered some heretical sacraments; so there is a full record of the last rites.

It began with Sergeant Velie knocking thrice upon the steel faces of Janus at five minutes past two o'clock on the afternoon of the first of January, and a thoroughly startled voice from within the holy of holies calling: "Who's there?" The Sergeant muttered an *Ave* and put his shoulder to the door. Three amazed, elderly male faces appeared. The heretics entered and the service began.

It is a temptation to describe in loving detail, for the satisfaction of the curious, the interior of the tabernacle—its stern steel furniture seizing the New Year's Day sun and tossing it back in the form of imperious light, the four-legged altar, the sacred vessels in the shape of beakers, the esoteric brown waters, and so on—but there has been enough of profanation, and besides the service is more to our point.

It was chiefly catechistical, proceeding in this wise:

INSPECTOR: Gentlemen, my name is Inspector Queen, I'm from Police Headquarters, this is my son, Ellery, and the big mugg on the door is Sergeant Velie of my staff.
BLACK: Police? Ed, do you know anything about—?
TEMPLE: Not me, Rodeny. Maybe Charlie, Ha-Ha...?
MASON: What is it, Inspector? This is a private clubroom—
INSPECTOR: Which one are *you?*
MASON: Charles Mason—Mason's Theater Chain, Inc. But—
INSPECTOR: The long drink of water—what's *your* name?
TEMPLE: Me. Edward I Temple. Attorney. What's the meaning—?

> INSPECTOR: I guess, Tubby, that makes you Rodney Black, Junior, of Wall Street.
> BLACK: Sir—!
> ELLERY: Which one of you gentlemen belonged to The Inner Circle of The Januarians?
> MASON: Inner what, what?
> BLACK: Circle, I think he said, Charlie.
> TEMPLE: Inner circle? What's that?
> SERGEANT: One of 'em's a John Barrymore, Maestro.
> BLACK: See here, we're three-fourths of what's left of the Class of Eastern '13...
> ELLERY: Ah, then you gentlemen don't know that Bill Updike is dead?
> ALL: Dead! *Bill?*
> INSPECTOR: Tell 'em the whole story, Ellery.

And so, patiently, Ellery recounted the story of the Inner Circle, William Updike's murder, and the vanished $200,000 in negotiable securities. And as he told this story, the old gentleman from Center Street and his sergeant studied the three elderly faces; and the theater magnate, the lawyer, and the broker gave stare for stare; and when Ellery had finished they turned to one another and gave stare for stare once more.

And finally Charlie Mason said: "My hands are clean, Ed. How about yours?"

"What do you take me for, Charlie?" said Temple in a flat and chilling voice. And they both looked at Black, who squeaked: "Don't try to make *me* out the one, you traitors!"

Whereupon, as if there were nothing more to be said, the three divinities turned and gazed bleakly upon the iconoclasts.

And the catechism resumed:

> ELLERY: Mr. Temple, where were you night before last between 11 p.m. and midnight?
> TEMPLE: Let me see. Night before last...That was the night before New Year's Eve. I went to bed at 10 o'clock.
> ELLERY: You're a bachelor, I believe. Do you employ a domestic?
> TEMPLE: My man.
> ELLERY: Was he—?
> TEMPLE: He sleeps out.

SERGEANT: No alibi!

INSPECTOR: How about you, Mr. Black?

BLACK: Well, the fact is... I'd gone to see a musical in town...and between 11 and 12 I was driving home...to White Plains...

SERGEANT: Ha! White Plains!

ELLERY: Alone, Mr. Black?

BLACK: Well... yes. The family's all away over the holidays...

INSPECTOR: No alibi. Mr. Mason?

MASON: Go to hell. *(There is a knock on the door.)*

SERGEANT: Now who would that be?

TEMPLE: The ghost of Bill?

BLACK: You re not funny, Ed!

ELLERY: Come in. *(The door opens. Enter Nikki Porter.)*

NIKKI: I'm sorry to interrupt, but she came looking for you, Ellery. She was terribly insistent. Said she'd just recalled something about The Inner Circle, and—

ELLERY: She?

NIKKI: Come in, Mrs. Updike.

"They're here," said Mrs. Updike. "I'm glad. I wanted to look at their faces."

"I've told Mrs. Updike the whole thing," said Nikki defiantly.

And Inspector Queen said in a soft tone: "Velie, shut the door."

But this case was not to be solved by a guilty look. Black, Mason, and Temple said quick ineffectual things, surrounding the widow and spending their nervousness in little gestures and rustlings until finally silence fell and she said helplessly, "Oh, I don't know, I don't know," and dropped into a chair to weep.

And Black stared out the window, and Mason looked green, and Temple compressed his lips.

Then Ellery went to the widow and put his hand on her shoulder. "You recall something about The Inner Circle, Mrs. Updike?"

She stopped weeping and folded her hands, resting them in her lap and looking straight ahead.

"Was it the names of the five?"

"No. Bill never told me their names. But I remember Bill's saying to me once: 'Mary, I'll give you a hint.'"

"Hint?"

"Bill said that he once realized there was something funny about the names of the five men in The Inner Circle."

"Funny?" said Ellery sharply. "About their *names?*"

"He said by coincidence all five names had one thing in common."

"In common?"

"And he laughed," Mrs. Updike paused. "He laughed, and he said: 'That is, Mary, if you remember that I'm a married man.' I remember saying: 'Bill, stop talking in riddles. What do you mean?' And he laughed again and said: 'Well, you see, Mary, *you're in it, too.*'"

"You're in it, too," said Nikki blankly.

"I have no idea what he meant, but that's what Bill said, word for word." And now she looked up at Ellery and asked, with a sort of ferocious zest: "Does any of this help, Mr. Queen?"

"Oh, yes," said Ellery gently. "All of it, Mrs. Updike." And he turned to the three silent Januarians and said: "Would any of you gentlemen like to try your wits against this riddle?"

But the gentlemen remained silent.

"The reply appears to be no," Ellery said. "Very well; let's work it out *en masse.* Robert Carlton Smith, J. Sanford Jones, Peter Zissing Brown, William Updike. Those four names, according to Bill Updike, have one thing in common. What?"

"Smith," said the Inspector.

"Jones," said the Sergeant.

"Brown," said Nikki.

"Updike!" said the Inspector. "Boy, you've got me."

"Include me in, Maestro."

"Ellery, please!"

"Each of the four names," said Ellery, "has in it, somewhere, the name of well-known college or university."

And there was another mute communion.

"Robert—Carlton—Smith," said the Inspector, doubtfully.

"Smith!" cried Nikki. *"Smith College,* in Massachusetts!"

The Inspector looked startled. "J. Stanford Jones.—That California university, *Stanford!"*

"Hey," said Sergeant Velie. "Brown. *Brown University,* in Rhode Island!"

"Updike," said Nikki, then she stopped. "Updike? There's no college called Updike, Ellery."

"William Updike was his full name, Nikki."

"You mean the 'William' part? There's a Williams, with an *s,* but no William."

"What did Updike tell Mrs. Updike? 'Mary, you're in it, too.' William Updike was in it, and Mary Updike was in it..."

"William and Mary College!" roared the Inspector.

"So the college denominator checks for all four of the known names. But since Updike told his wife the fifth name had the same thing in common, all we have to do now is test the names of these three gentlemen to see if one of them is the name of a college or university— and we'll have the scoundrel who murdered Bill Updike for the Inner Circle's fortune in securities."

"Black," babbled Rodney Black, Junior. "Rodney Black, Junior. Find me a college in that, sir!"

"Charles Mason," said Charles Mason unsteadily. "Charles? Mason? You see!"

"That," said Ellery, "sort of hangs it around your neck, Mr. Temple."

"Temple!"

"Temple University in Pennsylvania!"

Of course, it was absurd. Grown men who played at godhead with emblems and talismans, like boys conspiring in a cave, and a murder case which was solved by a trick of nomenclature. Eastern University is too large for that sort of childishness. And it is old enough, we submit, to know the truth:

ITEM: Edward I. Temple, Class of Eastern '13, did not "fall" from the thirteenth floor of The Eastern Alumni Club on New Year's Day this year. He jumped.

ITEM: The Patulcius Chair of Classics, founded this year, was not endowed by a wealthy alumnus from Oil City who modestly chose anonymity. It came into existence through the contents of The Inner Circle's safe-deposit box, said contents having been recovered from another safe-deposit box rented by said Temple in another bank on the afternoon of December thirty-first under a false name.

ITEM: The Januarian room was not converted to the storage of linen because of the expanded housekeeping needs of The Eastern Alumni Club. It was ordered so that the very name of the Society of the Two-Faced God should be expunged from Eastern's halls; and as for the stainless steel medallion of Janus which had hung on the door, the Chancellor of Eastern University himself scaled it into the Hudson

River from the George Washington Bridge, during a sleet storm, one hideous night this January.

Squeeze Play

Richard Prather

Richard Scott Prather (b. 1921) was born in Santa Ana, California. After attending Riverside Junior High School from 1940-41, Prather
joined the U.S. Merchant Marine a year later. He served in the Marines as
a fireman, oiler, and engineer until 1945. He married Tina Haggler that
year and served as an Air Force clerk until 1949, the year his first Shell
Scott novel, *The Case of the Vanishing Beauty,* was published. Prather
used the proceeds from that novel to buy an avocado farm and began
writing full-time. He wrote a large amount of Scott novels over the next
twenty-five years, including *Everybody Had a Gun* (1951), *Find the
Woman* (1951), *Pattern For Murder* (1952; written under a pseudonym
and rewritten as a Scott novel, *The Scrambled Yeggs*, in 1958), *Darling,
It's Death* (1952), *Always Leave 'Em Dying* (1954), *The Wailing Frail*
(1956), *Slab Happy* (1958), *Dig That Crazy Grave* (1961), *The Trojan
Hearse* (1964), *Kill Him Twice* (1965), *The Kubla Khan Caper* (1966),
and *The Sweet Ride* (1972). For health reasons, Prather moved to Scotts-
dale Arizona and did not publish again until 1986 when *The Amber Effect*
was printed. He received the Lifetime Achievement Award from The
Private Eye Writers of America that year. To date, he has written one more
Scott novel, *Shell-Shock* (1987), which seems to be a farewell to the
character and the series. Prather still resides in Arizona.

Whereas most hard-boiled detectives took themselves far too seriously, Prather's Shell Scott was always looking at the lighter side of
things. "Squeeze Play" is an exceptional example of Prather's breezy,
freewheeling prose.

PRETTY WILLIS WAS a killer as proud of his appearance as of his
gun, and he had no use for private detectives unless he was hitting them
over the head. Consequently he had no use at all for one Shell Scott.
But at four o'clock Tuesday afternoon he barged into my office in the
Hamilton Building and said flatly, "Get your coat, Scott. You're
leaving." It was an order.

I was watching guppies in the aquarium on top of my bookcase, so
all I knew at first was that there was a nasty-voiced slob behind me.

But I turned around, recognized him and said, "The hell you say. Bag your lip, Pretty."

His handsome face flushed. "You know who I am. You know better than to spring with a crack like that."

To Pretty both statements meant the same thing: If you knew who he was, you talked softly to him. We'd never met before, socially or unsocially, but I knew a lot of things about him and all of them except his appearance were nauseating.

He was handsome enough in a tortured sort of way. He stood almost my height, six-two, but I had twenty-five pounds over his one-eighty—not counting the gun which would be under his coat. Besides the gun and his weight-lifter's build, he had porcelain caps on his teeth, jet-black hair the precise color of Tintair number fourteen, and carefully manicured, too-shiny nails. His eyebrows were dark and neat, the space between them plucked as bare and empty as I imagined his mind was. Pretty Willis was possibly the vainest man in Los Angeles but also one of the toughest. He'd been in a number of brawls, and was still pretty only because he could take care of himself.

He said deliberately, "Snap it up. Hackman wants to see you. We hear you been looking for Leroy Crane." He was right. Mrs. Leroy Crane had been my client for about twenty-four hours now. She wanted me to find her husband—or, perhaps, late husband. Leroy was four days late. He worked—or had worked—as Hackman's accountant, so I figured Leroy was already starting to decompose.

Hackman was Wallace Hackman, Crook in capitals, with his fat fingers in everything from dope to sudden death. He was not only ruthless but stupid, and would never have got as high in the rackets as he had except for one thing: he didn't trust any man alive. He wouldn't give you the correct time if he could help it, and he didn't even trust his right-hand man, Pretty Willis, behind his back. His complicated little hierarchy was a lot like a communist club: crooks watching crooks who in turn watched other crooks, and all reporting to the top, Hackman.

Complicated, maybe, but as a result nobody had ever got enough on Hackman to haul him into court, much less put him behind bars. His previous accountant, who by the nature of his work would naturally have learned more than anybody else about the boss' business, had simply disappeared a couple years back—after which Leroy Crane got the well-paid, unhealthy job. It seemed likely that Hackman wouldn't want me to find Leroy.

Pretty Willis said, "Get a move on. Hack don't like to wait. And don't give me no more lip."

"You run along and pluck your eyebrows, Pretty," I said. "Tell your boss I'll see him when and if I get time." I wasn't exactly dying to see Hackman because a lot of times seeing Hackman and dying were practically the same thing.

Pretty walked up in front of me, stopped, started to say something and then strangled it in his throat. It's funny, but I wasn't thinking about much of anything except the best way to tie him up. I knew Pretty was handy with his hands—and feet and knees for that matter—but even if that was part of his business, it was also part of mine and had been from my Marine days down to here. I just wanted to be careful that I didn't mark him up. He would be mad enough at me for simply clobbering him, but there was no point in driving him insane. His face was to him what soft lingerie or French postcards are to some other guys; it was his fetish; he was in love with it. If I mashed his face, he'd kill me when he could, if he could. Actually, the best way to handle Pretty was with a gun, and I glanced toward my desk where the .38 Special and harness were draped over my coat.

I learned one thing for sure: You should never take your eyes off a guy like Pretty. While I was looking toward my gun, he knocked me down. I'd expected him to chat a bit more, but I had hurt his feelings so he just hauled off and caught me not only off guard, but behind the ear. I landed on my fanny, more surprised to be down there on the floor than hurt, and I was too surprised for too long.

Pretty swung his leg forward and the pointed toe of his shoe went into my stomach like a meal. It caught me in the solar plexus and I bent forward, grabbing for his leg, my sight blurring as tiny red and black spots danced in the air around me, and I got a grip on his foot and twisted. I did all of it just like the book says, but the book didn't say what happened when you were dizzy, paralyzed, and couldn't twist a wet noodle.

But I found out. I knew Pretty was way up there above me, that he'd be swinging his gun down toward my head, but it was like knowing the earth is moving; I couldn't do a thing to stop it—

When I came to I was on a soft couch, though I didn't realize even that at first. My head ached, and I couldn't remember what had happened or why my head should be throbbing. I felt my skull and found a large bump. There was a clue. Then I remembered and opened my eyes. A few feet from me, in an overstuffed chair large enough to hold his overstuffed bulk, was Hackman. That meant I must be in his suite on the top floor of L.A.'s new Hotel Statler.

"Hello, Hackman," I said. "Hello, you sonofabitch."

He chuckled. A lot of the top racket boys are pleasant, personable men, but not this oily, pudgy, baby-faced and round-bellied slug. I shut my eyes and shook my head to clear fog from my brain. I knew Hackman would want to talk about Leroy Crane, and I thought back to what Crane's wife had told me.

Yesterday Ann Crane, a cute little wide-eyed doll, had phoned me and I'd gone to see her. She'd cried and told me that three nights before, husband Leroy had phoned her and said he wouldn't see her for a few days. He had a big deal cooking and would make up for the separation—their first—with mink coats and diamonds. She hadn't heard from him since.

She'd convinced me not only that she had no idea what he'd been talking about, but that she was ready to crack up. I got a photograph of thin-faced, rather homely Leroy, learned all I could about him, including what his job was with Hackman, and through it all were her tears. Tears out of brown eyes, trailing down over soft cheeks, glistening on curved red lips.

After reaching an agreement about my fee I'd gone back to the office and put my lines out, let it be known in the right places that I was looking for Leroy. And then in had walked Pretty Willis.

I opened my eyes and said, "Get it off your chest, Hackman."

He glanced toward the door: "Wait outside, boys."

The "boys" were Pretty Willis and a little hood named Shadow who was so skinny and dishonest that he always weighed himself with his gun on. He must have helped Pretty lug me up here. When I saw Pretty, anger exploded inside me and I got to my feet, wobbling a bit. But before I could take a step toward him both men had gone out the door and closed it. I started after them but Hackman said, "Sit down. All I gotta do is grunt and you've had it."

I told him to shut up, but I sat down. He was right. If I'd had a gun, though, he might have been wrong. Hackman wheezed and jiggled, shifting from one monstrous buttock to the other, then he said, "Scott, I know you don't like me. And I got no love for you, neither. But we don't have to like each other to cooperate."

"Get to the point."

"I want Crane myself. In case you get to him before me, I want him, see? I can make it worth your while."

"Nuts. I wouldn't give you a drink in the desert. I wouldn't even give you conversation if you hadn't asked me so politely." I went on from there. I watched him get angry, watched his oily face shade from white into pink, and when I finished he knew for sure I wasn't going to give him a damned thing except trouble.

Suddenly he said, "Shut your face, Scott. And blow. Blow fast before you start leaking someplace besides your mouth." He leaned forward and said, "But understand this, Scott. I want Crane myself. And I mean to get him. You get in my way an inch, move one inch out of line, and I'll see that you get dead."

Some of the hot anger drained out of me because it finally had occurred to me that this was a strange conversation we were having if Leroy Crane were alive. And if Hackman was still looking for him, he almost surely *was* alive.

I thought about that for a moment, then said slowly, "So that's it. Crane powdered and now you're sweating."

In his own cute way he told me I was constipated. Then he went on, "You drop it. Stop looking for Crane. Forget you ever heard of him." He didn't make any more specific threats, but his voice was lower and the words came out like ice cubes. I started to say something else but Hackman said, "Get out," then raised his voice and shouted, "Pretty!"

Pretty Willis came inside followed by Shadow. There weren't any guns in sight, but I knew there would be if I wiggled. Hackman said, "Beat it, Scott. Don't forget nothing I told you."

I walked to the door and as I passed the two thugs I said pointedly, "Be seeing you, Pretty." He showed me his too-white teeth and chuckled, "I'm panicked." He and Shadow followed me to the outer door. Shadow opened it and I went through, then started to turn around for a last word. I didn't make it. While Pretty was behind me he must have taken his gun out. I assume that's what he slammed against the back of my skull.

I stumbled forward, fell to my hands and knees and there was barely enough strength in my arms to hold me up off the floor. Laughter grated behind me. I guess it took me about a minute to get to my feet and turn around, and by that time I was alone with my insanity. I left, went back to the office, found my gun still there and strapped it on, and returned to the Statler lobby before even a semblance of reason returned.

Half a dozen of Hackman's boys were scattered around in the chairs and divans. One of them stood up and the rest looked at me, grinning. There wasn't a thing I could do about it. I had been knocked down, kicked, threatened and sapped, and if I wanted to keep on living I had to take it—at least for a while longer.

But from then on I stopped sleeping except for short naps in my Cad or slumped over my office desk. I didn't go near my apartment. I looked for Leroy Crane. Every ex-con, every tipster and stoolie I'd ever had anything to do with got word one way or another from me that they could name their price if they gave me a lead to Crane. I saw Ann again, told her that her husband was at least alive, and that I'd find him, but I learned nothing new from her except that she was the cryingest babe I had ever seen. I kept my eyes peeled for any of Hackman's pals, and I looked for Pretty as hard as I looked for Leroy. For two long days nothing happened.

On Thursday afternoon my office phone rang and a woman's soft, lilting voice said, "Mr. Scott? I can take you to Leroy Crane. For a hundred dollars."

"You just made a hundred. Where and when?"

"Right now in room sixteen, Porter Hotel on L.A. Street."

"Is Crane there?"

"No, stupid. I am. Bring the C-note. Incidentally, my name's Billie."

I hung up and glared at the phone. Billie could be on the level, and probably was, but I didn't like it. A hundred dollars didn't seem like much payment for her information.

It was one of those mangy hotels on Los Angeles Street a block from Main. On the wrong side of Main. Somebody had thrown up in the narrow entrance at street level; worn wooden stairs shuddered as I walked up them into a dimly-lighted hallway that smelled like dead mice. The door of room sixteen looked as if it would turn into powder and termites if I knocked hard on it, so I tapped gently with my left hand, right hand curled around the .38's butt in my coat pocket. The door opened and I stared.

This was almost like getting kicked in the stomach again. It would be impossible to describe her exactly because there aren't any three-dimensional words, but she looked so warm and wild and wonderful that my mouth went down and then up like a small slow elevator while I listened to a voice like a breeze saying, "Come on in. I'm Billie. You bring the money?"

"Yeah. Hello. Yeah. I brought the money. Uh..."

The "Uh..." was because Billie wasn't wearing much of anything. She had on a robe which reached nearly to the floor and covered every inch of skin from the neck down, but it was thin enough to suit me, and that is pretty goddamned thin. She held the robe together with both hands—there was so much to cover that it took both hands—and stepped aside as I walked in.

I glanced around to make sure we were alone, then turned to look at the gal again. She was tall, with white skin as smooth as smoke, with mist-gray eyes, with long black hair and pleasantly full lips and things. She let me look, even seemed to help me a little, and I asked her, "Where do we go from here?"

"Nowhere if you don't have the hundred. Hand it over and I'll take you to Crane."

"Not in that outfit." I took two fifty-dollar bills from my pocket.

She laughed, walked past me and flopped on a rickety bed, plucking the two fifties from my hand as she went by. I was just starting to wonder what such a choice, expensive-looking tomato was doing in this dump, and where she thought she was going in that robe and nothing else, and I might have saved myself some trouble if I'd continued thinking like that. Only right then was when she flopped on the bed.

I'm sure she hadn't planned it quite the way it happened, because the bed springs broke. There was a great deal of activity for about two seconds there, and that was long enough for the guy to come up behind me. I hadn't been worried about anybody getting behind me because only the gal and I had been in the room and there weren't any adjoining doors—just the front door. Just the one I had my back to. Maybe I should have worried about that door behind me, considering what a phony deal this now seemed to be, but I was stupid. And if you were staring open-mouthed at a babe flying through the air with arms and legs waving at you, and bouncing to the sound of twanging springs, and no longer clutching a robe which had been thin enough to begin with, you, too, would be stupid.

But what tipped me was that the gal was paying no attention to either my face or her nudity, but was looking at a spot past my left shoulder. And maybe I heard something. I don't know now. I just know I ducked and dropped as the blow fell, and something jarred against my skull, glancing off and not getting me squarely enough to knock me out. It hurt, and it dazed me, but I still had enough sense left to reach behind me as I went down, get one hand on a trousers-covered leg and yank.

The leg slipped out of my hand as the guy fell, but I flipped over in time to see him sprawling on his back. He rolled over and jumped up again as I got my feet under me and stood up straight. It was Pretty Willis. I should have known. Every time a guy came up behind me and batted me it was Pretty Willis. Only this time I was facing him, looking at him.

The sap he'd used was on the floor, and he didn't have a gun in his hand—but he dug under his coat for one and I jumped for him. I slammed into him and my weight jarred him back against the wall as I drove my right fist forward, knuckles projecting to dig into the soft spot in his belly. Somehow his elbow got in the way, and then the hard heel of his other hand crashed under my chin, snapping my head back. I staggered slightly but in the same moment I sliced my right hand up in a tight arc, felt its edge crack against the bony structure of his face. I caught my balance, turned toward him and saw a trickle of blood under his nose, his lips pulled back tight over white teeth. He swung a hand at me and when I jerked my head aside his other fist came out of nowhere and exploded against my chin.

At least he hit me so hard that it felt like an explosion. All the colors in the room blended into a shimmering gray for a moment as I fell backwards. The floor thudded against my back. Then my vision cleared enough so I could see Pretty still bent over from the force of his swing, see him straighten up and leap toward me.

While I wasn't in the best shape of my life I could have rolled out of the way. But I didn't. I didn't even start to. Pretty had already started to dive toward me, hands extended, before I jerked my legs up off the floor and toward my chest, thinking even as I did it about the hell this bastard had given me. Then I drove my legs forward and my feet burst through his outstretched hands as if they were paper; my hard leather heels jarred into his face; and Pretty wasn't pretty any more. His body jerked, hung for a moment in the air, then dropped limply to the floor. Red stain flowed from his cheek, covered exposed white bone, seeped into the carpet.

I glanced over my shoulder at the girl, who was still on the bed, then I felt Pretty's neck to see if it was broken. It wasn't. I'll never know why it wasn't. I got up, walked to the bed and stood over Billie. She licked her lips, swallowed, stared up at me.

"Spill it," I said.

She shook her head, said nothing. I bunched her black hair in one hand. "Give me some straight answers or wind up like him. Take your pick, beautiful."

She bit her lips but didn't answer. Then she looked at Pretty. He lay on his back, face toward us. I knew I couldn't slug Billie around, but the expression of fright on her face gave way slowly to revulsion, and that gave me an idea.

I grabbed her, pulled her off the bed and twisted her arms behind her, then shoved her across the room, forced her to kneel by the unconscious man. She struggled to get away but I held her firmly and pressed her face closer and closer to his. When I let her go there was a smudge of blood on her cheek. She wiped it off, stared at her stained fingers, then spoke, trying to keep the sickness out of her voice, keep from actually becoming sick.

I was lucky to be talking to Billie because Hackman hadn't trusted even Pretty with the details I wanted to hear. But she knew it all—Billie was Hackman's woman. And she told me all of it. Leroy Crane had found out that Hackman had ordered the death of his previous accountant when said accountant learned too much about the boss. For more than a year now, Crane had kept a detailed record of every financial move Hackman had made—including taxes Hackman had paid and what he *should* have paid. Crane had originally started preserving his info as a guarantee of his own safety when and if Hackman decided that accountant Crane, too, had to go. It had started out like that but had turned into the old squeeze play, a shakedown.

Crane, with his typed information supported by a mass of documents and figures, had phoned Hackman—on that night when Crane hadn't showed up at home—and told Hackman he could have the file of information for a cool half million; otherwise Crane would turn the dope over to the income-tax boys and settle for the "informer's fee," the informant's share of delinquent taxes collected—while Hackman would wind up in the federal clink. After telling Hackman he would phone again in a week, Crane had hung up.

So Hackman had to get those papers, even if he had to pay a half-million dollars for them. But now he was trying to find Crane and work him over, beat the location of the papers out of him, then put a bullet into his brain. Crane, knowing what would happen to him if he were found, had dropped completely out of sight.

I asked Billie why Pretty had jumped me and she kept talking. "Hack knows now that you've been seeing a lot of Mrs. Crane. He didn't know that at first. This is too important for him to take any chance of a slip when he grabs her. So he had to make sure you were out of—"

"When he what? *Grabs* her?"

"Crane has the papers, but maybe he thinks more of his wife than he does of a half-million dollars." The trace of a smile curved her smooth lips as she said, "Crane must have thought nobody would bother his wife, at least not when he had all that stuff on the boss. But Crane was wrong if he did."

"When?" I said. "When are they—"

That slight smile again stopped me. "Oh," she said slowly, "they probably have her by now."

I turned and ran for the door, jumping over Pretty. I was clear down on the street and in my Cad before I thought of what it meant to leave him back there, unconscious but soon to be awake—and looking at his face. He was a little psycho anyway, and now he'd go off the deep end, crazy mad. He'd do his damndest to kill me, but there wasn't time to go back. There wasn't time for anything but Ann

There wasn't even time for Ann. When I reached her home she was gone. The door was ajar and a wrinkled carpet, a tipped-over end table were mute signs of a struggle.

It was four o'clock, Thursday afternoon. On Friday afternoon, at three o'clock, the party started coming to a head. I spent those intervening twenty-three hours without sleep, and I did everything I could to find Ann or Leroy, with no success. I looked for Pretty and Billie but didn't find them; I did find Hackman holed up in the Statler with half a dozen thugs around him, and not being suicidal I left him alone. There was one way left, and it was all I had so I took it.

For six hours now I'd been parked near the Statler where I could watch the exits. From what I knew of Hackman I was sure of one thing: he would, one way or another, get his hands on Crane's file of papers, but Hackman would also make sure they were his *own* hands. The only man alive with information which could put Hackman in prison was Crane. If Hackman let one of his underlings pick up the papers, that underling would then have in his hands enough to put the boss in jail or else squeeze him dry—and there was a very good chance the other boys around Hackman would squeeze a lot harder than Crane. I knew Hackman wouldn't trust any of his hoodlums with his right name if he could avoid it; he sure as hell wouldn't hand them the end of the noose around his neck. At least that's the way I had it figured; that was what I was counting on. If I kept my eye on Hackman, didn't lose him, I'd be in at the finish.

At three P.M., it started. Pretty Willis arrived.

He parked in a no-parking zone and ran into the hotel. I almost missed him, because I was watching for any sign of Hackman, and I would have missed Pretty if it hadn't been for his face. It was swathed in white bandages and he looked like something out of a horror picture as he ran limping across the sidewalk. Two minutes later Pretty came out—with Hackman. They drove away and I tailed them to Forty-Sixth Street, to a rooming house. They went inside, came back to their car

with Shadow, the skinny hood. And with Ann. They drove to Broadway and I followed, keeping a car between them and me, and the
farther they went the more puzzled I got. Shadow drove through the
business district, turned right beyond First, swung back into Main and
parked squarely in front of the City Hall. I didn't get it, but I double-
parked a few yards behind them, taking a chance they'd spot me,
because whatever was happening, I wanted to be close. Shadow stayed
in the car with Ann; Pretty and Hackman got out and started walking
up the stone steps of the Main Street entrance of City Hall. And then
it made sense.

Standing between high cement columns before the huge entrance
was Leroy Crane, tall and thin, thin-faced, haggard, with a leather
briefcase in one hand. He looked past the two men, toward the car,
toward Ann. At the top of the steps the three men talked, argued; Crane
shook his head, pointed toward the car.

It was clear enough now. Hackman was trading Leroy's wife for the
stuff in the briefcase, getting the noose off his neck without spending
a buck—and Leroy was the guy in the squeeze now. But Leroy was
playing it smart. He was going to make the trade, but not in a place
where he could be shot in the back. Behind Crane in the City Hall
lobby was a guard, a cop was standing halfway down the block, in the
building was everything from the Mayor to office workers to firemen
to hundreds of policemen.

After some more argument Hackman turned and waved to Shadow.
He and the girl got out of the car. Ann walked a few feet away, looking
all the time at her husband. I got out of the Cad, grabbed my gun and
started walking toward them, tightness swelling in my chest, stomach
knotting. For a moment their figures were still, as if frozen. There
seemed no movement at all and none of them had yet seen me. Then
Hackman took the briefcase from Crane, looked inside and pawed
briefly through its contents, shut it and gripped it tightly as he and
Pretty started down the steps. Shadow walked rapidly toward the car
and Ann started running toward the big entrance and her husband.

It was as if a rigid tableau had dissolved into separate lines of
movement, exept for the still figure of Crane, standing motionless and
looking toward Ann. And then came the explosion; then it happened;
then Main Street blew up in our faces.

Hackman spotted me.

He stopped, reached out and clutched Pretty's arm. From twenty feet
away and below him on the sidewalk I could see his fat, oily face get
white. Pretty turned his bandaged head and stared at me, his eyes wide

above the strips of gauze and tape. Hackman's mouth stretched open and he thrust both hands toward me, pulling his head into his neck, fat cheeks jiggling. But not Pretty, not that crazy bastard. All the hate boiled up in Pretty and overflowed when he saw me, and his mashed face twitched beneath the bandages as his hand went under his coat.

I yelled at him, told him to stop, but he didn't hear me or just plain didn't give a damn. I even let him get the gun in his hand, bring it out from under his coat, but when sunlight gleamed on the .45's rapidly swinging barrel, there wasn't any choice for me.

The first slug from my .38 caught him high on the chest and I squeezed the trigger again as he staggered just enough so my second shot missed him and the slug caromed off one of the high cement columns fronting City Hall. Pretty convulsively triggered his .45, but by then the gun was pointing down at the sidewalk. I heard the bullet crack viciously against the walk and whine away as I fired the third shot from my Colt. It was the last shot, too, because it caught him in the throat and sliced the jugular cleanly.

You've got to see something like that to believe it. You wouldn't think the red fountain of a man's blood would squirt so far through the air, leave such a long, wide, snakelike stream against the cement, a stream that spread wider and uglier even as Pretty fell into it. He hit the cement with his side, rolled over onto his face and sprawled across two of the steps, awkward, puppet-like, very messily dead.

I thought a slug had caught Hackman, because he stumbled and fell down the steps quivering like a life-size mound of Jello, but from the corner of my eye I saw him reach bottom squirming, face down, hands wrapped around the top of his head. He was just scared, sweating plasma.

And then there was nothing but cops. They came from everywhere exept out of the sky. There were uniformed cops, plain-clothes cops, cops from Robbery and Homicide and Forgery and maybe even the Juvenile division. There were cops milling about, and possibly jumping up and down, and sirens and squad cars converging, and this was for sure the damnedest commotion ever seen on lower Main Street. Well, what can you expect when you start shooting up City Hall?

Somewhere in there a policeman on my right raised a gun toward me and I swung around yelling as he fired. The slug went past me and I looked over my shoulder to see Shadow, a red stain on his chest, gun falling from his hand and clanking against the sidewalk just before Shadow fell too. There was a blurred glimpse of Ann clinging to Leroy on one of the middle steps, of uniforms, of shouting red faces; and one guy with halitosis got his face close to mine and swore at me, and I swore.

It might have been a minute or it might have been ten, but then the landscape sighed and settled, people stopped milling, Main Street settled down. There was much jawing and yakking and explaining, and cops looked at the papers in Leroy's briefcase and beamed happily; and there was weeping because naturally Ann was bawling away as usual, only this time it was different.

And everybody was hauled away, including me for an hour after which somebody patted me on the back and told me to get some sleep. I got in a word with Ann, alone now because her husband was in a cell, and I told her Leroy wouldn't get off scot-free but it shouldn't be bad, and she cried and thanked me.

I went out of City Hall free as a bird and walked to my car. A man was mopping up red stain from the big cement steps. I headed for home, for sleep, and on the way I thought about the case, about Hackman. He'd given me a lot of trouble, but now that it was over I actually felt sorry for him. Where he was going he'd want a lot of things, miss a lot of things—but most of all he was going to miss Billie.

But, then, she was a woman almost any man would miss. And I remembered her standing in the doorway, mist-gray eyes in her soft white face, a voice like whispering winds, a shape—a shape—

Come to think of it, she still owed me a hundred bucks.

Sleeping Dog

Ross Macdonald

Ross Macdonald (1915-1983), the natural successor of Chandler and Hammett, was born Kenneth Millar in Los Gatos, California. In 1919, his father abandoned the family, and Millar's mother moved to Canada. A product of a poor childhood, Millar graduated from the University of Western Ontario in 1938. That year, he married Margaret Strum. His daughter, Linda Jane Millar, was born a year later. He began graduate work at the University of Michigan in 1941, and joined the Naval Reserves during World War II. After his wife achieved success as a mystery novelist, Millar wrote *The Dark Tunnel* (1944) in a month. He produced three more novels under his own name—*Trouble Follows Me* (1946), *Blue City* (1947), and *Three Roads* (1948)—before publishing the first Lew Archer novel under the name John Ross MacDonald, *The Moving Target* (1949). Millar changed his pseudonym to Ross MacDonald with *The Barbarous Coast* (1956). In 1974, he received the Grand Master Award from the Mystery Writers of America. In 1981, he was diagnosed as having Alzheimer's disease, and died two years later. Among his most famous works are *The Drowning Pool* (1951), *The Way Some People Die* (1951), *The Doomsters* (1958), *The Galton Case* (1959), *The Far Side of the Dollar* (1965), *The Goodbye Look* (1969), *The Underground Man* (1971), *The Blue Hammer* (1976), and two short story collections: *The Name is Archer* (1955) and *Lew Archer, Private Investigator* (1977).

The Lew Archer stories were always concerned with what happened to the people involved as opposed to the crime themselves. "Sleeping Dog" is a good example of this, with its long-ago murder triggering off mayhem among the jet-set of California.

THE DAY AFTER her dog disappeared, Fay Hooper called me early. Her normal voice was like waltzing violins, but this morning the violins were out of tune. She sounded as though she'd been crying.

"Otto's gone." Otto was her one-year-old German shepherd. "He jumped the fence yesterday afternoon and ran away. Or else he was kidnaped—dognaped, I suppose is the right word to use."

"What makes you think that?"

"You know Otto, Mr. Archer—how loyal he was. He wouldn't deliberately stay away from me overnight, not under his own power. There must be thieves involved." She caught her breath. "I realize searching for stolen dogs isn't your metier. But you *are* a detective. and I thought, since we knew each other..." She allowed her voice to suggest, ever so chastely, that we might get to know each other better.

I liked the woman. I liked the dog, I liked the breed. I was taking my own German shepherd pup to obedience school, which is where I met Fay Hooper. Otto and she were the handsomest and most expensive members of the class.

"How do I get to your place?"

She lived in the hills north of Malibu, she said, on the far side of the county line. If she wasn't home when I got there. her husband would be.

On my way out, I stopped at the dog school in Pacific Palisades to talk to the man who ran it, Fernando Rambeau. The kennels behind the house burst into clamor when I knocked on the front door. Rambeau boarded dogs as well as trained them.

A dark-haired girl looked out and informed me that her husband was feeding the animals. "Maybe I can help," she added doubtfully, and then she let me into a small living room.

I told her about the missing dog. "It would help if you called the vets and animal shelters and gave them a description," I said.

"We've already been doing that. Mrs. Hooper was on the phone to Fernando last night." She sounded vaguely resentful. "I'll get him."

Setting her face against the continuing noise, she went out the back door. Rambeau came in with her, wiping his hands on a rag. He was a square-shouldered Canadian with a curly black beard that failed to conceal his youth. Over the beard, his intense, dark eyes peered at me warily, like an animal's sensing trouble.

Rambeau handled dogs as if he loved them. He wasn't quite so patient with human beings. His current class was only in its third week, but he was already having dropouts. The man was loaded with explosive feeling, and it was close to the surface now.

"I'm sorry about Mrs. Hooper and her dog. They were my best pupils. He was, anyway. But I can't drop everything and spend the next week looking for him."

"Nobody expects that. I take it you've had no luck with your contacts."

"I don't have such good contacts. Marie and I, we just moved down here last year, from British Columbia."

"That was a mistake," his wife said from the doorway.

Rambeau pretended not to hear her. "Anyway, I know nothing about dog thieves." With both hands, he pushed the possibility away from him. "If I hear any word of the dog, I'll let you know, naturally. I've got nothing against Mrs. Hooper."

His wife gave him a quick look. It was one of those revealing looks that said, among other things, that she loved him but didn't know if he loved her, and she was worried about him. She caught me watching her and lowered her eyes. Then she burst out, "Do you think somebody killed the dog?"

"I have no reason to think so."

"Some people shoot dogs, don't they?"

"Not around here," Rambeau said. "Maybe back in the bush someplace." He turned to me with a sweeping explanatory gesture. "These things make her nervous and she gets wild ideas. You know Marie is a country girl—"

"I am not. I was born in Chilliwack." Flinging a bitter look at him, she left the room.

"Was Otto shot?" I asked Rambeau.

"Not that I know of. Listen, Mr. Archer, you're a good customer, but I can't stand here talking all day. I've got twenty dogs to feed."

They were still barking when I drove up the coast highway out of hearing. It was nearly forty miles to the Hoopers' mailbox, and another mile up a blacktop lane that climbed the side of a canyon to the gate. On both sides of the heavy wire gate, which had a new combination padlock on it, a hurricane fence, eight feet high and topped with barbed wire, extended out of sight. Otto would have to be quite a jumper to clear it. So would I.

The house beyond the gate was low and massive, made of fieldstone and steel and glass. I honked at it and waited. A man in blue bathing trunks came out of the house with a shotgun. The sun glinted on its twin barrels and on the man's bald head and round brown, burnished belly. He walked quite slowly, a short, heavy man in his sixties, scuffling along in huaraches. The flabby brown shell of fat on him jiggled lugubriously.

When he approached the gate, I could see the stiff gray pallor under his tan, like stone showing under varnish. He was sick or afraid, or both. His mouth was profoundly discouraged.

"What do you want?" he said over the shotgun.

"Mrs. Hooper asked me to help find her dog. My name is Lew Archer."

He was not impressed. "My wife isn't here, and I'm busy. I happen to be following soybean futures rather closely."

"Look here, I've come quite a distance to lend a hand. I met Mrs. Hooper at dog school and—"

Hooper uttered a short, savage laugh. "That hardly constitutes an introduction to either of us. You'd better be on your way right now."

"I think I'll wait for your wife."

"I think you won't." He raised the shotgun and let me look into its close-set, hollow round eyes. "This is my property all the way down to the road, and you're trespassing. That means I can shoot you if I have to."

"What sense would that make? I came out here to help you."

"You can't help me." He looked at me through the wire gate with a kind of pathetic arrogance, like a lion that had grown old in captivity. "Go away."

I drove back down to the road and waited for Fay Hooper. The sun slid up the sky. The inside of my car turned oven-hot. I went for a walk down the canyon. The brown September grass crunched under my feet. Away up on the far side of the canyon, an earthmover that looked like a crazy red insect was cutting the ridge to pieces.

A very fast black car came up the canyon and stopped abruptly beside me. A gaunt man in a wrinkled brown suit climbed out, with his hand on his holster, told me that he was Sheriff Carlson, and asked me what I was doing there. I told him.

He pushed back his wide cream-colored hat and scratched at his hair-line. The pale eyes in his sun-fired face were like clouded glass inserts in a brick wall.

"I'm surprised Mr. Hooper takes that attitude. Mrs. Hooper just came to see me in the courthouse. But I can't take you up there with me if Mr. Hooper says no."

"Why not?"

"He owns most of the county and holds the mortgage on the rest of it. Besides," he added with careful logic, "Mr. Hooper is a friend of mine."

"Then you better get him a keeper."

The sheriff glanced around uneasily, as if the Hoopers' mailbox might be bugged. "I'm surprised he has a gun, let alone threatening you with it. He must be upset about the dog."

"He didn't seem to care about the dog."

"He does. though. *She* cares, so *he* cares," Carlson said.

"What did she have to tell you?"

"She can talk to you herself. She should be along any minute. She told me that she was going to follow me out of town."

He drove his black car up the lane. A few minutes later, Fay Hooper stopped her Mercedes at the mailbox. She must have seen the impatience on my face. She got out and came toward me in a little run, making noises of dismayed regret.

Fay was in her late thirties and fading slightly, as if a light frost had touched her pale gold head, but she was still a beautiful woman. She turned the gentle force of her charm on me.

"I'm dreadfully sorry," she said. "Have I kept you waiting long?"

"Your husband did. He ran me off with a shotgun."

Her gloved hand lighted on my arm, and stayed. She had an electric touch, even through layers of cloth.

"That's terrible. I had no idea that Allan still had a gun."

Her mouth was blue behind her lipstick, as if the information had chilled her to the marrow. She took me up the hill in the Mercedes. The gate was standing open, but she didn't drive in right away.

"I might as well be perfectly frank," she said without looking at me. "Ever since Otto disappeared yesterday, there's been a nagging question in my mind. What you've just told me raises the question again. I was in town all day yesterday so that Otto was alone here with Allan when—when it happened." The values her voice gave to the two names made it sound as if Allan were the dog and Otto the husband.

"When what happened, Mrs. Hooper?" I wanted to know.

Her voice sank lower. "I can't help suspecting that Allan shot him. He's never liked any of my dogs. The only dogs he appreciates are hunting dogs—and he was particularly jealous of Otto. Besides, when I got back from town, Allan was getting the ground ready to plant some roses. He's never enjoyed gardening, particularly in the heat. We have professionals to do our work. And this really isn't the time of year to put in a bed of roses."

"You think your husband was planting a dog?" I asked.

"If he was, I have to know." She turned toward me, and the leather seat squeaked softly under her movement. "Find out for me, Mr. Archer. If Allan killed my beautiful big old boy, I couldn't stay with him."

"Something you said implied that Allan used to have a gun or guns, but gave them up. Is that right?"

"He had a small arsenal when I married him. He was an infantry officer in the war and a big-game hunter in peacetime. But he swore off hunting years ago."

"Why?"

"I don't really know. We came home from a hunting trip in British Columbia one fall and Allan sold all his guns. He never said a word about it to me but it was the fall after the war ended, and I always thought that it must have had something to do with the war."

"Have you been married so long?"

"Thank you for that question." She produced a rueful smile. "I met Allan during the war, the year I came out, and I knew I'd met my fate. He was a very powerful person."

"And a very wealthy one."

She gave me a flashing, haughty look and stepped so hard on the accelerator that she almost ran into the sheriff's car parked in front of the house. We walked around to the back, past a free-form swimming pool that looked inviting into a walled garden. A few Greek statues stood around in elegant disrepair. Bees murmured like distant bombers among the flowers.

The bed where Allan Hooper had been digging was about five feet long and three feet wide, and it reminded me of graves.

"Get me a spade," I said.

"Are you going to dig him up?"

"You're pretty sure he's in there, aren't you, Mrs. Hooper?"

"I guess I am."

From a lath house at the end of the garden, she fetched a square-edged spade. I asked her to stick around.

I took off my jacket and hung it on a marble torso where it didn't look too bad. It was easy digging in the newly worked soil. In a few minutes, I was two feet below the surface, and the ground was still soft and penetrable.

The edge of my spade struck something soft but not so penetrable. Fay Hooper heard the peculiar dull sound it made. She made a dull sound of her own. I scooped away more earth. Dog fur sprouted like stiff black grass at the bottom of the grave.

Fay got down on her knees and began to dig with her lacquered fingernails. Once she cried out in a loud harsh voice, "Dirty murderer!"

Her husband must have heard her. He came out of the house and looked over the stone wall. His head seemed poised on top of the wall, hairless and bodiless, like Humpty Dumpty. He had that look on his face, of not being able to be put together again.

"I didn't kill your dog, Fay. Honest to God, I didn't."

She didn't hear him. She was talking to Otto. "Poor boy, poor boy," she said. "Poor, beautiful boy."

Sheriff Carlson came into the garden. He reached down into the grave and freed the dog's head from the earth. His large hands moved gently on the great wedge of the skull.

Fay knelt beside him in torn and dirty stockings. "What are you doing?"

Carlson held up a red-tipped finger. "Your dog was shot through the head, Mrs. Hooper, but it's no shotgun wound. Looks to me more like a deer rifle."

"I don't even own a rifle," Hooper said over the wall. "I haven't owned one for nearly twenty years. Anyway, I wouldn't shoot your dog."

Fay scrambled to her feet. She looked ready to climb the wall. "Then why did you bury him?"

His mouth opened and closed.

"Why did you buy a shotgun without telling me?"

"For protection."

"Against my dog?"

Hooper shook his head. He edged along the wall and came in tentatively through the gate. He had on slacks and a short-sleeved yellow jersey that somehow emphasized his shortness and his fatness and his age.

"Mr. Hooper had some threatening calls," the sheriff said. "Somebody got hold of his unlisted number. He was just telling me about it now."

"Why didn't you tell me, Allan?"

"I didn't want to alarm you. You weren't the one they were after, anyway. I bought a shotgun and kept it in my study."

"Do you know who they are?"

"No. I make enemies in the course of business, especially the farming operations. Some crackpot shot your dog, gunning for me. I heard a shot and found him dead in the driveway."

"But how could you bury him without telling me?"

Hooper spread his hands in front of him. "I wasn't thinking too well. I felt guilty, I suppose, because whoever got him was after me. And I didn't want you to see him dead. I guess I wanted to break it to you gently."

"This is gently?"

"It's not the way I planned it. I thought if I had a chance to get you another pup—"

"No one will ever take Otto's place."

Allan Hooper stood and looked at her wistfully across the open grave, as if he would have liked to take Otto's place. After a while, the two of them went into the house.

Carlson and I finished digging Otto up and carried him out to the sheriff's car. His inert blackness filled the trunk from side to side.

"What are you goung to do with him, Sheriff?" I asked.

"Get a vet I know to recover the slug in him. Then if we nab the sniper, we can use ballistics to convict him."

"You're taking this just as seriously as a real murder, aren't you?" I observed.

"They want me to," he said with a respectful look toward the house.

Mrs. Hooper came out carrying a white leather suitcase which she deposited in the back seat of her Mercedes.

"Are you going someplace?" I asked her.

"Yes. I am." She didn't say where.

Her husband, who was watching her from the doorway, didn't speak. The Mercedes went away. He closed the door. Both of them had looked sick.

"She doesn't seem to believe he didn't do it. Do you, Sheriff?"

Carlson jabbed me with his forefinger. "Mr. Hooper is no liar. If you want to get along with me, get that through your head. I've known Mr. Hooper for over twenty years—served under him in the war—and I never heard him twist the truth."

"I'll have to take your word for it. What about those threatening phone calls? Did he report them to you before today?"

"No."

"What was said on the phone?"

"He didn't tell me."

"Does Hooper have any idea who shot the dog?"

"Well, he did say he saw a man slinking around outside the fence. He didn't get close enough to the guy to give me a good description, but he did make out that he had a black beard."

"There's a dog trainer in Pacific Palisades named Rambeau, who fits the description. Mrs. Hooper has been taking Otto to his school."

"Rambeau?" Carlson said with interest.

"Fernando Rambeau. He seemed pretty upset when I talked to him this morning."

"What did he say?"

"A good deal less than he knows, I think. I'll talk to him again."

Rambeau was not at home. My repeated knocking was answered only by the barking of the dogs. I retreated up the highway to a drive-in where I ate a torpedo sandwich. When I was on my second cup of coffee, Marie Rambeau drove by in a pickup truck. I followed her home.

"Where's Fernando?" I asked.

"I don't know. I've been out looking for him."

"Is he in a bad way?"

"I don't know how you mean."

"Emotionally upset."

"He has been ever since that woman came into the class."

"Mrs. Hooper?"

Her head bobbed slightly.

"Are they having an affair?"

"They better not be." Her small red mouth looked quite implacable. "He was out with her night before last. I heard him make the date. He was gone all night, and when he came home, he was on one of his black drunks and he wouldn't go to bed. He sat in the kitchen and drank himself glassy-eyed." She got out of the pickup facing me. "Is shooting a dog a very serious crime?"

"It is to me, but not to the law. It's not like shooting a human being."

"It would be to Fernando. He loves dogs the way other people love human beings. That included Otto."

"But he shot him."

Her head drooped. I could see the straight white part dividing her black hair. "I'm afraid he did. He's got a crazy streak, and it comes out in him when he drinks. You should have heard him in the kitchen yesterday morning. He was moaning and groaning about his brother."

"His brother?"

"Fernando had an older brother, George, who died back in Canada after the war. Fernando was just a kid when it happened and it was a big loss to him. His parents were dead, too, and they put him in a foster home in Chilliwack. He still has nightmares about it."

"What did his brother die of?"

"He never told me exactly, but I think he was shot in some kind of hunting accident. George was a guide and packer in the Fraser River Valley below Mount Robson. That's where Fernando comes from, the Mount Robson country. He won't go back on account of what happened to his brother."

"What did he say about his brother yesterday?" I asked.

"That he was going to get his revenge for George. I got so scared I couldn't listen to him. I went out and fed the dogs. When I came back in, Fernando was loading his deer rifle. I asked him what he was planning to do, but he walked right out and drove away."

"May I see the rifle?"

"It isn't in the house. I looked for it after he left today. He must have taken it with him again. I'm so afraid that he'll kill somebody."

"What's he driving?"

"Our car. It's an old blue Meteor sedan."

Keeping an eye out for it, I drove up the highway to the Hoopers' canyon. Everything there was very peaceful. Too peaceful. Just inside the locked gate, Allan Hooper was lying face down on his shotgun. I could see small ants in single file trekking across the crown of his bald head.

I got a hammer out of the trunk of my car and used it to break the padlock. I lifted his head. His skin was hot in the sun, as if death had fallen on him like a fever. But he had been shot neatly between the eyes. There was no exit wound; the bullet was still in his head. Now the ants were crawling on my hands.

I found my way into the Hoopers' study, turned off the stuttering teletype, and sat down under an elk head to telephone the courthouse. Carlson was in his office.

"I have bad news, Sheriff. Allan Hooper's been shot."

I heard him draw in his breath quickly. "Is he dead?"

"Extremely dead. You better put out a general alarm for Rambeau."

Carlson said with gloomy satisfaction, "I already have him."

"You have him?"

"That's correct. I picked him up in the Hoopers' canyon and brought him in just a few minutes ago." Carlson's voice sank to a mournful mumble. "I picked him up a little too late, I guess."

"Did Rambeau do any talking?"

"He hasn't had a chance to yet. When I stopped his car, he piled out and threatened me with a rifle. I clobbered him one good."

I went outside to wait for Carlson and his men. A very pale afternoon moon hung like a ghost in the sky. For some reason, it made me think of Fay. She ought to be here. It occurred to me that possibly she had been.

I went and looked at Hooper's body again. He had nothing to tell me. He lay as if he had fallen from a height, perhaps all the way from the moon.

They came in a black county wagon and took him away. I followed them inland to the county seat, which rose like a dusty island in a dark green lake of orange groves. We parked in the courthouse parking lot, and the sheriff and I went inside.

Rambeau was under guard in a second-floor room with barred windows. Carlson said it was used for interrogation. There was nothing in the room but an old deal table and some wooden chairs. Rambeau sat hunched forward on one of them, his hands hanging limp between his knees. Part of his head had been shaved and plastered with bandages.

"I had to cool him with my gun butt," Carlson said. "You're lucky I didn't shoot you—you know that, Fernando?"

Rambeau made no response. His black eyes were set and dull.

"Had his rifle been fired?"

"Yeah. Chet Scott is working on it now. Chet's my identification lieutenant and he's a bear on ballistics." The sheriff turned back to Rambeau. "You might as well give us a full confession, boy. If you shot Mr. Hooper and his dog, we can link the bullets to your gun. You know that."

Rambeau didn't speak or move.

"What did you have against Mr. Hooper?" Carlson said.

No answer. Rambeau's mouth was set like a trap in the thicket of his head.

"Your older brother," I said to him, "was killed in a hunting accident in British Columbia. Was Hooper at the other end of the gun that killed George?"

Rambeau didn't answer me, but Carlson's head came up. "Where did you get that, Archer?"

"From a couple of things I was told. According to Rambeau's wife, he was talking yesterday about revenge for his brother's death. According to Fay Hooper, her husband swore off guns when he came back from a certain hunting trip after the war. Would you know if that trip was to British Columbia?"

"Yeah. Mr. Hooper took me and the wife with him."

"Whose wife?"

"Both our wives."

"To the Mount Robson area?"

"That's correct. We went up after elk."

"And did he shoot somebody accidentally?" I wanted to know.

"Not that I know of. I wasn't with him all the time, understand. He often went out alone, or with Mrs. Hooper," Carlson replied.

"Did he use a packer named George Rambeau?"

"I wouldn't know. Ask Fernando here."

I asked Fernando. He didn't speak or move. Only his eyes had changed. They were wet and glistening-black, visible parts of a grief that filled his head like a dark underground river.

The questioning went on and produced nothing. It was night when I went outside. The moon was slipping down behind the dark hills. I took a room in a hotel and checked in with my answering service in Hollywood. About an hour before, Fay Hooper had called me from a Las Vegas hotel. When I tried to return the call, she wasn't in her room and didn't respond to paging. I left a message for her to come home, that her husband was dead.

Next, I called R.C.M.P. headquarters in Vancouver to ask some questions about George Rambeau. The answers came over the line in clipped Canadian tones. George and his dog had disappeared from his cabin below Red Pass in the fall of 1945. Their bodies hadn't been recovered until the following May, and by that time they consisted of parts of the two skeletons. These included George Rambeau's skull which had been pierced in the right front and left rear quadrants by a heavy-caliber bullet. The bullet had not been recovered. Who fired it, or when or why, had never been determined. The dog, a husky, had also been shot through the head.

I walked over to the courthouse to pass the word to Carlson. He was in the basement shooting gallery with Lieutenant Scott, who was firing test rounds from Fernando Rambeau's .30/30 repeater.

I gave them the official account of the accident. "But since George Rambeau's dog was shot, too, it probably wasn't an accident," I said.

"I see what you mean," Carlson said. "It's going to be rough, spreading all this stuff out in court about Mr. Hooper. We have to nail it down, though."

I went back to my hotel and to bed, but the process of nailing down the case against Rambeau continued through the night. By morning, Lieutenant Scott had detailed comparisons set up between the test-fired slugs and the ones dug out of Hooper and the dog. I looked at his evidence through a comparison microscope. It left no doubt in my mind that the slugs that killed Allan Hooper and the dog Otto had come from Rambeau's gun.

But Rambeau still wouldn't talk, even to phone his wife or ask for a lawyer.

"We'll take you out to the scene of the crime," Carlson said. "I've cracked tougher nuts than you, boy."

We rode in the back seat of his car with Fernando handcuffed between us. Lieutenant Scott did the driving. Rambeau groaned and pulled against his handcuffs. He was very close to the breaking point, I thought.

It came a few minutes later when the car turned up the lane past the Hoopers' mailbox. He burst into sudden fierce tears as if a pressure gauge in his head had broken. It was strange to see a bearded man crying like a boy, and whimpering, "I don't want to go up there."

"Because you shot him?" Carlson said.

"I shot the dog. I confess I shot the dog," Rambeau said.

"And the man?"

"No!" he cried. "I never killed a man. Mr. Hooper was the one who did. He followed my brother out in the woods and shot him."

"If you knew that," I said, "why didn't you tell the Mounties years ago?"

"I didn't know it then. I was seven years old. How would I understand? When Mrs. Hooper came to our cabin to be with my brother, how would I know it was a serious thing? Or when Mr. Hooper asked me if she had been there? I didn't know he was her husband. I thought he was her father checking up. I knew I shouldn't have told him—I could see it in his face the minute after—but I didn't understand the situation until the other night, when I talked to Mrs. Hooper."

"Did she know that her husband had shot George?"

"She didn't even know George had been killed. They never went back to the Fraser River after 1945. But when we put our facts together, we agreed he must have done it. I came out here next morning to get even. The dog came out to the gate. It wasn't real to me—I was drinking most of the night—it wasn't real to me until the dog went down. I shot him. Mr. Hooper shot *my* dog. But when he came out of the house himself, I couldn't pull the trigger. I yelled at him and ran away."

"What did you yell?" I said.

"The same thing I told him on the telephone: 'Remember Mount Robson.'"

A yellow cab, which looked out of place in the canyon, came over the ridge above us. Lieutenant Scott waved it to a stop. The driver said he'd just brought Mrs. Hooper home from the airport and wanted to know if that constituted a felony. Scott waved him on.

"I wonder what she was doing at the airport," Carlson said.

"Coming home from Vegas. She tried to call me from there last night. I forgot to tell you."

"You don't forget important things like that," Carlson said.

"I suppose I wanted her to come home under her own power."

"In case she shot her husband?"

"More or less."

"She didn't. Fernando shot him, didn't you, boy?"

"I shot the dog. I am innocent of the man." He turned to me: "Tell her that. Tell her I am sorry about the dog. I came out here to surrender the gun and tell her yesterday. I don't trust myself with guns."

"With darn good reason," Carlson said. "We know you shot Mr. Hooper. Ballistic evidence doesn't lie."

Rambeau screeched in his ear, "You're a liar! You're all liars!"

Carlson swung his open hand against the side of Rambeau's face. "Don't call me names, little man."

Lieutenant Scott spoke without taking his eyes from the road. "I wouldn't hit him, Chief. You wouldn't want to damage our case."

Carlson subsided, and we drove on up to the house. Carlson went in without knocking. The guard at the door discouraged me from following him.

I could hear Fay's voice on the other side of the door, too low to be understood. Carlson said something to her.

"Get out! Get out of my house, you killer!" Fay cried out sharply. Carlson didn't come out. I went in instead. One of his arms was wrapped around her body; the other hand was covering her mouth. I got his Adam's apple in the crook of my left arm, pulled him away from her, and threw him over my left hip. He went down clanking and got up holding his revolver.

He should have shot me right away. But he gave Fay Hooper time to save my life.

She stepped in front of me. "Shoot me, Mr. Carlson. You might as well. You shot the one man I ever cared for."

"Your husband shot George Rambeau, if that's who you mean. I ought to know. I was there." Carlson scowled down at his gun, and replaced it in his holster.

Lieutenant Scott was watching him from the doorway.

"You were there?" I said to Carlson. "Yesterday you told me Hooper was alone when he shot Rambeau."

"He was. When I said I was there, I meant in the general neighborhood."

"Don't believe him," Fay said. "He fired the gun that killed George, and it was no accident. The two of them hunted George down in the woods. My husband planned to shoot him himself, but George's dog

came at him and he had to dispose of it. By that time, George had
drawn a bead on Allan. Mr. Carlson shot him. It was hardly a coincidence that the next spring Allan financed his campaign for sheriff.''

''She's making it up,'' Carlson said. ''She wasn't within ten miles of
the place.''

''But you were, Mr. Carlson, and so was Allan. He told me the whole
story yesterday, after we found Otto. Once that happened, he knew that
everything was bound to come out. I already suspected him, of course,
after I talked to Fernando. Allan filled in the details himself. He
thought, since he hadn't killed George personally, I would be able to
forgive him. But I couldn't. I left him and flew to Nevada, intending
to divorce him. I've been intending to for twenty years.''

Carlson said: ''Are you sure you didn't shoot him before you left?''

''How could she have?'' I said. ''Ballistics don't lie, and the ballistic
evidence says he was shot with Fernando's rifle. Nobody had access
to it but Fernando and you. You stopped him on the road and knocked
him out, took his rifle and used it to kill Hooper. You killed him for
the same reason that Hooper buried the dog—to keep the past buried.
You thought Hooper was the only witness to the murder of George
Rambeau. But by that time, Mrs. Hooper knew about it, too.''

''It wasn't murder. It was self-defense, just like in the war. Anyway,
you'll never hang it on me.''

''We don't have to. We'll hang Hooper on you. How about it,
Lieutenant?''

Scott nodded grimly, not looking at his chief. I relieved Carlson of
his gun. He winced, as if I were amputating part of his body. He offered
no resistance when Scott took him out to the car.

I stayed behind for a final word with Fay. ''Fernando asked me to
tell you he's sorry for shooting your dog.''

''We're both sorry.'' She stood with her eyes down, as if the past was
swirling visibly around her feet. ''I'll talk to Fernando later. Much
later.''

''There's one coincidence that bothers me. How did you happen to
take your dog to his school?''

''I happened to see his sign, and Fernando Rambeau isn't a common
name. I couldn't resist going there. I had to know what had happened
to George. I think perhaps Fernando came to California for the same
reason.''

''Now you both know,'' I said.

At the Old Swimming Hole

Sara Paretsky

Sara Paretsky (b. 1947) was raised in Kansas. She moved to Illinois to attend The University of Chicago. While working in an insurance company, Paretsky took a leave of absence to write her first novel, *Indemnity Only* (1982). Her other novels, all featuring detective V.I. Warshawski, include *Deadlock* (1984), *Killing Orders* (1985), *Bitter Medicine* (1987), *Blood Shot* (1988), and *Burn Marks* (1990). She has also contributed stories to *Raymond Chandler's Philip Marlowe* (1988) and to two *Women in Crime* anthologies. In 1990, Paretsky edited the Mystery Writers of America Anthology for that year. She presently lives in Chicago with her husband.
V.I. Warshawski, Paretsky's popular gumshoe, is more often than not called in to protect her friends and family. "At the Old Swimming Hole" is a prime example of this, as the detective comes to the aid of a high school friend involved in espionage, gambling, and murder.

THE GYM WAS DANK—chlorine and sweat combined in a hot, sticky mass. Shouts from the trainers, from the swimmers, from the spectators, bounced from the high metal ceilings and back and forth from the benches lining the pool on two sides. The cacophony set up an unpleasant buzzing in my head.

I was not enjoying myself. My shirt was soaked through with sweat. Anyway, I was too old to sit cheering on a bleacher for two hours. But Alicia had been insistent—I had to be there in person for her to get points on her sponsor card.

Alicia Alonso Dauphine and I went to high school together. Her parents had bestowed a prima ballerina's name on her, but Alicia showed no aptitude for fine arts. From her earliest years, all she wanted was to muck around with engines. At eighteen, off she went to the University of Illinois to study aeronautics.

Despite her lack of interest in dance, Alicia was very athletic. Next to airplanes, the only thing she really cared about was competitive

300

swimming. I used to cheer her when she was NCAA swimming champ, always with a bit of irritation about being locked in a dank, noisy gym for hours at a time—swimming is not a great spectator sport. But after all, what are friends for?

When Alicia joined Berman Aircraft as an associate engineer, we drifted our separate ways. We met occasionally at weddings, confirmations, bar mitzvahs (my, how our friends were aging! Childlessness seemed to suspend us in time, but each new ceremony in their lives marked a new milestone toward old age for the women we had played with in high school).

Then last week I'd gotten a call from Alicia. Berman was mounting a team for a citywide corporate competition—money would be raised through sponsors for the American Cancer Society. Both Alicia's mother and mine had died of cancer—would I sponsor her for so many meters? Doubling my contribution if she won? It was only after I'd made the pledge that I realized she expected me there in person. One of her sponsors had to show up to testify that she'd done it, and all the others were busy with their homes and children, and come on, V.I., what do you do all day long? I need you.

How can you know you're being manipulated and still let it happen? I hunched an impatient shoulder and turned back to the starting blocks.

From where I sat, Alicia was just another bathing-suited body with a cap. Her distinctive cheekbones were softened and flattened by the dim fluorescence. Not a wisp of her thick black hair trailed around her face. She was wearing a bright red tank suit—no extra straps or flounces to slow her down in the water.

The swimmers had been wandering around the side of the pool, swinging their arms to stretch out the muscles, not talking much while the timers argued some inaudible point with the referee. Now a police whistle shrilled faintly in the din and the competitors snapped to attention, moving toward the starting blocks at the far end of the pool.

We were about to watch the fifty-meter freestyle. I looked at the hand-scribbled card Alicia had given me before the meet. After the fifty-meter, she was in a 4x50 relay. Then I could leave.

The swimmers were mounting the blocks when someone began complaining again. The woman from the Ajax insurance team seemed to be having a problem with the lane marker on the inside of her lane. The referee reshuffled the swimmers, leaving the offending lane empty. The swimmers finally mounted the blocks again. Timers got into position.

Standing to see the start of the race, I was no longer certain which of the women was Alicia. Two of the other six contenders also wore red tank suits; with their features smoothed by caps and dimmed lighting, they all became anonymous. One red suit was in lane two, one in lane three, one in lane six.

The referee raised the starting gun. Swimmers got set. Arms swung back for the dive. Then the gun, and seven bodies flung themselves into the water. Perfect dive in lane six—had to be Alicia, surfacing, pulling away from all but one other swimmer, a fast little woman from the brokerage house of Feldstein, Holtz and Woods.

Problems for the red-suited woman in lane two. I hadn't seen her dive, but she was having trouble righting herself, couldn't seem to make headway in the lane. Now everyone was noticing her. Whistles were blowing; the man on the loudspeaker tried ineffectually to call for silence.

I pushed my way through the crowds on the benches and vaulted over the barrier dividing the spectators from the water. Useless over the din to order someone into the pool for her. Useless to point out the growing circle of red. I kicked off running shoes and dove from the side. Swimming underwater to the second lane. Not Alicia. Surely not. Seeing the water turn red around me. Find the woman. Surface. Drag her to the edge where, finally, a few galvanized hands pulled her out.

I scrambled from the pool and picked out someone in a striped referee's shirt. "Get a fire department ambulance as fast as you can." He stared at me with a stupid gape to his jaw. "Dial 911, damn it. Do it now!" I pushed him toward the door, hard, and he suddenly broke into a trot.

I knelt beside the woman. She was breathing, but shallowly. I felt her gently. Hard to find the source of bleeding with the wet suit, but I thought it came from the upper back. Demanding help from one of the bystanders, I carefully turned her to her side. Blood was oozing now, not pouring, from a wound below her left shoulder. Pack it with towels, elevate her feet, keep the crowd back. Wait. Wait. Watch the shallow breathing turn to choking. Mouth-to-mouth does no good. Who knows cardiopulmonary resuscitation? A muscular young man in skimpy bikini shorts comes forward and works at her chest. By the time the paramedics hustle in with stretcher and equipment, the shallow, choking breath has stopped. They take her to the hospital, but we all know it's no good.

As the stretcher-bearers trotted away, the rest of the room came back into focus. Alicia was standing at my side, black hair hanging damply to her shoulders, watching me with fierce concentration. Everyone else seemed to be shrieking in unison; the sound re-echoing from the rafters was more unbearable than ever.

I stood up, put my mouth close to Alicia's ear, and asked her to take me to whoever was in charge. She pointed to a man in an Izod T-shirt standing on the other side of the hole left by the dead swimmer's body.

I went to him immediately. "I'm V.I. Warshawski. I'm a private detective. That woman was murdered—shot through the back. Whoever shot her probably left during the confusion. But you'd better get the cops here now. And tell everyone over your megaphone that no one leaves until the police have seen them."

He looked contemptuously at my dripping jeans and shirt. "Do you have anything to back up this preposterous statement?"

I held out my hands. "Blood," I said briefly, then grabbed the microphone from him. "May I have your attention, please." My voice bounced around the hollow room. "My name is V.I. Warshawski; I am a detective. There has been a serious accident in the pool. Until the police have been here and talked to us, none of us must leave this area. I am asking the six timers who were at the far end of the pool to come here now."

There was silence for a minute, then renewed clamor. A handful of people picked their way along the edge of the pool toward me. The man in the Izod shirt was fulminating but lacked the guts to try to grab the mike.

When the timers came up to me, I said, "You six are the only ones who definitely could not have killed the woman. I want you to stand at the exits." I tapped each in turn and sent them to a post—two to the doors on the second floor at the top of the bleachers, two to the ground-floor exits, and one each to the doors leading to the men's and women's dressing rooms.

"Don't let anyone, regardless of *anything* he or she says, leave. If they have to use the bathroom, tough—hold it until the cops get here. Anyone tries to leave, keep them here. If they want to fight, let them go but get as complete a description as you can."

They trotted off to their stations. I gave Izod back his mike, made my way to a pay phone in the corner, and dialed the Eleventh Street homicide number.

II

Sergeant McGonnigal was not fighting sarcasm as hard as he might have. "You sent the guy to guard the upstairs exit and he waltzed away, probably taking the gun with him. He must be on his knees in some church right now thanking God for sending a pushy private investigator to this race."

I bit my lips. He couldn't be angrier with me than I was with myself. I sneezed and shivered in my damp, clammy clothes. "You're right, Sergeant. I wish you'd been at the meet instead of me. You'd probably have had ten uniformed officers with you who could've taken charge as soon as the starting gun was fired and avoided this mess. Do any of the timers know who the man was?"

We were in an office that the school athletic department had given the police for their investigation-scene headquarters. McGonnigal had been questioning all the timers, figuring their closeness to the pool gave them the best angle on what had happened. One was missing, the man I'd sent to the upper balcony exit.

The sergeant grudgingly told me he'd been over that ground with the other timers. None of them knew who the missing man was. Each of the companies in the meet had supplied volunteers to do the timing and other odd jobs. Everyone just assumed this man was from someone else's firm. No one had noticed him that closely; their attention was focused on the action in the pool. My brief glance at him gave the police their best description: medium height, light, short brown hair, wearing a pale green T-shirt and faded white denim shorts. Yes, baggy enough for a gun to fit in a pocket unnoticed.

"You know, Sergeant, I asked for the six timers at the far end of the pool because they were facing the swimmers, so none of them could have shot the dead woman in the back. This guy came forward. That means there's a timer missing—either the person actually down at the far end was in collusion, or you're missing a body."

McGonnigal made an angry gesture—not at me. Himself for not having thought of it before. He detailed two uniformed cops to round up all the volunteers and find out who the errant timer was.

"Any more information on the dead woman?"

McGonnigal picked up a pad from the paper-littered desk in front of him. "Her name was Louise Carmody. You know that. She was twenty-four. She worked for the Ft. Dearborn Bank and Trust as a junior lending officer. You know that. Her boss is very shocked—you probably could guess that. And she has no enemies. No dead person ever does."

"Was she working on anything sensitive?"

He gave me a withering glance. "What twenty-four-year-old junior loan officer works on anything sensitive?"

"Lots," I said firmly. "No senior person ever does the grubby work. A junior officer crunches numbers or gathers basic data for crunching. Was she working on any project that someone might not want her to get data for?"

McGonnigal shrugged wearily but made a note on a second pad—the closest he would come to recognizing that I might have a good suggestion.

I sneezed again. "Do you need me for anything else? I'd like to get home and dry off."

"No, go. I'd just as soon you weren't around when Lieutenant Mallory arrives, anyway."

Bobby Mallory was McGonnigal's boss. He was also an old friend of my father, who had been a beat sergeant until his death fifteen years earlier. Bobby did not like women on the crime scene in any capacity—victim, perpetrator, or investigator—and he especially did not like his old friend Tony's daughter on the scene. I appreciated McGonnigal's unwillingness to witness any acrimony between his boss and me, and was getting up to leave when the uniformed cops came back.

The sixth timer had been found in a supply closet behind the men's lockers. He was concussed and groggy from a head wound and couldn't remember how he got to where he was. Couldn't remember anything past lunchtime. I waited long enough to hear that and slid from the room.

Alicia was waiting for me at the far end of the hall. She had changed from her suit into jeans and a pullover and was squatting on her heels, staring fiercely at nothing. When she saw me coming, she stood up and pushed her black hair out of her eyes.

"You look a mess, V.I."

"Thanks. I'm glad to get help and support from my friends after they've dragged me into a murder investigation."

"Oh, don't get angry—I didn't mean it that way. I'm sorry I dragged you into a murder investigation. No, I'm not, actually. I'm glad you were on hand. Can we talk?"

"After I put some dry clothes on and stop looking a mess."

She offered me her jacket. Since I'm five-eight to her five-four, it wasn't much of a cover, but I draped it gratefully over my shoulders to protect myself from the chilly October evening.

At my apartment Alicia followed me into the bathroom while I turned on the hot water. "Do you know who the dead woman was? The police wouldn't tell us."

"Yes," I responded irritably. "And if you'll give me twenty minutes to warm up, I'll tell you. Bathing is not a group sport in this apartment."

She trailed back out of the bathroom, her face set in tense lines. When I joined her in the living room some twenty minutes later, a towel around my damp hair, she was sitting in front of the television set changing channels.

"No news yet," she said briefly. "Who was the dead girl?"

"Louise Carmody. Junior loan officer at the Ft. Dearborn. You know her?"

Alicia shook her head. "Do the police know why she was shot?"

"They're just starting to investigate. What do you know about it?"

"Nothing. Are they going to put her name on the news?"

"Probably, if the family's been notified. Why is this important?"

"No reason. It just seems so ghoulish, reporters hovering around her dead body and everything."

"Could I have the truth, please?"

She sprang to her feet and glared at me. "It is the truth."

"Screw that. You don't know her name, you spin the TV dials to see the reports, and now you think it's ghoulish for the reporters to hover around?...Tell you what I think, Alicia. I think you know who did the shooting. They shuffled the swimmers, nobody knew who was in which lane. You started out in lane two, and you'd be dead if the woman from Ajax hadn't complained. Who wants to kill you?"

Her black eyes glittered in her white face. "No one. Why don't you have a little empathy, Vic? I might have been killed. There was a madman out there who shot a woman. Why don't you give me some sympathy?"

"I jumped into a pool to pull that woman out. I sat around in wet clothes for two hours talking to the cops. I'm beat. You want sympathy, go someplace else. The little I have is reserved for myself tonight.

"I'd really like to know why I had to be at the pool, if it wasn't to ward off a potential attacker. And if you'd told me the real reason, Louise Carmody might still be alive."

"Damn you, Vic, stop doubting every word I say. I told you why I needed you there—someone had to sign the card. Millie works during the day. So does Fredda. Katie has a new baby. Elene is becoming a grandmother for the first time. Get off my goddamn back."

"If you're not going to tell me the truth, and if you're going to scream at me about it, I'd just as soon you left."

She stood silent for a minute. "Sorry, Vic. I'll get a better grip on myself."

"Great. You do that. I'm fixing some supper—want any?"

She shook her head. When I returned with a plate of pasta and olives, Joan Druggen was just announcing the top local story. Alicia sat with her hands clenched as they stated the dead woman's name. After that, she didn't say much. Just asked if she could crash for the night—she lived in Warrenville, a good hour's drive from town, near Berman's aeronautic engineering labs.

I gave her pillows and a blanket for the couch and went to bed. I was pretty angry: I figured she wanted to sleep over because she was scared, and it infuriated me that she would'nt talk about it.

When the phone woke me at 2:30, my throat was raw, the start of a cold brought on by sitting around in wet clothes for so long. A heavy voice asked for Alicia.

"I don't know who you're talking about," I said hoarsely.

"Be your age, Warshawski. She brought you to the gym. She isn't at her own place. She's gotta be with you. You don't want to wake her up, give her a message. She was lucky tonight. We want the money by noon, or she won't be so lucky a second time."

He hung up. I held the receiver a second longer and heard another click. The living room extension. I pulled on a dressing gown and padded down the hallway. The apartment door shut just as I got to the living room. I ran to the top of the stairs; Alicia's footsteps were echoing up and down the stairwell.

"Alicia! Alicia—you can't go out there alone. Come back here!"

The slamming of the entryway door was my only answer.

III

I didn't sleep well, my cold mixing with worry and anger over Alicia. At eight I hoisted my aching body out of bed and sat sneezing over some steaming fruit juice while I tried to focus my brain on possible action. Alicia owed somebody money. That somebody was pissed off enough to kill because he didn't have it. Bankers do not kill wayward loan customers. Loan sharks do, but what could Alicia have done to rack up so much indebtedness? Berman probably paid her seventy or eighty thousand a year for the special kinds of designs she did on aircraft wings. And she was the kind of client a bank usually values. So what did she need money for that only a shark would provide?

The clock was ticking. I called her office. She'd phoned in sick; the secretary didn't know where she was calling from but had assumed home. On a dim chance I tried her phone. No answer. Alicia had one brother, Tom, an insurance agent on the far south side. After a few tries I located his office in Flossmoor. He hadn't heard from Alicia for weeks. And no, he didn't know who she might owe money to.

Reluctantly Tom gave me their father's phone number in Florida. Mr. Dauphine hadn't heard from his daughter, either.

"If she calls you, or if she shows up, *please* let me know. She's in trouble up here, and the only way I can help her is by knowing where she is." I gave him the number without much expectation of hearing from him again.

I did know someone who might be able to give me a line on her debts. A year or so earlier, I'd done a major favor for Don Pasquale, a local mob leader. If she owed him money, he might listen to my intercession. If not, he might be able to tell me whom she had borrowed from.

Torfino's, an Elmwood Park restaurant where the don had a part-time office, put me through to his chief assistant, Ernesto. A well-remembered gravel voice told me I sounded awful.

"Thank you, Ernesto," I snuffled. "Did you hear about the death of Louise Carmody at the University of Illinois gym last night? She was probably shot by mistake, poor thing. The intended victim was a woman named Alicia Dauphine. We grew up together, so I feel a little solicitous on her behalf. She owes a lot of money to someone: I wondered if you know who."

"Name isn't familiar, Warshawski. I'll check around and call you back."

My cold made me feel as though I was at the bottom of a fish tank. I couldn't think fast enough or hard enough to imagine where Alicia might have gone to ground. Perhaps at her house, believing if she didn't answer the phone no one would think she was home? It wasn't a very clever idea, but it was the best I could do in my muffled, snuffled state.

The old farmhouse in Warrenville that Alicia had modernized lay behind the local high school. The boys were out practicing football. They were wearing light jerseys. I had on my winter coat—even though the day was warm, my cold made me shiver and want to be bundled up. Although we were close enough that I could see their mouthpieces, they didn't notice me as I walked around the house looking for signs of life.

Alicia's car was in the garage, but the house looked cold and unoccupied. As I made my way to the back, a black-and-white cat darted out from the bushes and began weaving itself around my ankles, mewing piteously. Alicia had three cats. This one wanted something to eat.

Alicia had installed a sophisticated burglar alarm system—she had an office in her home and often worked on preliminary designs there. An expert had gotten through the system into the pantry—some kind of epoxy had been sprayed on the wires to freeze them. Then, somehow disabling the phone link, the intruder had cut through the wires.

My stomach muscles tightened, and I wished futilely for the Smith & Wesson locked in my safe at home. My cold really had addled my brains for me not to take it on such an errand. Still, where burglars lead shall P.I.s hesitate? I opened the window, slid a leg over, and landed on the pantry floor. My feline friend followed more gracefully. She promptly abandoned me to start sniffing at the pantry walls.

Cautiously opening the door I slid into the kitchen. It was deserted, the refrigerator and clock motors humming gently, a dry dishcloth draped over the sink. In the living room another cat joined me and followed me into the electronic wonderland of Alicia's study. She had used built-in bookcases to house her computers and other gadgets. The printers were tucked along a side wall, and wires ran everywhere. Whoever had broken in was not interested in merchandise—the street value of her study contents would have brought in a nice return, but they stood unharmed.

By now I was dreading the trek upstairs. The second cat, a tabby, trotted briskly ahead of me, tail waving like a flag. Alicia's bedroom door was shut. I kicked it open with my right leg and pressed myself against the wall. Nothing. Dropping to my knees I looked in. The bed, tidily covered with an old-fashioned white spread, was empty. So was the bathroom. So was the guest room and an old sun porch glassed in and converted to a solarium.

The person who broke in had not come to steal—everything was preternaturally tidy. So he (she?) had come to attack Alicia. The hair stood up on the nape of my neck. Where was he? Not in the house. Hiding outside?

I started down the stairs again when I heard a noise, a heavy scraping. I froze, trying to locate the source. A movement caught my eye at the line of vision. The hatch to the crawl space had been shoved open; an arm swung down. For a split second only I stared at the arm and the gun in its grip, then leaped down the stairs two at a time.

A heavy thud—the man jumping onto the upper landing. The crack as the gun fired. A jolt in my left shoulder, and I gasped with shock and fell the last few steps to the bottom. Righted myself. Reached for the deadlock on the front door. Heard an outraged squawk, loud swearing, and a crash that sounded like a man falling downstairs. Then I had the door open and was staggering outside while an angry bundle of fur poured past me. One of the cats, a heroine, tripping my assailant and saving my life.

IV

I never really lost consciousness. The football players saw me stagger down the sidewalk and came trooping over. In their concern for me they failed to tackle the gunman, but they got me to a hospital, where a young intern eagerly set about removing the slug from my shoulder; the winter coat had protected me from major damage. Between my cold and the gunshot, I was just as happy to let him incarcerate me for a few days.

They tucked me into bed, and I fell into a heavy, uneasy sleep. I had jumped into the black waters of Lake Michigan in search of Alicia, trying to reach her ahead of a shark. She was lurking just out of reach. She didn't know that her oxygen tank ran out at noon.

When I woke finally, soaked with sweat, it was dark outside. The room was lit faintly by a fluorescent light over the sink. A lean man in a brown wool business suit was sitting next to the bed. When he saw me looking at him, he reached into his coat.

If he was going to shoot me, there wasn't a thing I could do about it—I was too limp from my heavy sleep to move. Instead of a gun. though, he pulled out an ID case.

"Miss Warshawski? Peter Carlton, Federal Bureau of Investigation. I know you're not feeling well, but I need to talk to you about Alice Dauphine."

"So the shark ate her," I said.

"What?" he demanded sharply. "What does that mean?'

"Nothing. Where is she?"

"We don't know. That's what we want to talk to you about. She went home with you after the swimming meet yesterday. Correct?"

"Gosh, Mr. Carlton. I love watching my tax dollars at work. If you've been following her, you must have a better fix on her whereabouts than I do. I last saw her around 2:30 this morning. If it's still today, that is."

"What did she talk to you about?"

My mind was starting to unfog. "Why is the Bureau interested in Miss Dauphine?"

He didn't want to tell me. All he wanted was every word Alicia had said to me. When I wouldn't budge, he started in on why I was in her house and what I had noticed there.

Finally I said, "Mr. Carlton, if you can't tell me why you're interested in Miss Dauphine, there's no way I can respond to your questions. I don't believe the Bureau—or the police—or anyone, come to that—has any right to pry into the affairs of citizens in the hopes of turning up some scandal. You tell me why you're interested, and I ll tell you if I know anything relevant to that interest."

With an ill grace he said, "We believe she has been selling Defense Department secrets to the Russians."

"No," I said flatly. "She wouldn't."

"Some wing designs she was working on have disappeared. She's disappeared. And a Soviet functionary in St. Charles has disappeared."

"Sounds pretty circumstantial to me. The wing designs might be in her home. They could easily be on a disk someplace—she did all her drafting on computer."

They'd been through her computer files at home and at work and found nothing. Her boss did not have copies of the latest design, only of the early stuff. I thought about the heavy voice on the phone demanding money, but loyalty to Alicia made me keep it to myself—give her a chance to tell her story first.

I did give him everything Alicia had said, her nervousness and her sudden departure. That I was worried about her and went to see if she was in her house. And was shot by an intruder hiding in the crawl space. Who might have taken her designs. Although nothing looked pilfered.

He didn't believe me. I don't know if he thought I knew something I wasn't telling, or if he thought I had joined Alicia in selling secrets to the Russians. But he kept at me for so long that I finally pushed my call button. When the nurse arrived, I explained that I was worn out and could she please show my visitor out? He left but promised me that he would return.

Cursing my weakness, I fell asleep again. When I next woke it was morning, and both my cold and my shoulder were much improved. When the doctors came by on their morning visit, I got their agreement to a discharge. Before I bathed and left, the Warrenville police sent out a man who took a detailed statement.

I called my answering service from a phone in the lobby. Ernesto had been in touch. I reached him at Torfino's.

"Saw about your accident in the papers, Warshawski. How you feeling?...About Dauphine. Apparently she's signed a note for $750,000 to Art Smollensk. Can't do anything to help you out. The don sends his best wishes for your recovery."

Art Smollensk, gambling king. When I worked for the public defender, I'd had to defend some of his small-time employees—people at the level of smashing someone's fingers in his car door. The ones who did hits and arson usually could afford their own attorneys.

Alicia as a gambler made no sense to me—but we hadn't been close for over a decade. There were lots of things I didn't know about her.

At home for a change of clothes I stopped in the basement, where I store useless mementos in a locked stall. After fifteen minutes of shifting boxes around, I was sweating and my left shoulder was throbbing and oozing stickily, but I'd located my high school yearbook. I took it upstairs with me and thumbed through it, trying to gain inspiration on where Alicia might have gone to earth.

None came. I was about to leave again when the phone rang. It was Alicia, talking against a background of noise. "Thank God you're safe, Vic. I saw about the shooting in the paper. Please don't worry about me. I'm okay. Stay away and don't worry."

She hung up before I could ask her anything. I concentrated, not on what she'd said, but what had been in the background. Metal doors banging open and shut. Lots of loud, wild talking. Not an airport—the talking was too loud for that, and there weren't any intercom announcements in the background. I knew what it was. If I'd just let my mind relax, it would come to me.

Idly flipping through the yearbook, I looked for faces Alicia might trust. I found my own staring from a group photo of the girls' basketball team. I'd been a guard—Victoria the protectress from way back. On the next page, Alicia smiled fiercely, holding a swimming trophy. Her coach, who also taught Latin, had desperately wanted Alicia to train for the Olympics, but Alicia had had her heart set on the U of I and engineering.

Suddenly I knew what the clanking was, where Alicia was. No other sound like that exists anywhere on earth.

V

Alicia and I grew up under the shadow of the steel mills in South Chicago. Nowhere else has the deterioration of American industry shown up more clearly. Wisconsin Steel is padlocked shut. The South Works are a fragment of their former monstrous grandeur. Unemployment is over thirty percent, and the number of jobless youths lounging in the bars and on the streets had grown from the days when I hurried past them to the safety of my mother's house.

The high school was more derelict than I remembered. Many windows were boarded over. The asphalt playground was cracked and covered with litter, and the bleachers around the football field were badly weathered.

The guard at the doorway demanded my business. I showed her my P.I. license and said I needed to talk to the women's gym teacher on confidential business. After some dickering—hostile on her side, snuffly on mine—she gave me a pass. I didn't need directions down the scuffed corridors, past the battered lockers, past the smell of rancid oil coming from the cafeteria, to the noise and life of the gym.

Teenage girls in blue shirts and white shorts—the school colors— were shrieking, jumping, wailing in pursuit of volleyballs. I watched the pandemonium until the buzzer ended the period, then walked up to the instructor.

She was panting and sweating and gave me an incurious glance, looking only briefly at the pass I held out for her. "Yes?"

"You have a new swimming coach, don't you?"

"Just a volunteer. Are you from the union? She isn't drawing a paycheck. But Miss Finley, the coach, is desperately shorthanded— she teaches Latin, you know—and this woman is a big help."

"I'm not from the union. I'm her trainer. I need to talk to her—find out why she's dropped out and whether she plans to compete in any of her meets this fall."

The teacher gave me the hard look of someone used to sizing up fabricated excuses. I didn't think she believed me, but she told me I could go into the pool area and talk to the swim coach.

The pool dated to the time when this high school served an affluent neighborhood. It was twenty-five yards long, built with skylights along the outer wall. You reached it through the changing rooms, separate ones with showers for girls and boys. It didn't have an outside hallway entrance.

Alicia was perched alone on the high dive. A few students, boys and girls, were splashing about in the pool, but no organized training was in progress. Alicia was staring at nothing.

I cupped my hands and called up to her, "Do you want me to climb up, or are you going to come down?"

She shot off the board in a perfect arc, barely rippling the surface of the water. The kids watched with envy. I was pretty jealous, myself— nothing I do is done with that much grace.

She surfaced near me but looked at the students. "I want you guys swimming laps," she said sharply. "What do you think this is—summer camp?"

They left us reluctantly and began swimming.

"How did you find me?"

"It was easy. I was looking through the yearbook, trying to think of someone you would trust. Miss Finley was the simple answer—I remembered how you practically lived in her house for two years. You liked to read *Jane Eyre* together, and she adored you.

"You are in deep trouble. Smollensk is after you, and so is the FBI. You can't hide here forever. You'd better talk to the Bureau guys. They won't love you, but at least they're not going to shoot you."

"The FBI? Whatever for?"

"Your designs, sweetie pie. Your designs and the Russians. The FBI are the people who look into that kind of thing."

"Vic. I don't know what you're talking about." The words were said with such slow deliberateness that I was almost persuaded.

"The $750,000 you owe Art Smollensk."

She shook her head, then said, "Oh. Yes. That."

"Yes, that. I guess it seems like more money to me than it does to you. Or had you forgotten Louise Carmody getting shot?...Anyway, a known Russian spy left Fermilab yesterday or the day before, and you're gone, and some of your wing designs are gone, and the FBI thinks you've sold them overseas and maybe gone East yourself. I didn't tell them about Art, but they'll probably get there before too long."

"How sure are they that the designs are gone?"

"Your boss can't find them. Maybe you have a duplicate set at home nobody knows about."

She shook her head again. "I don't leave that kind of thing at home. I had them last Saturday, working, but I took the diskettes back..." Her voice trailed off as a look of horror washed across her face. "Oh, no. This is worse than I thought." She hoisted herself out of the pool. "I've got to go. Got to get away before someone else figures out I'm here."

"Alicia, for Christ's sake. What has happened?"

She stopped and looked at me, tears swimming in her black eyes. "If I could tell anyone, it would be you, Vic." Then she was jogging into the girls' changing room, leaving the students in the pool swimming laps.

I stuck with her. "Where are you going? The Feds have a hook on any place you have friends or relations. Smollensk does, too."

That stopped her. "Tom, too?"

"Tom first, last, and foremost. He's the only relative you have in Chicago." She was starting to shiver in the bare corridor. I grabbed her and shook her. "Tell me the truth, Alicia. I can't fly blind. I already took a bullet in the shoulder."

Suddenly she was sobbing on my chest. "Oh, Vic. It's been so awful. You can't know...you can't understand...you won't believe..." She was hiccuping.

I led her into the shower room and found a towel. Rubbing her down, I got the story in choking bits and pieces.

Tom was the gambler. He'd gotten into it in a small way in high school and college. After he went into business for himself, the habit grew. He'd mortgaged his insurance agency assets, taken out a second mortgage on the house, but couldn't stop.

"He came to me two weeks ago. Told me he was going to start filing claims with his companies, collect the money." She gave a twisted smile. "He didn't have to put that kind of pressure on—I can't help helping him."

"But, Alicia, why? And how does Art Smollensk have your name?"

"Is that the man Tom owes money to? I think he uses my name—Alonso, my middle name—I know he does; I just don't like to think about it. Someone came around threatening me three years ago. I told Tom never to use my name again, and he didn't for a long time, but now I guess he was desperate—$750,000, you know....

"As to why I help him...You never had any brothers or sisters, so maybe you can't understand. When Mom died, I was thirteen, he was six. I looked after him. Got him out of trouble. All kinds of stuff. It gets to be a habit, I guess. Or an obligation. That's why I've never married, you know, never had any children of my own. I don't want any more responsibilities like this one."

"And the designs?"

She looked horrified again. "He came over for dinner on Saturday. I'd been working all day on the things, and he came into the study when I was logging off. I didn't tell him it was Defense Department work, but it's not too hard to figure out what I do is defense-related—after all, that's all Berman does; we don't make commercial aircraft. I haven't had a chance to look at the designs since—I worked out all day Sunday getting ready for that damned meet Monday. Tom must have taken my diskettes and swapped the labels with some others—I've got tons of them lying around."

She gave a twisted smile. "It was a gamble: a gamble that there'd be something valuable on them and a gamble I wouldn't discover the switch before he got rid of them. But he's a gambler."

"I see....Look, Alicia. You can only be responsible for Tom so far. Even if you could bail him out this time—and I don't see how you possibly can—there'll be a next time. And you may not survive this one to help him again. Let's call the FBI."

She squeezed her eyes shut. "You don't understand, Vic. You can't possibly understand."

While I was trying to reason her into phoning the Bureau, Miss Finley, swim coach-cum-romantic-Latin-teacher, came briskly into the locker room. "Allie! One of the girls came to get me. Are you all—" She did a double-take. "Victoria! Good to see you. Have you come to help Allie? I told her she could count on you."

"Have you told her what's going on?" I demanded of Alicia.

Yes, Miss Finley knew most of the story. Agreed that it was very worrying but said Allie could not possibly turn in her own brother. She had given Allie a gym mat and some bedding to sleep on—she could just stay at the gym until the furor died down and they could think of something else to do.

I sat helplessly as Miss Finley led Alicia off to get some dry clothes. At last, when they didn't rejoin me, I sought them out, poking through half-remembered halls and doors until I found the staff coaching office. Alicia was alone, looking about fifteen in an old cheerleader's uniform Miss Finley had dug up for her.

"Miss Finley teaching?" I asked sharply.

Alicia looked guilty but defiant. "Yes. Two-thirty class. Look. The critical thing is to get those diskettes back. I called Tom, explained it to him. Told him I'd try to help him raise the money but that we couldn't let the Russians have those things. He agreed, so he's bringing them out here."

The room rocked slightly around us. "No. I know you don't have much of a sense of humor, but this is a joke, isn't it?"

She didn't understand. Wouldn't understand that if the Russian had already left the country, Tom no longer had the material. That if Tom was coming here, she was the scapegoat. At last, despairing, I said, "Where is he meeting you? Here?"

"I told him I'd be at the pool."

"Will you do one thing my way? Will you go to Miss Finley's class and conjugate verbs for forty-five minutes and let me meet him at the pool? Please?"

At last, her jaw set stubbornly, she agreed. She still wouldn't let me call the Bureau, though. "Not until I've talked to Tom myself. It may all be a mistake, you know."

We both knew it wasn't, but I saw her into the Latin class without making the phone call I knew it was my duty to make and returned to the pool. Driving out the two students still splashing around in the water, I put signs on the locker room doors saying the water was contaminated and there would be no swimming until further notice.

I turned out the lights and settled in a corner of the room remote from the outside windows to wait. And go over and over in my mind the story. I believed it. Was I fooling myself? Was that why she wouldn't call the Feds?

At last Tom came in through the men's locker room entrance. "Allie? Allie?" His voice bounced off the high rafters and echoed around me. I was well back in the back shadows, my Smith & Wesson in hand; he didn't see me.

After half a minute or so another man joined him. I didn't recognize the stranger, but his baggy clothes marked him as part of Smollensk's group, not the Bureau. He talked softly to Tom for a minute. Then they went into the girl's locker room together.

When they returned, I had moved part way up the side of the pool, ready to follow them if they went back into the main part of the high school looking for Alicia.

"Tom!" I called. "It's V.I. Warshawski. I know the whole story. Give me the diskettes."

"Warshawski!" he yelled. "What the hell are you doing here?"

I sensed rather than saw the movement his friend made. I shot at him and dived into the water. His bullet zipped as it hit the tiles where I'd been standing. My wet clothes and my sore shoulder made it hard to move. Another bullet hit the water by my head, and I went under again, fumbling with my heavy jacket, getting it free, surfacing, hearing Alicia's sharp, "Tom, why are you shooting at Vic? Stop it now. Stop it and give me back the diskettes."

Another flurry of shots, this time away from me, giving me a chance to get to the side of the pool, to climb out. Alicia lay on the floor near the door to the girls' locker room. Tom stood silently by. The gunman was jamming more bullets into his gun.

As fast as I could in my sodden clothes I lumbered to the hitman, grabbing his arm, squeezing, feeling blood start to seep from my shoulder, stepping on his instep, putting all the force of my body into my leg. Tom, though, Tom was taking the gun from him. Tom was going to shoot me.

"Drop that gun, Tom Dauphine." It was Miss Finley. Years of teaching in a tough school gave creditable authority to her; Tom dropped the gun.

VI

Alicia lived long enough to tell the truth to the FBI. It was small comfort to me. Small consolation to see Tom's statement. He hoped he could get Smollensk to kill his sister before she said anything. If that happened, he had a good gamble on her dying a traitor in their eyes—after all, her designs were gone, and her name was in Smollensk's files. Maybe the truth never would have come out. Worth a gamble to a betting man.

The Feds arrived about five minutes after the shooting stopped. They'd been watching Tom, just not closely enough. They were sore that they'd let Alicia get shot. So they dumped some charges on me—obstructing federal authorities, not telling them where Alicia was, not calling as soon as I had the truth from her, God knows what else. I spent several days in jail. It seemed like a suitable penance, just not enough of one.

Case Studies

The Detective:
A Selective Chronology

1747 • Zadig

Voltaire's *Zadig* features a main character who uses rational thought to solve problems; a forerunner to the intellectual detective.

1828 • Vidocq

Eugene Francois Vidocq, founder of the *police de sûreté,* publishes his memoirs. They are read by Poe, Le-Blanc, and Gaboriau, who use Vidocq as an inspiration for their own fictional creations.

1841 • C. August Dupin

"The Murders in the Rue Morgue" by Edgar Allen Poe is published; it's hero, C. Auguste Dupin, is the first official detective hero.

1863 • Inspector Lecoq

The Lerouge Case by Emil Gaboriau introduces Inspector Lecoq, the first police detective hero.

1870 • Inspector Datchkey

Charles Dickens dies after writing the middle chapters of *The Mystery of Edwin Drood,* a novel whose detective hero, Inspector Datchkey, is supposedly another character in disguise. Despite several attempts, the mystery of who killed Edwin Drood—and Datchkey's identity—remain unsolved.

321

1881 • Sherlock Holmes

"A Study in Scarlet," by Arthur Conan Doyle, introduces the most famous detective of all, Sherlock Holmes.

1886 • Nick Carter

A group of writers collaborate on the first Nick Carter dime novel; this style of daredevil/detective will dominate the genre until the 1920's.

1893 • Sexton Blake

A group of British writers collaborate on the first Sexton Blake adventure. Blake becomes the longest-running detective series in the history of the world.

1894 • Martin Hewitt

The Strand Magazine, anxious to keep the readers it gained with the recently completed series of Sherlock Holmes stories, commisions Arthur Morrison to write a series with his character, Martin Hewitt.

1901 • "The Old Man in the Corner"

The Baroness Emmuska Orczy writes a series of stories featuring "The Old Man in the Corner," a hero whose sedentary ways are reminiscent of Nero Wolfe.

1905 • Arsene Lupin
     • Van Dusen, the "Thinking Machine"

Maurice LeBlanc introduces Arsene Lupin in the pages of *Je sais tout* magazine. He is the precursor of such "gentleman thieves" as the Toff and the Lone Wolf. "The Problem of Cell 13" by Jacques Futrelle is serialized in *The American.* Its sleuth, Augustus S.F.X. Van Dusen, the Thinking Machine is considered the first "scientific detective," and appears in forty-five stories before his creator's death aboard the Titanic.

1907 • Fleming Stone
• Dr. Thorndyke

Carolyn Wells publishes the first Fleming Stone story in *Lippincott* magazine—she would later become the genre's first anthologist. Richard August Freeman publishes *The Thumb Mark*, which features the highly erudite Dr. John Thorndyke.

1910 • Father Brown

G.K. Chesterton's Father Brown makes his debut in "The Blue Cross."

1911 • Uncle Abner
• Fantomas

Melville Davisson Post introduces Uncle Abner, a Southwestern judge who is the first "folksie" detective. Fantomas, the first anti-hero in detective literature (and idol of the Surrealists), makes his debut in a French magazine of the same name.

1912 • Craig Kennedy
• Astrogen Kirby

Arthur B. Reeve's collection, *The Silent Bullet,* introduces Craig Kennedy, "The American Sherlock Holmes." Gerett Burgess' *The Master of Mystery* takes the "gentleman thief" one step further by making his hero, Astrogen "Astro the Clairvoyent" Kirby an unrepentant con-man who solves crimes while bilking the public!

1913 • Trent

Trent's Last Case by Edmund Bentley introduces the gentleman detective Trent, who is the first detective to fall in love—and to fail to solve a case.

1915 • J.P. Davenant
• Barny Cook

Lord Fredric Hamilton and Henry J. O'Higgins both create their own version of the "boy detective." Hamilton calls his J.P. Davenant; O'Higgins names his Barny Cook. The magazine *Nick Carter Stories* becomes *Detective Story* with its 160th issue, making it the first detective pulp magazine.

1917	*Mystery Magazine,* the pulp magazine that features many of Agatha Christie's early stories, premieres.
1920 • Hercule Poirot • Reggie Fortune	Agatha Christie's first book, *The Mysterious Affair at Styles* is published, giving the reading public its first glimpse of the Belgian detective Hercule Poirot. H.L. Mencken, needing money, publishes the first issue of *Black Mask,* the magazine that will found the "hard-boiled" school of detective fiction. H.C. Bailey, the biggest proponent of the "clever plot," introduces Reggie Fortune, in *Call Mr. Fortune.*
1922 • Antony Gillingham	A.A. Milne's attempt at a detective novel, *The Red House Mystery*, includes the first humorous detective, Antony Gillingham.
1923 • Lord Peter Wimsey • Race Williams • The Continental Op	*Whose Body?* by Dorothy L. Sayers introduces Lord Peter Wimsey. Carol John Daly's Race Williams, the first hard-boiled series detective, is introduced in *Black Mask.* The unnamed "Continental Op," by former Pinkerton operative Dashiell Hammett, debuts in the October issue of the same magazine.
1924 • Anthony Gethryn	Philip MacDonald's sleuth Anthony Gethryn solves the mystery of *The Rasp* in his first case.
1925 • J.G. Reeder • Charlie Chan	Edgar Wallace, better known for his garish, gothic crime thrillers, publishes the first book featuring his amatuer detective, *The Mind of Mister J.G. Reeder.* Earl Derr Bigger's Hawaiian detective Charlie Chan, created in reaction to the many negative oriental

characters in modern mysteries, is featured in his first case, *The House Without a Key.*

1926 • Philo Vance

S.S. Van Dine's detective Philo Vance is introduced in *The Bensen Murder Case.* The erudite bibliophile would appear in twelve novels and serve as the template for Ellery Queen.

1928 • Simon Templar
       "The Saint"

Leslie Charteris' Simon Templar, the most popular of the "gentlemen thieves," makes his debut in *Enter the Saint.*

1929 • Ellery Queen
     • Albert Campion

Fredrick Dannay and Manfred Lee create Ellery Queen for *The Roman Hat Mystery,* a novel originally written to win a mystery-writing contest. Margery Allingham's Albert Campion is introduced in *The Crime at Black Dudley.*

1930 • Sam Spade
     • Jane Marple
     • The Shadow

Dashiell Hammett introduces one of the most famous detectives of all time in *The Maltese Falcon,* Sam Spade. Agatha Christie's other sleuth, the elderly Miss Jane Marple, appears for the first time in *Murder at the Vicarage.* Street and Smith hire an ex-magician's assistant named William Gibson to write a series of novels based on their popular radio host, The Shadow.

1931 • Hildegarde Withers

The Penguin Pool Murders is the first novel to feature Stuart Palmer's feisty school teacher sleuth, Hildegarde Withers.

1933 • Gideon Fell
     • Inspector Maigret
     • Perry Mason

Raymond Chandler's first story, "Blackmailers Don't Shoot," appears in *Black Mask;* the unnamed detective in the story is a rough version of Philip Marlowe. John Dickinson Carr writes his first novel featuring a detective based on G.K. Chesterton called Gideon Fell, *Hag's Nook*. George Simenson writes his first novel featuring Inspector Maigret. Earle Stanley Gardner's *The Case of the Velvet Claws* features a lawyer named Perry Mason; Gardener forgets about the character—until his editor asks him to turn it into a series.

1934 • Nero Wolfe
     • Dan Turner
     • Sir Henry Merrivale
     • Nick & Nora Charles

Rex Stout's *Fer-de-Lance* features the sedentary and brilliant Nero Wolfe and his "Watson," Archie Goodwin. Robert Leslie Bellum's first Dan Turner story, "Murder By Proxy," appears in *Spicy Detective Tales*. Turner will become the most popular pulp detective of all, appearing in more stories than any other pulp detective, and becoming the subject of a grudgingly positive article by S.J. Perlman. John Dickinson Carr's other famed detective, Sir Henry Merrivale, solves *The Plague Court Murders*. Dashiell Hammett introduces Nick and Nora Charles in *The Thin Man*, two characters in the formal detective tradition.

1935 • Nigel Strangeways

Poet Cecil Day Lewis writes the first Nigel Strangeways novel, *A Question of Proof*, under the pseudonym Nicholas Blake.

1936 • John Appleby
     • Lemmy Caution

Oxford don Michael Innes' first John Appleby novel, *Death at the President's House*, is released in England. The title, referring to the president of a college, is changed to *Seven Suspects* for its American release at the

behest of the United States govern-
ment. Private detective and journalist
Peter Cheyney writes *This Man is
Dangerous* on a bet. Its hero, Lemmy
Caution, will appear in several novels
and will be the hero of the Jean-Luc
Goddard film *Alphaville.*

1938 • Captain MacGrail

Richard Sale's "Perseus Had a Hel-
met" featured police captain
MacGrail, a detective whose cases frequently have a supernatural element.
He will become the forerunner of such
"psychic detectives" as George Ches-
bro's Mongo and Edward Hoch's Simon Ark.

1939 • Philip Marlowe
 • Cool & Lam
 • John J. Malone
 • Mike Shayne

Philip Marlowe, the epitome of the
hard-boiled detective, makes his entrance in *The Big Sleep.* Earle Stanley
Gardener's *The Bigger They Come* is
the first novel featuring Bertha Cool
and Donald Lam. Cool is the first—
and, for a long time, only—hard-
boiled female detective. Craig Rice
(Georgiana Ann Randolph) writes the
first book to feature alcoholic lawyer
John J. Malone, *Eight Faces at Three.*
Rice will later collaborate with Stuart
Palmer on some stories that team up
Malone with Palmer's sleuth, Hilde-
gard Withers. Brett Halliday's Miami
gumshoe Mike Shayne appears for the
first time in *Dividend on Death.*

1941 • Hannah Van Doren

Black Mask veteran Dwight V. Ba-
bock surprises his fans by producing *A
Homicide for Hannah,* the first in a
series featuring the decidedly upbeat
"Gorgeous Ghoul," true crime writer
Hannah Van Doren.

1945 • Taylor & Freeman

Lawrence Treat's *V as in Victim,* featuring the police detectives Taylor and Freeman, is published, making it the first modern police procedural.

1946 • Max Thursday

Wade Miller—the psuedonym of Robert Wade and Bill Miller—introduce Max Thursday in *Deadly Weapon.* Thursday is unusual in his staunch refusual to carry firearms and his compassionate outlook, and appears to be the precursor of Lew Archer.

1947 • Mike Hammer

Mickey Spillaine's ultra-violent Mike Hammer is introduced in *I, the Jury.*

1948 • Shell Scott

Richard Prather publishes his first detective satire with Shell Scott, *The Case of the Vanishing Beauty.*

1949 • Lew Archer

Lew Archer, a more humane variation of the hard-boiled detective, is introduced in Ross MacDonald's *The Moving Target.*

1953 • Ed Noon

The Tall Delores, by Michael Avallone, unleashes the befuddling Ed Noon; easily one of the most bizarre detective series ever written.

1955 • Simon Ark
     • Gideon

"Village of the Dead," the first published story of the highly prolific Edward D. Hoch, introduces the psychic detective Simon Ark. Hoch will later go on to produce a story a month for *Ellery Queen's Mystery Magazine,* and introduce other series detectives: police detective Captain Leopold, gentlemen thief Nick Velvet, frontier lawman Ben Snow, and country doctor Sam Hawthorne among them. John Creasey, the most prolific crime novelist ever (over 560 novels spread out over 28 psuedonyms), publishes the first of the influential Gideon series of procedurals, *Gideon's Day.*

1956 • The 87th Precinct
• Mitch Alliston

Ed McBain's *Cop Hater,* the first novel featuring the 87th Precinct, is published. Jim Thompson's sole series character, con-man Mitch Alliston, debuts in the surprisingly witty "The Cellini Challis."

1959 • Coffin Ed Johnson &
Grave Digger Jones

The first of Chester Himes' violent novels featuring Coffin Ed Johnson and Grave Digger Jones, *The Crazy Kill,* is published in America only after its success in France the year before attracts interest.

1962 • Adam Dalgliesh

P.D. James' wonderfully complex poet/detective Adam Dalgliesh is introduced in *Cover Her Face.*

1964 • Travis McGee
• Kate Fansler
• Rabbi Small

John D. MacDonald's Travis McGee is introduced in four novels published over the course of the year, quickly gaining MacDonald a legion of fans. *In the Last Analysis* is the first adventure of Amanda Cross' collegiate sleuth Kate Fansler. Harry Kemelman's Rabbi David Small, the spiritual descendant of Father Brown, debuts in *Friday the Rabbi Slept Late.*

1965 • Sid Halley
• Virgil Tibbs

Popular thriller writer Dick Francis introduces his only series character, retired jockey turned private eye Sid Halley, in *Odds Against. In the Heat of the Night* is the first novel to feature John Ball's dynamic black detective, Virgil Tibbs. The book will win that year's Edgar for best novel, and a film based on it will be awarded the Academy Award for best picture.

1966 • Pharoah Love — George Baxt introduces Pharoah Love, a homosexual detective, in *A Queer Kind of Death*.

1970 • Sargent Cribb
     • Shaft — Peter Lovesy's Sargent Cribb, a Victorian police detective, debuts in the highly detailed *Wobble to Death*. Shaft, a black hard-boiled detective, debuts in Ernest Tidyman's novel of the same name.

1971 • Nameless Detective — Bill Pronzini's Nameless Detective, a character patterned after the Continental Op, is introduced in *The Snatch*.

1973 • Spenser — Robert Parker creates the Boston detective Spenser in *The Godwulf Manuscript*. This character will go on to become one of the most popular detectives of all time.

1974 • Irwin M. Fletcher — Gregory MacDonald's first novel, *Fletch*, introduces the light-hearted investigative reporter Irwin M. Fletcher.

1976 • Matt Scudder — Lawrence Block, who also created Bernie the Burglar and Evan Tanner, introduces his most popular creation, Matt Scudder, with *In the Midst of Death*.

1980 • Harry Stoner — Harry Stoner, "the best private eye of the 80s," is introduced in Jonathan Valin's *The Lime Pit*. Stoner becomes the first series detective to premeditatedly kill somebody in *Extenuating Circumstances*, ten years later.

1982 • V.I. Warshawski — Sara Paretsky takes time off from her insurance company to write *Indemnity Only*. The novel introduces V.I. Warshawski, one of the first and best of the female hard-boiled detectives.

1983 • Nate Heller
• Eliot Ness
• Devlin Tracy

True Detective features two "characters" who will star in their own series written by Max Allen Collins: Nate Heller and Eliot Ness. *Destroyer* co-creator Warren Murphy reworks his defunct series Digger to create the popular investigator Devlin Tracy in *Trace*.

1985 • Carlotta Carlyle

Linda Barnes' "Lucky Penny" introduces Carlotta Carlyle, and wins both the Edgar and Shamus for that year.

The Contributions of Edgar Allan Poe

Robert A.W. Lowndes

Just how far back back in time the mystery tale goes is a moot question, and the question of how far back goes the tale wherein a mystery is solved by the use of reason, rather than magic or divination, is also open. The Book of Daniel contains two episodes which make very respectable detective stories: "Bel and the Dragon," and "Susanna." However, these two stories, as far as we know, were not written as fiction or understood by their readers to be fiction. We must come far forward in time from those days, to the nineteenth century to be exact, to find the beginnings of what we now consider the detective story, wherein a fictional character solves a fictional mystery through the use of inductive and deductive reasoning—ratiocination, as this operation was called in the early nineteenth century. Such a story might indeed include thrilling events and action, but in no way does the solution of the mystery depend upon action. The detective may need to take steps in order to achieve justice, but the physical action derives from the solution to the mystery, at which the detective has arrived either by a combination of inspecting the premises and listening to or reading reports, or on the basis of reports alone, without ever having stirred from his chair.

The date to remember is April 1841 (in those days magazines were not dated ahead), and the publication to honor is *Graham's Magazine,* published in Philadelphia. It was here that readers saw "The Murders in the Rue Morgue," by an author who was already well known to followers of magazines: Edgar Allan Poe. This was the first of three tales of ratiocination devolving about a character named C. Auguste Dupin, whom Ellery Queen justly honors as "the world's first fictional detective in a modern sense." A little more than a year and a half later, the second Dupin tale, "The Mystery of Marie Rogêt," appeared as a three-part serial in *The Ladies' Companion*, November and December 1842 and February 1843. (Remember that one-month hiatus; it will become important later.) The final story, "The Purloined Letter," appeared in *The Gift*, late in 1844. An examination of these three tales will indicate the range of Poe's inventions in the detective story.

The first thousand or so words of "The Murders in the Rue Morgue" are devoted to an introductory essay on analysis. Some sort of introductory material preceding what can properly be called the start of a story was common apparatus for 19th century authors; but most of Poe's stories (as opposed to pieces which are sometimes included among the "tales" but are little more than essays or whimsies) either start at once or begin after no more than a paragraph or two of introduction. This preliminary essay, then, is unusual for Poe. Whether he employed it for his own benefit (feeling his way, as it were, in a new type of story), whether he felt that the reader needed this introduction in order to comprehend or sympathize with what the author was doing, or whether it represents a combination of the two previous suggestions, is something I'll gladly leave to the experts. Having read it with care, I can assure you that today's reader does not need it at all. There is nothing in it that is not accomplished better in the course of the story, once the story starts. The introduction ends with this brief paragraph: "The narrative which follows will appear to the reader somewhat in the light of a commentary upon the propositions just advanced."

Now the story begins, with the introduction of Monsieur C. Auguste Dupin. "This young gentleman was of an excellent, indeed of an illustrious family, but, by a variety of untoward events, had been reduced to such poverty that the energy of his character succumbed beneath it, and he ceased to bestir himself in the world, or to care for the retrieval of his fortunes." Our narrator meets Dupin in an obscure library where both are in search of the same "very rare and very remarkable" volume. They find they are kindred souls in a sufficient number of ways so that they decide to share quarters, so long as our narrator stays in Paris. "...and as my worldly circumstances were somewhat less embarrassed than his own, I was permitted to be at the expense of renting, and furnishing in a style which suited the rather fantastic gloom of our common temper, a time-eaten and grotesque mansion, long deserted through superstitions into which we did not inquire, and tottering to its fall in a retired and desolate portion of the Faubourg St. Germain.''

We see at once that the world's first private detective is an unusual person of unusual tastes and temperament; with Poe, it could hardly be otherwise. "Had the routine of our life at this place been known to the world, we should have been regarded as madmen—although, perhaps, as madmen of a harmless nature.'' My own feeling is that this represents more of the author's characteristic gestures—his routine manner of describing an intelligent and educated gentleman with whom he hoped to capture the readers' attention—than carefully thought-out harmony between story and character. The pair leave their quarters only at night, while "At the first dawn of the morning we closed all the massy shutters of our old building; lighted a couple of tapers which, strongly perfumed, threw out only the ghastliest and feeblest of rays. By the aid of these we then busied our souls in dreams—reading, writing, or conversing, until warned by the clock of the advent of the true Darkness. Then we sallied forth into the streets,...seeking, amid the wild lights and shadows of the populous city, that infinity of mental excitement which quiet observation can afford.'' Apparently this was before eyestrain was invented.

Nonetheless, despite the fact that the original portrait of Dupin is overdone (and later must be modified so that he can accomplish what he must accomplish), this very opening had tremendous influence upon subsequent authors of detective fiction. Sherlock Holmes, Father Brown, Hercule Poirot, Philo Vance, Sir Henry Merrivale, and Nero Wolfe—to list but a few—are all, to one degree or another, bizarre characters. And Dr. Doyle found that he had to modify a great deal of the description of Holmes' limitations as well as some of his habits (as presented in *A Study in Scarlet)* in order to fit him into later stories.

Poe goes on for slightly more than 800 words about the weird living style of the narrator and Dupin, then launches an episode wherein Dupin demonstrates his skill in induction and deduction, startling the narrator with a comment which would seem to indicate that Dupin could read his thoughts. Sherlock Holmes, you will remember, startled Dr. Watson at their first meeting, and Watson later compares Holmes to Dupin. Whereupon: "Sherlock Holmes rose and lit his pipe. 'No doubt you think that you are complimenting me in comparing me to Dupin,' he observed. 'Now, in my opinion, Dupin was a very inferior fellow. That trick of his of breaking in on his friends' thoughts after a quarter of an hour's silence is really very showy and superficial. He had some analytical genius, no doubt; but he was by no means such a phenomenon as Poe seemed to imagine.'" *(A Study in Scarlet,* Chapter II.)

But as Michael Harrison notes in his essay on Dupin ("Dupin: The Reality Behind the Fiction," in *The Exploits of the Chevalier Dupin,* Mycroft & Moran 1968), Doyle is really drawing a red herring across the reader's path, hoping thus to distract him from the size of the debt he actually owes to Poe and, in this first Holmes story, to "The Murders in the Rue Morgue" in particular. As Harrison indicates, Doyle was just beginning at that time, and was worried about being dismissed as a mere imitator of Poe; had he started writing about Sherlock Holmes after he was well established, he might have been more generous. (Later in *A Study in Scarlet,* Holmes tells Watson that his is a unique profession: the world's first consulting detective. For after all, Dupin was a fictional character.)

It is not until after the thought-reading episode that we get to the crime: Dupin and the narrator see an account "Extraordinary Murders" in the evening paper. However, the material preceding this point and dealing with the first meeting between the narrator and Dupin is not superfluous, however awkward some of the attempts to make Dupin himself seem extraordinary. The two friends follow the newspaper accounts for a time, then when the arrest of a particular person is announced, Dupin asks the narrator's opinions. He replies: "I could merely agree with all Paris in

considering them an insoluble mystery. I saw no means by which it
would be possible to trace the murderer."

We shall see later on in the story that the narrator, while not adept
at ratiocination to anything like the extent of Dupin, is nonetheless
able to observe and to ask intelligent questions. The difference
between Dupin and the narrator in these tales is nowhere near the
difference between Holmes and Watson. Of course our detective
must be ahead of his Boswell (otherwise the story might as well be
written from the viewpoint of the detective himself); but the
difference between Dupin and the narrator in Poe's tales, and
between Holmes and Watson, is particularly interesting. Poe was
writing for readers who were on the whole far better educated and
addicted to thought than the general public for which Doyle wrote.
The magazines to which Poe contributed were read by the "gentle"
class, and only incidentally here and there by members of the
general populace. But in late 19th-century England, the popular
magazines, though priced for the most part beyond the means of the
lower classes (the so-called penny dreadfuls were for them), had a
much broader circulation. It was not only Doyle's need to show but
also the reader's need to see how extraordinary Holmes was that
required Watson to be rather lazy-minded and decidedly slow on
the uptake—outside of his profession, that is.

The beautiful thing about Holmes' line "You know my methods,
Watson" is that Watson really did know Holmes' methods, but he
didn't know he knew them. He employed them constantly as a
doctor, but it never occurred to him to use them outside the practice
of medicine.

Whether consciously or not, Doyle used a technique which was
perfectly appropriate for his general readership. He makes Watson
a little denser than the reasonably well informed and alert reader,
so that while the reader is perhaps rarely able to beat the great
detective to the solution of the mystery, at least he's better than
Watson. In respect to acumen, later authors have made their
narrators pretty much either the Watson or the colleague-of-Dupin
sort: Agatha Christie's Captain Hastings, whom she dropped after
awhile for good reason, is more stupid than Watson (although he

improves a bit after his marriage), and Archie Goodwin, while not up to Nero Wolfe's level, is at least as intelligent as the companion of Dupin.

Both Sherlock Holmes and Hercule Poirot said that their Boswells inspired genius, and we must suspect that one reason these sleuths are so fond of their companions is that the two masters appear so brilliant by comparison; in his heart each of the detectives realizes that he isn't as wonderful as his "friend and colleague" thinks he is. On the other hand, while Nero Wolfe has a certain fondness for Goodwin, he keeps Archie around because Archie is alert, intelligent and useful, more like the Poe than the Doyle type of narrator.

After the newspaper accounts of "The Murders in the Rue Morgue" comes a discussion of the police and their limitations. "The Parisian police, so much extolled for *acumen*, are cunning, but no more. There is no method in their proceedings, beyond the method of the moment....The results attained by them are not unfrequently surprising, but, for the most part, are brought about by simple diligence and activity. When these qualities are unavailing, their schemes fail."

There is in these tales a certain amount of competition and rivalry between Dupin and G——, the Prefect of Police, but neither is really contemptuous of the other. Dupin respects the police on their level of competence, and acknowledges readily that they can do better than he on *most* crimes; for most crimes are very ordinary affairs, perpetrated by people with little imagination, and thus readily susceptible to diligence and cunning. But when the police are up against the extraordinary crime, the criminal with both intelligence and imagination, their methods are often inadequate. Poe does not lean heavily on exalting Dupin by presenting G—— and the police as imbeciles.

Sherlock Holmes, on the other hand, is usually at loggerheads with Scotland Yard, and rarely has a good word for Lestrade and the others. They, quite humanly, resent Holmes' airs (in addition to his very presence which is itself something of an insult to them); but they cannot always withhold a grudging respect for him, and eventually Scotland Yard men will mourn his apparent death.

Agatha Christie plays it both ways. Poirot already has the respect of the police on both sides of the Channel before the time of the first case that Captain Hastings records *(The Mysterious Affair at Styles)*, but at times he has difficulty with a particular police detective (like Giraud in *Murder on the Links)* who considers him a conceited has-been. Miss Marple never has trouble with the police: to criticize them would be out of character for her. Willard Huntington Wright (S.S. Van Dine) wrote *The Benson Murder Case* as a burlesque, so the police are utter idiots. Philo Vance is a close friend of District Attorney Markham, and after one brief misunderstanding wins the respect of Sergeant Heath. As Wright began to find that he enjoyed writing murder mysteries he became less satirical, but I don't recall that the police ever go beyond the simplest level of competence in the series. Nero Wolfe and Archie Goodwin are in an endless feud with police authorities, who are constantly trying to get Wolfe's license revoked. Sir Henry Merrivale is a clown as well as a genius, but in general John Dickson Carr/Carter Dickson leans more toward Poe's rather than Doyle's method of handling the police. Father Brown, as a priest, renders unto Caesar that which is Caesar's.

But all the outstanding detectives of fiction who appear in a series of novels follow Poe in one respect: the murder or mystery is almost always an extraordinary one, not susceptible to the usual routine of diligence and cunning which at its best results in the solution of most crimes. Admittedly I have just presented a judgment disguised as a definition: I define outstanding fictional detectives as those who appear in cases of extraordinary crimes, requiring the methods of a Dupin, a Holmes, a Poirot or a Father Brown. My definition excludes crime stories where the only extraordinary element is the amount of violence, stupidity and sordidness that can be strung out before a simple and uninteresting "mystery" is solved. (Blood and horror are not barred *ipso facto:* "The Murders in the Rue Morgue" is as gruesome as any of the mindless gangster epics.)

To return to "The Murders," Dupin draws different conclusions than did the police from the facts available, one such conclusion being that there is something to be observed at the scene of the crime which the police did not notice. We do not know yet whether something right under their eyes escaped them, or whether they failed to look for something which hardly anyone would have noticed. These are two different possibilities, and Poe and his followers employed them both singly and in combination.

Another important element we find here is that it becomes necessary for the detective to observe at firsthand. (As we shall see, Dupin will solve a later case without stirring from his chair.) In the short story form we often find detectives who arrive at their solutions by sheer ratiocination, such as Miss Marple in *The Tuesday Club Murders* and a number of stories collected in other volumes; but in her novel-length cases she is required to move around a bit. Sherlock Holmes, for all his pipe-smoking and armchair deductions, is highly active in chasing down clues. Poirot scorns legwork that a police detective can do just as well, gets others to do most of the sniffing, and relies upon his gray cells—after, of course, getting everyone involved to talk at length about all sorts of matters seemingly unrelated to the crime. Father Brown goes around to a certain extent but is more of a Dupin than a Holmes. Nero Wolfe tries to give us the impression that he never leaves his brownstone, but it is astonishing how frequently he actually does go out; nonetheless his is the "gray cells" method, with Archie and subordinate private detectives such as Saul Panzer gathering the needed information preparatory to the climactic session in Wolfe's office.

When Dupin personally investigates the scene of the murders in the Rue Morgue, he discovers what he was looking for: a method of entering the murder room which was not considered possible. He knows now what he seeks as well as the type of person he seeks, and arranges for the person to come to him rather than going out to look for the party. There is a private confrontation and a confession, and Dupin's report to the police results in the release of the man who had been arrested and charged with the crime.

What was unique about "The Murders in the Rue Morgue"? Let us recapitulate some of the many elements in it that would be carried forward, or at least onward, by Poe's successors.

1. C. Auguste Dupin is a private citizen, neither presently nor formerly a policeman, nor associated with the police in their work.

2. Dupin is an eccentric, with a genius for induction and deduction as applied to human behavior.

3. Dupin has not made a special study of crime and criminal methods beyond the extent to which an ordinary well-read person of his time would have done so.

4. We see Dupin through the eyes of a close friend and associate, whose capabilities are above average, but lesser than Dupin's.

5. Dupin is attracted by the extraordinary features of the crime in the Rue Morgue; ordinary crimes do not interest him.

6. The case is a locked-room mystery.

7. Several important clues are presented squarely to the reader in the initial accounts of the crime that Dupin and the narrator read in the papers. The number of clues is not important; what is important is that the reader is given a fair chance to see an essential part of the truth before the detective reveals it.

8. But even if the reader follows these clues to a logical conclusion, the crime still appears to be impossible.

9. Dupin has apparently reached a tentative conclusion from reading the newspaper accounts. However, if this conclusion is correct, the police have overlooked something that is there to be seen.

10. Dupin arranges to examine the scene of the crime with the consent of the police. Relations between him and the Prefect show mutual respect and reasonable amity.

11. Dupin considers police methods adequate for most crimes, which are committed by people with very little imagination. He is interested only in the unusual cases, for which routine methods are inadequate. He acknowledges that the police can do better in the routine cases than can he.

12. Dupin is spurred to solve the riddle of the Rue Morgue by the fact that a person of whose innocence he is certain has been arrested and charged with the murders.

13. Dupin satisfies himself by an examination of the scene of the crime that his hypothesis is correct. The reader is shown the evidence, and, if astute, now knows essentially as much as Dupin does.

14. Dupin does not at once present his findings to the police, but sets a trap for the person he seeks.

15. Dupin does not turn this party over to the police after he has heard the entire story, a good deal of which he has deduced.

16. Dupin presents the police with just enough data to insure the release of the wrongly arrested gentleman.

17. Even if the astute reader has solved the puzzle in essence before Dupin reveals the whole truth, there are aspects of the final summation which are likely to surprise, and the summing-up is therefore rewarding to read. (My opinion is that in a well-done puzzle detective story, even the most alert and ingenious reader never figures out the whole truth as revealed at the end.)

18. There are no subplots in the story.

19. Dupin and the narrator neither run into danger nor are threatened with violence.

20. "The Murders in the Rue Morgue" is a short story. A writer before Poe's time would probably have made the same material into a long novel, filling it out with extraneous matter. Poe's story,

however, contains nothing inessential except the introduction, which was necessary in this pioneering instance.

Had Poe never written another Dupin story, "The Murders in the Rue Morgue" would still be a monument for everyone today who loves the puzzle type of mystery tale, wherein the puzzle is solved by reason rather than physical violence, and the reader is given the clues he needs to solve the puzzle himself if he is astute enough. But in fact Poe did write more than one Dupin story; so let us look at what he did in the second story, "The Mystery of Marie Rogêt."

This, I am told, is the least popular of the three tales, although I should think that the person who enjoys true crime stories as I enjoy mystery-puzzle fiction would find it the best of the three. A young girl named Mary Cecilia Rogers had been murdered in the vicinity of New York. At the time Poe wrote his second Dupin tale, the crime had not been solved. So, fascinated by his own theories of ratiocination, Poe set out again to do something which (to my knowledge) had never been done in fiction before. He essayed to solve not a crime that had taken place in the dim past but a still-unsolved mystery of the present—one which might even be solved between the time his story was being printed and the time it came to the reader's attention. Poe was risking disaster for his theories.

For what Poe did was to take the Mary Rogers case and transpose each separate element of it, using nothing more than newspaper accounts. As the brief introduction to the tale states in part: "The 'Mystery of Marie Rogêt' was composed at a distance from the scene of the atrocity, and with no other means of investigation than the newspapers afforded. Thus much escaped the writer of which he could have availed himself had he been on the spot and visited the localities."

Mary Rogers became Marie Rogêt, the essential facts of the real murder were duplicated in detail and the inessential facts were paralleled. Poe both draws the reader's attention to what he is really doing and disguises his objective in the brief introduction, where he speaks of coincidences which may seem almost supernatural but which actually are quite natural in the light of what he terms the "Calculus of Probabilities." And, he says, a prime recent example of such coincidence is the case of Mary Cecilia Rogers; for, *mirabile dictu,* a nearly exact parallel took place in Paris, "about two years after the atrocity in the Rue Morgue." And its solution was one of the most brilliant exploits of the narrator's friend, C. Auguste Dupin.

The crime is not extraordinary, but rather common and sordid. Why then does Dupin bother with the Marie Rogêt case? "The first intelligence of the murder was brought us by G——, in person.... He had been piqued by the failure of all his endeavors to ferret out the assassins. His reputation—so he said with a peculiarly Parisian air—was at stake. Even his honor was concerned. The eyes of the public were upon him; and there was really no sacrifice which he would not be willing to make for the development of the mystery...."

Dupin gets his information from the police, from newspaper accounts, and from editorials in the papers. He makes no investigation of the scene of the crime, and he proposes his solution from the armchair. At the end of Dupin's solution appears the following paragraph, placed in square brackets.

"For reasons which we shall not specify, but which to many readers will appear obvious, we have taken the liberty of here omitting, from the MSS. placed in our hands, such portion as details the *following up* of the apparently slight clew obtained by Dupin. We feel it advisable only to state, in brief, that the result desired was brought to pass; and that the Prefect fulfilled punctually, although with reluctance, the terms of his compact with the Chevalier....—Eds.

The "Eds." is generally taken as referring to the editors of *The Ladies' Companion,* in which "Marie Rogêt" was originally published; I cannot but wonder, though, whether the paragraph did not appear in Poe's own original manuscript. Since the Mary Rogers case was still open, surely Poe would have realized that, assuming his solution correct, revelation of the details whereby the essential clues should be followed up might serve to insure the culprit's escape.

An interesting feature of "Marie Rogêt" is that Poe therein punctures common notions about the behavior of corpses under water; this element too has been widely followed by subsequent authors. Of course, the question whether Dupin's certainties as to the facts are actually any less fallacious or superstitious than the opinions he is puncturing remains moot. New superstitions drive out old ones, and the notion that what drives out an old superstition cannot possibly be superstition itself is among the greatest of superstitions.

Poe, as noted above, took a considerable risk in publishing this story; for not only did he lack the advantage of examining the locale himself, but he was in danger of being misled by the sort of sloppy reporting that one frequently finds in the papers at any time in the history of journalism. Nevertheless, we are assured in a footnote to the story as it appears in book form that "the confessions of *two* persons (one of them the Madame Deluc of the narrative) made, at different periods, long subsequent to the publication, confirmed, in full, not only the general conclusion, but absolutely *all* the chief hypothetical details by which that conclusion was attained."

On the basis of this note, most readers of "Marie Rogêt" have accepted Poe's claim that he solved the actual murder of Mary Cecilia Rogers. But new light has recently been shed on this subject by John Walsh in his book *Poe the Detective* (Rutgers University Press, 1968). A former newspaperman, Mr. Walsh searched through the files of newspapers published in New York and New Jersey in 1841/42—i.e., Poe's own source material—and familiarized himself with the area of New York City where Mary Rogers lived and worked. Contemporary maps and woodcuts of the Hoboken-Weehawken area gave further assistance, so that it was possible for him to come up with nearly as much material as Poe had, as well as some that Poe did not have. Walsh then made a close examination of Poe's story in the light of known or probable events in the author's life during 1841-42, and compared the original magazine version of the story's final sections with the version later reprinted in hard covers, with numerous footnotes added. His conclusion is that Poe's claim to have solved the case in his story amounts not to a triumph of ratiocination but of flummery. The footnotes added to the hardcover reprint, plus a few ingenious alterations (both additions and deletions) in the text of the reprint, have given a misleading impression for well over a century.

At least that is Mr. Walsh's thesis, and the late Prof. Thomas Ollive Mabbott, who wrote the Introduction to *Poe the Detective,* found it convincing; as I do myself, mainly for the following reasons. (1) The issue of *The Ladies' Companion* which carried part three of the story was not January 1843 but February 1843. The first two installments appeared in the issues of November and December 1842, and there was a January 1843 issue; why then was Poe's final installment held up a month? Walsh's researches indicate that fresh material in the Mary Rogers case which threatened to refute Poe's solution came to light just around the time the final installment of "Marie Rogêt" was due to be printed. The most likely theory seems to be that publication was held up so that Poe could do a quick revision incorporating the newly discovered material. (2) Although Poe's original manuscript cannot be found, two slightly different texts exist. In his book Walsh prints the text we are familiar with, plus the alterations (the additions and deletions), so that we can see where the two versions differ, and correlate the variant texts with the footnotes which made Poe's claim so convincing to both readers and scholars up to the present time. (3) Walsh confirms my suspicion that Poe himself wrote the bracketed paragraph quoted above, which is signed *"Eds."* in the hardcover text. (Which raises the question, which never before occured to me, Watson that I am: might not Poe have written *all* the footnotes?)

But regardless of whether or not it solved the actual murder of Mary Rogers, "The Mystery of Marie Rogêt" gives us some more firsts for Poe.

21. Dupin is the first fictional private detective to appear in a series of stories.

22. The police come to Dupin, imploring his help.

23. Dupin solves the mystery upon data brought to him, without leaving his quarters, thereby becoming the first armchair detective.

24. Dupin questions no one other than the Prefect, and solves the case solely on official data and newspaper accounts.

25. In this second appearance, Dupin is no longer presented as a bizarre character but only as a slightly eccentric fellow.

26. Dupin presents the police with data enabling them to apprehend the culprit, but takes no part himself in following up his deductions.

27. In the course of discussing the case, Dupin undertakes to explode popular notions on matters often connected with crime.

"The Purloined Letter," last of the Dupin series, is easily the best in a number of ways, but not in all ways. It is the best written, judged by the modern taste. "The Murders in the Rue Morgue" could not help but arouse suspicion that it was merely an invention to illustrate Poe's theory of analysis rather than an episode in the career of C. Auguste Dupin. An equal suspicion of ulterior motives lies behind "The Mystery of Marie Rogêt": Poe is so full of enthusiasms and messages, so quick with fables which "prove" his contentions! But "The Purloined Letter" has no such flaws; it starts at once, in Dupin's quarters, one autumn evening.

By a most interesting coincidence, the narrator and Dupin have just been discussing the two previous cases when Monsieur G——, the Prefect of Police, enters. What is more, he enters at the end of the very first paragraph. The game is afoot, as a spiritual son of Dupin will say.

In several pages of animated dialogue, we learn that the Prefect's problem is a stolen letter for which all search thus far has been futile but which must be recovered. Dupin says he can only suggest that the Prefect and his men search once again, even more thoroughly, the premises where the letter must be hidden.

"I have no better advice to give you," said Dupin. "You have, of course, an accurate description of the letter?"

"Oh, yes!"—And here the Prefect, producing a memorandum-book, proceeded to read aloud a minute account of the internal, and especially of the external, appearance of the missing document. Soon after finishing the perusal of this description, he took his departure, more entirely depressed in spirits than I had ever known the good gentleman before.

It is generally contended that the reader has no fair chance to solve the mystery of the letter's hiding-place; and so far as the precise spot is concerned, I would agree. But it seems to me that the reader is given a fair enough opportunity to grasp the principle of concealment that is the point of the story.

A month passes, then the Prefect drops around to Dupin's quarters again, and admits that he is completely stumped. He again searched the premises of the man who stole the letter, as Dupin suggested, but to no avail. (There is no doubt who the culprit is, nor is there anything to be gained by arresting the man, for a royal scandal will ensue if the existence of the letter becomes known.)

Dupin asks if there is a reward for the return of the letter, and the prefect replies: "...I wouldn't mind giving my individual check for fifty thousand francs to anyone who could obtain me the letter. The fact is, it is becoming of more and more importance every day; and the reward has been lately doubled. If it were trebled, however, I could do no more than I have done."

After a little badinage, wherein the Prefect repeats that he would *really* give fifty thousand francs to anyone who could aid him in the matter, Dupin gets up, produces his checkbook, and replies: "In that case,... you may as well fill me up a check for the amount mentioned. When you have signed it, I will hand you the letter."

After the Prefect has signed the check, Dupin, "unlocking an *escritoire,* took thence a letter and gave it to the Prefect. This functionary grasped it in a perfect agony of joy, opened it with a trembling hand, cast a rapid glance at its contents, and then, scrambling and struggling to the door, rushed at length unceremoniously from the room and from the house, without having uttered a syllable since Dupin had requested him to fill up the check." And herewith G—— exits from the series, for he does not return to learn how Dupin obtained the letter or where it had been hidden. Several pages of question and answer between the narrator and Dupin fill us in.

From this dialogue we learn something of Dupin's past, of the days prior to those misfortunes that left him in the rather sorry condition in which the narrator first met him in "The Murders in the Rue Morgue." Dupin's narration shows him taking action for once, and rather dangerous action; however, he had deduced in advance how to look for the letter, and that, of course, is the answer to the riddle. Although it has become astonishingly easy to locate the letter, recovering it is another matter, and Dupin resorts to assistance to create a diversion just long enough so that he can substitute a facsimile for the letter.

Although Dupin's explanation covers more pages than were taken to come to the delivery of the letter to the Prefect, Poe continues to hold the reader's interest. The pace slows a little, as it must when an illustrated lecture is being given; but the slow-down is more than compensated for by the suspense and the revelation of Dupin's character. Although it is actually somewhat longer than it appears to be, "The Purloined Letter" remains a remarkably swift-moving short story. From it we may add the following features to our list.

28. New facets of Dupin's character are revealed.

29. An element of humor (the practical joke on the Prefect) is worked in without appearing strained.

30. Dupin has a personal score to settle with the culprit.

31. The essential problem is not how to reveal but how to help officially conceal the existence of a crime.

32. Since the health of the state is involved, "The Purloined Letter" is a cloak-and-dagger story of intrigue in addition to being a genuine puzzle mystery.

My list of elements that subsequent authors derived directly or indirectly from Poe's Dupin stories comes to 32. It is a sizeable list, and I know of no subsequent author who has added half so much again to the list. Even if some of the elements can be traced back to writers predating Poe, he was the first to put them all together in a shorter total of words than you will find in any of the best novels that came after him.

The Simple Art of Murder

Raymond Chandler

Fiction in any form has always intended to be realistic. Old-fashioned novels which now seem stilted and artificial to the point of burlesque did not appear that way to the people who first read them. Writers like Fielding and Smollett could seem realistic in the modern sense because they dealt largely with uninhibited characters, many of whom were about two jumps ahead of the police, but Jane Austen's chronicle of highly inhibited people against a background of rural gentility seem real enough psychologically. There is plenty of that kind of social and emotional hypocrisy around today. Add to it a liberal dose of intellectual pretentiousness and you get the tone of the book page in your daily paper and the earnest and fatuous atmosphere breathed by discussion groups in little clubs These are the peoplc who make best-sellers, which are promotional jobs based on a sort of indirect snob-appeal, carefully escorted by the trained seals of the critical fraternity. and lovingly tended and watered by certain much too powerful pressure groups whose business is selling books, although they would like you to think they are fostering culture. Just get a little behind in your payments and you will find out how idealistic they are.

The detective story for a variety of reasons can seldom be promoted. It is usually about murder and hence lacks the element of uplift. Murder, which is a frustration of the individual and hence a frustration of the race, may, and in fact has, a good deal of sociological implication. But it has been going on too long for it to be news. If the mystery novel is at all realistic (which it very seldom is) it is written in a certain spirit of detachment; otherwise nobody but a psychopath would want to write it or read it. The murder novel has also a depressing way of minding its own business, solving its own problems and answering its own questions. There is nothing left to discuss, except whether it was well enough written to be good fiction, and the people who make up the half-million sales wouldn't know that anyway. The detection of quality in writing is difficult enough even for those who make a career of the job, without paying too much attention to the matter of advance sales.

The detective story (perhaps I had better call it that, since the English formula still dominates the trade) has to find its public by a slow process of distillation. That it does do this, and holds on thereafter with such tenacity, is a fact; the reasons for it are a study for more patient minds than mine. Nor is it any part of my thesis to maintain that it is a vital and significant form of art. There are no vital and significant forms of art; there is only art, and precious little of that. The growth of populations has in no way increased the amount; it has merely increased the adeptness with which substitutes can be produced and packaged.

Yet the detective story, even in its most conventional form, is difficult to write well. Good specimens of the art are much rarer than good serious novels. Rather second-rate items outlast most of the high velocity fiction, and a great many that should never have been born simply refuse to die at all. They are as durable as the statues in public parks and just about that dull. This is very annoying to people of what is called discernment. They do not like it that penetrating and important works of fiction of a few years back stand on their special shelf in the library marked "Best-Sellers of Yesteryear," and nobody goes near them but an occasional shortsighted customer who bends down, peers briefly and hurries away; while old ladies jostle each other at the mystery shelf to grab off some item of the same vintage with a title like *The Triple Petunia Murder Case,* or *Inspector Pinchbottle to the Rescue.* They do not like it that "really important books" get dusty on the reprint counter, while *Death Wears Yellow Garters* is put out in editions of fifty or one hundred thousand copies on the news-stands of the country, and is obviously not there just to say goodbye.

To tell you the truth, I do not like it very much myself. In my less stilted moments I too write detective stories, and all this immortality makes just a little too much competition. Even Einstein couldn't get very far if three hundred treatises of the higher physics were published every year, and several thousand others in some form or other were hanging around in excellent condition, and being read too. Hemingway says somewhere that the good writer competes only with the dead. The good detective story writer (there must after all be a few) competes not only with all the unburied dead but with all the hosts of the living as well. And on almost equal terms; for it is one of the qualities of this kind of writing that the thing that makes people read it never goes out of style. The hero's tie may be a little off the mode and the good gray inspector may arrive in a dogcart instead of a streamlined sedan with siren screaming, but what he does when he gets there is the same old futzing around with timetables and bits of charred paper and who trampled the jolly old flowering arbutus under the library window.

I have, however, a less sordid interest in the matter It seems to me that production of detective stories on so large a scale, and by writers whose immediate reward is small and whose need of critical praise is almost nil, would not be possible at all if the job took any talent. In that sense the raised eyebrow of the critic and the shoddy merchandizing of the publisher are perfectly logical The average detective story is probably no worse than the average novel, but you never see the average novel. It doesn't get published. The average—or only slightly above average—detective story does. Not only is it published, but it is sold in small quantities to rental libraries, and it is read. There are even a few optimists who buy it at the full retail price of two dollars, because it looks so fresh and new, and there is a picture of a corpse on the cover. And the strange thing is that this average, more than middling dull, pooped-out piece of utterly unreal and mechanical fiction is not terribly different from what are called the masterpieces of the art. It drags on a little more slowly, the dialogue is a little grayer, the cardboard out of which the characters are cut is a shade thinner, and the cheating is a little more obvious; but it is the same kind of book. Whereas the good novel is not at all the same kind of book as the bad novel. It is about entirely different things. But the good detective story and the bad detective story are about exactly the same things, and they are about them in very much the same way. There are reasons for this too, and reasons for the reasons; there always are.

I suppose the principle dilemma of the traditional or classic or straight-deductive or logic-and-deduction novel of detection is that for any approach to perfection it demands a combination of qualities not found in the same mind. The cool-headed constructionist does not also come across with lively characters, sharp dialogue, a sense of pace and an acute use of observed detail. The grim logician has as much atmosphere as a drawing-board. The scientific sleuth has a nice new shiny laboratory but I'm sorry, I can't remember the face. The fellow who can write you a vivid and colorful prose simply won't be bothered with the coolie labor of breaking down unbreakable alibis. The master of rare knowledge is living psychologically in the age of the hoop skirt. If you know all you should know about ceramics and Egyptian needlework, you don't know anything at all about the police. If you know that platinum won't melt under about 2800 degrees F. by itself, but will melt at the glance of a pair of deep blue eyes when put close to a bar of lead, then you don't know how men make love in the twentieth century. And if you know enough about the elegant flânerie of the pre-war French Riviera to lay your story in that locale, you don't know that a couple of capsules of barbital small enough to be swallowed will not only kill a man—they will not even put him to sleep, if he fights against them.

Every detective story writer makes mistakes and none will ever know as much as he should. Conan Doyle made mistakes which completely invalidated some of his stories, but he was a pioneer, and Sherlock Holmes after all is mostly an attitude and a few dozen lines of unforgettable dialogue. It is the ladies and gentlemen of what Mr. Howard Haycraft (in his book *Murder for Pleasure*) calls the Golden Age of detective fiction that really get me down. This age is not remote. For Mr. Haycraft's purpose it starts after the first World War and lasts up to about 1930. For all practical purposes it is still here. Two-thirds or three-quarters of all the detective stories published still adhere to the formula the giants of this era created, perfected, polished and sold to the world as problems in logic and deduction. These are stern words, but be not alarmed. They are only words. Let us glance at one of the glories of the literature, an acknowledged masterpiece of the art of fooling the reader without cheating him. It is called *The Red House Mystery,* was written by A. A. Milne, and has been named by Alexander Woollcott (rather a fast man with a superlative) "one of the three best mystery stories of all time." Words of that size are not spoken lightly. The book was published in 1922, but is quite timeless, and might as easily have been published in July 1939, or, with a few slight changes, last week. It ran thirteen editions and seems to have been in print, in the original format, for about sixteen years. That happens to few books of any kind. It is an agreeable book, light, amusing in the *Punch* style, written with a deceptive smoothness that is not as easy as it looks.

It concerns Mark Ablett's impersonation of his brother Robert, as a hoax on his friends. Mark is the owner of the Red House, a typical laburnum-and-lodge-gate English country house, and he has a secretary who encourages him and abets him in this impersonation, because the secretary is going to murder him, if he pulls it off. Nobody around the Red House has ever seen Robert, fifteen years absent in Australia, known to them by repute as a no-good. A letter from Robert is talked about, but never shown. It announces his arrival, and Mark hints it will not be a pleasant occasion. One afternoon, then, the supposed Robert arrives, identifies himself to a couple of servants, is shown into the study, and Mark (according to testimony at the inquest) goes in after him. Robert is then found dead on the floor with a bullet hole in his face, and of course Mark has vanished into thin air. Arrive the police, suspect Mark must be the murderer, remove the debris and proceed with the investigation, and in due course, with the inquest.

Milne is aware of one very difficult hurdle and tries as well as he can to get over it Since the secretary is going to murder Mark once he has established himself as Robert, the impersonation has to continue on and fool the police. Since, also, everybody around the Red House knows Mark intimately, disguise is necessary. This is achieved by shaving off Mark's beard, roughening his hands ("not the hands of a manicured gentleman"—testimony) and the use of a gruff voice and rough manner. But this is not enough. The cops are going to have the body and the clothes on it and whatever is in the pockets. Therefore none of this must suggest Mark. Milne therefore works like a switch engine to put over the motivation that Mark is such a thoroughly conceited performer that he dresses the part down to the socks and underwear (from all of which the secretary has removed the maker's labels), like a ham blacking himself all over to play Othello. If the reader will buy this (and the sales record shows he must have) Milne figures he is solid. Yet, however light in texture the story may be, it is offered as a problem of logic and deduction. If it is not that, it is nothing at all. There is nothing else for it to be. If the situation is false, you cannot even accept it as a light novel, for there is no story for the light novel to be about. If the problem does not contain the elements of truth and plausibility, it is no problem; if the logic is an illusion there is nothing to deduce. If the impersonation is impossible once the reader is told the conditions it must fulfill, then the whole thing is a fraud. Not a deliberate fraud, because Milne would not have written the story if he had known what he was up against. He is up against a number of deadly things, none of which he even considers. Nor, apparently, does the casual reader, who wants to like the story, hence takes it at its face value. But the reader is not called upon to know the facts of life; it is the author who is the expert in the case. Here is what this author ignores:

1. The coroner holds formal jury inquest on a body for which no competent legal identification is offered. A coroner, usually in a big city, will sometimes hold inquest on a body that *cannot* be identified, if the record of such an inquest has or may have a value (fire, disaster, evidence of murder, etc). No such reason exists here, and there is no one to identify the body. A couple of witnesses said the man said he was Robert Ablett. This is mere presumption, and has weight only if nothing conflicts with it. Identification is a condition precedent to an inquest. Even in death a man has a right to his own identity. The coroner will, wherever humanly possible, enforce that right. To neglect it would be a violation of his office

2. Since Mark Ablett, missing and suspected of the murder, cannot defend himself, all evidence of his movements before and after the murder is vital (as also whether he has money to run away on); yet all such evidence is given by the man closest to the murder, and is without corroboration. It is automatically suspect until proved true.

3. The police find by direct investigation that Robert Ablett was not well thought of in his native village. Somebody there must have known him. No such person was brought to the inquest (The story couldn't stand it.).

4. The police know there is an element of threat in Robert's supposed visit, and that it is connected with the murder must be obvious to them. Yet they make no attempt to check Robert in Australia, or find out what character he had there, or what associates, or even if he actually came to England, and with whom (If they had, they would have found out he had been dead three years.).

5. The police surgeon examines the body with a recently shaved beard (exposing unweathered skin), artificially roughened hands, yet the body of a wealthy, soft-living man, long resident in a cool climate. Robert was a rough individual and had lived fifteen years in Australia. That is the surgeon's information. It is impossible he would have noticed nothing to conflict with it.

6. The clothes are nameless, empty, and have had the labels removed. Yet the man wearing them asserted an identity. The presumption that he was not what he said he was is overpowering. Nothing whatever is done about this peculiar circumstance. It is never even mentioned as being peculiar.

7. A man is missing, a well-known local man, and a body in the morgue closely resembles him. It is impossible that the police should not at once eliminate the chance that the missing man *is* the dead man. Nothing would be easier than to prove it. Not even to think of it is incredible. It makes idiots of the police, so that a brash amateur may startle the world with a fake solution.

The detective in the Case is an insouciant gent named Antony Gillingham, a nice lad with a cheery eye, a cozy little flat in London, and that airy manner. He is not making any money on the assignment, but is always available when the local gendarmerie loses its notebook. The English police seem to endure him with their customary stoicism; but I shudder to think of what the boys down at the Homicide Bureau in my city would do to him.

There are less plausible examples of the art than this. In *Trent's Last Case* (often called "the perfect detective story") you have to accept the premise that a giant of international finance, whose lightest frown makes Wall Street quiver like a chihuahua, will plot his own death so as to hang his secretary, and that the secretary when pinched will maintain an aristocratic silence; the old Etonian in him maybe. I have known relatively few international financiers, but I rather think the author of this novel has (if possible) known fewer. There is one by Freeman Wills Crofts (the soundest builder of them all when he doesn't get too fancy) wherein a murderer by the aid of makeup, split second timing, and some very sweet evasive action, impersonates the man he has just killed and thereby gets him alive and distant from the place of the crime. There is one of Dorothy Sayers' in which a man is murdered alone at night in his house by a mechanically released weight which works because he always turns the radio on at just such a moment, always stands in just such a position in front of it, and always bends over just so far A couple of inches either way and the customers would get a rain check. This is what is vulgarly known as having God sit in your lap; a murderer who needs that much help from Providence must be in the wrong business. And there is a scheme of Agatha Christie's featuring M. Hercule Poirot, that ingenious Belgian who talks in a literal translation of school-boy French, wherein, by duly messing around with his "little gray cells," M. Poirot decides that nobody on a certain through sleeper could have done the murder alone, therefore everybody did it together, breaking the process down into a series of simple operations, like assembling an egg-beater. This is the type that is guaranteed to knock the keenest mind for a loop. Only a halfwit could guess it.

There are much better plots by these same writers and by others of their school. There may be one somewhere that would really stand up under close scrutiny. It would be fun to read it, even if I did have to go back to page 47, and refresh my memory about exactly what time the second gardener potted the prize-winning tearose begonia. There is nothing new about these stories and nothing old. The ones I mentioned are all English only because the authorities (such as they are) seem to feel the English writers had an edge in this dreary routine, and that the Americans, (even the creator of Philo Vance—probably the most asinine character in detective fiction) only made the Junior Varsity.

This, the classic detective story, has learned nothing and forgotten nothing. It is the story you will find almost any week in the big shiny magazines, handsomely illustrated, and paying due deference to virginal love and the right kind of luxury goods. Perhaps the tempo has become a trifle faster and the dialogue a little more glib. There are more frozen daiquiris and stingers ordered, and fewer glasses of crusty old port; more clothes by *Vogue,* and décors by the *House Beautiful,* more chic but not more truth. We spend more time in Miami hotels and Cape Cod summer colonies and go not so often down by the old gray sundial in the Elizabethan garden. But fundamentally it is the same careful grouping of suspects, the same utterly incomprehensible trick of how somebody stabbed Mrs. Pottington Postlethwaite III with the solid platinum poignard just as she flatted on the top note of the Bell Song from *Lakmé* in the presence of fifteen ill-assorted guests; the same ingenue in fur-trimmed pajamas screaming in the night to make the company pop in and out of doors and ball up the timetable; the same moody silence next day as they sit around sipping Singapore slings and sneering at each other, while the flat-feet crawl to and fro under the Persian rugs, with their derby hats on.

Personally I like the English style better. It is not quite so brittle, and the people as a rule, just wear clothes and drink drinks. There is more sense of background, as if Cheesecake Manor really existed all around and not just the part the camera sees; there are more long walks over the Downs and the characters don't all try to behave as if they had just been tested by MGM. The English may not always be the best writers in the world, but they are incomparably the best dull writers.

There is a very simple statement to be made about all these stories: they do not really come off intellectually as problems, and they do not come off artistically as fiction. They are too contrived, and too little aware of what goes on in the world. They try to be honest, but honesty is an art. The poor writer is dishonest without knowing it, and the fairly good one can be dishonest because he doesn't know what to be honest about. He thinks a complicated murder scheme which baffles the lazy reader, who won't be bothered itemizing the details will also baffle the police, whose business is with details. The boys with their feet on the desks know that the easiest murder case in the world to break is the one somebody tried to get very cute with, the one that really bothers them is the murder somebody only thought of two minutes before he pulled it off. But if the writers of this fiction wrote about the kind of murders that happen, they would also have to write about the authentic flavor of life as it is lived. And since they cannot do that, they pretend that what they do is what should be done. Which is begging the question—and the best of them know it.

In her introduction to the first *Omnibus of Crime,* Dorothy Sayers wrote: "It (the detective story) does not, and by hypothesis never can, attain the loftiest level of literary achievement." And she suggested somewhere else that this is because it is a "literature of escape," not "a literature of expression." I do not know what the loftiest level of literary achievement is; neither did Aeschylus or Shakespeare; neither does Miss Sayers. Other things being equal, which they never are, a more powerful theme will provoke a more powerful performance. Yet some very dull books have been written about God, and some very fine ones about how to make a living and stay fairly honest. It is always a matter of who writes the stuff, and what he has in him to write it with. As for literature of expression and literature of escape, this is critics' jargon, a use of abstract words as if they had absolute meanings. Everything written with vitality expresses that vitality; there are no dull subjects, only dull minds. All men who read escape from something else into what lies behind the printed page; the quality of the dream may be argued, but its release has become a functional necessity. All men must escape at times from the deadly rhythm of their private thoughts. It is part of the process of life among thinking beings. It is one of the things that distinguish them from the three-toed sloth; he apparently—one can never be quite sure—is perfectly content hanging upside down on a branch, and not even reading Walter Lippmann. I hold no particular brief for the detective story as the ideal escape. I merely say that *all* reading for pleasure is escape, whether it be Greek, mathematics, astronomy, Benedetto Croce, or *The Diary of the Forgotten Man.* To say otherwise is to be an intellectual snob, and a juvenile at the art of living.

I do not think such considerations moved Miss Dorothy Sayers to her essay in critical futility.

I think what was really gnawing at her mind was the slow realization that her kind of detective story was an arid formula which could not even satisfy its own implications. It was second-grade literature because it was not about the things that could make first-grade literature. If it started out to be about real people (and she could write about them—her minor characters show that), they must very soon do unreal things in order to form the artificial pattern required by the plot. When they did unreal things, they ceased to be real themselves They became puppets and cardboard lovers and papier mâché villains and detectives of exquisite and impossible gentility. The only kind of writer who could be happy with these properties was the one who did not know what reality was. Dorothy Sayers' own stories show that she was annoyed by this triteness; the weakest element in them is the part that makes them detective stories, the strongest the part which could be removed without touching the "problem of logic and deduction." Yet she could not or would not give her characters their heads and let them make their own mystery. It took a much simpler and more direct mind than hers to do that.

In the *Long Week-End,* which is a drastically competent account of English life and manners in the decade following the first World War, Robert Graves and Alan Hodge gave some attention to the detective story. They were just as traditionally English as the ornaments of the Golden Age, and they wrote of the time in which these writers were almost as well-known as any writers in the world. Their books in one form or another sold into the millions, and in a dozen languages. These were the people who fixed the form and established the rules and founded the famous Detection Club, which is a Parnassus of English writers of mystery. Its roster includes practically every important writer of detective fiction since Conan Doyle. But Graves and Hodge decided that during this whole period only one first-class writer had written detective stories at all. An American, Dashiell Hammett. Traditional or not, Graves and Hodge were not fuddy-duddy connoisseurs of the second rate; they could see what went on in the world and that the detective story of their time didn't; and they were aware that writers who have the vision and the ability to produce real fiction do not produce unreal fiction.

How original a writer Hammett really was, it isn't easy to decide now, even if it mattered. He was one of a group, the only one who achieved critical recognition, but not the only one who wrote or tried to write realistic mystery fiction. All literary movements are like this; some one individual is picked out to represent the whole movement; he is usually the culmination of the movement. Hammett was the ace performer, but there is nothing in his work that is not implicit in the early novels and short stories of Hemingway. Yet for all I know, Hemingway may have learned something from Hammett, as well as from writers like Dreiser, Ring Lardner, Carl Sandburg, Sherwood Anderson, and himself. A rather revolutionary debunking of both the language and material of fiction had been going on for some time. It probably started in poetry; almost everything does. You can take it clear back to Walt Whitman, if you like. But Hammett applied it to the detective story, and this, because of its heavy crust of English gentility and American psuedo-gentility, was pretty hard to get moving. I doubt that Hammett had any deliberate artistic aims whatever; he was trying to make a living by writing something he had first hand information about. He made some of it up; all writers do; but it had a basis in fact; it was made up out of real things. The only reality the English detection writers knew was the conversational accent of Surbiton and Bognor Regis. If they wrote about dukes and

Venetian vases, they knew no more about them out of their own experience than the well-heeled Hollywood character knows about the French Modernists that hang in his Bel-Air château or the semi-antique Chippendale-cum-cobbler's bench that he uses for a coffee table. Hammett took murder out of the Venetian vase and dropped it into the alley; it doesn't have to stay there forever, but it was a good idea to begin by getting as far as possible from Emily Post's idea of how a well-bred debutante gnaws a chicken wing. He wrote at first (and almost to the end) for people with a sharp, aggressive attitude to life. They were not afraid of the seamy side of things; they lived there. Violence did not dismay them; it was right down their street.

Hammett gave murder back to the kind of people that commit it for reasons, not just to provide a corpse; and with the means at hand, not with hand-wrought duelling pistols, curare, and tropical fish. He put these people down on paper as they are, and he made them talk and think in the language they customarily used for these purposes. He had style, but his audience didn't know it, because it was in a language not supposed to be capable of such refinements. They thought they were getting a good meaty melodrama written in the kind of lingo they imagined they spoke themselves. It was, in a sense, but it was much more. All language begins with speech, and the speech of common men at that, but when it develops to the point of becoming a literary medium it only looks like speech. Hammett's style at its worst was almost as formalized as a page of Marius the Epicurean; at its best it could say almost anything. I believe this style, which does not belong to Hammett or to anybody, but is the American language (and not even exclusively that any more), can say things he did not know how to say or feel the need of saying. In his hands it had no overtones, left no echo, evoked no image beyond a distant hill. He is said to have lacked heart, yet the story he thought most of himself is the record of a man's devotion to a friend. He was spare, frugal, hardboiled, but he did over and over again what only the best writers can ever do at all. He wrote scenes that seemed never to have been written before.

With all this he did not wreck the formal detective story. Nobody can; production demands a form that can be produced. Realism takes too much talent, too much knowledge, too much awareness. Hammett may have loosened it up a little here, and sharpened it a little there. Certainly all but the stupidest and most meretricious writers are more conscious of their artificiality than they used to be. And he demonstrated that the detective story can be important writing. *The Maltese Falcon* may or may not be a work of genius, but an art which is capable of it is not "by hypothesis" incapable of anything. Once a detective story can be as good as this, only the pedants will deny that it *could* be even better. Hammett did something else, he made the detective story fun to write, not an exhausting concatenation of insignificant clues. Without him there might not have been a regional mystery as clever as Percival Wilde's *Inquest,* or an ironic study as able as Raymond Postgate's *Verdict of Twelve,* or a savage piece of intellectual double-talk like Kenneth Fearing's *The Dagger of the Mind,* or a tragi-comic idealization of the murderer as in Donald Henderson's *Mr. Bowling Buys a Newspaper,* or even a gay and intriguing Hollywoodian gambol like Richard Sale's *Lazarus No. 7.*

The realistic style is easy to abuse: from haste, from lack of awareness, from inability to bridge the chasm that lies between what a writer would like to be able to say and what he actually knows how to say. It is easy to fake; brutality is not strength, flipness is not wit, edge-of-the-chair writing can be as boring as flat writing; dalliance with promiscuous blondes can be very dull stuff when described by goaty young men with no other purpose in mind than to describe dalliance with promiscuous blondes. There has been so much of this sort of thing that if a character in a detective story says, "Yeah," the author is automatically a Hammett imitator.

And there are still quite a few people around who say that Hammett did not write detective stories at all, merely hard-boiled chronicles of mean streets with a perfunctory mystery element dropped in like the olive in a martini. These are the flustered old ladies—of both sexes (or no sex) and almost all ages—who like their murders scented with magnolia blossoms and do not care to be reminded that murder is an act of infinite cruelty, even if the perpetrators sometimes look like playboys or college professors or nice motherly women with softly graying hair. There are also a few badly-scared champions of the formal or the classic mystery who think no story is a detective story which does not pose a formal and exact problem and arrange the clues around it with neat labels on them. Such would point out, for example, that in reading *The Maltese Falcon* no one concerns himself with who killed Spade's partner, Archer (which is the only formal problem of the story) because the reader is kept thinking about something else. Yet in *The Glass Key* the reader is constantly reminded that the question is who killed Taylor Henry, and exactly the same effect is obtained; an effect of movement, intrigue, cross-purposes and the gradual elucidation of character, which is all the detective story has any right to be about anyway. The rest is spillikins in the parlor.

But all this (and Hammett too) is for me not quite enough. The realist in murder writes of a world in which gangsters can rule nations and almost rule cities, in which hotels and apartment houses and celebrated restaurants are owned by men who made their money out of brothels, in which a screen star can be the fingerman for a mob, and the nice man down the hall is a boss of the numbers racket; a world where a judge with a cellar full of bootleg liquor can send a man to jail for having a pint in his pocket, where the mayor of your town may have condoned murder as an instrument of money-making, where no man can walk down a dark street in safety because law and order are things we talk about but refrain from practicing; a world where you may witness a hold-up in broad daylight and see who did it, but you will fade quickly back into the crowd rather than tell any one, because the hold-up man may have friends with long guns, or the police may not like your testimony, and in any case the shyster for the defense will be allowed to abuse and vilify you in open court, before a jury of selected morons, without any but the most perfunctory interference from a political judge.

It is not a very fragrant world, but it is the world you live in, and certain writers with tough minds and a cool spirit of detachment can make very interesting and even amusing patterns out of it. It is not funny that a man should be killed, but it is sometimes funny that he should be killed for so little, and that his death should be the coin of what we call civilization. All this stuff is not quite enough.

In everything that can be called art there is a quality of redemption. It may be pure tragedy, if it is high tragedy, and it may be pity and irony, and it may be the raucous laughter of the strong man. But down these mean streets a man must go who is not himself mean, who is neither tarnished nor afraid. The detective in this kind of story must be such a man. He is the hero, he is everything. He must be a complete man and a common man and yet an unusual man. He must be, to use a rather weathered phrase, a man of honor, by instinct, by inevitability, without thought of it, and certainly without saying it. He must be the best man in his world and a good enough man for any world. I do not care much about his private life; he is neither a eunuch nor a satyr; I think he might seduce a duchess and I am quite sure he would not spoil a virgin; if he is a man of honor in one thing, he is that in all things. He is a relatively poor man, or he would not be a detective at all. He is a common man, or he could not go among common people. He has a sense of character, or he would not know his job. He will take no man's money dishonestly and no man's insolence without a due and dispassionate revenge. He is a lonely man and his pride is that you will treat him as a proud man or be very sorry you ever saw him. He talks as the man of his age talks, that is, with rude wit, a lively sense of the grotesque, a disgust for sham, and a contempt for pettiness. The story is his adventure in search of a hidden truth, and it would be no adventure if it did not happen to a man fit for adventure. He has a range of awareness that startles you, but it belongs to him by right, because it belongs to the world he lives in.

If there were enough like him, I think the world would be a very safe place to live in, and yet not too dull to be worth living in.

The Detective Story as a Historical Source

William O. Aydelotte

One would hardly go to the detective story for an accurate picture of modern life. If a historian five hundred years hence were to base a reconstruction of our twentieth-century civilization solely on the evidence contained in detective stories, he might reach strange conclusions. He would probably infer that the most prominent features of our culture were inefficient or corrupt police forces, a multitude of private detectives, sometimes urbane and sometimes hard-boiled, and a constant series of domestic crimes occuring principally in large country houses and committed exclusively by people of the most harmless and respectable outward appearance. What little realism detective stories possess lies on the surface and does not extend to the characters or to the action. The notion that they give a literal representation of modern society may be rejected at the outset. Far from being realistic, they constitute one of the most conventionalized of literary forms, being exceeded in this respect perhaps only by the comic strip.

This does not argue, however, that detective novels are completely dissociated from the age in which they are written. On the contrary, their immense popularity—it is alleged that one out of every four new works of fiction published in the English language belongs to this category—suggests that they are an impressive portent of our cultures. Their popularity is not likely to be accidental. If we can ascertain the reason for it, we may be able to grasp the link between detective literature and the society of which it forms a part.

I suggest that the widespread and sustained popularity of detective stories is principally due to the very elements which make them unrealistic, to their conventions. These conventions (which will be analyzed at length in the course of this essay) have been fairly constant in the century-long history of the *genre,* amid all the variations of setting and technique. A substantial number of them appear even in the stories of Poe. The long persistence and regular recurrence of these stereotypes afford at least a presumption that they are essential to the detective story's continued vogue. Their role is of course clear. They are wish-fulfillment fantasies designed to produce certain agreeable sensations in the reader, to foist upon him illusions he wants to entertain and which he goes to this literature to find.

The charm of detective stories lies neither in originality nor in artistic merit, though they may possess both these qualities. It consists rather in the repetition of a formula that through trial and error has been found pleasing. We read these books, not to have a new experience, but to repeat in slightly different form an experience we have had already. Thus, for example, the "surprise" ending is not really a surprise. It is the ending we expect and demand, and we would feel outraged if any other kind of ending were offered to us. It is true that many of these works introduce elements of novelty in the background and setting, and that the best of them unquestionably show considerable skill in writing and construction. Such amenities, however, serve not so much to change the formula as to render it more palatable to the highbrow. The educated part of the detective-story audience shows no unwillingness to accept the formula but merely a fastidious distaste for its cruder expressions.

The interest of detective stories to the historian is that they shed light on the people who read them. By studying the fantasies contained in this literature, one may gather a description of its readers, in terms of their unsatisfied motivational drives. Thus these books are the more illuminating the more unrealistic and inaccurate they are. It is precisely by their inaccuracies that they reveal attitudes and emotions of the audience to which they cater. To the historian concerned with popular opinion, this audience is of particular interest for two reasons. In the first place it is large—the detective story is a mass medium—and in the second place it is extremely varied. Detective novels appeal to different types of readers, highbrows as well as lowbrows. They are read with avidity by intellectuals who despise soap operas and are repelled by the success stories in popular magazines. Some critics even assert that they are written primarily for intellectuals, a claim which is of course invalid in view of the breadth and extent of their circulation. The reading of this literature is, rather, a widespread habit to which the educated also adhere.

The extent and variety of the detective-story audience argue a surprising degree of unity in our culture, at least in respect to the demand for the particular fantasies which this literature purveys. Since these books appeal, not only to many people, but to many different kinds of people, they presumably reflect attitudes and needs that are widely distributed. A study of the stereotypes in the detective story may, therefore, reveal to us attitudes and opinions which, if not universal, at least occur in our age with significant frequency.

Primarily, the detective story presents a view of life which is agreeable and reassuring. By ingenious and long-tested devices, it persuades the reader that the world it describes is simple and understandable, that it is meaningful, and that it is secure.

(1) In place of the complex issues of modern existence, people in a detective story have very simple problems. Life goes along well except for the single point that some crime, usually, in modern stories, a murder, has been committed. (There are some exceptions, particularly among the Sherlock Holmes stories, which are not wholly typical of the modern form of the *genre*: many of these contain no murder, and some involve no crime at all, merely a puzzle.) From this act follow most of the troubles which the sympathetic characters must endure: they may, for example, come under temporary suspicion of murder, or they may have a misunderstanding with their loved ones. Troubles are objectively caused by an external circumstance, the murder, which can and will be resolved, whereupon the troubles will disappear. Once the solution has been reached, most of the other difficulties are ended and the characters go away happy, never apparently to be vexed by

the minor worries and neuroses of modern man. The mess, confusion, and frustration of life have been reduced to a simple issue between good and evil, virtue and wickedness. And virtue triumphs.

To carry the argument to the next stage, the simplification of the problem is matched by a corresponding simplification of the solution. Here we come to one of the most universal conventions in the *genre,* the essential clue, the unique significant detail that unlocks the mystery. The detective story makes a distinction between essential and non-essential facts. As Sherlock Holmes puts it, "It is of the highest importance in the art of detection to be able to recognize, out of a number of facts, which are incidental and which vital. Otherwise your energy and attention must be dissipated instead of being concentrated." ("The Reigate Puzzle.") In the unreal world of the detective story, we depart from the intricate currents of causation in life as we know it, and find instead that a whole elaborate plot may be unravelled by discovering the one relevant detail. Furthermore, the factual nature of this detail lends an air of concreteness to the solution: we are led to feel it is the only solution, inevitable, unique, completely certain.

(2) By other commonly used devices the detective story makes life more meaningful and endows the events it describes with significance, even with glamor. To say that detective stories provide a thrill which compensates for the dullness of their readers' lives is only the beginning of the story. It is true that they offer the excitement of adventure, and also capitalize on popular indignations or fetishes in the manner of other types of sensation literature. But they do more than this. In many subtle ways they help their readers to believe in the existence of a richer and fuller world.

Even the sordid surroundings of crime make their contribution to the atmosphere of richness and meaning. As G. K. Chesterton says, this form of literature succeeds often in getting the romance and poetry of the city, and "the investigator crosses London with something of the loneliness and liberty of a prince in a tale of elfland."

Comparable effects are achieved in other ways. Consider, for example, the following quotation, in which Sherlock Holmes is explaining one of his solutions: "I am only, of course, giving you the leading results now of my examination of the paper. There were twenty-three other deductions which would be of more interest to experts than to you." ("The Reigate Puzzle.")

This is one of many passages in which Conan Doyle contrives to suggest there is a great world of intellectual phenomena, beyond the range of the average man, but really existent for all that and within the competence of the superior mind. Thus, for other illustrations, Holmes deduces a whole life-history from the appearance of a hat or a watch. ("The Blue Carbuncle," "The Sign of Four.") The implication is that life is not the simple and drab affair we ordinarily encounter, but something more extensive and more interesting.

To add further to the reader's sense of new frontiers of meaning and significance, the detective story manages in various ways to cast a glamor on its characters and to convey to the reader that these people count, that they matter in the world. Such an illusion is achieved, for example, when the action takes place in the classical setting of the large English country-house with its atmosphere of butlers and scullery-maids, lawns and shrubberies, French windows and guest-wings, and large house parties of elegant guests.

(3) Finally, the detective story introduces us to a secure universe. We find here an ordered world obedient to fixed laws. The outcome is certain and the criminal will without fail be beaten by the detective. In this world man has power to control his own affairs and the problems of life can be mastered by human agency.

Even the handling of the theme of death contributes to this feeling of security. One might not at first expect a form of literature which deals with death by violence to have the cheerful and encouraging effect I have attributed to the detective story. Yet murder is an almost universal feature of these books. From the point of view of literary construction, of course, a murder is useful for the plot and provides the suitable starting-point for an investigation. But there is another reason for including it.

This is that the detective story, by its peculiar treatment of death, contrives to minimize the fear of it. Death is always presented in a rather special way. It is something that happens to somebody else, not to anyone we like or identify ourselves with. The victim, though he is ultimately avenged, is not allowed to be a sympathetic character. The reader's emotions must not become engaged on his behalf. At the least the victim is killed off before his personality has been developed far enough for the reader to take an interest in him or to like him. More often the victim is clearly unattractive, a man who has been injuring the lives of a number of the other characters (which also helps the plot by increasing the list of possible suspects), and his death is good riddance. In many cases, the murder turns out to be the best thing that could have happened. After everything has been straightened out, the lovers, if any, are brought together, the detective has had a chance to prove his worth, all the other characters are now freed from the guilt of his murder, since this guilt has now been thrown on an acceptable scapegoat, and everyone is set for a cheerful future.

The detective story uses crime not to make life more horrible but to make it more cheerful. The despair and horror it seems to offer the reader are presented in a very manageable form and really subserve, not a pessimistic view of life, but a view that is exactly the opposite. Its concern with crime and the seamy side of life misleads the observer as to its true impact. Its message is essentially agreeable, almost to the point of being saccharine.

The agreeable view of life presented in the detective story is deepened and enlarged by the actions of its two most important characters, the criminal and the detective. Each plays a standardized role that affords a special kind of satisfaction to the reader. We will consider the criminal first.

The criminal is a scapegoat. He is the cause of and can justly be blamed for all the troubles of the detective-story world, the murder and everything that follows from it. The detective story evades the complex issues of life and saves us the effort of analyzing the sources of our difficulties and frustrations by presenting every problem as one of personal morality. The criminal therefore must be a single individual, who can eventually be identified. A detective novel where the murder was due to "conditions" of some sort, and where no individual was responsible, would be quite unsatisfactory.

But the criminal is not only a scapegoat, he is also something more deeply gratifying, a scapegoat that can be beaten. His great charm is that he is conquerable and will infallibly be conquered. He appears for most of the story as a colossus, formidable in his cunning and power. But his strength, though great, is futile, only sham strength. His position is actually unreal, for he has no place nor meaning in an ordered world. If you look closely, the criminal is a miscrable creature. He can do little ultimately against organized society which is rapidly closing in on him. If we are terrified of him for a while, because of his apparent cunning and dexterity, that simply enhances the relief we feel when he gets beaten, and also the satisfaction we have in knowing all the time, in our inmost hearts, that he is going to be beaten.

Besides this, I believe the criminal also fulfills another and more subtle purpose. He relieves our feelings of aggression, not only by becoming an object of them himself, but also in a second and quite different way, by committing the murder. As I tried to show earlier, it not infrequently happens that the murder is a good thing; the victim is a menace to the sympathetic characters and the murder starts off the train of events that leads finally to the happy ending. In novels where this is the case, the criminal, by killing the victim, performs a service to society, a service we would not wish, however, to have performed by any sympathetic character because of the penalty that must ensue. The criminal, though he is made to act from selfish and unworthy motives and must therefore be punished, still gratifies us by committing the act we are glad to see done. He shares something of the ambiguous character of the scapegoat of mythology who is both a friend and enemy to society, who commits the act of sin or disobedience that helps us all and then removes the taint or penalty attached thereto by himself undergoing the punishment, a punishment that is occasionally even inflicted by the beneficiaries.

Perhaps the most gratifying function of the detective story, and one that is also achieved through the agency of the criminal, is the illusion the reader obtains of being released from guilt and dissociated from the murderer. This illusion is achieved by bringing a number of the most prominent characters, including any with whom the reader might perhaps identify himself, temporarily under suspicion. For this purpose, the criminal must be a member of the closed circle, the small group affected by or concerned with the crime, so that the possibility of an outside murderer will be excluded and any member of this little society may therefore conceivably be guilty. (Here again the Holmes stories constitute a partial exception to the convention that has crystallized in our own day: in very few cases are there several suspects, and in some cases the criminal is an outsider who does not appear till caught.) The criminal must also be the least likely person, revealed only in the surprise ending, so that, since the identity of the murderer is kept a secret until the end, no single character in the closed circle can be assumed to be assuredly free from guilt. By such means the fear of guilt is temporarily intensified and the reader's relief at the identification of the criminal is increased.

Once the criminal is discovered, everyone else is at once freed from the burden of possible guilt. The suspicious actions of the other characters now turn out to have a perfectly innocent explanation. Yet the temporary suspicion directed against them was in a sense justified, for many of them benefited from the crime and would perhaps have liked to commit it if they could have escaped the consequences. For that reason, their relief is the greater. The satisfaction of the "innocent" characters and the reader at being released from guilt is all the more poignant because they do not deserve it; in thought and feeling, if not in action, they are also guilty. Therefore our gratification when the murder is committed does not conflict with our satisfaction at being ultimately freed from guilt, but on the contrary enhances it.

Besides all this, the criminal has one additional function. He contributes to the illusion of the power of the detective. His crime is thought out in great detail, is indeed perfect except for the single flaw discernible only to the detective's penetrating eye. The botched crime of real life is unknown to the detective story. The criminal shows incredible self-possession and address, and conducts himself with such poise and assurance that he is not suspected until the end. In all this he is a worthy antagonist and gives the detective full scope to demonstrate his talents. However, though the crime is so difficult that it can be solved only by the detective, the detective almost invariably does succeed in solving it. He always has the particular bit of esoteric knowledge or the particular type of intuition that turns out to be just what is needed, the one and only thing that will clear up this particular mystery. The point, as we may now perceive, is that the crime is tailored to fit the detective. It finally proves to be exactly the kind of crime that is best suited to his peculiar and unique talents. The criminal actually serves the detective by offering him just the kind of problem that he is best equipped to deal with. Though a skilful writer seeks to maintain the illusion, the crime is really a setup, and the detective solves it because the author has contrived everything to that end.

The detective contributes even more than the criminal to the good view of life set forth in these books. He makes the world simple, comprehensible, and orderly by discovering the essential clue and solving the murder. He understands the meanings and possibilities of life and reveals its vistas to us. He gives us security, certainty and protection. By unearthing the criminal he sets in motion the scapegoat mechanism which shifts the burden of guilt from our shoulders. He can do all these things because he has control over the world we know and the destinies of men in it.

The most prominent feature of the detective is his power and strength. The fact that he is also represented as an intellectual need not lead us astray about this. He is not the feckless intellectual of popular culture, the absent-minded professor, the man who is cloistered, impractical and ineffective. On the contrary, his talents are used for a concrete practical end, the apprehension of the murderer. Intellect is for him simply a path to power, a means of controlling the external world.

Furthermore, his power is not solely intellectual. There is a tradition that he must be physically as well as mentally competent. Detectives in American stories of the hard-boiled school are supposed to be handy with their fists. Sherlock Holmes, though to some extent a recluse and at times a drug-addict, is an expert singlestick player, boxer, and swordsman. Peter Wimsey, no he-man, is still a famous athlete whose proficiency as a cricketer gives away his identity in "Murder Must Advertise." Even the effeminate Poirot shows a courage and alertness in ticklish situations which fit him a little bit into the type of the hero of adventure. Besides this, the detective works not just by intellect and logic but also by intuition. He often senses something wrong in a situation, and this sense prevents him from acting mistakenly or making a fool of himself, even though the whole truth is not yet revealed to his intellect. He plays his hunches, and they are apt to be right.

To make the detective appear a figure of power the police, like the criminal, are drummed into his service. By their very inadequacy or opposition to him they do more to display his qualities than they could by giving him the most efficient cooperation. The convention of the inept police force helps to establish the unique excellence of the detective, his ability to do things nobody else can do. Thus the superiority of the detective to the police has been a common feature of detective literature from Poe's Dupin to Gardner's Perry Mason. It has become especially prominent in recent books, especially American ones such as those of Geoffrey Homes or Dashiell Hammett. Despite some notable exceptions like Inspector Alleyn or Inspector French, there have been relatively few policeman-heroes, and a substantial number of these are police officers only in name who in practice perform something like the role of a private detective. Ellery Queen plays a lone hand and summons in his father's cohorts only for special tasks; the solution is his work and not theirs. Maigret, too, works mostly alone and excites the enmity or disapproval of his colleagues. In one of the latest of the series, he has retired from the *Sûreté*.

Since our present interest in the detective story is its impact on the reader, the important question to ask about the detective is what kind of fantasy he evokes in the reader's mind. At first glance the issue might seem to be whether the reader's relation to the detective is one of identification or dependence. We might attempt, as Louise Bogan suggests would be possible, to divide detective stories into those written for sadists and those written for masochists. Yet this first and most obvious way of putting the question does violence to the complexity of the reader's emotions and reactions, which for any book are likely to be not simple but ambiguous and multiple. As a matter of fact, identification and dependence do not exclude each other; each refers to a different aspect of the reader's reaction, and both are possible at the same time.

I suggest that the reader probably does identify himself with the detective, make the detective an extension of his ego, but only in very general terms. The detective is on our side. His actions are beneficial to us, and we feel ourselves in some degree represented in them. On the other hand, this representation occurs at a distance. The reader may identify himself with the detective to the extent that he gets a vicarious thrill of power when the detective solves the mystery. But I doubt that he identifies himself with the detective to the larger extent of trying to solve the murder himself. The reader is audience. He is like the spectator at a football game, identifying himself with his team, feeling a personal triumph if they win, yet always aware that it is the players and not himself who do the work on which his satisfaction is based. Though the reader both identifies and depends, the emphasis is on the latter, the significant relationship is dependence.

I would argue, to support this, that the reader does not generally compete intellectually with the detective. A detective story is not an invitation to intellectual exercise or exertion, not a puzzle to which the reader must guess the answer. On the contrary, the claim of detective stories to be puzzle literature is in large part a fraud, and the reader, far from attempting to solve the mystery himself, depends on the detective to do it for him.

This is an extremely controversial point. Many detective stories claim to put all the clues in the reader's hands, to show him everything the detective sees, so that the reader has an equal chance to make something out of it. This is the so-called "gentlemen's agreement," the supposedly best modern practice, according to which, says Miss Sayers, readers demand to be put "on an equal footing with the detective himself, as regards all clues and discoveries." Mr. R. Austin Freeman, who also insists that the satisfaction a detective story offers the reader is primarily an intellectual one, argues that the principal connoisseurs of this literature are theologians, scholars and lawyers. To please this audience of subtle and skilled dialecticians, he thinks a good detective story must have above all two things: accuracy as to external facts, and freedom from fallacies of reasoning.

Unfortunately many detective stories, including some of the best-known ones, have neither one nor the other. Critics have amused themselves for some time now by pointing out errors of fact and deduction in the Sherlock Holmes tales. And the same weaknesses can be found in many other works. If we applied to detective stories the critical attention we give to serious literature, we would find a surprising number that simply do not hang together intellectually. This point is the theme of an important article by Raymond Chandler in the December, 1944, issue of the *Atlantic*. Mr. Chandler examines a number of the most famous detective novels of all time, "The Red House Mystery," "Trent's Last Case," "Busman's Honeymoon," "Murder in the Calais Coach," and demonstrates conclusively that none of them is free from important fallacies of reasoning, and that they will not stand up for a moment under strict analysis.

The point should not, however, be pushed too far, for there is a certain amount to be said on the other side. It might be argued that the four stories selected by Mr. Chandler for comment are not a fair sample of the best writing in the *genre*. Furthermore, the very fact that the detective story is popularly regarded as puzzle literature has no doubt influenced writers to try to create puzzles that are fair. Some of these books, particularly including Mr. Freeman's, are well written and articulated, and in fact detective literature at its best demands a good deal in the way of strict construction and technical proficiency, and is not easy to write. Also, I have found a number of readers who insist that they read detective stories as puzzles, and are often able to determine the identity of the murderer in the middle of the story by logical deduction from the clues. And yet, without going into the question of the extent to which these readers may be deceiving themselves, I would doubt that the majority of readers discover the murderer by logical processes of thought before the denouement, and I would doubt that this is even possible in a large number, perhaps the majority, of detective stories.

Any writer of detective fiction who tries to adhere to the "gentlemen's agreement" faces the problem well put by Miss Sayers, "How can we at the same time show the reader everything and yet legitimately obfuscate him as to its meaning?" I submit that what this "legitimate obfuscation" often amounts to is that either the clues are *not* all given to the reader or, if they are, this is not done in a significant way that will enable him to determine their meaning.

The reader, if he guesses correctly at all, does so not by reasoning from the evidence, but rather by selecting the least probable character, the person the evidence does not point to. The reader's solution is a guess and not a deduction. It is on the level of the speculations of the woman in the Thurber story who knew that, whoever might have murdered Duncan, the deed could not possibly have been done by Macbeth because he was too obvious a suspect, a patent red herring.

For the detective story to have a solution that could readily be guessed by the majority of readers would go clean against the whole nature and character of the *genre*. The solution has to come as a surprise. A story has no punch when the reader can guess the murderer before the denouement. Furthermore, the purpose of the detective novel, as we saw from other evidence, is to comfort the reader, create agreeable illusions for him. If these books described themselves primarily as tests of the reader's intelligence, which the reader would flunk if he did not guess the murderer before the end,

The Detective Story as a Historical Source 379

many readers would scarcely find detective stories comforting. For, if the puzzles are so difficult that they can be worked out by the most intelligent readers only with some effort, they would be far beyond the less intelligent but more numerous remainder of the audience.

Detective stories are not a test of the reader's intelligence but, at the most, a means of creating in the reader a delusion that he is intelligent and that, by following the steps in the analysis, he has somehow displayed intellectual proficiency. All too often, the "gentlemen's agreement" means in practice nothing more than that the *appearance* of fair play is to be maintained. The good writing, if any, helps to create and maintain this illusion.

This effort to maintain the illusion of the reader's intelligence is simply a device to keep decently concealed what I consider to be the basic feature of the detective story, the reader's dependence on the detective. Our attitude toward dependence is apt to be ambivalent: we may need it, and at the same time resent having to confess this need or having it called to our attention. The pretense that the detective story is an intellectual puzzle helps to hide the feeling of dependence which the reader goes to these books to find but which he hates to acknowledge.

In any case, there seems little doubt about the dependence of the reader, as of all the characters in the story, upon the detective-hero. The attraction of this literature is that, though the problem may be beyond the powers of the reader or of any of the characters in the story, we can always depend on the detective to step in and solve it. We get satisfaction from seeing him do this even before we know how he is going to bring it off, for the interest lies not in the steps of the analysis but in the certainty of the solution. Thus the reader may get a little bored in the middle of the book when one theory after another is tried and discarded, but when Dr. Fell says he now pretty well knows who the murderer was, when Poirot says he of course identified the murderer two days ago and is only waiting to settle the details, when Holmes says the crime is simple and obvious and presents no difficulty—the reader's interest is quickened by a thrill of excitement.

The characters in the book, like the reader, prove to be passive under the detective's control. By the end they sometimes become his puppets, doing what he planned without knowing he meant them to. In the denouement scene, a character will make an important statement, or act in a particular manner, or even commit suicide, and after it is all over people will realize that the detective planned it just that way. The detective's interference with the lives of the other characters is almost as self-confident as that of a deity, and the reader is supposed to love it.

The passiveness of the reader is underlined by one of the most famous devices of all, the narration of the story by a confidant, a foil to the detective, of which Dr. Watson is the outstanding example. The reader sees the story through the eyes of Watson or Hastings or whoever it may be, and also shares the confidant's sense of security and stability which comes from his dependence on the detective.

The confidant, though he may be of various types, is generally somewhat stupid, inferior to the detective, and the detective pokes fun at his blunders and obtuseness. But the confidant doesn't object to this. Even Dr. Watson, though he does at times rebel against Holmes' superior manner, shows an almost masochistic streak. He doesn't mind being ordered around by Holmes without explanation; in fact, he gets a thrill out of it. He is delighted to be proved wrong and to have his stupidity shown up. For all this enhances his belief in the infallibility of the detective. The detective becomes a kind of father-image to whom the narrator is occasionally opposed but in general submissive. The Watson-Holmes relationship gives an opening for the instincts of hero-worship .

But what is the historical importance of this? How can such a description as I have attempted here of fantasies and the motivations to which they correspond, even if it is made much more accurate and extensive, be translated into terms of society and politics? The answer to this question, suggested at the beginning of this paper, may now be given more fully. The point of all I have been saying is that the detective story is hokum, a means of arousing in the reader a belief in contrary-to-fact conditions, an opiate and a drug, which protects the reader from the facts of life by covering him with veils upon veils of illusions. The historical value of the detective story is that it describes day-dreams, and describes them with a wealth of documentation extending into innumerable volumes. A knowledge of people's day-dreams may enable us to progress to an understanding of their desires. In this way, a careful study of literature of this kind may reveal popular attitudes which shed a flood of light on the motivation behind political, social, and economic history.

The method can be illustrated on the basis of the preliminary survey attempted here, and I will now, finally, indicate by a couple of suggestions how it might work. To take a negative point first, even this cursory examination will enable us to dismiss as uncritical and altogether false the thesis, which has been hazarded by not a few writers, that the detective story is in some fashion a flower of democracy and an embodiment of the democratic way of life. The argument used to support this view is that these books have appeared almost exclusively in democratic countries, chiefly England and America, while by contrast the writings of Agatha Christie and Edgar Wallace were banned by Hitler as "decadent." The reason alleged is that this kind of literature can flourish only in a society where there is due process of law, a non-faulty procedure for handling evidence, public sympathy on the side of order, and an effective police dedicated to finding the truth by objective means.

This argument, in the light of what has so far been said is obviously nonsense. It is not true, incidentally, that detective literature has appeared solely in democratic societies, for Vidocq published his "Memoirs" in the age of Louis Philippe and Gaboriau wrote mostly under the Second Empire. Nor does the development of effective police forces seem relevant, since the fictional detective works separately from or even against the police, who are represented as anything but effective.

Even if we grant, what is for the most part true, that the *genre* has flourished mainly in England and the United States, it does not follow that it is an illustration of democratic sentiment or a symbol of democratic culture. Our analysis of the detective story would lead to a somewhat less reassuring view. The whole tenor of these books appears to be that they show an enormous demand for gratification, on the level of fantasy, of basic drives which apparently cannot be satisfied in our western society on the level of ordinary reality, and which have an application going rather beyond democratic institutions. The resemblance of the fantasies of dependence and aggression in the detective novel to the two principal political figures of totalitarianism, the dictator and the scapegoat, has been pointed out before this.

Though the detective story appears non-political on the surface, the roles of its two protagonists are saturated with political meanings. The criminal, by the very fact that he is the least likely person, justifies the reader's suspicion that all men, including those who appear most innocent, are really his potential enemies. The reader gets a tremendous vicarious satisfaction when the criminal is identified, for this denouement confirms to the reader that he is right to suspect everybody. The criminal is a fantasy developing out of a competitive, uncohesive society. He is a personalization of our grievances, as we like to personalize them in the atmosphere of political or social crisis in real life. We have toward the criminal the same or comparable feelings that we have toward any one of the commonly accepted scapegoats of our day, the Jew, the labor agitator, Wall Street, the "radical," the capitalist, or whatever other image we have formed the habit of using. And we like to attribute to these bogeymen, as we do to the criminal, sham strength instead of real strength, and to think of them as major threats which, however, we will somehow always be able to counter.

The detective, on the other hand, has many characteristics in common with the modern political leader or agitator. He simplifies life, makes sense out of it and gives it meaning. His strength is real, unlike the criminal's pseudo-strength, for it is based not just on externals but on intuition and a sense of community with the right things in the universe. Like the agitator in Professor Lowenthal's article (in *The Public Opinion Quarterly,* Fall, 1948), he is conservative and objects not to the system but to certain people, the criminal or criminals, who seem to be endangering it. And yet the detective is not really a part of the established framework of society, for he neither belongs to the police, the official guardians of the law, nor is he a member of the closed circle or group within which the plot develops. Thus, though he moves in an ordered universe, the order is not that of the police or other regular authorities, but an order that is discovered and imposed by him. The detective may have a kind of democratic aura, for he frequently rises from the ranks and is not distinguished by birth, and although he moves unperturbed among the highly placed he is not one of them. Yet he is indispensable, for he alone can solve the riddle. Therefore the authorities (the family or the police) perforce surrender the controls to him, sometimes reluctantly and occasionally with sharp protest. One could argue that all these qualities add up to a dictator, that the detective is the extra-legal superman who is called in to accomplish by extraordinary measures what is impossible within the traditional organization of society.

Thus a case could be made to show that the detective story is no monument to the strength of democracy but rather a symptom revealing its weaknesses, the insupportable burdens it places on the individual. The detective story does not reflect order, but expresses on the fantasy level a yearning for order; it suggests, then, a disordered world, and its roots are to be sought in social disintegration rather than in social cohesion.

All this is not to suggest that the impulses catered to in this literature made their first appearance in history in the nineteenth century, and never existed before. On the contrary, the fantasies of the detective story appear in recognizable form in the popular culture of other ages, in folklore for example, and the drives they reveal are therefore by no means recent in origin but might rather be regarded as traditional elements of the human character as it has developed in our civilization. Nostalgia for the dependent relationships of childhood is hardly a novelty of our own age. The significant thing is rather that so many people of our age, roughly the era of democratic liberalism, have seemingly come to depend on an enormous literature for the development and even the artificial stimulation of these fantasies. This literature offers disturbing evidence of psychological tensions, and of the prevalence in our modern western culture of elements of character-structure which do not provide adequate support for democratic institutions. The hypothesis toward which a study of these books might tend is that the political arrangements in a democracy, in contrast to the political arrangements in more authoritarian types of government, are simply not adequate to take up this strain.

But perhaps we should beware of taking evidence of this sort too tragically, or of deducing from detective stories nothing but a pessimistic moral. The condemnation of detective stories as drugs or cheap escapism may be pedantic. For, if they are a symptom, they can also be a cure. If we credit the Freudian view that socially dangerous impulses can be got rid of by removing them to the level of fantasy, then detective stories could be described as a harmless safety valve, a wholesome therapy serving a desirable social purpose. And yet one may wonder if this commonly accepted view is entirely correct, if fantasy and real life are actually so unrelated. To some extent we may build our real life around our fantasy and, if this is so, sensation literature may not so much rid us of dangerous drives as reinforce and reshape them.

In any case, if detective stories are not so sinister as they at first appear from analysis, neither are they as frivolous as some critics have judged them. The drives they cater to are compelling and basic, and relate ultimately to the struggle for self-preservation. It is the universal nature of their theme which explains the size and variety of their reading audience. The intellectual, who scorns the cheap fantasies of the popular magazines, is not likely to be able to forgo the fantasies which give him hope for his survival in an alien world. Detective stories deal, in their own way and on their own level, with the most essential and urgent problems in the human situation.

Acknowledgements

Permission to reprint the following stories is gratefully acknowledged to the following:

ALFRED A. KNOPF INC. for "Lamb to the Slaughter" by Roald Dahl. Copyright © 1953 by Roald Dahl. Reprinted from *Someone Like You* by Roald Dahl, by permission of Alfred A. Knopf Inc.

THE BOWLING GREEN UNIVERSITY POPULAR PRESS for "The Detective Story as Historical Source" by William O. Aydelotte, and "The Contributions of Edgar Allan Poe" by Robert A.W. Lowndes. From *The Mystery Writer's Art.* Copyright © 1970 by The Bowling Green University Press. Reprinted by permission.

DOMINICK ABEL LITERARY AGENCY, INC. for "At the Old Swimming Hole" by Sara Paretsky. Copyright © 1986 by Sara Paretsky. Originally published in *Mean Streets: The Second Private Eye Writers of America Anthology,* edited by Robert J. Randisi. Published by Mysterious Press. Used by permission.

DONALD I. FINE INC. for "Exactly What Happened" by Jim Thompson. From *Fireworks: The Lost Writings,* edited by Robert Polito and Michael Mc-Cauley. Copyright © 1988 by The Estate of Jim Thompson. Used by permission of Donald I. Fine, Inc.

JOHN FARQUHARSEN LTD. for "First Offense" by Ed McBain. Copyright © October 1955 by Flying Eagle Publications, Inc., renewed December 1983 by Evan Hunter. Used with permission of John Farquharson Ltd.

HAROLD OBER ASSOCIATES INC. for "The Four Suspects" by Agatha Christie. From *The Tuesday Club Murders.* Copyright © 1928, 1929, 1930, 1931 by Agatha Christie Mallowan. Copyright renewed 1956, 1960 by Agatha Christie Mallowan. "Sleeping Dog" by Ross Macdonald. Originally published in the April 1965 issue of *Argosy.* Copyright © 1965 by the Margaret Millar Survivor's Trust. Reprinted by permission of Harold Ober Associates, Inc.

HOUGHTON MIFFLIN COMPANY for "The Simple Art of Murder" by Raymond Chandler. From *The Simple Art of Murder* by Raymond Chandler. Copyright © 1950 by Raymond Chandler. Copyright © renewed 1978 by Helga Greene. Reprinted by permission of Houghton Mifflin Co.

Index to Volumes I-V

A cumulative index to authors and stories

387